Dragons' Rebirth

Danielle Paquette-Harvey

1984 –

This is a work of fiction. Names, characters, places, and incidents either are the product of the author's imagination or are used fictitiously. Any resemblance to actual people, living or dead, events, or locales is entirely coincidental. **No part of this book may be used to train AI.**

Cover design by Danielle Paquette-Harvey, stock pictures bought with the appropriate licenses, all rights reserved to Danielle Paquette-Harvey.

Drawings by Danielle Paquette-Harvey

Cover by Danielle Paquette-Harvey

ISBN (paperback) 978-1-998458-11-0

First Edition: April 2026

Published by: Danielle Paquette-Harvey

http://daniellephauthor.com

https://www.instagram.com/daniellephauthor

Subscribe to my mailing list so you don't miss anything!

daniellephauthor.com

Follow me

- Facebook: Danielle Paquette-Harvey
- Instagram: daniellephauthor

Other books by the author

All my books are available on Amazon.

Audiobooks

- The Vampire's Pet

$0.99 Short stories collection

- The Vampire's Pet
- The Vampire's Pet Part Two
- The Werewolf's Revenge

Longing mates Series

Considered for a movie adaptation!

A powerful, alluring vampire prince. The strong daughter of the Alpha. Born enemies, tied by an unbreakable bond.

Worldwide Best Sellers. Read the series that started it all.

1. Age-Old Enemies - ISBN 978-1777572136

2. A Beloved Sin - ISBN 978-1777572150
3. The Fallen - ISBN 978-1-7782178-5-2

Related to the Longing Mates series

Read the **Award-Winning** fantasy romance today!

The Goddess's Wards: Origins of the werewolf-witches rogue pack - ISBN 978-1-7782178-8-3

Blood and Kisses Series

1. Cursed King - ISBN 978-1-7388313-2-6
2. The Awakening – ISBN 978-1-998458-00-4
3. Dragons' Rebirth – ISBN 978-1-998458-11-0
4. The King at World's End – Coming soon

Half-angel's Daughter Series

1. Devoured by Darkness – coming soon

Danielle Paquette-Harvey

Dragons' Rebirth

Contents

Y'vagroth
Naiad Shrine
Moon Elve's
Lands
Delos
St.-Selena
Kreligraz
Leila's
Pack
Melian Nymph
Sacred Grove
St-Lawrence River
Valley of Nysa
Sleeping
Lake

Darton Seacastle
Carlpar Mountai
Mytvathyr
Mumbur
Ancient Crystal Field
Nokorath Hills
Desolation Hills

"Even Gods are afraid to die."
C.D. McKenna, The Vorelian Saga

Chapter 1 (Elaine)

Scorchfire

The order of time had been violated. The magical balance of the world had been disrupted, and it was my duty to restore it. The artifact's pieces lay shattered on the ground from the lightning strike. My legs trembled from the sustained effort of using the Rods of Origins. It took all that I had to stay upright.

The portal had been forcibly closed. In the deafening silence, I stared into the queen's eyes beside me, unsure if it had worked. Despite my magical power, I would have failed without her help. I wiped my sweaty hands on my clothes and held my breath, waiting. The ground started shaking all around us, and stones fell from the ceiling. An ear-shattering roar escaped from Scorchfire's throat.

The dragon was alive.

I was overcome with relief. So much depended on Scorchfire's rebirth. Elven magic would be saved. I wondered if the magic's withering that had occurred would be reversed. I realized that I knew very little about the connection between our magic and that of the dragons, except that they were linked.

My relief quickly faded. The furious beast shook his head and tail in all directions. Benches flew, and I ducked just in time to avoid one larger than my head. The dragon spread his wings. Though the room was huge, it was small compared to this majestic beast.

He wanted his freedom. Judging by the damage he was causing, he would soon have it, too. I tried to jump to avoid the tip of his tail, but my legs wouldn't obey me, and I was thrown sideways by his mighty blow. The impact knocked the wind out of me momentarily. Black spots appeared before my eyes.

I coughed up blood and realized that the dragon's resurrection would lead to my downfall. If only Oswald were here with me, we could contain it. I should have waited until he was awake, but it was too late now for regrets.

I wanted to cast a spell to calm Scorchfire, but I was out of mana. My heart pounded with fear. I had no choice but to retreat to a secluded corner. My embedded jewels activated automatically, raising a protective shield around me. Each time a projectile came my way, blue magical sparks appeared above me. I was grateful for my jewels, my last line of defense.

A strange, unknown, foreign sensation washed over me. My head hurt, as if it were about to split in half. I felt a presence intrude into my head and tried to fight it, but I was too weak.

Perplexed, I listened. Words echoed loudly in my mind: *"Zarvok Drel'kaan."*

My eyes caught a glimpse of Scorchfire, and I held my breath in shock when I realized that he was talking to me. I had no idea how that was possible. The dragon spoke in an ancient language I didn't understand. I read about mental links in ancient texts, but I had never thought much of them. It was mostly lore and nothing more. I wanted to answer him, but I didn't know how. All my efforts to concentrate were useless. I was too exhausted.

The connection was instantly cut off when the dragon roared. He stood there, enormous in all his glory. Samantha looked tiny next to him. Scorchfire could easily crush her, but she didn't seem impressed. The tip of her sword was embedded in the beast's chest. "Nooooo!" I cried.

I couldn't afford to lose him, especially since elven magic was tied to his life. In a final effort, I rushed toward the vampire queen, throwing myself at her. She easily pushed me away with a wave of magic; my embedded jewels raised a shield to cushion my fall again. Debris flew under the impact. Without the shield, I certainly would have broken a rib.

I had to face the facts. I was no match for her, not in my current state.

I watched helplessly as Samantha fought Scorchfire. It made no sense. Why would anyone try so hard to revive a beast only to kill it?

Scorchfire fought fiercely against her, breathing fire and attacking with his tail and paws. He may not have had claws—they had been plundered when he was dead—but he had teeth, which he repeatedly used to bite the queen. He sent her flying against the wall with a headbutt, but she quickly got back up. I was stunned to see how easily Samantha recovered from each of his blows and pushed him back despite his being a behemoth.

It was impressive, yet scary to watch them lunge at each other relentlessly. I had to do something to help Scorchfire. Suddenly, I found it. My gaze fell on the massive entrance doors. If I could open them, Scorchfire could escape and be free. I dragged myself slowly through the chapel; my body protested with every movement. Every piece of debris was an obstacle, slowing me down even more. The dragon's roars, the queen's screams, and the sound of benches crashing against the walls echoed around me. It felt like an eternity had passed by the time I finally arrived.

The smell of burning reached my nostrils. I turned around and saw that the benches were on fire. The centuries-old dry wood fed the flames greedily. It was already spreading to the base of the curtains. My gaze rose to the ceiling, which was supported by large wooden beams. Once the fire reached those, it would be too late to save the chapel. The ceiling would collapse, and everyone under it would die.

I had to get out of there, and fast.

The room was already unbearably hot. The stone walls glowed red where the fire raged most fiercely. I stayed close to the floor to avoid inhaling too much smoke, holding a piece of my tunic up to my nose.

In the center, Samantha stood motionless, possessed by a magical power unlike anything I had ever felt before. She was a much more formidable enemy than I had thought. I had underestimated her.

Just as I finally reached the door levers, I heard an ear-piercing scream. I turned around and saw Samantha covered in blood, wounded but victorious. She stood over Scorchfire. The dragon was dying—*again*. The creature's magic transferred into

Samantha like a bright purple stream. The queen savored her triumph, jubilant with pleasure at the dragon's death.

With his last breath, a wave of serenity washed over me, and words flooded my mind: *"Ruun to ruun. Mor'thuun noth."*

I collapsed to the ground, crying out in despair. The fire consumed everything around me, as if fate itself were determined to erase all traces of what had just happened. All those efforts . . . Scorchfire had been the only hope to save elven magic.

I felt our mental connection shatter when the beast took his last breath.

Samantha stood up and looked at me sharply. Her gaze fell on the walls. She sent magical waves into the room, effortlessly extinguishing the fire, as if it were nothing more than an inconvenience, while she slowly advanced toward me. There was no trace of a smile or kindness. This was her true face. She was a strong, hateful, and ruthless queen. Dark, like all vampires.

Desperate to save my people, I had allowed myself to be trapped in this deadly alliance with evil. Now, weakened and without magic, I would die without fulfilling my duty as Grand Wizard.

An intense power radiated from her as she came closer. I couldn't die—not like this. In desperation, I activated the lever to open the doors. This was my only chance. I had to run and save myself.

The lever clicked. The heavy doors began to open slowly, with a muffled clatter, as the gears turned. Too slow. Cool air seeped into the chapel as the doors opened, making me shiver as it touched the sweat beading on my skin. The sound of people feasting outside reached my ears, even though I couldn't see them yet. Samantha could reach me now, but the opening in the doors was still too small for me to run out—if I could even run in my state.

Suddenly, the chapel door that led to the castle swung open. Two out-of-breath guards entered.

"Your Majesty!" they shouted, clearly terrified.

Samantha turned toward them, annoyed. "What is it?"

"Dragons," the one on the left breathed. "Dragons are all over the sky. They're attacking the city."

I didn't know what to make of their words. Scorchfire had just died at Samantha's hands. He was the last dragon, whom we had only just resurrected, only to steal his second chance away.

"Zarvok Drel'kaan.

Ruun to ruun. Mor'thuun noth."

The words were engraved in my memory, even though I didn't understand their meaning.

The space between the doors widened, granting me visibility. Instead of a starry sky, dragons soared, dozens of them, their target the once-grand city of Ichoryllia. The buildings were on fire. Lightning and ice flashed everywhere—a magical storm of the elements that was bent on destruction. The screams that I had initially mistaken for those of a celebration were in fact the cries of vampires running through the streets. Houses were being destroyed. It was chaos.

"Impossible," I breathed.

Samantha gripped my arm with a steel-like force, preventing me from moving. "Lock her in her room!" she ordered the guards furiously. "I'll deal with her later. For now, I must prepare our defenses."

The guards took me away from the queen. Struggling was useless. Once my mana had recovered, I could devise a plan to escape. I didn't comprehend how those dragons appeared out of nowhere, but it brought hope to my heart. Dragons lived. The elven race and its magic would survive.

Chapter 2 (Samantha)

Fires From the Sky

Frustration filled me as I rushed out of the cathedral. The sudden dragon invasion prevented me from enjoying the fact that I had absorbed another of Alastor's essences. It didn't make sense. I had resurrected only *one* dragon, and I had killed it.

Now, these cursed creatures were everywhere, destroying *my kingdom*.

The only problem was that I had no idea how to defend the city. There had been dragon attacks on the kingdom centuries before, but it was only one beast each time. Even then, an entire army was needed to eliminate it.

I hurried down the hallway. Servants rushed past me in all directions. Panic was everywhere. I was out of breath when I reached the war strategy room. Viktor must have arrived a few seconds before me. He was walking to the back of the room when I entered. He turned at the sound of the doors opening and smiled when he saw me.

"There you are," he whispered, his voice filled with relief.

I walked over to him and enjoyed his embrace. "Your clothes are stained with blood. Are you okay?" he asked, concerned.

Memories of the fight flooded back: Scorchfire sinking his fangs into my flesh. In the adrenaline rush, I had forgotten about my wounds. Although not mortal due to my vampiric nature, they were still there, reminding me that the beast had not gone down easily.

"It's okay. Most of it isn't my blood. My vampire powers will heal these soon."

Viktor nodded, looking reassured. Dreven, one of my high-ranked Miłonblooders, entered the room with Lysander, followed by Caspian, one of our best generals. His dark brown hair fell in curls to his chin, framing his face. His white shirt contrasted with his dark amber skin.

"Your Majesty," he said hastily, unrolling a large map and placing it on the war room table made from a single slab of a two-hundred-year-old oak tree. Lysander brought an inkwell and a quill from a nearby desk to take notes.

The map was stained with blood at the top and bottom, but it was the most complete one we had. I made a mental note to ask for a new one once all this was over. We had a good mapmaker who worked with the best animal skins in town.

Caspian had drawn marks on the map with ink. "The fort has been destroyed, but most of the soldiers escaped and are safe. The houses to the east have been partially destroyed or burned down. We have received reports of more than fifty wounded citizens and dozens of dead. More than twenty people are reported missing, but we expect that number to rise."

Caspian's fingers shifted to the next area while Lysander scribbled everything on a parchment. "There have been reports of multiple fires to the west of the city. It seems dragons have mainly attacked from the air with magic and fire in that area. We don't yet know how many people have perished. The soldiers and the militia are working together to extinguish the fires."

"Have you sent the mages out?" I asked. We didn't have many, but we did have a couple of them in town—a handful of elves who had decided to set up shop in Ichoryllia years ago.

"Yes," Caspian replied. "They're all casting spells to try to repel the dragons and protect the city's market square."

"We could use the few enchanted shields we have to protect the most important stores," suggested Lysander.

We only had a handful, but it would be useful against the dragons' magic. I nodded. "Yes, let's protect the food and healing supplies shops first."

The market square was an essential part of the town. Rebuilding the city would be much more difficult if it were destroyed.

Viktor sighed. "Do we even know where those dragons come from? I thought they were extinct."

I shook my head. "I wish I knew, but it doesn't matter right now. We need to defend ourselves."

He nodded. "You're right. We can figure it out later."

Caspian continued, "To the south, the outer walls are destroyed. A few dragons landed on the ground and are attacking the soldiers directly. This is where we're taking the hardest hit."

"Then that's where we'll help," I declared. I wouldn't be a cowardly queen who hides when battle comes. With the powers I've absorbed to fulfill Alastor's prophecy, I should be able to inflict some damage.

Viktor held my gaze, a fire burning within. "We could send the battalion of volunteers we've assembled," he suggested.

I shook my head. "I sent the battalion to Krelgraz a few days ago. They should have reached the island by now."

He cursed. "Right. I had forgotten about that."

If I had known the dragons were going to attack us, I would have kept the battalion in town. In total, we had recruited about a hundred volunteers to go to battle against the orcs. There were people of different races and ages: humans, vampires, and some elves. Some were prisoners bargaining for their freedom, while others were experienced fighters. The battalion was stronger than I had anticipated, and we had trained them well before sending them out. They would have been a great help against the dragons.

"How many soldiers do we have?" I asked.

Caspian answered after a moment's thought, "A little over four thousand, but they're spread throughout the town. To the south, I'd say about two thousand."

I was hoping for more. "It will have to do," I answered.

"I have contacted our fellow Miłonblooders," Dreven added. "Some of them are already fighting as their houses were attacked, but they're all reporting to duty."

"Good."

Lysander added, "I have contacted the Thieves' Guild. Their leader, Vince, vowed to protect the town. They may be thieves, but this is their home."

"Nice thinking. Assassins and thieves will prove themselves useful in battle," Viktor said.

"Indeed," replied the old servant. "And they have access to a wide array of poisons."

I summarized, "This brings us to about five thousand men spread throughout the city. Dreven, gather the Miłonblooders and tell them to head south. Lysander, do the same for the Thieves' Guild. This will give us an extra force against the dragons that have landed."

They all nodded. "Yes, Your Majesty!"

They headed out, leaving me alone with Viktor. He grabbed my hand, landing a soft kiss on top of it, and stared deeply into my eyes. "Promise me you'll be safe."

I smiled. "Don't worry about me."

He nodded. "I'll try, but I'll stay close to you on the battlefield. That way, I can take a blow in your stead."

His words struck me to the heart. I had never thought much of others, but I realized now that I didn't want him to leave my side. I shook my head. "You don't need to do this. I need you to stay alive."

He smiled, his canines showing slightly. I loved it when they did. "I'll try my best not to get killed, then," he answered.

Outside, the scream of a dragon tore through the night. There was no time to lose. I rushed to the armory, Viktor following. Caspian was already in his steel armor, which was painted with the city's emblem: a red sword piercing a skull and dripping blood.

He handed us our royal armors. Viktor's helmet covered his entire face, leaving only holes for him to see and breathe through. It was heavy, but offered maximum protection. Mine was made of reinforced leather, unlike his steel-made attire. It was designed for speed and movement. I did not wear a helmet. This combination of armor allowed me to freely use my magical powers.

I have absorbed three of Alastor's essences. I didn't yet know how to harness this power, but I was convinced that I would discover how on the battlefield.

We passed through the castle courtyard, finding the sky was streaked with fire and wings. War horns blared in the distance. Plumes of gray smoke rose into the sky. Houses reduced to ashes glowed red in the night. Towers were cracked and leaning, threatening to collapse. The cobblestone streets were littered with broken roof pieces and loose rocks. Blood and ash mixed in the gutters, forming a blackish-red mixture that flowed across the ground. It was horrible to see my kingdom in such a state.

We strode through it all as quickly as possible. We avoided flying so as not to be attacked by dragons and headed south on foot.

We passed what had once been a square, but all that remained were rubble and broken bodies. A group of vampires knelt in a heap beside the ruins, clutching corpses—children, lovers, and charred people.

One man staggered up from the ashes, his face caked with soot and blood. He held a jagged spear of scrap metal and trembled with rage.

"You did this . . ." he rasped, his voice breaking, pointing an accusing finger at me. "You brought this on us!"

I clenched my teeth. This man had no idea of what I had gone through for this kingdom and Alastor. These were the words of a desperate, grief-stricken man. I bellowed, "How dare you speak to your queen like that?"

The man ran at me. In an instant, Viktor stepped forward. His blade sang, and the man fell—cleanly, gentle even. Silence ensued, broken only by the thud of the body and the soft weeping of those left behind.

My eyes flicked across the people—these broken shadows of citizens. "You would do well to remember where your loyalty remains," I warned in a low voice.

The citizens stared without a sound, frozen in shock by what had happened. I didn't wait for them to respond and continued walking, stepping over the bloodied stone and the man's body, into the smoke where the dragons still roared.

The closer we got to the southern border, the louder the sounds of battle became: the clanging of swords striking hard scales and the cries of men being attacked by the beasts. The smell of burnt skin, mixed with sweat and blood, hung in the air, carried by the breeze. I wrinkled my nose and pressed on.

The ruins of the southern wall came into view, along with the sight of two imposing dragons. My breath caught. One was midnight blue with white opal eyes, the other was deep green with purple eyes. They looked to be at least fifty feet long and as tall as houses. They beat their massive wings, generating gusts of wind that caused soldiers and debris to fall. Their tails swung, and the soldiers jumped to avoid being hit. There were circles of burned dirt on the ground, along with the remains of charred bodies.

The blue dragon roared in anger, the sound resonating through my chest. “I’m going for that one,” I shouted.

“Then I’ll take the green,” Caspian answered.

Viktor added, “I’ll go with the queen.”

We split up and joined the soldiers who were already fighting the beasts. The blue dragon surged forward, snapping his jaws at me as we passed. I dove to the side, avoiding the attack. I sent a wave of magic at the beast’s flank, and the creature screeched. A group of soldiers and Miłonblooders launched a fierce attack on the dragon. Viktor slashed at the beast with his sword. The training he had undergone in recent weeks showed. He skillfully maneuvered to avoid being hit and managed to pierce the dragon’s hard scales.

Alastor’s essence flowed through my veins as I bombarded the dragon with magic spells. He was granting me his strength and grace to defeat the beast, but the dragon was stronger than I had imagined and offered great resistance. Killing Scorchfire had been easier—this one was ten times stronger.

We only managed to hold him off, rather than inflict real damage. Meanwhile, Caspian and the army were fighting hard against the green dragon. It was smaller—possibly a juvenile—and wounded. I watched my general leap into the air to attack it. Blood oozed from its wounds, and it howled in pain, shaking the ground with its cry.

I couldn’t watch for long before the blue dragon lunged at me again. I barely had time to cast a protective spell around myself and Viktor before the beast breathed burning fire at us. The heat was unbearable, even under the protective bubble. Sweat beaded on my forehead, but I continued to cast my spell, pushing back the dragon’s breath with great effort.

It was either that or get killed.

A soldier next to me caught fire and began screaming while rolling on the ground. He managed to extinguish them, but staggered away, clearly shaken by what had just happened.

I lost track of time as we battled on for hours. Exhaustion began to show on our soldiers. Their reflexes slowed, and some sought shelter among the debris to rest briefly. This couldn't go on forever. Even I, despite all the power I had absorbed, was breathing heavily.

The sun began to rise on the horizon. Suddenly, a scream tore through the battlefield, drowning out all other sounds. Everyone froze for a moment as our eyes fell on the source of the cry—the green dragon. Around the beast lay about half of our army, dead and lying in pools of blood. Dozens of soldiers surrounded the beast, still alive. The dragon was bleeding from several wounds. One of its wings had been severed and lay further away. Caspian stood triumphantly, covered in blood and holding his sword in the beast's eye.

I shifted my attention back to the blue dragon with renewed confidence. The remaining soldiers joined us in the fight. Pumped up on adrenaline, we already believed ourselves to be victorious against these two. The swords were being readied, and I recited the words to cast a spell, but just as we were about to attack, the dragon launched into the sky. I expected it to breathe fire or dive toward us. To my utter amazement, though, the dragon rose higher, abandoning the fight.

Silence fell, sudden and wrong. The fires still crackled. The wounded still screamed. But the dragons no longer attacked. All the others still in the sky did the same. Some flew away into the distance, others remained high above the city, circling like vultures. They hovered, distant shapes beyond the reach of spell or arrow. They showed no further signs of hostility. It was as if they were watching, waiting for something. But what?

"Do you think killing one of them caused this?" Viktor asked as he removed his helmet. He was as shocked as I was.

I shook my head. "No, I think that whatever called them here must have called them back."

"You think so?" Viktor asked thoughtfully.

I shrugged, exhausted from fighting for hours. "We'll find the answer, but for now . . ." My gaze swept around me. The soldiers could barely stand. There were dead bodies to burn. The dragon's corpse had to be dealt with. Walls and buildings needed repair, and citizens needed rescue. There was so much to do, yet we were all on the verge of collapse. "For now, we've earned a moment of rest."

Caspian, who had joined us during the conversation, nodded and ordered the soldiers to retreat, wash up, and eat.

The walk back to the castle seemed to take forever. Despite being exhausted, we helped a few people along the way. Ash still drifted through the air, but the fires had quieted. The streets were filled with sobbing. Some people searched through the rubble, while others dug graves with their bare hands. Some were too numb to move, staring at the desolation. The heart of the vampire city, once proud and tall, now sat hunched under a sky still haunted by the dragons' shadows.

Only the north side of the city and the castle had been spared. I wondered if it was luck or if the beasts had intentionally avoided attacking the castle. Servants awaited us when we arrived.

"Patrol the town. Help the wounded however you can. Make a list of the gold and resources needed for reconstruction," I told them. They nodded and prepared to do as I said.

Viktor, Caspian, and I stood in the throne room for a moment. The air was still, frozen by the emotions of what had just happened. Even the dust particles suspended in the air seemed to be waiting for the shock to pass. I just wanted to wash the dried blood and dirt from my skin and under my nails, but we still needed to talk. Suddenly, the events of the night hit me like a wave. It was so overwhelming that I was afraid I would drown. A light breeze entered the room, carrying the pungent smell of destruction, but I was too shaken to really notice. Lost in thought, I remembered the man's attack and his accusation, vivid and real.

"They blame me," I whispered, clenching my teeth to keep the tears of anger from flowing. These accusations were unfair. They didn't know all I had sacrificed. "After everything I've done for them, all my efforts to restore Alastor— They spat on my name when I fought for the greater good."

"They're scared," Viktor said softly. "Scared people cling to blame like a raft in a storm. It gives them the illusion of control."

A lot had happened since I became queen of Ichoryllia. I stared at my general. "Do *you* blame me?"

He paused. "I blame the dragons, the gods who woke them, and whoever sent them to our town."

I gave a dry, bitter smile. "How diplomatic of you," I said, my words as sharp as a sword.

Viktor cut in before Caspian could answer, breaking the tension. "We need to reassure them and show them that you're there to protect the kingdom."

Caspian looked serious, his arms crossed. He was more concerned about the kingdom's safety than about politics and opinions. "The dragons are still circling in the sky. We must prepare ourselves in case they attack again."

He was right. It was essential to prepare for another attack. By Alastor, I hoped that wouldn't happen. However, preparing for it would also reassure the population. Still, I felt like I was being asked to perform miracles. "The town is half destroyed, and our surviving men who are still alive are wounded. How do you expect me to do that?" I asked.

Silence. Then, hesitantly, Caspian took a breath. "There is . . . a relic. A shield. Not a literal one, but a ward. It was crafted during the first war between mortals and dragons, thousands of years ago. It's a relic imbued with the will of the last winged saint."

I narrowed my eyes at the general. If such a powerful relic existed, it would have been found already. "The winged saints are nothing but a myth."

He retorted. "A myth that left behind something we could use against the dragons. It would make the citizens feel protected and restore their faith in you, Your Majesty."

I didn't have many options. The city was defenseless against so many dragons, and I was fortunate that the damage wasn't more extensive. If this relic were real, searching for it could be very advantageous. I sighed. "Where is it?"

"It's said to be hidden in the drowned ruins of the Skyfall Temple, beyond the marshes to the northwest."

The marshes were several days away, and I couldn't trust anyone to go and retrieve it. Such power could turn any soldier or general—my gaze fell on Caspian—into a threat to my throne. I would have to find a way to enter the submerged ruins and retrieve the relic without dying. However, doing so could secure my reign, protect the kingdom, and give me the time and power I needed to fulfill Alastor's prophecy. It was worth the risk.

"Alright, I'll rest and prepare to head there."

Viktor commented, "It's a long journey. You can't be gone for that long. Send someone else—"

"No," I interrupted, my voice more aggressive than I would have liked. The strain from the earlier fight was taking its toll on me. I was done with this conversation. I lowered my tone, determined to go and wash. "I need to do this myself. Alastor will guide me. You take care of the kingdom while I'm gone."

I hoped to reassure him, but Viktor frowned. "What if it kills you?"

I took a deep breath as the weight of my decision settled on my shoulders like a crown of stone. "Then let my bones become the shield the city needs."

Chapter 3 (Erendriel)

The Sun Kingdom

It was early morning when I opened my eyes, and light streamed into my room through the gap in the curtains. For once, dawn didn't come bearing the weight of a crown, but rather the shimmer of promise. I was eager to see the results of my experiments.

I fastened my robes. The green silk hung comfortably on my body, and the golden embroidery glinted like fine chainmail. I grabbed the rune from my dresser and studied its symbol before slipping it into my pocket. Its familiar presence made me feel better. I looked into the mirror. The years had yet to leave their mark on me, and my silver hair, tied back and clasped with an onyx circlet, still gave me the air of a god among mortals.

I smiled. Today wouldbe productive.

I was eager to get to the mages' tower. I had provided them with four *volunteers* the day before. They were easy to find, and they didn't have a choice, anyway. I couldn't wait to see how the runes would affect them. I had left all the bags of runes for them to experiment with. All except one rune, which I kept with me in my pocket at all times.

I descended the eastern stairway, taking my time. My mood was too fine to rush.

In the great hall, the morning feast awaited me. On the table were roasted nuts, grapes, and honey bread. Mathias was already seated, hunched over his plate, with his long blond hair braided. He usually ate before me, but I had gotten up earlier than usual.

"Your Majesty," he said, rising and bowing quickly. I beckoned him to sit down.

"I'll help myself," I said as I broke off a piece of bread.

Mathias looked at me, surprised. "You're up . . . cheerful. That's rare, especially for someone expecting war."

He was right. The nightmares and the war against the dwarves had weighed heavily on my mood, as well as the voices that had been pressing me to spill more blood. Humans and werewolves had declared war on us. I should have had plenty to be nervous about, but the prospect of my experiments yielding the desired results was stronger than anything else. I slid into the seat beside him. "Perhaps it's because I finally have weapons the world has never seen," I declared.

He raised a brow. Mathias knew about my ongoing experiments with the magical runes. "Was it successful?"

"Perhaps. I'm off to see the results right after breakfast."

Mathias paused, swallowing his bite of sun fruit. “Well, that’s worth a toast, or at least another piece of bread.”

We sat in silence for a moment. Birdsong came in through the open window and filled the space between us. I enjoyed the warmth and the momentary calm. Mathias pushed his empty plate aside and headed for the large sideboard at the far end of the room. On top was the rolled-up map of the world.

“Any news of the elite warriors we sent?” I asked as he brought the map to the table.

He shook his head. “No, but at this rate, they should have reached their target by now. We should receive news tonight.”

I hoped they killed every werewolf. “Good. That will teach those beasts to declare war on us.”

Mathias nodded and unrolled the map across the table.

“Have they bought the woman yet?” I asked.

“We have sent our agents, but haven’t heard back yet,” he answered nonchalantly. Emerald was my key to power over Nathan. The sooner we acquired her, the sooner I had a way to get rid of the hybrid. I would be damned if I let the prophecy come true.

Mathias cleared his throat, and I returned my attention to the map. He pointed to it and spoke eagerly. “I have consulted our generals, as you requested. The human kingdom and the werewolf packs are both located to the west of our city. They can’t get through the mountains surrounding the Valley of Nysa. They’re most likely to travel up northeast and approach from the west. It’s the quickest route.”

It made sense, but still, I didn’t like it. I was sure they had a better strategy. Surprising your opponent was the best way to gain the upper hand in a war. I knew that from experience. Only an inexperienced general would follow what Mathias was suggesting. "That's what they want us to think. It's too obvious."

I studied the map and tapped my fingers north of our city. "They can't come from the north because the river is too wide to cross on foot, and they have no fleet."

I traced the forest down from Mytvathyr with my finger. "On the other hand, they could take a detour hidden in the forest, and come from the south, hoping to ambush us."

I turned my eyes to the dwarf city I'd just conquered to the northeast. "It would be an even bigger detour, but they could bypass our city and attack Mumbur directly to take it from us. It's unlikely, but it's an option that shouldn't be overlooked."

He nodded. "We still have troops there."

"But we destroyed much of the city's defenses while attacking. I haven't heard from my generals stationed there in a few weeks, so I'm unsure of the state of the city. They might not be able to push the enemy back, and we can't afford to leave Mytvathyr undefended."

"So what do we do?"

"We'll send lookouts. If they detect that troops are heading for Mumbur, our mages will launch a wall of fire at the enemy army, destroying them in the desert before they reach the city."

Yesss, rejoiced the voice in my head. Mathias had a horrified look. "But that will likely destroy everything in the area, making the roads impracticable for commerce. The citizens might starve."

I shrugged. "They'll either get resources from the port or die. Sacrifices are sometimes necessary."

"Wouldn't that make the citizen resent us?" asked Mathias.

I dismissed his concerns with a wave of my hand. "We've already crushed their army. There's practically no one left who could oppose us."

My gaze shifted southward on the map to the town of Ichoryllia. "I sent a message to the vampire queen yesterday. Any news?"

Mathias shook his head. "Still no reply, Your Majesty."

I grunted. "They'll wait until the rivers run red before lifting a finger. Still, they're our allies."

A servant arrived then, bowing low. "Your Majesty, there is someone at the gate. Prince Vaelarion of the Sun Kingdom."

The name surprised me. We had very limited contact with that elven kingdom. They lived far to the east, on another continent, so it had probably taken them several weeks to get here. They certainly didn't come all this way for nothing. I already had enough on my plate without worrying about them.

I nodded graciously, hiding my emotions. "Prepare the audience chamber and keep him waiting. I'll see him after my breakfast."

The servant left the room. I took another bite of bread, but it now tasted bland. News of the elf prince's visit had ruined my appetite. I left the food on the table and motioned to Mathias.

"We'll talk about this later."

The elf nodded, and I left for the audience chamber.

The scent of citrus tea filled the room when I arrived. Prince Vaelarion was sitting in a comfortable pink upholstered armchair with his back to the door. It had been the previous queen's favorite chair, and I had kept it as a reminder of the days when I used to come and play here as a child.

I took a deep breath, preparing myself for what was to come. The prince certainly wasn't there for a chat about the weather. I walked around the chair and sat down behind the massive wooden desk.

Prince Vaelarion's eyes lit up when he saw me. I hadn't seen him in over a century, and he looked exactly as I remembered: too tall, too graceful, and too rigid. His armor sparkled in the light, an orange flame encrusted in the center, untouched by war—a perfect symbol of his house. A house that, for all its ancient honor, contributed nothing to the present struggle.

"King Erendriel," he said with the stiffness of diplomacy. "Thank you for receiving me."

"Akael," I said with equal hollowness. "I trust your journey was safe?"

"We sailed along safe trade routes, those monitored by all the maritime kingdoms, and avoided pirates."

Surely, he must have traveled with several dozen men. One didn't cross the ocean on a boat alone. Still, the prince had come alone to the castle. Our kingdoms were at peace, but it was unusual for a prince to visit without at least one personal guard accompanying him.

"That is good to hear. I will ask the servants to bring refreshments to your crew."

The prince shook his head. "That won't be necessary, Your Majesty. They remained at the port of Mumbur. Some of my men have gone into town to buy supplies while the others wait for my return on the ship."

The commercial port of Mumbur was the main point of entry to our continent. Since Mytvathyr was further inland, people would drop anchor at the dwarf city and then continue their journey on foot or horseback.

Akael hesitated. "I came because I am seeking a mage who works for you: Elaine."

I tensed slightly. *"Wench,"* whispered the voice, but I ignored it. Elaine hadn't returned from the vampire kingdom yet, and I hoped she had been dealt with.

"What do you want with her?" I asked. I wasn't sure if she was dead, and I wouldn't want her powers to fall into someone else's hands. She was far too powerful, far too dangerous.

The prince tensed. "It is a matter for the Sun Kingdom to discuss with her. I assure you, Your Majesty, we mean no harm to your kingdom," he added quickly.

He brushed it off too easily, which annoyed me. He had traveled across the ocean for this. Whatever he wanted with her, he wouldn't get it.

"I'm afraid she's not here," I continued smoothly. "She left weeks ago. She traveled to the dwarven kingdom. She had magical matters to attend to. Her powers were needed to help the king and queen of the dwarves. She'll return when she's finished."

He studied me for a moment too long. I returned his gaze without flinching. If he knew I was lying, he didn't say anything.

"I'll wait for her return," he said.

I cursed inwardly. As a member of the royal family, I was obliged to accept his request and offer him hospitality. Otherwise, I would be breaking a royal etiquette established centuries ago. How tedious.

"Of course," I replied, smiling thinly. "As long as you like. I'll have my servants prepare a room for you."

"You have my sincerest gratitude, Your Majesty," replied the prince with a slight bow of his head.

I needed to leave this room and get the prince out of my sight before I lost whatever patience I had left. I would need Mathias to keep a close eye on our *guest*. One wrong move and I'd deal with him myself. I couldn't eliminate the prince without causing diplomatic problems with the Sun Kingdom, but I knew how to navigate political problems. I would send him right back to his crew on the ship, and then back home at the first opportunity.

"Now, if you'll excuse me, I have matters to attend to," I said, standing up. I didn't wait for an answer and left the room.

Mathias was waiting outside the room. I gave him instructions and left. By midday, I had made my way to the mages' tower. The lower levels of the tower housed rooms that no one talked about, the ones where my experiments took place.

The magic runes we had found in the dwarf kingdom proved to be very effective when embedded in animals. I remembered how difficult it had been to kill the living armor that the dwarves had created with them. By implanting them in people, I could create the most powerful army ever. Strong enough to defend us in the war against humans and werewolves, and to prevent the Oracle's prophecy from coming true.

The stones were colder there, and the air reeked of blood, salt, and change. Guards were stationed every few rooms. The nature of this floor was for experiments and torture, so it was preferable to keep it highly guarded.

Jules greeted me with a deep bow. His robes were stained with greenish ink and dried blood. "Your Majesty. The results are . . . varied."

I approached the first cell. The body was swollen, and the veins were blackened. Elven, male. His face was frozen in silent agony.

"Rejected?"

"Violently."

I grunted. These weren't the results I was hoping for. The second prisoner, a half-wolf, was still alive. He writhed and gasped, his claws digging into the stone beneath him. His transformation had failed halfway through. His limbs were out of proportion. His eyes flickered with madness.

"Dispose of him."

Jules nodded and signaled for the nearest guards to put the man out of his misery. The stationed guards lifted their blades through the bars without hesitation. A scream followed the slicing sound, accompanied by the melody of blood dripping to the floor. I moved on to the third cell. It was empty and had already been cleaned.

And the fourth . . .

My breath caught for just a moment.

The elf in the final cell had survived. He had not only survived, but also changed. His body was lean and taut with new muscle. His skin shimmered faintly, and light flowed through veins that now glowed like emerald fire. His eyes opened as I approached, not with fear, but awareness. *Uncanny intelligence*. His eyes were steady, following every movement with a depth of awareness no living thing should possess.

"Do you remember your name?" I asked.

"Taron," he said. "I was a soldier before I was made a prisoner."

I remembered him. A sad story, really. He was a good, loyal soldier who was caught stealing in the palace. It was a shame to have to imprison him. I stared at him with the look only a king could give: full of authority and imposing respect.

"You have a chance to redeem yourself. You are something more now."

He nodded. "I feel it."

Jules stepped beside me. "Enhanced cognitive reflexes and acute magical sensitivity. His strength is greatly enhanced, and his pain tolerance is . . . extraordinary."

That was exactly the kind of result I needed. With enough transformed soldiers, I was sure I would win the war, even with fewer troops than my enemies had.

"Any idea why this one survived while the others died?" I asked Jules. If we could pinpoint that, then I could build an army in no time.

Jules shrugged. "I'm afraid not, Your Majesty."

"State information about yourself," I said to the transformed soldier.

"My name is Taron. Magic level M-3. I was born to elven parents. I learned to wield a sword at a young age. I'm not sure what else you wish to know, Your Majesty."

Although one subject wasn't enough to determine the parameters for success, it was still a start.

"Have him prepped for training. I want him combat-ready within a week."

Jules bowed again.

"All the failed subjects. Note their race, age, and magical levels. I want to narrow down who makes a good candidate and who doesn't."

"Yes, of course," Jules replied.

"More subjects will arrive today. Take them all. Every prisoner. Tell them they've volunteered." I turned back toward the stairs. "We need survivors."

If we could achieve a higher success rate, I would crush the humans and werewolves. Then I'd find the hybrid and put an end to him. I had barely returned to the upper hall when I heard the pounding of boots.

A guard came running, red-faced and panting. "My king!"

I turned around, hoping it wasn't another visiting prince.

"What is it?" I asked, keeping my tone calm.

"Dragons. Two. East of the city. They were seen above the marshes."

My blood ran cold.

I climbed the tower steps two at a time. The higher I climbed, the more the air changed—becoming sharper and more electric. The wind tugged at my cloak as I stepped out onto the viewing platform.

And there they were.

Two massive shapes wheeled in the sky. One was emerald, and the other was bronze. Their wings beat like thunder, slow and deliberate. They weren't flying directly toward us, but they were close enough to smell the fear in our city.

I remembered Elaine's words. She had said that we needed to resurrect the dragons to save our magic. Was this her doing?

Whether it was or not, it was good news. I would tell the citizens that their magic had been saved and that they didn't have to worry anymore. I would take the credit. They would rejoice and remain loyal to me.

"Beautiful," Mathias murmured as he joined me.

"Terrifying," I corrected. Dragons were great for what they represented, but they were deadly.

He nodded. "They're not attacking."

"Not yet," I pointed out.

They veered westward and disappeared behind the horizon. My heart pounded. If there were two of them, then I assumed there were more. As long as one remained alive, the elven magic should be safe.

"Send word to the outposts. Prepare the ballistae. If they come too close, we'll shoot them down."

Mathias looked uncertain. "Are we ready for that?"

It was a gamble, but we had no choice but to defend our city if the creatures attacked. "No, but we will be."

As the wind howled louder, I closed my eyes and let it whip through my hair. Dragons in the sky. I had thought that sight impossible. It was both comforting and terrifying. I knew their presence was required for elven magic to survive, but they were also powerful creatures that could destroy our city. They would rule the sky, and who knows what lands they would choose to settle in? One more thing to worry about. But that would have to wait.

War was coming.

And I had to be ready.

Chapter 4 (Caleb)

Burning Blood

I flew through the night sky, holding Summer tightly. Lost in her jasmine scent, the sound of her heart was reassuring. She held to me faintly, but her clenched fingers reminded me that she was alive. That was all that mattered. I had no idea how we would escape Aeris, but I didn't care. We would find a way. The first thing to do was to take care of my mate.

All kinds of thoughts raced through my head as I flew. I realized that the goddess's magic, which had been omnipresent before, had still not returned since I had sealed the bond with Summer. The magic was still there, but very weak and nearly unreachable. It was as if the sacred bond of the Moon Goddess had pushed back Aeris's magic. I remembered her mentioning that she was Selena's half-sister. I wasn't too sure about their family rank or hierarchy, but I was grateful that my connection with the dreaded goddess was broken. I hoped it would prevent her from knowing my location. It would give me a head start to escape her wrath.

I had a plan. It wasn't fully formed yet, but it was the best I could think of in the few hours I decided to flee with my mate. We flew north where the moon elves had their lands, but I had also once heard about a distant kingdom. I knew little about them, but I had heard that they welcomed people from different races. Surely, either the moon elves or that kingdom would welcome us.

I wasn't sure if they would allow us to settle permanently in their city, but I was certain they would at least let me take care of Summer while she healed.

There was another reason I had chosen to fly north: it was far from the vampire city. I was sure Aeris would check my home first. With a little luck, the goddess wouldn't think to look for us so far north, and we'd have some time to rest before she found us.

It wasn't ideal. I didn't want my mate to spend her life fleeing an angry goddess. What a terrible mate I was, dooming her to a life of running away.

"I'm happy with you." Those sweet, tender words echoed in my mind. They dispelled my doubts and stopped me from blaming myself.

I kissed the top of her head and held her tighter. *"You're right,"* I replied through our bond.

Her eyes widened as she looked at me. "Your eyes," she said weakly.

I was so preoccupied with her health that I wondered what she suddenly meant. "What's wrong with them?"

"They're not silver anymore!"

I frowned. "What?"

She whispered with a smile, "They're blue with silver flickers running through them."

I was shocked, but happy at the same time. I wouldn't have wanted to be stuck with silver eyes forever, constantly reminding me of the mistake I had made in bonding with Aeris.

Then I realized that Summer had only known me when I had silver eyes. "Do you like it?" I asked.

Her hand brushed against my cheek with affection. "Yes, they're beautiful!"

Warmth spread through my chest at her words. I looked up from Summer. The stars were beautiful, and a feeling of serenity filled me. A breeze rose and brushed my skin. Suddenly, the sky filled with dragons. I blinked to see if I was dreaming, but they were really there, filling the sky as far as the eye could see. It made no sense. Vampires had perfect vision at night. I would have seen them if they had been there. Dragons couldn't just appear out of thin air. Weren't they extinct? I was stunned.

"What the . . . ?"

I narrowly avoided a red dragon that was charging toward me at full speed. Even though I was powerful, these creatures were incredibly fast and terrifying. I didn't understand how such creatures could blink into existence like that. There were so many of them that I had to dodge them everywhere I went. Summer let out a scream. I couldn't continue like this, or we would both be dead. I briefly considered going around them, but there were so many that I couldn't see how I could avoid them.

The red dragon came back for more. I changed course, but it followed. I cursed. It had decided that I was its next meal, and I disagreed.

"It'll be okay," I promised to Summer, as I dove to avoid the beast. It was close behind me. I was grateful that I was stronger than a regular vampire, because otherwise I wouldn't have stood a chance.

I dodged left and right, constantly changing course to avoid the fire the dragon breathed at me. The air heated, and the night lit up as the fire passed close to me—too close for my liking. I was in a deadly celestial waltz with this beast, and I had no idea how to get rid of it. Holding my wounded mate in my arms, I was unable to fight back.

I needed to land.

I desperately scanned the ground below, looking for a safe place. These were wretched lands, Krelgraz. Even dragons knew better than to land here, except the one chasing me. Finally, I spotted a deserted beach, away from orcs. It would have to do. I couldn't run from the dragon forever.

I dove toward the beach at full speed, twisting and turning to avoid being an easy target, and the beast had no trouble keeping up. I kept full speed even as the ground drew closer. It was dangerous, irresponsible, and deadly, but it was my best option. Summer's hands tightened around my arms. She hid her face in my chest. Her heart beat frantically, reverberating across my entire being. The details of the beach became clearer. I hoped I wasn't making a mistake. Fortunately, a few meters before reaching the ground, the dragon spread its wings to slow down, as I had hoped. In doing so, it gained altitude, and I gained a few seconds' lead over the beast.

But it was too late.

I couldn't stop so quickly. I changed course to avoid crashing directly into the ground. I narrowly avoided hitting the beach, the sand kicked up by the wind generated from my passage. I continued along the coast, trying to slow down.

I knew I didn't have much time before the dragon would attack. I doubted it would give up that easily. I spotted some large rocks and a wrecked ship. There was not much left of the boat, just half a wooden hull with some pieces still standing. It wasn't much, but it would have to do. I flew behind the debris and set Summer down on the ground. She should be out of sight, and hopefully, the dragon wouldn't find her.

"Stay here, don't move," I instructed.

Her eyes widened, as if she had already guessed my plan. "What are you going to do?" she asked me, her lips trembling.

"There's no way the dragon will give up that easily. If I stay with you, we'll both get killed."

Terror was evident in Summer's eyes. "No! Don't do it! It'll kill you," she pleaded.

I smiled at her words. "Don't forget that I'm a demigod. I'll survive."

I tried to sound confident, but I didn't know if I could kill such a beast on my own. One thing I was certain of, though, was that there was no way I was going to let the dragon kill my mate. It was my duty to protect her.

"I'll never forgive you if you die," she warned.

I laughed and kissed her tenderly. There was no time to enjoy the moment as an angry roar tore through the night. I broke our kiss and hurried out from behind the debris.

There it was, flying low, scanning the beach for me. Its furious yellow eyes glowed in the night sky, the moonlight reflecting off its red scales. I went as far as I could from where Summer was hiding. The dragon spotted me almost immediately and accelerated. It dove toward the ground, its claws ready to grab its prey.

Now that my arms were free, I could defend myself. I focused on the beast, not wanting to miss a single movement. The wind whistled, and sand swirled beneath the dragon's path. I dodged it, but felt the leathery membrane of its wing brushed against my shoulder. My heart raced when I realized how close it had been to me.

I could have flown after it, but it would have been futile; dragons were masters of the air. I was stronger on the ground. If I wanted any chance of winning, I had to force the creature to land.

The dragon repeated its tactic several times, and I dodged each time. I noticed a large piece of wood jutting out of the sand—a possible oar from the wreck. Either way, it would serve as an improvised weapon. The dragon dove once more. I was about to strike it with the oar when it suddenly breathed fire. My first instinct was to run, but I wasn't fast enough. I used my vampire powers to create a protective bubble around myself. It wasn't one of my most powerful abilities, but it was enough to keep me from being burned. However, the oar I was holding caught fire. With its broken end, it looked like a flaming spear. The dragon roared in frustration and flew away. The waves whistled against the sand, smoking where the dragon's flame had touched it.

The beast dove again, and I rolled to avoid it. I managed to scratch the underside of its wing, burning it with the tip of my weapon. The dragon roared and stopped a little further away. Sand rose several feet into the air as the beast's claws dug into the ground, and its wings stretched wide to slow its movement. The dragon turned back toward me, its fury still palpable. The underside of its wing had a trail of blackened, damaged skin that looked fragile, as if it could tear at any moment.

The red dragon crouched low, but it was still much bigger than me. It snarled, smoke curling from its nostrils, and while it couldn't speak to me, I could feel it challenging me to move forward. When I didn't move, the dragon roared an earth-shattering cry and charged at me.

I took flight and avoided the attack.

Then *pain.* I had misjudged the distance, or perhaps the dragon had changed course. Its tail slammed into my side. The piece of wood I was holding flew straight into the water. The sound of my bones breaking echoed through the air before I was thrown into a dune. I closed my eyes and let out a scream.

I had endured worse in the past. I couldn't die here and leave Summer alone. I coughed blood and stood, despite my broken ribs. The dragon didn't wait. It surged forward with its jaws wide open, letting loose a torrent of flames. I rolled, narrowly missing the fire. I used the pain and the fury to fuel my energy. I felt my mate's fear and courage, giving me renewed strength.

I raised my hand to attack the creature with magic, but it charged. Sand spurted from beneath its weight as the dragon attacked me, blocking its view momentarily. I took advantage of the distraction and leaped, reappearing above the dragon. I quickly reached for the dagger hidden in my boot, and I drove it into the dragon's neck with all my might. Its flesh was hard as stone, but I managed to lodge it into the beast. The dragon shrieked. Blood sprayed across my chest—dragon blood.

The dragon thrashed, flinging me to the ground and dislodging the dagger from its neck. I snarled when I hit the rocks hard. When I tried to move my arm, I realized my shoulder was dislocated. I crawled to one knee and dragged myself toward the fallen dagger. I looked up to the beast. It would kill me, I could feel it.

My fangs lengthened at the smell of blood. It was so irresistible, gripping me by the throat, drawing me in like never before. I knew it was a bad idea, but I couldn't fight it.

They said dragon blood was forbidden, filled with magic. To feed from these beasts would be the downfall of any vampire. But then again, I wasn't just *any* vampire. I dipped my finger in the dragon blood on my chest and licked it.

Just a taste.

I shuddered. My back arched. Magic pulsed, slow and burning, like swallowing a star. It mixed with my vampiric magic, the remnants of the cold goddess's magic, and my mate bond. It was intoxicating, powerful, devastating.

Too much magic, in just one lick. I was made a slave to this magic in a single lick, unable to resist it. I was filled with a yearning. I wanted more. I *needed* more—even if it killed me.

My voice was hoarse, trembling, "So, this is what burns inside you."

The dragon charged this time. Not soaring, not gliding, just raw force. I raised a magical shield around me, but it shattered under the dragon's weight. I was thrown, skipped across the beach, and landed with a crunch near the rocks. My mind went blank for an instant, and I heard a shout in my head, *"Caleb!"*

Before I could rise, the dragon pinned me with one clawed foreleg. Its sulfurous, hot breath washed over my face. Perhaps it wanted to eat me or scare me, but I just smiled. I sank my canines right into its foreleg. The dragon's eyes went wide. Fire shot uncontrollably from its maw, and its limbs thrashed violently, trying to make me let go, but I held on tight. Each sip tasted like lava. It hurt like hell, but the power was exhilarating. I continued to drink even though it felt like my insides were burning. The ancient power was inside me, raw and savage. With each swallow, the pain increased. I didn't know how long I could survive.

Then I heard her. *"Caleb, stop! Don't leave me."* The power the blood had over me vanished.

Summer.

I couldn't leave her. I took a step back as steam rose from my skin. My fingers trembled, not from weakness but from the fire still burning through me. The taste of dragon blood lingered on my tongue, mixed with something more.

Memory. Pain. Pride.

The dragon stirred, weakened from the blood loss. I tensed, afraid it would attack me again. Instead, it grunted with effort and dug its claws into the wet sand, beginning to rise. Its wounded wing frayed like fabric grazed by thorns. I watched the beast fly toward the sky, away from the island. Its good wing made up for the injured one.

I stood alone on the beach. The adrenaline from the fight left me, and I collapsed. Memories of the dragon's blood flooded my mind, and of stolen secrets. A storm was coming. Not of rain or wind.

Of wings. Of flame. Of vengeance.

Now was not the time for old wars. We needed to ally and to prepare. I wasn't sure what, but it was coming soon. And when the time came, I needed allies, or I would fall.

Two arms encircled me, and the scent of jasmine. I wrapped my uninjured arm around Summer.

"I was so scared of losing you," she said, hot tears gliding down her cheeks.

I cuddled my nose in the crook of her neck, losing myself in her scent. "I would never leave you," I whispered, but we both knew it was a lie. I could have died, and I almost did, if not for her call. The dragon's blood, its magic, had enthralled me. My veins were still hot with the beast's fire.

"Let's find a spot to rest," I said.

"The shipwreck was deserted. It should give us cover," she suggested.

I nodded. Never in my life had I felt so tired. I was bruised, and my ribs hurt with every movement I made. I winced as I stood, suddenly remembering my shoulder was dislocated. I took a deep breath and popped it back into place, a grunt escaping my mouth as it did. I followed Summer to the shipwreck, resting my weight against her as I walked. This wasn't how this should have gone—her having to help me when I was supposed to protect her.

She smiled. "Stop thinking like that and let me take care of you. My wolf is proud to be able to help her mate."

I stopped at her words, then smiled. I had to remember I wasn't alone anymore. I no longer made the rules.

"Yes, little wolf."

She chuckled as we walked through the night.

Chapter 5 (Nathan)

Alliance

I spent the day with the Dark Forest pack and enjoyed my first meal in 334 years. It felt amazing to taste things other than blood. Not that I disliked it. Blood was rich and tinted with a distinct taste of the person it came from—divine even. But discovering the sweet taste of cherries, the sour taste of lemon, or how butter melts on your tongue was a whole different thing. I learned the bitter taste of rosemary and how spices can turn a piece of meat from good to mouthwatering. I grimaced when I tried pumpkin but indulged in raspberries. I had missed so much in these past years and wanted to discover it all.

I knew I needed to leave at the end of the day, and I was eager to find Emerald. I missed her terribly! I couldn't wait to have her back in my arms. Now that my wolf was awake, I no longer had to drink only blood, and I was stronger than ever, able to use both my vampire and wolf powers. I was finally strong enough to go and get her back. Since it was the pack that had allowed me to awaken my wolf, it was only natural to take the time to celebrate this meal with them. This was, in a way, a farewell as I'd be gone for a while.

We were almost done eating when an injured gray wolf entered the pack house, accompanied by two Betas. Etienne, the Alpha, rose, a frown on his face.

"What is going on?"

The first Beta explained, "We found her at the border of our territory. She wasn't aggressive, but she seems to be stuck in her wolf form."

Etienne got closer and assessed the wolf's wounds. He frowned. "It's deep. She's been poisoned with silver."

A gasp rose from the pack. *Silver.* Werewolves and vampires were affected by it. It was an inconvenience to vampires, weakening our powers, but it was deadly to werewolves. As a hybrid, I suspected that silver affected me more than regular vampires, but I had never experienced it.

"Is it too late?" asked a man.

"Let me have a look," said a woman as she pushed through the people. Her long brown hair was braided. Her blue eyes narrowed on the injured wolf as she studied her. She may have looked young, but she had the confidence of someone who had a lifetime of experience.

"It's already in her bloodstream, but she's not fully affected yet. Quickly, bring me my knife and poison kit," she instructed a teen. He had red hair, and his face was covered in freckles; he looked no more than twelve or fourteen years old. He ran out of the pack house to fetch what the woman had asked for.

"Do you think she'll make it, Amelia?" asked the Alpha.

The woman nodded. “She’s strong. She won’t die, but I must hurry, or she’ll be stuck in her wolf form forever. I need to remove as much as I can.”

“I need two volunteers. The others need to leave,” Etienne instructed everyone.

“I’ll help,” I said, feeling the urge to. These people had helped me when they could have cast me out. I was in debt to them.

“Me too,” said Simeon.

The Alpha nodded. “Good. The rest of you, leave. Amelia will need her utmost concentration for this.”

The pack house emptied in seconds. As the last person left, the teen arrived out of breath. He held a big black leather bag. Amelia gestured for the teenager to come closer. “Good, you did well, Ethan.”

She opened the bag and looked through it. She got a rune-encrypted dagger and some reagents, as well as a long tube.

“You two,” she said to Simeon and me. “I need you to hold her on her back, make sure to immobilize her paws. If she moves while I do this, she’ll get hurt even more.”

I grabbed the front paws while Simeon grabbed the back ones. My eyes fell on Ethan. “Is he staying?” I asked, wondering if it was common in the pack for someone so young to see something like this.

All eyes fell on me. “Of course, he’s staying,” snapped Amelia. “He’s my apprentice.”

Etienne paced further into the room, leaving Amelia plenty of space to do her work. “First, we need to cast the *slow ailment* spell, so that her blood flow reduces.”

“I know this one!” exclaimed Ethan enthusiastically.

"You want to do it?" she asked.

The teen nodded eagerly. He pronounced words in a language I didn't know, and a soft breeze whirled around us. His attention returned to Amelia when he was done.

"Good job," she praised. She pointed with her finger at the upper abdomen of the wolf. "We will need to cut here. Near the heart, but not too close."

As she said this, she slashed the wolf's abdomen. The wolf whimpered and tried to break free from our grip, but I applied great force, making sure to hold her in place. I expected a surge of blood, but to my surprise, almost none escaped.

"Thanks to your spell, she will survive the surgery without dying from blood loss. Now, see that glistening silver vein?"

I stared at what she was pointing to. The vein, instead of being blue like the others, was grayish and shone like metal.

"That vein here contains silver. Many veins are probably affected. As you know, silver conducts magic. Therefore, the alteration spell must be cast on the affected veins to corrode the silver. Doing so will remove the toxicity of silver, leaving only debris that the body will naturally eliminate."

The lad listened carefully, unimpressed by the sight before him, like he'd seen this a hundred times. Meanwhile, the wolf kept whimpering in agony. She looked as if she would pass out, and I worried she might die before they were done.

"Shouldn't we hurry?" I suggested.

Amelia looked at me with a stern look. "Don't interrupt. I know what I'm doing."

The Alpha's hand rested on my shoulder. "Trust her, Nathan. She's been doing this since she was a pup."

I shut my mouth, hoping that the woman would be done quickly and the injured wolf would be saved. "Now, when I say so, you will apply the calendula leaves on her wound."

The teenager picked up a jar of leaves without hesitation and grabbed a handful. Amelia recited words, pointing her fingers at the infected veins. They immediately turned black and rigid, along with the muscles surrounding them. Ethan crushed the leaves in his hands and applied them to the veins and muscles. They softened and returned to their normal state, still slightly black, under the leaves' influence. They continued this process on all the silver veins.

When they were finished, Amelia said, "The thread and the needle."

Ethan obeyed. The she-wolf cried out, and her chest heaved as the needle pierced her flesh. Amelia was unfazed and continued her work, closing the wound.

"You can let go," she said to Simeon and me. I did as she said, realizing then how tightly I had been holding the wolf. I was expecting the she-wolf to react or try to escape, but she didn't even move. I imagined she was exhausted.

"How is she?" I asked.

Amelia took the wolf's pulse. "She's weak, but the silver has been corroded by the magic, so the toxicity is gone. Her werewolf's healing powers will return. She should survive."

I breathed a sigh of relief.

"Let's bring her to the bed in that room," said Etienne, pointing to the room where I had stayed the night before.

I picked her up, trying not to pull at her wound, and found her light and easy to carry. I gently placed her on the bed. She didn't emit any sounds, lost in a deep slumber.

Back in the main room, Etienne had a serious look on his face. "Who would do such a thing? It has been forbidden to use silver since the great war between vampires and werewolves thousands of years ago."

"The great war?" asked Ethan.

The Alpha nodded. "Yes. During that time, vampires had used silver against werewolves, carefully crafting weapons with it."

"Aren't vampires affected by silver, too?" asked Ethan.

"It's not deadly to them, and they wore protective clothing to avoid contact. We lost many great warriors during that war, and when the peace treaty was signed, it was decided to forbid the use of silver in war, as well as other reagents deemed too dangerous. I can't believe someone would do such a thing."

"We'll ask her when she wakes up," suggested Amelia.

"How long do you think it's going to take?" I asked.

The woman thought for a moment. "I think that a few hours should be enough for her body to remove most of the toxin so that she can regain consciousness."

I nodded. I wanted to go looking for Emerald, but as a werewolf hybrid, I was at risk of being attacked with silver. Knowing who had carried out this attack could save my life. At least I'd know who was likely to attack me with it.

"What you did was impressive," I commented.

The woman smiled. "Thank you. I'm but a witch who aims to heal everyone."

"A witch?" I asked. The memory of Beatrix came to mind. That wicked woman had poisoned me to put me to sleep and had sex with me while I was unconscious in order to conceive a child.

I studied Amelia. The Alpha trusted her, and she had just saved an injured wolf. She seemed to be well-liked by the pack, unlike Beatrix, who was a recluse. Maybe Amelia was trustworthy.

"Don't look so surprised," the woman said with a smile. "I come from a long line of werewolves blessed with the power of magic. My mother trained me my whole life so that I can take on her role as the healer of the pack before she passed away—just like I'm training my son, Ethan."

The lad had a proud look on his face. Just then, the doors burst open and a tall, red-haired man entered the pack house.

"Dad!" Ethan greeted as he hugged his father.

"I heard you and your mom healed an injured wolf," he said. "Good job!"

We continued chatting. It was a hot day, and the room was humid. Etienne explained that Ethan's father was one of the pack's lookouts. The Alpha also explained the lineage of werewolf witches born in the pack, explaining that they have always been healers.

I had lost track of time when I heard a faint whimper coming from the room. We all rushed in. The injured wolf had turned back to her human form. She had long brown hair and ebony skin, her body mostly hidden under the covers. Amelia took her pulse and smiled. "This is good. She's way better already."

Just then, the woman whispered, "Help."

"You are safe," said Amelia. "We rescued you. You're in the pack house."

The woman's eyes suddenly went wide as she gasped, as if breathing for the first time after almost drowning. She looked right and left in panic, then realized she was safe and relaxed.

"You are in the Dark Forest pack," said Etienne calmly. "I am the Alpha."

The woman put a hand on her heart. "It is an honor to meet you, Alpha. I am Brooke, of the Luscious Woods pack."

"The Luscious Woods pack? I'm afraid I'm not familiar with them," said Etienne.

"That's understandable," replied Brooke. "Our pack is just north of the Valley of Nysa. We usually trade with the werewolves' pack that resides in the valley or further to the north."

Etienne nodded. "My Betas found you near the border of our pack, injured. Do you remember what happened?"

Brooke's chocolate-brown eyes widened. "Elven warriors attacked me. They had arrows dipped in liquid silver. I was in my wolf form to run faster. I dodged several arrows, but was finally hit. They caught up with me and injected me with liquid silver. I struggled and bit the elf holding me as hard as I could, and I broke free. I ran with all my might until I reached your pack, which was my original destination."

We all stared at her in disbelief. It was true that I didn't like Erendriel, but the elves were generally a peaceful nation. To hear they would attack werewolves with liquid silver was hard to believe. This behavior was frowned upon.

"This is all shocking," the Alpha said. "Anyone who attacks with silver is an enemy. I will have to reevaluate the pack's relations with the elves. In the meantime, why did you want to reach us?"

"I have a message from my Alpha, Joey. The elven king has taken the dwarf kingdom, so we have declared war on them. The humans have accepted an alliance with us. We aim to rally every werewolf pack to our cause."

"They have taken Mumbur?" asked Etienne in disbelief. I was as surprised as he was. It had been centuries since the last great war. I had worked so hard to keep the nations at peace, as my parents before me. After all that effort, the world was crumbling back into war. A vein pulsed in my neck. It was revolting.

Brooke nodded. "Yes, and the vampires have allied themselves with the elves."

It was disheartening to hear this. To think that my nation, *my kingdom*, had allied itself to the elves in this conflict. It was unthinkable. And now, we were at the beginning of another great war. All those years of diplomatic efforts were wasted because of one man's folly.

"These are dark times. We will join forces with your pack," Etienne said gravely.

Brooke smiled. "We plan to deal with the elven king first, and then deal with the vampires."

The Alpha turned to me. "Nathan, what do you think of all this?"

I clenched my fists. "What the elven king did was an atrocity, both the silver and the attack on the dwarves. I have spent my entire life keeping the peace. It is inconceivable that the vampires would ally themselves with the elves. I would never have tolerated Erendriel's actions if I were still king."

The werewolf appeared pleased. "Do you intend to claim back your throne?"

The answer was obvious. "Of course! I am the rightful ruler of Ichoryllia."

Etienne nodded. "That's what I thought. Then, we will attack the elves, but after, we will help you get back your throne."

Brooke added, "I would need to consult with our Alpha, but I think he will support the plan."

Pride filled me. "Then it will be an honor to have you by my side when I reclaim my throne, but there is one thing I need to do before. Emerald is being held in a slave shop in Ichoryllia. She is my top priority."

"I support you in getting your mate back," said Etienne.

Emerald. My vassal. My mate.

The sooner I got there, the sooner I could get her out of the slave shop. The fact that she was in Ichoryllia was problematic, though. With the kingdom under Samantha's control and rewards offered for my head, I would have to find a way to sneak in without being seen.

"The day is getting late," I said, "but I want to leave now. I have to get Emerald back."

"Simeon will accompany you," Etienne said. "Gather intel on the vampire city. It will be useful to us when the time comes."

Simeon nodded. "Yes, my Alpha, but I must request something."

Etienne raised a brow. "What is it?"

"I would like to bring my mate Raphael with me. We have sealed our bond, and I can't bear to be away from him. My wolf will go crazy. "

The Alpha nodded. "A newly sealed bond can do that, indeed. You do understand that the vampire city is dangerous to humans, don't you?"

Simeon's dark eyes shone with conviction as he spoke, "Yes. But I will make sure to protect him."

"Then do as you will. You will leave with Nathan."

Brooke interjected, "I want to come, too."

But Amelia shook her head. "You're too weak. You need to recuperate more."

"In the meantime," added the Alpha, "we will send a communication to the Luscious Woods pack and inform them that you're safe. We'll coordinate our plan of attack on the elves with them."

"Right, let's go get Raphael and prepare to leave," said Simeon.

I nodded and followed him out of the pack's house. We quickly got there as it was only three houses away from Etienne's. It was a small, wooden house, a shadow to the other, much larger homes. There was an old, broken wooden wheel leaning against the wall, and climbing plants grew from the ground on it. White flowers bloomed, decorating the wheel. I waited outside while Simeon went to fetch Raphael. The worst of the heat and humidity was beginning to subside, but you could still hear the cicadas. A cool, gentle breeze blew, bringing welcome relief. I hoped the night would be cool. A child ran by, kicking a ball. I smiled at his innocence, remembering a time when life was easier.

Simeon and Raphael exited the house, holding hands. The human smiled at me, his blond hair still slick with water. "I am so excited to be accompanying you!" he said, gesturing while he spoke.

"It will be dangerous," Simeon reminded him. His brown eyes fixed on the human so that he would understand how serious he was.

Raphael brushed it off. "I know, but it will be fine. Come on."

Simeon rolled his eyes, and I stifled a laugh at the human's carefree attitude, true to himself.

Chapter 6 (Elaine)

Prisoner

I woke up disoriented. What time was it? I had no idea. I vaguely remembered the guards dragging me to my room after our fight in the cathedral. The rest was a blur. I had no memory of entering my room or going to bed. The guards must have transported me.

I sat up, pushing the heavy blanket off me. My legs were heavy, and my arms ached. Memories of Scorchfire flashed in my mind, along with his words.

Zarvok Drel'kaan.

Ruun to ruun. Mor'thuun noth.

They resonated deep within my soul. I had to discover their meaning. But more than that, I had to find what caused the dragons' rebirth. I didn't believe in miracles or fate, even less so in gods. There had to be an explanation, and I would find it.

My head spun when I tried to stand. My belongings were scattered on the floor next to the bed. Considering where I was and how the queen had treated me the day before, I found myself lucky that they hadn't taken them. I quickly searched through my things. They had taken my sword, but it didn't matter. My magic was all I needed. My lips curved into a smile when I felt a hard object hidden under a cloth. They hadn't seen the artifact that I had found in the crystal fields. I didn't know what it was, but anything that could help me get out of here was welcome.

I examined it more closely as I hadn't had the chance to do so earlier. The tip was sharp and slightly hooked. It was shorter than a sword, more like a long knife. It looked as if it were made for rituals as much as for war. I wiped the dirt off the blade and realized it was made from high-quality steel. The handle was warm to the touch. Looking closer, I realized it was covered with dragon-scale patterns. It almost looked like it was made of interlaced strips of hardened beast hide, blackened and scaled. I gasped. I had never heard of such an object. It must have been created several centuries ago, maybe more. What mattered was that it looked sturdy and in good shape. I could probably use it as a weapon to help me escape once I've come up with a plan.

The latch on the door slid open. I quickly hid the knife at the bottom of my bag. A servant entered, barely glancing at me. He held a tray with a piece of bread and a cup of water. I'd only been served by Lysander so far. He was a young vampire but walked with a hunched back and a submissive attitude. Behind him stood three well-armed guards. They glared hard, ready to react to the slightest threat.

"Your meal," said the servant, setting the tray down by the door.

"I want to see my friend," I said eagerly. It had been several days since I'd seen Oswald. He was probably trapped in his room, like me. I needed to tell him everything that happened. We needed to leave this place together and return home.

"You can't leave your room," the servant replied coldly. "Queen's orders."

The servant turned and prepared to leave. I rushed at him and grabbed his arm. He gasped, and his frightened gaze met mine. Two of the three guards immediately entered, swords drawn. I quickly felt the blade of a sword against my throat.

"Let me go," breathed the servant.

I obeyed, clenching my teeth to hide my anger and swallow the words that wanted to come out. I hated vampires, but I didn't stand a chance against four vampires, three of whom were guards.

"I am a guest of the queen," I reminded them as politely as I could.

"It seems the situation has changed," the servant replied quickly, rubbing his wrist.

"I am a representative of King Erendriel. His Majesty will hear my report, and he will not be pleased with the way his Grand Wizard has been treated!"

"That's the queen's problem, not mine. I'm only following orders," the servant replied without even looking at me, before leaving.

The guards waited until the servant was gone before lowering their swords and leaving, too. I heard the latch click behind them.

So that was it.

I had suspected that the room was just a way of keeping me in the castle. Now, I had confirmation that it was a prison cell in disguise. Still . . . I wouldn't be staying. I concentrated on casting a *sending* spell, which would allow me to send a message to Oswald. We had to devise a plan to escape together. But try as I might, I couldn't do it. That's when I realized that my mana was still empty. My energy usually replenished within a few hours at most. For it to still be empty meant that the room was magically enchanted to block mana regeneration. We had rooms like this in the elven castle to hold mage prisoners, to prevent them from using their spells, but I wouldn't have thought there would be rooms like this in the vampire castle. I thought it was a specialty of our race. I swore. So she had planned this all along. Wicked queen, wicked vampires. They were all the same.

I was out of ideas. I went to the wall that was behind my bed. I knew Oswald was in the room next to mine. I listened carefully but heard no sound. I banged as hard as I could against the wall with my fist, my knuckles hurting from it, and shouted, "Oswald! Answer me!" I waited, but all I heard was silence. I wondered if he was all right.

Hunger gripped my stomach, and I turned back to the tray. Bread and water. A far cry from the feast we'd been served on our arrival.

I took the tray and sat down at my bedroom window to eat. The bread was dry, but the water helped to wash it down. I was so hungry that I didn't care. I busied myself observing the events unfolding outside. Under the gray day, the city stretched out from the foot of the castle. Undamaged houses stood among the ruins of burned-down structures. The contrast was striking. The destruction was precise. In the streets, people rummaged through the debris, casting frightened glances at the sky. The dragons still flew, but they no longer attacked the city. They seemed to be simply wandering around, as if to remind us of their presence. The further north I looked, the more the city had been spared. In some places, you could almost believe nothing had happened if it weren't for the shadows of the beasts over the city.

I watched the dragons fly, clouds parting as they passed. The wind carried them along as water carried boats. It all seemed so peaceful to me. My attention turned to a magnificent white dragon with purple-tinged wings. The beast exuded grace and power. I probably should have been afraid, but I could only marvel.

I recalled the legend of Celestia and the sacred dragon Aurelion, and their forbidden love that had given birth to the elves. Thousands of years later, we were still connected, with elven magic depending on them. And now, there was the mystery of the sudden return of the dragons when Scorchfire was killed a second time. There was so much I didn't know.

A thirst for discovery overwhelmed me. I was dying to find out everything about these ancient beasts.

Chapter 7 (Erendriel)

Army of Mutants

The last two waves of volunteers helped us identify a few criteria that enabled us to select candidates more effectively and achieve better results. It seemed that the subject's magic level had a direct impact on the outcome. The higher the magic level, the stronger the creature created, and above all, the greater the chances that they would retain their consciousness. This last point was crucial and made the difference between a mindless monster and a soldier with a purpose.

Elves, due to their magical nature, were, of course, the ones who responded best to the transformation. Humans were of no interest—they all perished because they had no magic. As for werewolves, the results were variable. I had not yet identified what made the operation successful. Some had survived and retained their sanity, while others had transformed into bloodthirsty, deformed beasts seized by a rage to destroy everything. I hadn't thrown the beasts away, opting to keep them in cages, certain that they might be useful eventually. I was disappointed that there were no vampires among my prisoners. I would have loved to see what effect the runes would have on them. I still had several prisoners left to experiment on, and I was still hoping to figure out why some retained their elven form, while others grew extra limbs.

My army of mutants grew with each passing day. They stayed in cages for a day or two while we assessed their level of intelligence and obedience. Then they were moved. The savage beasts in the dungeon, waiting to be useful. Those who had retained their sanity were sent to the barracks to train and prepare for war.

I hoped I would find the key to achieving the best results before running out of prisoners. The next ones to be transformed would be the soldiers, but I didn't want to suffer any losses. I had enough runes to transform every soldier so that they all became enhanced, and I intended to do so.

I was busy writing down my notes on parchment with a cup of lukewarm tea on my desk. I would ask Mathias to bring me some freshly boiled water to reheat it when he returned. He had gone to look after the servants and ensure everything was in order.

I picked up the next parchment and read it. It was only one sentence: *"The woman has been captured."*

A relaxed smile crossed my face. Good. She was an important part of my plan to destroy Nathan and prevent the Oracle's prophecy from happening.

I picked up another one. This one was about our defenses in case we were attacked. I hadn't yet seen any humans or werewolves trying to attack the city, but my watchers were on the lookout. The dragons hadn't returned to the city, much to my relief. No one was ready to fight them, so I preferred to avoid it. I had enough on my plate with the war. I expected an attack any day.

There was a knock at the door.

I put my quill down in the inkwell and sat up straighter in my chair. I had spent several hours here and had lost track of time.

"Come in," I said loud enough to be heard.

The door opened. Prince Akael's green eyes met mine, and I immediately regretted that Mathias wasn't there to deal with him. *"Cumberworld,"* whispered the voice, and I agreed with her. I had done everything in my power to avoid dealing with this prince. I had even declined the royal meals that he had invited me to.

I had heard that he was wandering around the castle asking questions. He was looking for more information about Elaine, as I had been told, but other than that, he never tried to enter restricted areas and didn't break any rules. Nothing that would allow me to send him back to his kingdom.

I had sent messages to Mumbur. The guards reported that the prince's crew was respectful and spent a substantial amount of gold in the shops and taverns of Mumbur. I had no real reason to send him back overseas, much to my regret.

"Akael," I said without bothering to get up. The elf's hair fell in curls on either side of his face as he bowed. The red of his hair enhanced the green of his eyes, his freckles emphasizing the fire that burned within him.

"I have come to express my immense gratitude for your hospitality, Your Majesty."

Bland pleasantries, I thought to myself.

“Although I have not had the pleasure of spending more time in your company,” he continued, “I have come to announce my departure.”

I really didn’t expect him to say that.

“Your departure?” I asked, feigning sadness. In fact, I found it rather suspicious. “Have you had the opportunity to meet my Grand Wizard?” It was hard to believe that the elf would leave after weeks of traveling without seeing Elaine.

“No, Your Majesty, but I have been informed that she will be with the dwarves for several weeks, if not longer.”

“Is that so?” I asked, stunned. I had kept Elaine’s whereabouts a secret. Only Mathias and a few others knew that she had been sent to the vampire city. As for the others, even if they had noticed her absence, they would not dare to ask about it. So who could have said that to him when Elaine’s presence among the dwarves was a complete lie?

The prince continued, “Unfortunately, I cannot afford to wait that long. I have obligations awaiting me in the Sun Kingdom. I will send a message to your mage by owl when I return home.”

I was speechless. It was the best I could have hoped for. I would be rid of this unwanted visitor and no longer have to watch his every move.

“Well, I’m very sorry to see you leave,” I replied, pretending to be sincere, “but I understand. I wish you a safe return to your kingdom.”

“Thank you, Your Majesty,” he replied.

At that moment, Mathias entered the room behind the prince. I smiled when I saw the kettle of boiling water he was carrying without my having to ask him. My chancellor knew me well.

"Prince Vaelarion," he stammered. "I didn't mean to interrupt a royal meeting."

"Ah, Mathias! Come in. You're not disturbing us," I replied. "The prince was only announcing his departure."

Mathias set the serving tray on my desk and added boiling water to my cup. He turned back to the prince. "I'm sorry to see you go," he said sincerely. "The servants had grown accustomed to your morning visits."

The prince smiled. "I will not forget the hospitality I have received at your castle. Now, if you will excuse me, I must prepare to leave."

"Of course," I replied. "May Deep Sashelas, the god of the seas, guide your ship."

Akael nodded and left my office. I inhaled the fruity aroma wafting from my cup. A sense of relief washed over me at the thought of being rid of my guest. Mathias stood before me, awaiting an order. I picked up the cup and savored a sip, taking the time to appreciate the peach-and-apple-blossom tea on my tongue.

"Mathias," I finally said after a moment. "Send spies to ensure that the prince's ship leaves the port of Mumbur and that he is on board."

The chancellor nodded. "It will be done, Your Majesty."

He reached into the inside pocket of his jacket. "You received a letter early this morning from our elite warriors." He handed me a tightly rolled scroll tied with a hemp cord, which I took eagerly. I had been waiting several nights for news and was surprised not to have received any before. I unrolled the scroll and read:

"The operation is a success. Dozens of werewolves have been killed. The silver burned them from within and blocked their powers of regeneration.

A few managed to escape us, but they are exceptions.

We continue to discreetly intercept werewolves in the forest, avoiding going directly to the packs where we would be outnumbered.

We await your orders."

This was great news. However, it would only be a matter of time before the werewolves really understood what was going on and tried to track and kill my elite warriors. I had to move them before they were discovered.

"Prepare a letter. If they believe they have been detected, they should return to the kingdom. I do not want to risk them as they are our best soldiers."

Mathias nodded. "Yes, Your Majesty."

He bowed and took his leave. I grabbed my cup of tea and made my way to the balcony. The air was heavy with humidity. It would rain later. We hadn't had rain lately, and I was grateful that we'd have some soon. Some plants and even some trees had begun to wither because of the drought. I hoped for a major storm. There was nothing I loved more than sitting sheltered under the awning and admiring the display of lightning scorching the sky, and hearing the rumble of thunder reverberating across the land.

A large bird flew toward me with a parchment tied to its talons—undoubtedly a peregrine falcon. It perched itself on the high pole near my door. I grabbed the message with eagerness. My generals used peregrine falcons for urgent messages. Once the message was removed, the bird flew away to the royal aviary, where it knew it would be served fresh meat.

I rejoiced upon reading the message. Ancient writings had been discovered in the ruins deep in the mines, and our mages in Mumbur had managed to decipher them. They believed that these writings came from the Oracle and concerned the prophecy. I had to go there immediately.

Chapter 8 (Caleb)

Overcome by Fever

I had only slept a few hours, consumed by the fire of the dragon's blood. The draconic magic mocked me and my audacity in drinking from such a sacred beast. Rather than finding rest, I found myself trapped in dreams of destruction. Each time, I woke with a start, drenched in sweat. Finally, when the first light of day began to appear, I gave up on the idea of resting.

I managed to push myself up painfully into a sitting position. My ribs weren't healed, my arm still throbbed, and I felt nauseous. I was feverish, and my head spun. I couldn't remember ever feeling this much pain before. My healing powers should have restored me, but clearly the dragon magic was blocking them.

Summer was still sleeping peacefully beside me. She lay tangled in the first rays of sunlight, which caressed her skin. Even in her sleep, she was temptation wrapped in silk. Her dark hair fell around her like spilled ink. Her lips were slightly parted, as if she were whispering secrets meant only for me. Desire rose within me as I imagined those deep brown eyes slowly opening and smoldering with lust.

I shook my head. She needed more sleep. As a werewolf, she would recover from the blood loss faster than a human, but she had stayed up late last night to take care of me. I remembered waking up between two nightmares, delirious. She cradled me to chase away the pain, her wolf purring with love.

I bit back the pain to avoid making a sound as I got up. I wanted to assess our current state. I sought to leave this dreaded island as quickly as possible. It was a miracle that orcs hadn't ambushed us during the night . . . or Aeris. I was sure she was looking for me.

Getting up, I was pissed at how much I was hurting—I was a demigod, a force to be reckoned with, not a coward. I would be damned before I let something like this stop me.

I ignored my body and walked a few steps further. I took a deep breath and launched myself into the sky. The orcs weren't far. I could see one of their outposts nearby, and their city was just a little further. We were south of the island. If we decided to travel on foot, we would have to circle the island to avoid attracting their attention or stepping into traps, which would take too long. If we traveled by air, they might shoot arrows or throw rocks at us. I would have to fly very high to be out of reach, but it would be faster.

A burning pain suddenly overwhelmed me, and my breath turned shallow. My hands shook. I didn't know what was happening to me, but I was losing altitude fast. I tried to regain control of my body as the ground approached far too quickly. I swore. I could already imagine the pain of hitting the ground and the sound my bones would make as they broke. That is, if I survived. But as suddenly as it had started, the burning sensation subsided, and I managed to stop myself just before hitting the ground. Tears streamed down my cheeks despite myself, and I collapsed. I grabbed handfuls of sand between my fingers, clenching them in anger at my lack of control over my own body. What was happening to me? I was stronger than this. I was a feared assassin. A demigod, capable of taking out anyone. And yet . . . A lump formed in my throat. It wasn't my style to cry, and I hated myself for doing it. I hated feeling weak and helpless.

The beach was engulfed in flames. A fire burned inside me, filled with anger. A dragon flew overhead. Dozens of animals fled from the destructive flames. My heart pounded, and sweat poured down my body. Run. I had to run. If I stayed there, I would die, but I was frozen in place. The dragon suddenly fixed its gaze on me, its yellow eye tracking my every move.

Then everything disappeared. I blinked, not believing what I was seeing. The beach was as serene as it had been before. I was covered in sweat, and I struggled to calm my shaking hands. It had been nothing but a hallucination. Summer was next to me. I had no idea how long she had been there, but I imagined she arrived while I was hallucinating.

"What are you doing?" Summer shouted, frantic. "Are you trying to kill yourself while I'm asleep?"

She was more furious than I had ever seen her.

"I wanted to see where we were and plan our next steps."

"Did you forget the fever you've had all night? I cradled you in my arms for hours, afraid to lose you. And you . . ." She stopped, staring at me, her lip quivering. "You're in no shape to be flying!" she cried angrily, hot tears streaming down her cheeks.

The waves lapped at the beach, and a duck flew over our heads, landing in the water of the river. I stopped. There were thousands of things I wanted to tell her: that I wanted to protect her, that I didn't want to wake her up, and I thought I was feeling better. But the words wouldn't come up, and I hoped she could feel it through our bond. The only words I could whisper, disarmed by her tears, were filled with a raw guilt. "I'm sorry."

I had never felt so vulnerable, and her face softened. "Try to understand. I only say this because I don't want to lose you, and I love you," she insisted.

Her words were gentle and promised something I had lost hope of finding. My armor melted in the warmth of her feelings, and my heart spoke before my brain even had time to understand. "I love you, too."

She launched herself at me in a hug. I groaned as she squeezed me, my ribs still hurting. She loosened her grip a little so as not to hurt me. Her luscious lips met mine, and her kiss was deep and needy, full of passion. She stepped back suddenly, as if only realizing it, and frowned. "You're even hotter than last night. Are you alright?"

I shook my head. "I should have known better than to drink dragon blood. I don't know what came of me."

"I know, I felt it through our bond. It enthralled you."

"I didn't think it would have such an effect on me. I thought I was stronger."

She sighed. "What am I going to do with you? I guess all I can do is nurse you back to health."

"I guess it's the price to be bonded to someone like me," I remarked.

She giggled. "Moon Goddess help me."

She told me to follow her, waiting patiently as I walked more slowly than she did because of my condition.

The wind suddenly shifted, bringing a stench of sweat, iron, and decay. The sound of boots and clanking metal accompanied the smell. We turned around and came face-to-face with a group of six grotesque creatures—orcs. They were tall and wore leather armor patched with chains and animal tusks. Their skin was ash-colored.

They were too close, and I was in no condition to run.

"You could get away," I whispered to Summer. She was probably fit enough to run or even change into her wolf form and flee.

A growl escaped her chest. Her wolf disagreed. "There's no way I'm leaving you here," she replied firmly.

One of the orcs stepped forward, dragging a rusted axe across the ground. A smile spread across his lips, revealing tusks yellowed by age and dirt.

"You on orc territory. You come with us," he said in a guttural voice.

The others approached as well, forming a large circle around us, blocking any possible escape routes. Their movements were slow and deliberate as they watched our every move. One had a large net, while another swung a chain with sharp hooks. Others had clubs made of bone and metal.

"I can't fight," I told Summer through our bond. Our only advantage was that we could talk without the orcs hearing us.

"I know, and I'm not strong enough to take them all," she replied. It was clear we only had one option left.

Seeing that we weren't moving, the orcs began to grow impatient. The one who had stepped forward first, the one I believed to be the leader, raised his axe threateningly toward us. I raised my hands, the movement causing me to wince as my ribs still ached.

"Alright, we surrender," I said as loudly as I could. It felt cowardly, but it was necessary. Summer raised her hands too, showing her palms.

The leader shouted something in a language I didn't understand. Immediately, the other orcs rushed us, and we were soon trapped in the large net, bound by chains with the sharp hooks digging into our skin, drawing trickles of blood.

"Is this really necessary?" I complained.

The orc leader responded with a punch to my stomach, and I immediately regretted the question. "Silence," he roared as we began to walk.

We followed him in silence. He led us away from the river, toward the center of the island. As we moved forward, the bushes grew taller and larger, and wider trees surrounded us. We were now walking on a rocky, blackish path, surrounded by a gray forest.

Unfortunately, this was the forest known to have been destroyed by the orcs—at least, that's what people said. But here, in the middle of this forest, it appeared very much alive, despite its lack of color. The long branches of the trees looked skeletal, and they tried to grab us as we passed. The animals, though few in number, were filled with unusual anger. It was as if the nature of the orcs had corrupted the lands and their inhabitants. An evil forest.

"Faster," growled one of the orcs, pushing me in the back.

I stopped looking around and focused on my steps. I had no idea how to get out of this. I hoped they weren't taking us to the central city, which was said to be huge, but rather to one of the small encampments I had seen nearby.

Although short, the walk seemed to take forever. In my feverish state, my head spun and my vision blurred. I had to stop several times to keep from losing my balance and falling, the orcs shoving me to move forward.

Fortunately, we soon saw crude buildings ahead of us. To my great relief, it was a small settlement; no more than a dozen tents made of animal skins held together with pieces of wood and large bones. Metal spikes held the shelters in place. A basic palisade surrounded the camp, consisting of logs of varying sizes with sharpened ends, tied together with strips of cloth and skin.

Weapons lay scattered around the camp. A handful of orcs watched us with predatory eyes. In the center of the camp, a fire burned with a large cauldron nearby. A thought suddenly crossed my mind: I hoped we weren't their dinner. I didn't know if they had the habit of eating their prisoners, but I certainly hoped not.

At the back of the camp was a crude wooden enclosure covered with animal skins, designed to hold prisoners. A large metal pole stood in the center with chains attached to it. They tied us with chains and left without a word. We had enough slack to stand up or lie down, but not enough to try to escape. At least we were together.

I collapsed on the ground. My body was exhausted from the effort. Summer knelt beside me. "Oh my gosh, how hot can your body get?" she whispered, concerned.

I wanted to say something, but I couldn't find the strength. I couldn't fight the dreamless sleep that took over me.

Chapter 9 (Nathan)

Masters of the Shadows

We had been traveling for several days, stopping only when necessary. Simeon had no trouble keeping up, but Raphael was human. He was slower than we were and needed more rest. Simeon carried him when he was too tired to continue. This allowed us to cover a great distance. On the third day, when the sun was high in the sky, Ichoryllia rose on the horizon.

My beloved kingdom. I had spent my whole life devoting myself to its people, trying to make it a better place, just as my parents had before me.

My heart shattered when it came into sight. Rather than the beautiful city I remembered, this one was in ruins. The southern wall was in shambles, the culprit's body still lying on the floor: a dragon. They were harvesting its meat and scales. Even from afar, I could see people massing to cut a piece for themselves. There were dozens of guards, trying to keep everything in order. The stench of death hung in the air and drifted up to where we were.

I crouched behind bushes. I kept my voice low even though we were far enough that no one would hear us. "There are way too many people here. Let's go through the north entrance of the town."

The men nodded. "Good idea. Let's hope there's not another dragon body up north."

The idea hadn't crossed my mind. "If that's the case, then we'll find a place where the wall is destroyed so we can sneak into the city without being noticed."

We stayed under the cover of the forest and slowly made our way around the city. Thankfully, the rest of Ichoryllia was in better shape than the south side of it. I wondered if my people were fine, if Samantha had helped them, or if she stayed in the castle, ignoring the people's pleas. I didn't even know the state of the castle. My entire being pleaded to march in there and take care of my kingdom, but I couldn't. The picture of Emerald flashed through my mind, her deep green eyes staring at me when we were alone. I hoped the beasts hadn't destroyed the slave store.

Wait for me, I'm coming.

The sun lowered in the sky, but its rays were still strong when we arrived on the north side. The forest was dense, and the ground was dotted with golden rays and shadows. I accidentally stepped on a mushroom, the rich, earthy smell filling my nostrils as I crouched down to get a better look at the city. My fingers sank into the soft, moist moss on the tree trunk next to me, where I had leaned. I was grateful to see there were no dragon corpses on this side of Ichoryllia. The wall was in good condition. However, there were more guards than usual with many caravans and people—probably because they couldn't enter through the other entrance.

"How are we going to enter?" asked Raphael. He was crouched beside Simeon, who was still staring at the town.

Posters with my picture were surely still plastered all over the city, offering a great reward for my capture. Anyone would recognize me if I showed myself, and I couldn't count on anyone's loyalty, not even the guards. After all, they were in Samantha's service. She ruled the kingdom through fear and punished treason with cruelty. She had control over the guards and the Miłonblood-ers. That was enough to ensure the obedience of a large part of the population as well.

My thoughts turned to Lysander. He had served my father throughout his reign and had been like a second father to me. I could trust him. He had proven his loyalty over hundreds of years. If I could find him, he would smuggle me into the city.

A whisper of movement broke the moment. Arrows hissed through the air. Simeon pushed his mate away. The arrows narrowly avoided them. I stood up, carefully scanning the forest for our attacker. Simeon's wolf snarled. "Get out, you coward! I won't let you touch him!" he shouted around.

I caught the scent of moving shadows. They were swift—masters of the forest. An elven warrior. He was dressed in leather, moving like the wind, shifting with the trees and nature, using the forest as his disguise. Simeon was already fighting with one when another came out of seemingly nowhere to attack Raphael. The human had no chance in a fight against magical creatures. He wasn't trained for combat. I stepped between them and blocked the blow with my sword.

"Hide," I ordered him. A second warrior joined the one I was fighting off. I parried their blows easily enough. It seemed that my combined vampiric-werewolf powers made me stronger than I thought.

I heard a grunt. I turned my head just for a moment to see Simeon's arm being cut with a knife by his attacker. He staggered, a second blow nicking his thigh. "Silver. They're using silver!" he shouted, but I already suspected this from the wounded wolf at the pack.

My movements were fluid, almost unnatural, as I ducked and sidestepped every attack, but I wouldn't get rid of the elves this easily. My sword plunged through the larger one's armor, causing blood to spurt out. I sent a wave of vampiric powers at the other, causing him to recoil sharply. The taller one launched at me full force, but he wasn't fast enough. I dodged his attack, then took advantage of the fact that his side was unprotected to impale him with my sword, all the way through to his heart. He fell with a huff.

The elf warrior frowned as he looked at me, then exclaimed, "You are the former king of Ichoryllia."

I smiled wickedly. "Then you know me."

He stammered, taking a step back. "You . . . You are too powerful."

"Let me show you how powerful I am," I suggested, approaching him.

"I must warn the king," cried the elven warrior before fleeing.

I could have gone after him, but I turned my attention to Simeon. He needed my help. His fight had become chaos. He spun, slashing, lunging, but he was too wounded and slow to hit his assailant, likely from the silver. Further away, I spotted Raphael. The human was hiding behind a bush, pinned by fear.

I didn't wait and lunged at the elf who was fighting my friend. The elf didn't expect it, but parried my blow with respectable strength. I imbued my sword with my vampiric strength and struck him with all my might. The blade sank into the bone of his wrist. The elf pulled, desperately trying to save his hand. When I finally managed to pull the blade out of his wrist, the elf grabbed his limp hand and took a step back. He didn't hesitate and ran away before I could strike again. I could have caught him, but it was more important to deal with the werewolf lying before me.

I called Raphael to come as I assessed Simeon's state. He was badly wounded by silver. It didn't look as severe as the injured wolf at the pack the other day, but he needed to be treated, and quickly.

Raphael put his arms around his mate, tears rolling down his cheeks. "I can't lose him," he sobbed.

I scanned the forest around us, finding no more elves. Was there anyone in Ichoryllia skilled enough to treat Simeon? I didn't think the royal physicians knew much about werewolves. I could always ask them to continue without me. Werewolves weren't liked by all vampires, but they would be able to go and find a healer. Just as I was thinking this, the werewolf fainted, ruining my idea. Raphael couldn't carry him alone, and I couldn't show my face in the city.

"Looks like you could use some help," said a deep voice behind me. I turned around, wondering how I hadn't noticed him a few moments earlier. A tall, bald vampire stood in the shadow of a tree. He wore a black shirt and brown leather pants. Though his tone was friendly, I didn't trust him.

"Were you standing there the whole time?" I asked.

He nodded. "I know better than to throw myself in a melee with elven assassins, werewolves, and the ex-king."

He knew who I was, which meant he could be in for the reward. "What do you want?"

The man pointed to Simeon, who was worsening by the minute. "Looks like your friend needs some help."

He was right, but I didn't like this. "What tells me I can trust you?" I asked.

The man shrugged. "Nothing, but it looks like he won't make it if you don't."

I hated how right he was. I clenched my fists into balls. He was alone. I could take him on if he attacked. "You didn't even tell me who you are, and you expect me to follow you blindly?"

The man chuckled. "The fact you don't know who I am means I've been doing a good job. The name's Vince. I'm the guild master of the Thieves' Guild."

My blood ran cold. The Thieves' Guild. I had searched high and low to find them when I was king. Even with my best people, they were always a step ahead of us.

"Why would an outlaw like you help us? You're probably after the reward for my head, if anything."

The man scoffed. "I'm not surprised you'd think so. In fact, one of our members was looking for you a while ago. You may have met Caleb, a seasoned assassin. Anyway, I hear there's a good sum of money to find you . . . *dead or alive*," he added, emphasizing the last words. "I had thought about trying to get my hands on the reward at the time, but I changed my mind and decided to help you out."

A red-feathered bird flew from a branch between us, breaking the tension for a fleeting moment. "Why?" I asked.

"The members of the Thieves' Guild are family—all of them, whether vampire or human, but the new laws the queen has instated pose a threat to all our human members. Have you seen the state of this city? Even the orcs are attacking now! I want the queen out. You're here to reclaim your throne, aren't you?"

"I am, but I need to find someone first," I answered.

The man nodded. "I understand, and I won't ask what it's about. We don't ask questions in my line of business. Let me help you, then you'll help me by removing the wench that's making my family miserable."

It felt wrong. Could he really be trusted? Probably not in the long run, but, for the time being, he needed me, and I needed him. Simeon whimpered.

"He's going to die!" said Raphael, panicked.

"Looks like I don't really have a choice anyway," I said.

"Good answer," replied the guild master. "Follow me."

I picked up the injured werewolf in my arms and followed Vince through the forest, Raphael following. We walked away from Ichoryllia, and I wondered for a moment if we were being led into a trap. I felt vulnerable, and I hated it, but Simeon's condition was deteriorating, and I worried about him. "You know someone who can treat a werewolf hurt by silver?" I said as we walked.

"Don't underestimate us. We're used to dealing with all kinds of injuries and poisons. We have connections," he answered casually as we walked.

We crossed a small stream and walked through ferns and other plants. There were no trails here, but Vince looked like he had been here thousands of times. We finally arrived at a small cave, which was barely big enough for us to stand in. The stone was permanently wet, covered by a small layer of argillaceous soil. We were barely inside when the temperature dropped significantly.

"Where are you taking us?" I asked.

Vince turned toward us. "Where do you think? To the guild."

I thought of all the times I had searched for it as a king, and now, I was now being led to it. Before I could even think of trying to remember its location, Vince added, "We change the entrance spots regularly."

"How do you do that? You dig up caves?" I joked.

"You can't imagine the labyrinth of tunnels that runs beneath Ichoryllia. It's easy to find a new one to use as an entrance, blocking the old one."

I knew what he was talking about. I had heard about the tunnels under the city. They had been dug by ancient rulers several millennia ago. People who went in there never returned and were reported missing. I had always thought I should send a few guards to survey and map the tunnels, but no one wanted to go. There were rumors of monsters living in there and ghosts haunting them, or both if you asked the right person. I had told myself I would go someday, but I never got the chance, always too busy with royal duties.

We walked for some time. The cave changed paths a few times. We came to crossroads and followed Vince blindly. Eventually, the cave's structure changed, and rather than walking on slippery rocks covered with clay, the walls were now made of stones and bricks. I realized we were now in the city's sewers. The stench of rotten eggs filled my nose, and I gagged. Still, we followed the guild master.

At one point, we arrived at a ladder. "Can you climb?" asked Vince.

"Not with him in my arms, but I can fly up," I answered.

"Good, then go first," he commented.

I flew up the ladder. The stench lessened. The tunnels here were large, made of brickwork. The ceilings were arched and dripping with condensation, the old mortar between the bricks blackened with centuries of moisture. Faint lanterns burned with smoky oil, their dim glow casting long shadows along the walls, enough to guide those who belonged but to keep uneasy intruders in the half-dark. The tunnels were vast and interconnected, a secret city beneath the town.

Two thugs were at the top, frowning at me. The first one was tall and had a scar running from his cheek to his ear, and the second one was smaller. He wore a thick black beard and a mustache. He was chubbier but looked like he could pack a punch. They were both humans, and I could take them on if I didn't have Simeon in my arms.

"Who are you?" the first one asked.

"I'm here with the guild master," I said, wanting to avoid trouble.

Raphael slowly climbed the ladder, out of breath. "I don't see him," he replied.

Vince finally climbed the ladder up. "Had I known this guy would take so long to climb, I would have gone first," he said. "Stand down, Joe, Frank. These are our guests, and we need a healer."

Frank, the smaller one, nodded and bolted. Joe relaxed and let us pass.

"Let's get to the living area. We'll put him in a bed," said Vince as he led us through the guild's tunnels.

I observed the Thieves' Guild as we walked. After all this time, it was unreal to think I was here now. Each chamber had been repurposed to suit the guild's needs: armory rooms, treasure vaults, living quarters, and even taverns and kitchens. Some rooms acted as markets for the underworld. Fences sold jewelry and gems, tailors stitched fine cloaks from stolen silks, apothecaries peddled powders and tinctures of questionable legality, and black-market scribes forged documents in the dim light of flickering candles. At the heart of the maze lay the guild master's hall. A long table dominated the chamber, surrounded by high-backed chairs carved from stolen wood. Maps of the city sprawled across the tabletop, marked with routes, safehouses, and targets. The guild master's seat was slightly raised, backed by shadows and flanked by lieutenants. It was even more impressive than I had thought.

But rather than the group of brutes I had imagined, I saw some kids, teenagers, and adults who looked like they were refugees. Some took care of the young ones, and others taught skills. They shared everything they had. Many had barely anything to go by. Yes, there were some loot piles, but most of the stuff was far from being a fortune. Armors and basic weapons, crude furniture, tattered clothes, and some food. This was far from what I had in mind when I was trying to arrest them as king.

As if reading my mind, Vince spoke, "A lot of orphans end up here. We take them in, give them what they need to grow, and teach them how to survive. We only take what we need. The rest, everything you heard during your reign, are contracts that we accept, given by the wealthy. Those dirty jobs that they don't want to do? They hire us to do it. It pays well, so we do it. Sure, we've stolen nice things, and we ain't innocent, but overall, we do what we need to survive."

I was speechless. I had been brought up to hate these people and to believe they were heartless murderers. This was far from what I had thought, and now I wasn't sure what to think anymore. Vince brought us to a large living area containing multiple beds. One of them held an old woman who was sleeping.

"Put him in this bed," Vince said, gesturing to the bed beside her. "This is Dana. She lived in the streets, a beggar. One day, a rich lady decided that she was unhappy to see her near her mansion. She asked us to eliminate her, but instead, we brought her here. Now she has a place to call home. She likes to take care of everyone as if they were her grandchildren."

I rested Simeon in the bed. The werewolf was feverish and didn't stir. Raphael sat worryingly on the side of the bed.

"This way," said Vince to someone outside the room. Frank entered, followed by an old man with white hair and a hooked nose. His face bore several scars, although he did not appear to be a fighter with his thin frame. He carried a black briefcase.

"This is Joseph. He'll be able to heal him," said Vince, making room for the man at Simeon's bedside.

Joseph opened the briefcase, revealing an assortment of vials and tools. "Do you know what's wrong with him?" the older man asked.

"He was attacked with silver," I said.

"Hmm, we need to hurry," he muttered, taking a large syringe out of his case. He took a vial and drew the contents into the syringe. This didn't look like what the healer had done at the werewolf pack.

"What are you doing?" I asked. "Shouldn't you be casting a spell or applying leaves to the veins?"

The man snorted. "Do I look like I have magical powers? I'm human, but this potion I have will neutralize the silver flowing through his veins. I bought it on the black market from a reputable alchemist."

I stared at the man, mouth agape. Sure, most humans didn't have magical powers, but I had hoped that he had a way to conjure magic, or maybe that he'd be a hybrid. It didn't matter. As long as his remedy worked, that was all that mattered. He found a vein easily, his movements showing years of experience. He injected the liquid into Simeon's arm.

"Now we wait for it to take effect," he said, satisfied.

"How long will that take?" asked Raphael.

"His fever should go down quickly, but it will take a few hours before his condition improves noticeably."

Vince nodded. "Thank you, Joseph." He looked at Raphael. "You can take a bed in the room and stay for the night."

"Thank you. I wouldn't want to leave him alone," Raphael replied, appearing noticeably grateful.

My thoughts turned to my mate—I couldn't wait any longer. I needed to get back to her as soon as possible.

"Raphael, I have to go on alone. Stay with Simeon, ensure he recovers completely, and obtain the information the Alpha asked for. I have to go look for Emerald."

"I understand," he replied seriously. "Simeon would agree too. Stay safe."

I nodded and turned to Vince. “Can you help me get into town discreetly? I need to go to the slave shop, near the destroyed windmill.”

The guild master smiled. “Of course. Follow me.”

I followed Vince through the tunnels. We returned the way we had come, then took another route. People watched us pass, some whispering among themselves, but I ignored them. “These people were born without luck,” Vince muttered as we walked by. Vampires and humans sat in these chambers, most of them concealed with hoods and hiding in the shadows.

It bothered me to see all those people, stuck in these tunnels, leading a life of stealing and killing. I had to find a way to properly regulate their activities and steer them away from crime when I returned to the throne.

“Have you ever thought of becoming royal guards?” I asked.

The guild master laughed. “Are you kidding me? Do you imagine me with armor going to fight outlaws?”

“I mean, like a special force squad.”

“I haven’t heard about any special forces,” retorted the vampire as he bent down to avoid a low-hanging pipe.

I did the same and said, “There isn’t, but there could be one. We could ally, and you wouldn’t need to be an outlaw. We could find some use for the Thieves’ Guild. Assassins could prove useful to the kingdom.”

The man stopped and turned, a smile on his face. “Look, this has been my whole life, and for many others, it’s all they know. I’m not so keen on an alliance, but we can talk about it once you reclaim your throne.”

I knew it wouldn't be easy to win that battle, but it was something to go by. "Deal. Once I reclaim my throne, we can talk. How will I contact you?"

"I'll find you." With that, he pointed to a tunnel that went to the right and uphill. "Follow that path. It won't take you directly to the destroyed windmill, but it will take you to the streets nearby. You'll need to walk the rest in the city. Be careful, the queen has eyes everywhere."

I snickered. "Don't worry. I'll be careful."

I followed the path he had indicated.

Chapter 10 (Samantha)

The Marshes

I knelt before Alastor's statue. With everything that had just happened, I needed to collect my thoughts. I closed my eyes and recited the prayer. A sense of peace washed over me as I communed with him. *"My dear Alastor, how I need your grace. I don't understand why the dragons attacked. I did everything you asked. I'm collecting your essences as fast as I can."*

I waited. In the past, he had come to me and answered, but this time, only silence followed. I took a deep breath. *"I'm nervous about going to find the relic in the sunken temple, but I understand that this is a test you are sending me. I will not disappoint you."*

As I spoke these words, an unknown spell echoed in my mind. It instantly engraved itself in my memory, as if I had always known it. Then, a warning: *"You will be able to breathe underwater, but the duration varies, and it costs a lot of mana, so you will only be able to cast it a limited number of times."*

I froze. He had heard me, had even given me what I needed to succeed, but his warning resonated within me. I would have to be careful. I wouldn't want to find myself without mana as the spell's effect wore off. "Thank you," I whispered.

I got up. I had a lot to take care of before leaving for the marshes. Repairs to the city would take much longer than expected. Soldiers had finished clearing debris from the main squares and major streets, so wagons could now pass through, which would help remove the remaining rubble more quickly. The death toll was in the hundreds, and so were the missing. I had not made a speech to reassure the population as it would have been pointless. They were all busy surviving and searching for their loved ones. People dug through their ruined houses to find gold coins to buy food, which was in short supply. We needed to hurry and reestablish trade routes so that farmers' grain could reach the bakeries. All in all, it would be a long road before our great city was restored.

Soldiers had knocked down the large clock tower, which was damaged by the dragons and was threatening to collapse on the few houses that had been spared around it. We destroyed it floor by floor, taking care to drop the pieces onto ruins and establish a safety perimeter. It was utterly sad to see this idyllic monument of our great city fall to pieces. We would rebuild a new one when all this was over.

The images of the dragon attack haunted me whenever I closed my eyes. Viktor had tried to change my mind, but I couldn't stop thinking about the destruction they had brought. I had brought back *one* dragon. Just one. How did there end up being so many?

Rage filled me. They had devastated my kingdom. I had to find out the source of what had happened, and I knew exactly who could help me with this.

I headed for the rooms shielded against magic. Elaine was the perfect person to do this research. She wouldn't have a choice but to do my bidding. The guards were at her door, as I had requested, and they straightened at my arrival.

"Your Majesty!" they said respectfully.

"I'm entering," I told them.

They bowed their heads, and one of them hurried to remove the latch from the door and open it. There she was, at the window of her room. Her white and purple hair was dirty, her gaze defeated. I hadn't let her leave her room, not even to wash. The risk of her mana regenerating outside these walls was too great. I had initially thought of killing her, but I figured she might be useful.

The elf turned toward me. Her face changed to one of terror. "No!" she screamed, reaching for her bag on the floor.

Her weapons had been confiscated, and the door was already closed behind me. I waved my hand. "I'm not here for your life."

She stopped, stunned, dropping whatever she was holding in the bag. I could hear her heartbeat slowing down, but she remained motionless, waiting for me to speak.

"What do you know about dragons?" I asked.

Her mouth opened slightly, and she thought for a moment before answering. "What do you mean?"

I pinched my lips in annoyance, crossing my arms. "The dragons. You've seen them. We resurrected Scorchfire, and now there are dozens of them."

Her gaze turned toward the window before returning to me. "Ah, that! Yes. Of course I've seen them."

"How is that possible?" I pressed. "My patience is very short, so I recommend you answer quickly."

"I'd be happy to answer," she hastened to say, "but I don't know any more than you do. I was on a mission to bring Scorchfire back to life, just like you, before you murdered him." Her last words were filled with resentment, but I couldn't care less about what she thought.

"Come on, you're a mage. I can't believe you don't know. Where they nested, their eggs, anything."

She shook her head. "I know a little bit, but I concentrated most of my research on dragon magic and the cause of Scorchfire's death. It was my main research," she explained.

"That's bothersome," I replied, thinking out loud. I had hoped she would have an answer. I couldn't risk the citizens going into an uproar over fear of the dragons once I left. I also didn't want her to know that I'd be gone. She had to believe I was there so that she wouldn't try to run away. I gave my order, "I'll have the servants bring you all the books on dragons from the library, and you can find out what happened."

She gawked. "Why would I do that?"

"What else do you have to do? Watch the birds?" I retorted. When she didn't answer anything, I added, "You are a mage, aren't you?"

She nodded slowly.

"There you go. You can be useful, and who knows, maybe I'll spare your life." It was a blatant lie. I would get rid of her the minute I didn't need her anymore, but I wanted her to cling to some hope so that she would do as I needed.

"Maybe you'll let me leave?" she asked.

I smirked. "I'll consider it," I lied.

I exited the room. The guards still stood there. A servant passed by, carrying food to the kitchens, so I stopped him. "Go to the library and grab all the books we have about dragons and bring them to Elaine."

He had bowed his head low. "Yes, Your Majesty."

"You have the right to bring her additional books if she asks for them, but she can't go to the library herself under any circumstances."

I turned to the guards as well to make sure they heard me. They nodded in acknowledgment. Satisfied, I made my way to my study. Viktor was there, looking at parchments. He wore a black shirt that clung to him in the way that I loved, highlighting his strong physique.

"You're looking rather nice today," I told him.

He looked up from the scroll he was holding, a smile stretched across his face. "Thank you, my queen."

"What are you looking at?" I asked, pointing to the parchment.

"The reports from the guards. There was another orc attack this morning but the guards were able to repel them and avoid casualties. The corpses of the dead have been burned. There's still the matter of the dragon corpse at the south wall. The guards have been cutting it into pieces and handing it to the citizens. This provides a lot of meat, and it's also a great way to dispose of the body. It's better to take advantage of this while it's not rotten."

"You're learning fast and reasoning as a true king," I praised him. He had studied extensively to compensate for not having a royal education as a child.

"It is my duty," he answered proudly.

A knock echoed, but I knew who it was before even opening it. I could recognize my pet's scent anywhere. Jason stood before me, his brown eyes locked on the floor. "Forgive my intrusion, but someone wishes to see you," he said respectfully.

I was surprised–he wasn't the one to deal with visitors. "Where is Lysander?" I asked. He should be the one handling this.

Jason looked at me calmly. He was accustomed to my presence now and wasn't nervous anymore when I came to him, making his blood even more delectable. Just the thought of it aroused desire in me. He probably realized this, too, as his cheeks turned red. "He went to the town to do some shopping. He said he'd be back by nightfall. The servants are trying to make up for his absence, but I stepped in and helped." He hesitated, fiddling with his fingers. "I didn't ask for permission, I hope it's all right."

I smiled, pleased with his response. I moved closer to him, inhaling the delicious scent of his human skin, captivated by his heartbeat. My teeth lengthened, and I instinctively licked my lips. I could see the obvious signs I had learned to recognize in him, knowing that he wanted it too, which made him irresistible. Viktor stood up and put his arm around me, breaking the tension between us.

He whispered in my ear, his tone so low humans couldn't hear, "Do you wish me to leave you alone so you can feed? I could take a feeding too from my pet, if you're taking a break."

His offer was tempting, though I had drunk not long ago. I was careful not to drink too many times in a week or risk my pet having the effects of blood loss or falling sick. It was more gluttony and yearning than anything. Plus, someone wanted to see me. I shook my head slightly to Viktor, then returned my attention to the human before me.

"It's fine, Jason. Thank you for helping out."

The man looked relieved by my answer. "Who wishes to see me?" I asked.

"A man with a dark hood. He says he knows the whereabouts of Nathan."

I tensed. I hadn't heard from Nathan in a very long time. The memory of his hazel eyes, which I hated, came back to me. I resented him for getting away from me; I wanted him to disappear for good. I held my head up, trying to hide emotions from showing on my face. "Lead me to him."

Viktor locked his arm with mine as we followed Jason through the corridors. He showed us to a small room that we usually reserved for noble guests visiting the palace. In addition to a bed, there was a small desk and a sofa.

"I will be waiting here in case you need me," said my pet.

I nodded, and we entered the room.

When we arrived, the guest was sitting on the couch, resting his elbows on his thighs, clasping his hands, his gaze fixed on the floor. His long black cape spread out beside him, his hood hiding his eyes. I sensed that he was a vampire. He stood up when we arrived, keeping his eyes at a height where the large hood hid them. I noticed he was small, but couldn't see his face.

"Your Majesty," he said in a high-pitched tone. I expected a deeper voice.

Looking at him, it was evident he belonged away from the castle. I could have bet he was a criminal just by looking at him. I preferred to stay away from people like him. Viktor held me tighter, as if to reassure me and show me that he was there for me.

"Who are you?" I asked defensively.

The vampire cleared his throat. "Let's just say that I stick to the shadows."

His answer exasperated me. I knew he was right. I didn't really need to know his name. Still, it was disrespectful, and I wanted him to answer me.

"Your queen asks for it," I challenged.

He ignored me and continued, "I have seen Nathan. He is in town."

I gritted my teeth, refraining from showing any reactions. I hated how he didn't seem to care about my title. Still, the news of Nathan being back was something I'd need to deal with.

"So, the hybrid king has returned to die in the ashes of his own kingdom. Bring me his head, and I will grant you land, power, or gold, plenty of gold."

The man shrugged. "I don't care for land or power. I have all the gold I need."

Judging by the way he said it, it was clear that I wouldn't be able to convince him. Too bad, it would have been nice to have someone else do the dirty work for me. "Where did you see him?" I asked.

"I've seen him in places where royalty doesn't belong. Down below, where only shadows roam. Wait for him to come back to the surface. I don't want anything in return for the information that I bring. I just want him gone from my hunting ground."

I didn't know many vampires who spoke of hunting grounds, except for crooks and murderers. This made him a very untrustworthy informer.

"Petty information if you don't even tell me where to fetch him."

"It's not as if you knew he was in town before I told you," the vampire warned. "Maybe I should have waited for him to show up at the palace and watch him kill you."

The vampire annoyed me to no end. If anyone else had spoken to me like that, I would have had them executed on the spot. I toyed with the idea of doing it once I'd gotten all the information I needed.

"Why should I trust you?" I asked. He could have been here to set me up. If he was so involved in shady business, I couldn't expect him to be honest.

He answered casually, "I have nothing to gain from lying about this. I want him gone."

"Fair enough. But he could be anywhere. It's not like I can have soldiers running around the town, especially after the attack."

"I have heard he is interested in going to the slave shop," the stranger replied.

I wondered what he could be trying to get his hands on there. Then I remembered he couldn't drink anything but human blood. Did that mean he didn't have his vassal with him? Now *that* was something I could use against him.

"You're useful after all," I replied.

"Do you want me to deal with Nathan?" asked Viktor.

"I would like that, yes," I replied. I returned my gaze to the vampire. He held something in his hand. I didn't have the time to see what it was that he had thrown it; the glass shattered against the stone floor at my feet.

A pale vapor bloomed instantly, curling upward and quickly filling the room. It carried no scent at first, only a sudden pressure in the lungs, a weight that crushed breath before pain could follow.

I inhaled sharply—and choked.

Viktor reacted a heartbeat later, coughing, the sound harsh and wrong. The poison clawed inward, seizing breath, turning the air into a suffocating wall.

"Window," he rasped.

We moved together, instinct taking over. Stone scraped as I wrenched the window open. Cold air rushed in, scattering the vapor in frantic tendrils. The poison thinned, fled, dissolved. We took a deep breath of pure, toxin-free air. When the haze finally cleared, the room stood empty.

The door was ajar. Jason stood in the doorway, looking panicked. "Are you all right, Your Majesty?" he asked frantically.

"Where is he?" I asked.

It took Jason a split second to figure out who I was talking about. "He walked out, saying the discussion was over. I didn't think anything was unusual until I heard coughing and opened the door."

Anger rose in me at the realization that the vampire had used this as a distraction to escape. He knew I'd discard him once I had no use for his information anymore. Only shards of glass lingered on the floor.

I knelt, the skirt of my dress whispering against the floor. I brushed my fingers through the shattered glass. I stilled. Dust clung to my skin, too fine for ash, too bright for powder. It had a bluish tint in the light.

My expression hardened when I recognized what it was.

Viktor had joined me, already knowing just by looking at it. "Wolfsbane," he said. "Distilled."

Not the kind of amateur you find among shady dealers on street corners. The refined, high-quality kind that you find in the royal vault. I rubbed the dust between my fingers. It resisted, oily in a way no common poison ever was. Alchemically bound to disperse fast, but to linger just long enough.

"Volatile suspension," I murmured. "Inhalation-activated and neutralized by fresh air." My hand closed slowly into a fist. "That formula was never released."

"No," Viktor agreed. His gaze lifted to the open window and the empty doorway. "It was sealed in the castle's vault."

Silence settled heavily. The implication crept in like frost. The thief had stolen from us. He had selected the one thing that wouldn't kill us and would provide the best diversion so he could run away.

I rose, brushing the residue from my hand. "He knew what it would do."

"Yes," Viktor said quietly. "He must have had someone on the inside. An informant."

Meanwhile, Jason stood there, speechless. "Do you need me to do something?" he asked hesitantly.

I shook my head. "This is not a task for a pet. I'll choose someone trustworthy and find the traitor. In the meantime, see that this vampire never returns to the palace. Tell the guards to keep an eye out for him and kill him on the spot if he's seen around the palace."

Jason bowed and left the room to carry out my orders immediately. I would feel better if we caught the vampire. "We have to find out how he got into the vault," I added to Viktor.

He nodded. "Do you think he was lying about Nathan?" he asked.

I shook my head. "No. He looks like he wants Nathan gone. I think he just wanted to make sure he could leave freely."

"That makes sense. Why do you think Nathan wants to go to the slave store?" asked Viktor pensively.

I remembered that he didn't know the ex-king as well as I did. "He needs humans. He can't eat or drink anything other than blood."

Viktor paced in the room, grabbing a book on the bookshelf nonchalantly, not really looking at it. It was a habit of his. He needed to move while he thought. "So what? We guard the slave store?"

I shook my head. "That's too obvious. He'll expect the store to be guarded."

"Hum . . ." Viktor put the book back and walked to the desk to play with the feather in the inkwell. "How about we lure him somewhere else? We can set up a bait. Something he won't be able to resist."

I sat in the chair beside the desk. "Luring him away from the slave store could be a good idea to catch him off guard, but how will you set up a bait he can't resist?" I asked.

Viktor smiled. "We know he wants humans. Let's create a convoy of slaves to be sent as sacrifices to appease the dragons. We'll pick dozens of humans so he can smell their scent, too. He'll be drawn to it. That's where we'll kill him."

Innocent people would be killed, and I was sure Nathan wouldn't be able to resist the urge to save them. It could also serve to show people that we are trying to appease the dragons. It was a cruel and perfect idea. "I love it! Let's guard the slave shop just in case he tries to go there as well."

He nodded. I added, "I will leave this in your capable hands. That, and shedding light on the traitor who gave the thief information. I am leaving tonight to get the relic."

Viktor grabbed my hand and kissed the top of it. "It will be done, my queen."

A few hours later, I was ready to go. I wore black leather armor that hugged my frame and a small hood. A knife hung at my belt in its sheath. I should be able to conceal my identity dressed this way. With what had happened to the city, I wouldn't want the people to know I was leaving, even for just a few days. It wouldn't have been well seen if they knew.

Viktor embraced me, his manly scent surrounding me. For an instant, I wished I could lose myself in him and forget about the worries of the kingdom, but I had chosen to be a priestess. Alastor was my main priority. I needed to restore him, and to do that, I had to fulfill his prophecy. Getting the relic was only a slight delay on my agenda. It was necessary to maintain control over the people.

"Are you sure you want to go alone?" he asked.

I nodded. "I will be more stealthy if I go alone. Don't worry about me. I am powerful. Also, I need you on the throne to deal with everything else."

He kissed me, and I savored him fully, knowing I would be away for a few days. "Take good care of the kingdom while I'm gone," I whispered.

He nodded and walked me to the castle gates. The heavy gates creaked open just wide enough for me to slip through. Cloaked in the shadow of the early evening, I moved swiftly, my steps soundless on the worn cobblestones.

The town slept uneasily. Above were the dragons' looming shadows, even in the dusk, reminding us of their presence. A constant threat. A reminder of why I was searching for a relic, and of my failure to protect my city.

A few vampires ventured into the dark streets, but due to the recent dragon attack, the streets were almost empty. I could see the signs of the destruction inflicted on the town: broken shutters, charred beams, and faces peering through cracked windows, too frightened to come out. The damage was profound, and people were shaken, even in places that had been spared from the attack. I kept my gaze low. My heart raced at the sudden thought that maybe the dragons would notice me, see through the disguise, and attack me. I looked up for a moment. They remained on their circling path, undisturbed. I breathed a sigh of relief and made my way to the outer wall, hurrying my steps. The night guards at the outer wall scarcely noticed me, mistaking me for another shadow passing through.

Once beyond the boundary of stone and gate, the air shifted. The damp breath of the forest reached first, carrying the scent of pine and earth. The moonlight threaded through bare branches, reflecting a soft silver glow on the edges of my armor. I paused at the treeline, casting a final look back at the silhouette of towers rising above the wounded town. No guards, no attendants, no dragons, no crown, only a woman stepping into danger by her own choice.

I turned from the walls and vanished beneath the cover of the trees, swallowed by the woods where no one would follow. The forest closed around me like a shroud. The knots in my shoulders relaxed, and my fingers loosened at the thought that the dragons couldn't pass on the narrow path. I was safe. At least, temporarily.

A carpet of damp leaves blanketed the ground, muffling my steps. My hand brushed past tangled roots and hanging moss, guiding me deeper along a path few remembered. Caspian had shown me old, half-faded maps that indicated the way, in old books whose pages crumbled at the touch. The Skyfall Temple was once said to be where the winged saints lived. They said that the summit formed a bridge between the Elysian Plains and the world of the living. Kings consulted the saints for advice on their problems. But the temple collapsed thousands of years ago after an attack by kings seeking to take control, led by a traitor. History had long forgotten the traitor's identity or how he had gained entrance. The tale goes that he spent months forging alliances, planning his attack. Slowly, he turned all the rulers against the saints, spreading lies and deceptions. When the time came, they launched an assault on the temple, seeking control for themselves and entrance to the Elysian Plains. The saints couldn't allow for such a thing to happen and had no choice but to destroy their own temple, effectively cutting off the bridge to the afterlife.

All of the saints fled just before the temple crumbled into the waters below, but one: Alexander. Some say he was trapped in the ruins and couldn't flee. Others say that he stayed voluntarily to watch over the world of the living, sacrificing himself for mortals. Still others say that he was simply unable to return to the Elysian Plains and had given up hope. In any case, according to legend, it was he who made a shield, a relic, that could protect mortals. There was no actual description of the relic, nor were there any books with sketches of what it looked like, only vague tales recounted that the relic remained in the sunken temple. I knew I would recognize it when I saw it. I would find the relic.

The trees grew denser the farther I went, their trunks like silent sentinels standing watch. Owls stirred overhead, their eyes staring eerily as I passed by. A shiver ran down my spine. I followed the old markers; stones half-buried in earth, the faint groove of wagon ruts worn smooth by centuries of neglect. The air grew heavier with each step, tinged with the smell of stagnant water.

At last, the woods began to thin, giving way to a stretch of marshland that sprawled across the northwest. Mist clung to the stems in pale, shifting veils. The ground sucked faintly at the leather of my boots with every step. Black pools mirrored the stars above, broken only by the ripple of frogs vanishing into the water. Frogs were the least of my worries, though. I knew these marshes were the home of the marrowyrms, a giant serpent-like creature that feeds on flesh.

I struggled to take a deep breath. The air felt heavy, layered, and hard to escape, and carried the smell of stagnant water and algae, reeking of decaying vegetation. I wrinkled my nose. It was strange to think that no one had come here for several centuries. It gave an eerie feeling, as if the whole place was both alive and dying.

I paused at the edge of a narrow plank path, weathered and half-rotted, stretching into the mist. According to the ancient maps I had seen, the temple should be further, toward the center of the marshes. A broken column sticking out of the water was probably the direction I needed to take to reach it. I drew my cloak tighter around my shoulders and pressed forward, leaving the safety of the forest for the treacherous quiet of the swamp.

I walked carefully along the wooden path. It moved with every step I took, and I wondered if it was safe given its condition. Of course, I could have flown, but I wanted to save my mana for when I arrived at the temple. I would need a lot of mana to cast the water-breathing spell that Alastor had taught me. Since I didn't know how many hours I would spend in the temple, I preferred not to take any chances. Drowning would be a stupid way to die, especially when I was so close to fulfilling the prophecy.

The water stirred beside me. At first, it was only a ripple, spreading wide across a pool of blackness. Then a shadow uncoiled beneath the surface, vast and patient. My heart raced when I saw the faint gleam of scales. A marrowyrm. I clenched my fists as it rose before me, its head breaching the surface with a hiss, yellow eyes glowing like lanterns in the fog. It moved swiftly, the water exploding as it raised itself on its tail. The serpent was twice as high as I was, its body as thick as an oak trunk, water cascading off its scales like rainfall. Its roar was deep, creating an intense vibration that shook my bones. That thing was hungry, and it had decided that I was its meal.

It struck without warning. I threw myself to the side, sending mud flying all around me. In doing so, I fell off the other side of the wooden planks and into the marsh. The water was cold and deep. I could see nothing but darkness, vines, and pieces of decaying vegetation. Panic seized me. Water was the marrowyrn's natural habitat, where it was agile and fast.

Through the muddy water, I saw the silhouette of its long, sinuous body swimming nearby. The water bent around its body, revealing its shape. I was dead if I didn't get out of the water, but the wooden planks had broken under the creature's attack. I swam as fast as I could, desperately searching for a place to escape. Soon, I felt a large rock in front of me, near the surface of the water, and climbed on. It was large enough for me to take a few steps, allowing me to move around. My feet were still in the water, but at least I could stand. I would be able to defend myself this way.

I got my knife from its sheath. It was small compared to the beast's sheer size, but better than nothing. I steadied my breath and tried to calm myself so that my hand wouldn't shake.

The serpent lunged again, jaws gaping wide enough to swallow me whole. I rolled beneath its strike, slashing at the underside of its throat. Scales deflected the blade, but it still bit deep enough to draw a hiss of pain from the marrowyrm. The creature reared, its tail sweeping across the mire, striking me square in the chest and hurling me into the vines at the end of the rock, right on the edge of falling back into the water. Pain lanced through my ribs. The air left my lungs in a choking gasp, mud flooding my mouth. I clenched the vines in my hands to stop myself.

I knelt and coughed. The creature growled, reminding me that it had no intention of letting go. I rose.

It was clear I couldn't get out of this one without my powers. There was no point in saving my mana for the temple if I got killed before I got there.

With one hand, I held my knife, and with the other, I traced the prayer to Alastor with my fingers. Concentrating on myself, I gathered the forces from his essences: the dwarf, elf, and dragon. *May his will guide me.* I thrust the knife forward, hoping it would get imbued with his power. My initial surprise was soon replaced with delight when I saw searing lines of fire racing through the swamp. Alastor had heeded my call. The marrowyrn shrieked as flame met water near its body, steam boiling up in choking clouds. It thrashed, its coils tearing up earth and dead vegetation alike.

Seizing the moment, I leaped onto its back, driving the glowing knife between its scales. The serpent writhed violently, but I clung on, dragging the blade deeper until fire coursed through the wound. With a final, shuddering bellow, the creature collapsed. The marrowyrn started sinking slowly into the mire that birthed it. I hurried and removed my dagger from it and got back onto the rock to avoid sinking with it.

Silence returned, broken only by my ragged breath. Mist swirled aside, revealing what the serpent had guarded: broken pillars of stone rising crookedly from the marsh, half-sunken but unmistakable—the remains of the Skyfall Temple. The water lapped hungrily at its entrance, dark and bottomless.

Chapter 11 (Caleb)

Flames

I opened my eyes. I was hot and sweaty. I remembered more bad dreams. Lately, it was always about dragons. I remembered this one was about all of *us*, dragons, uniting under the One that was prophesied. I wasn't sure what this meant, but I clearly remembered thinking I was one of them. I could feel the blood of the dragon burning in me. It was invading my dreams, torturing me. I was weak, weaker than I had ever felt.

The grunts of the orcs nearby reminded me of where I was. It was early morning, judging by the light filtering through the tent where we were chained. Besides me was Summer, her cheeks red and wet from tears. In her stare, I could read relief and anger. She pulled on the slack of her chains, getting as close as she could to me.

"It's about time you woke up!" she exclaimed, her sentence ending in a high pitch before she sobbed again. Through our bond, I could feel all the sadness she had felt pierce my stomach. I was speechless, frozen by such despair. I wanted to hold her, but couldn't get myself to move. She added, "It's been four days! Do you know how worried I have been?"

I was stunned by her words. In four days, Aeris could have easily found us. I was sure she would have no trouble raiding an orc camp to get to me, especially after the betrayal I committed. The fact that she wasn't there confirmed that the link that allowed her to know where I was had been broken. She wouldn't have wasted that much time if she knew my location. I tried to sit up, but I was too weak.

The flap opened with force. Summer barely had time to stand before rough hands seized her arms and wrenched them behind her back.

"Leave her alone," I roared, struggling with all my might to get up, but couldn't.

Orcs poured in like a tide.

Their guttural laugh filled the tent as they pointed at me. "He awake," one said. "We just have one."

I was angry with myself for being this weak, but I had to resign myself to watching them mistreat my mate. One of them struck her across the face, not hard enough to knock her out. I growled angrily. One of the orcs restrained me to make sure I wouldn't intervene, even if I was too weak to stand. Summer's wolf growled angrily, and I felt her fury through our bond. As much as she wanted to fight, they were too strong and too many against her. Another forced her to her knees. The floor bit into her skin.

"Hold her," one growled.

She struggled. A fist tangled in her hair and yanked her head back. He pressed something against her lips.

"No—" she choked.

They forced her mouth open.

She gagged, convulsed, but they pinched her nose, held her jaw until swallowing was no longer a choice. When they released her, she collapsed forward, coughing, breath tearing out of her chest.

The orcs laughed and then exited the tent. One of them turned before leaving, adding, pointing to me, "Next time, you drink too." Their footsteps faded.

When they were gone, Summer dropped to her knees. She put a finger in her throat until she vomited the full contents of her stomach, once, twice, leaving her gasping, weak, shaking.

She wiped her mouth with trembling fingers. I was close enough that I grabbed her hand and pulled to help me sit up.

"I'm sorry," I whispered. "I'm so sorry I couldn't defend you."

She shook her head. "Don't worry about it. They've been doing it while you were out. I prefer to vomit the poison than to keep it."

"I'm so useless," I said more to myself than her.

"Don't say that!" she countered, reaching for me.

"I don't deserve you," I whispered.

She smiled, her hand gently caressing my cheek. She felt cool against the fever that rampaged through me. "I've seen your past through our bond. You've endured a lot of hardships; you deserve something nice in your life."

"But I've made a lot of bad choices," I replied.

"I'm the gift fate has sent to make up for everything that's happened to you. You can choose to be different."

I froze, surprised by her words. I had been an assassin for centuries. The stars lit up the night sky, but it remained dark, unchanged. My heart twitched when I looked at her. Who was I kidding? I'd do anything for her. I'd change if it were still possible. I'd be the partner she needed me to be, even if it meant that I stopped being an assassin. Maybe I didn't believe it was possible, but she believed it, and that was enough.

"You're right," I whispered, "I have a choice now. I'll do whatever it takes to make you happy."

In her eyes, I could see my future. If I made it through this fever, we would build our lives together on *her* terms. So be it if I didn't kill anymore—she was all that I needed.

"Can you stand?" she asked.

I pushed on my shoulders, determined to sit and rise, but my body refused to cooperate. My head spun as soon as I made the slightest effort to move. Defeated, I shook my head. Summer clenched her teeth, but I could feel her worry through our bond.

"You're too weak, you need blood to regain strength."

She pulled on her chains as much as she could, until her arm reached my lips. "Hurry, before the orcs enter the tent. And before you refuse, I'll be fine as long as you don't take too much."

Her heavenly scent of jasmine awakened the hunger in me. I felt her veins pulse with blood. She was right, I had to feed. I would have preferred my first feed from her as a mate to be a sweet, intimate, sensual moment, but I had to drink now and regain my strength. We had to leave this prison, or we'd never live to build our future together.

I sank my teeth into her arm and hummed as the first drop of her blood touched my tongue. Summer let out a single long moan that filled me with desire. I intoxicated myself with her nectar, reveling in her, bound by body and soul, feeling her urges and pleasure. As our hearts beat in unison, I pushed a promise into her mind: *"I'm going to worship you as you deserve when we get out of here."*

I was careful not to drink too much, not wanting to weaken her. She sighed languidly as I pulled my fangs from her arm, leaving my tongue to heal the skin. "I'll remember your promise," she breathed, her eyes still heavy with yearning, her moist lips rubbing against my earlobe.

Outside, the sound of the orcs suddenly changed. The sound of screams and the clash of swords came to us. Something was happening. This was an opportunity to escape.

Adrenalin filled me, mixed with the blood I'd just drunk. I pushed with effort and managed to stand up. My ribs still weren't healed, and sharp pain filled me at the movement, but I didn't let it show.

Summer smiled. "Are you feeling better?" she asked, though I suspected she knew that I was hiding the discomfort.

I took a moment assess myself. I was still burning with a fever. "A little. Enough to stand."

"That's a start," she replied.

We were still chained to the pole. We needed to get out of here. Whatever was distracting the orcs, we had to take advantage of it. "Let's see if I can do something about these," I said.

It was foolish to think I could conjure my magic in this state, but I had to try.

I concentrated as best I could, trying to find the remnants of Aeris's magic within me. Even though our bond was broken, the magic I had absorbed from her lingered, despite the suffocating omnipresence of draconic magic. I found a fragment, cold and hard, and focused on it. I molded the magic, forcing it into my hands, amplifying it, making it bend to my will. My fingers turned cold, overcoming the fever for a fleeting moment. I grabbed my chains and Summer's. I watched the magic slowly spread, coating the metal, frosting it little by little as it went. When the first links were frozen, I pulled as hard as I could. The effort was considerable, and Summer supported me to prevent me from falling, but I finally managed to break the frozen metal, and the chain links scattered the ground.

It was a small victory, and the first we had had in days, but it was far from over. I would rejoice once we were far away from here.

We approached the tent exit with care. Every movement took tremendous effort. My legs shook from the exertion. I pushed to Summer through our bond, afraid to make any noise, *"If the goddess is here, we run as fast as we can."*

There was no way we could outrun Aeris if she were there, but we had to try *something*. Summer agreed through our bond.

I held my breath as I poked my head out of the tent to see what was happening. Fortunately, the entrance was deserted. The guards had gone to fight the cause of the raucous. After spending so much time in the darkness of the tent, I had to blink against the smoke-choked dawn.

What struck me immediately was the stench of blood. Death hung thick in the air. The orc camp was in ruins. Orc bodies lay in the furrows between the tents everywhere. Tents were collapsed or burned, their hide walls curling in on themselves. The fire pit was scattered with charred meat and severed limbs, and the great warg pens had been destroyed. At this rate, it was a miracle our tent was still up.

We made our way through the debris until we reached a gap between the tents that let us see what was happening. A sense of relief filled me when I realized that Aeris wasn't the cause of the carnage. Dozens of soldiers were fighting the orcs. I couldn't make them out, but my predatory instinct could tell that some were human, dressed in sophisticated armor. Screams danced across the carnage. I wanted to help them, but I was too weak.

"Let's go," whispered Summer. I nodded and followed her.

We made our way through the debris, keeping a low profile. My breath was ragged, and I had to slow down a few times as black dots clouded my vision. One orc, still clinging to life, reached for my ankle with a blood-slick hand. I kicked it aside and pressed forward. We slipped past broken armor racks and stepped over corpses. Every breath was a knife in my broken ribs. Freedom was close now.

Then, through the haze of smoke and noise, we heard grunts. Human voices.

I froze, pushing Summer behind me instinctively, though I could barely stand. Figures emerged from the treeline—soldiers in battered armor, weapons raised, wary eyes scanning the carnage.

"Hold!" one called, a woman with a captain's band across her chest plate. She was covered in grime, so much so that I wouldn't be able to tell what she looked like. Her sword dripped dark blood—orc blood.

Summer rose her trembling hands. "We're prisoners," she rasped.

The captain studied us, then motioned to a soldier behind her. "They need healing. Bring them to the camp."

The weight of the efforts crushed my legs. I collapsed. Two soldiers rushed forward to catch me.

"You're safe now," the captain said, scanning the battlefield behind them. "The camp's fallen. We'll get you to ours. You'll get food, water, rest."

I looked back one last time at the broken bones of the orc camp, the place that had nearly become our grave.

I drifted in and out of consciousness as the soldiers carried me away. There were very few conditions that a vampire could not treat with blood. What if it were incurable? No power was worth this. I'd been stupid, and I was going to pay the price. The dragon's blood, still boiling inside me, mocked. I was delirious for sure, but it felt like I was hearing words breathed out: *"Vrak Drel'kaan Zarvok."*

Then everything went black.

I woke up. The first thing that hit me was the smell of herbs. In my mouth lingered a disgusting taste. I couldn't put my finger on what it was, then I remembered the soldiers. I must have fainted, and they brought me here. I was too weak to move, but I could see herbs, potions, and several beds. I guessed that this must be the infirmary.

I heard Summer's voice. She was a little further, and I couldn't see her from where I was. "Is he going to be okay?" she asked.

"The potion I concocted should be able to heal him," a man replied. "However, the magic flowing in his veins is beyond my powers. I've never seen magic this strong."

Summer asked, "Do you think it's magic from the dragon blood he drank?"

The man remained silent for a moment, then cursed. "If he drank dragon blood, there's nothing I can do for him. Dragon blood isn't just full of magic; it has a will of its own—living. It will decide his fate."

Summer gasped. There was a silence, and man's words sank in. Dragon blood was alive. I shuddered at the thought. The man said he couldn't do anything about the dragon magic, but at least the potion would heal my body. It would be a start.

"How do you know so much about dragon blood?" Summer asked.

"As an herbalist, I have spent my entire life treating various ailments. One day, I met an elf whose blood had been mixed with dragon blood by a mad sorcerer. He passed on all his knowledge to me."

I wanted to talk to them, to let them know I was awake, but my mouth was parched. I tried to summon some sounds, but couldn't.

"Let's hope for the best, then," Summer replied. She sounded worried. I heard steps and hoped they would come closer, but I realized they were going away.

The man talked, "I just gave him another dose of the potion a few minutes ago. Let's give him some time to rest, and let the drink do its magic on him. Let's return in a few hours to assess his state."

"Thanks, Darryl," said Summer before leaving. I didn't want her to leave. I wanted my mate by my side, but it was getting hard to stay awake. I could feel the potion having some effect on me. I felt less feverish. Or was it the dragon blood that had decided to let me survive? What was I even thinking . . . I closed my eyes, surrendering myself to the slumber.

I could smell the scent of jasmine before I even opened my eyes. My lips curled up in a smile. She was there.

Her eyes lit up with joy when I opened my eyes. "You're awake!"

The disgusting taste was still in my mouth, but I felt grateful for it as I didn't feel feverish anymore. I reached out to take Summer's hand. The pain in my ribs was much less. They weren't quite mended, but it only hurt like a bruise, which was a big improvement.

"I hope I wasn't out for days," I told her, only half-joking. I wouldn't have wanted to make her worry like last time, but judging by her mood, I would bet that it wasn't that long.

"It's only been a few hours."

Around me were a few beds. Wounded soldiers were lying on them. Some were alone, others had company. A slender man approached after tending to the bed next to me. His black hair was tied in a bun. "I see you're awake. That's good. I wasn't sure what the draconic magic would decide," he said with a smile.

I could feel that my vampiric powers were slowly returning to me, and the burn of dragon's blood was gone. With a little more time, I hoped my healing powers would return to how they used to be.

"Thank you for saving me," I told Darryl. I could hear his heartbeat and smell the scent of his skin.

The man shrugged. "I'm getting used to saving people on the brink of death. It reminds me of that time when I saved the king! Or ex-king now, but if you ask me, he's the only king I'll ever follow."

"What happened?" I asked.

"The poor guy was barely alive when he got to me. He was poisoned, and I didn't know if he would survive. I don't know how he got poisoned, but it was strong, meant to kill. It took a while for me to save him."

I was shocked. He had been the one to save Nathan, to prevent me from killing my target, but it all felt like a lifetime ago. I had found my mate and was running from an angry goddess. The dragons were on the brink of war if I was to trust the visions I'd been having. The dragon's words came back to mind. *"Vrak Drel'kaan Zarvok."* I had no idea what it meant, but I knew it was important.

"You are very talented," I commented to the man.

He nodded. "Thank you. I'm just doing my job."

"How did you get here?" Summer asked.

Darryl let out a long breath. "It's a long story. My sister got kidnapped by orcs, or so I had been told by an elven woman. I haven't seen her in years. My father left with her when I was just a baby to join the Miłonblooders. When I heard she was trapped here, I enrolled in the vampire queen's battalion to close the gate to the Underworld. That's what we are: Queen Samantha's army, here to defeat the orcs."

Summer gasped at the mention of the gate, but my mind was stuck on the vampire queen. She was ruthless. She wouldn't send people here unless she stood to gain personally.

"Why would the queen send a battalion? Krelgraz has been infected by orcs for centuries," I asked.

"The orcs have been attacking Ichoryllia," Darryl explained. "The queen was fine when they were only attacking the human town or the werewolves' pack. Now that they're attacking the vampires, she needs them gone."

It all made sense now. With the city under attack, she had no choice but to do something about it, or else the citizens would eventually rise against her.

Nevertheless, one battalion against an island crowded with orcs just waiting for an opportunity to spill some blood was a suicide mission. And this poor man, ready to die for his sister. My stare fell on Summer. I'd do the same if she was kidnapped by orcs. I remembered what I saw when I drank the dragon blood: a war was coming, and it was time to find allies. This man had just saved my life; it would be ungrateful to leave without helping him. I'd worry about Aeris when my debt was paid.

"We'll help you," I said. Summer's eyes went wide. Darryl smiled.

"Thank you. I will welcome all the help I can get, but first, you should rest. We can talk more tomorrow."

I nodded. As much as I wanted to go now, I was still healing and didn't feel like I could walk around just yet.

"I'm sorry to leave you alone," I told Summer.

She shook her head. "It's fine. I have been shown to a tent. You can join me once you're healed enough."

A moment later, her lips were on mine. She tasted like paradise, and I longed to be alone with her.

"Alright, you love birds," Darryl joked. "You'll get time alone as soon as you can stand."

He handed me a potion, and I realized I had no idea how long he had been holding it. The smell coming from it was distinctly the one he had been given to me. I wrinkled my nose.

"I'll return in the morning," said Summer as she exited the tent.

Alone with Darryl, I drank the medicine, hopeful for tomorrow.

Chapter 12 (Elaine)

The Stranger

It had been several days, maybe weeks. I had lost count. I had tried to go to Oswald's room again, but the guards always stopped me before I could even leave my room. I kept questioning the servants about him, but they never answered or acknowledged me. I still couldn't get my mana back. It was frustrating.

The only thing that kept me busy was the pile of books in my room. I had been terrified when the queen had visited the other day. I was sure she was there to finish what she had wanted to do on the day we resurrected Scorchfire. I was surprised to discover that she didn't want to kill me. I guess that the dragons' rebirth had bought me some time, but I was no fool. She would eliminate me once I'd found the answers she sought.

I had already read half of the books. Some dealt with things I already knew about dragons, but others contained information about dragon riders, whose existence I was unaware of before today. My contacts with dragons had been limited. I had always been told to stay away from dragons, that they were dangerous creatures. In the end, I had only seen Scorchfire once before he was killed. The king had wanted to learn how to obtain draconic magic and exploit it for himself, so it had been my main research topic. There was so much to discover about those creatures, and we didn't have that many books about them in our library.

However, I wasn't closer to understanding why the dragons had returned, and I still hadn't found a way to escape my prison. It was true that I was powerless for the moment; without my spells or a weapon, I was no stronger than a human, and they knew it. I was waiting for my moment.

I turned my attention outside. Which was my only other distraction besides the books. Last night, I heard noise coming from the city. The smell of fire wafted through my window, and I suddenly wondered if it was the dragons again. The noise quickly stopped, so I figured it must have been something else, but I couldn't see anything from my view.

The debris had been removed from the main streets. People had started walking outside again, glancing warily at the sky as they went by, and helping those in need. It was a reminder of how resilient people could be. Despite the city's state, they were still trying to get on with their lives and help rebuild. I had heard from whispering staff that the body of a dragon lay at the south wall, but my room's window was north. I wished I could have seen it.

The latch on my door moved, but I didn't even look. The servant always brought the tray of food and left immediately. When I didn't hear the door close, I turned around.

At the door stood a man—a human. It was the first time I'd seen him. He was well-dressed, which was unusual, since the queen despised humans. His dark brown eyes looked at me from the doorway. I rose to my feet, and he said in a deep voice, "Don't come forward."

I obeyed, filled with curiosity and not wanting him to leave. "Who are you?"

He ignored my question. "I've come to bring you a message. Your friend is dead."

My limbs went cold.

"You mean Oswald? Are you sure?" I asked, my heart beating wildly. I couldn't believe it—that was impossible.

He clenched his fists. "He was killed. I felt you deserved to know."

He exited as quickly as he had entered. I fell to my knees as the lock clicked back into place. I'd thought of that possibility in the darkest corners of my mind, unwilling to fully acknowledge it. I hadn't heard any sounds coming from his room, but I had hoped . . . Oswald was dead. A cry escaped my lips as I hit the floor with my fist. All the years we'd spent together—*gone*. And now, what was left? I had only a bag of belongings, my studded leather enchanted robe, and I was trapped in a golden prison, unable to cast spells or return home.

The dragons were restored, and elven magic was saved. As a Grand Wizard, that had been my main goal, but it had come at a terrible cost.

"My Lady. Please, wake up."

The voice was warm and melodious. I opened my eyes and saw an elf kneeling beside me. His curly red hair was tied back, and his deep green eyes were fixed on mine. A reassured look appeared on his freckled face when he saw that I was awake.

"Are you okay?" he asked, but I was too mesmerized by the sensation coursing through me to respond. It was soothing and hot, and I yearned for it never to stop. I had never felt anything like this before.

"Um, yes, I think so," I stammered.

The smile he gave me lit up my heart, and all my worries vanished for a moment. He held out his hand to help me up. Magic flowed through our fingers, sparks and fire mingled, light and pure.

"I looked everywhere for you," he confessed as I stood up. Behind him stood the same human servant who had been there before. The one who had told me of Oswald's death.

"You have?" I asked, confused.

"You don't have time for questions," the human servant said. "The queen might be out of the castle for a few days, but if the guards spot us, we're all dead."

"Jason is right," the elf answered. "Please, we must hurry. I will explain everything later."

I was more than ready to leave this place. Once on my feet, I grabbed my bag and followed the elf. As I passed Jason, I whispered, "Thank you."

The man replied, "If you get caught, you never saw me."

I didn't understand why he was doing it, but I understood the gravity of his words. I nodded seriously.

I took a deep breath as soon as I left the room. It was as if a huge weight had been lifted from my shoulders. The relief was instantaneous, and I felt my mana begin to restore itself. I rejoiced. The corridors were not protected against mages. It would take time, but I would be able to cast spells again.

"This way," the elf murmured to me, grabbing my hand.

I followed, not knowing where we were going. I only knew it was freedom, and that was enough. I knew I could trust him.

He done this a thousand times, turning left or right without hesitation, only looking to see if the corridors were empty. We went down a dead-end corridor. He put his ear against the last door to the left and listened. When he was satisfied, he opened the door. It opened onto a small room, as narrow as a closet, but it seemed to stretch on forever.

"Quick, into the servant's passages," he insisted.

I followed him, and he closed the door behind me. Candles lit the hallway.

"How do you know there won't be any servants to catch us?" I asked.

"I don't," he replied, "but it's better that servants see us than guards."

He was right. Servants would be easier to persuade them if we needed to. "Are you aware that I don't have enough mana to fight?" I asked. I wanted to make sure he knew he couldn't count on me.

He let go of my hand, and I immediately missed his contact. His eyes slightly glowed green in the darkness. "I wouldn't let anything happen to you," he said with such assurance that he stole my breath away. I blushed slightly and nodded.

Further ahead, the corridor turned left. I realized we were probably inside the castle's outer wall. At this point, the corridor was wider, wide enough for two people to walk side by side. Just as we turned the corner, we saw two vampiresses in front of us. The first was carrying a basket full of laundry, and the second was carrying brooms. Both jumped when they saw us. The elf stood in front of me as a shield, his arm raised defensively.

"If you attack, you're dead," he said.

The two women shook their heads. "The traitor drove out our king. We have no interest in telling her. We are only keeping our jobs to feed our families."

He relaxed his stance slightly. "You must not tell anyone that you saw us," he ordered with the confidence of someone accustomed to giving orders.

The vampiress holding the laundry replied, "We won't, but beware, some are loyal to the queen."

"We will, thank you," said the elf. I nodded in agreement. The vampiresses moved aside to let us pass. We continued for a while, and I was no longer quite sure where we were in the castle.

"I have so many questions," I admitted.

"I know. Let us get to safety first," he answered.

"Can I at least know your name?" I asked.

"Akael," he said.

I repeated the name in my mind. It was perfect. At one point, I saw light coming from a corridor that turned to the right.

"Ah, this is the place Jason mentioned," said my rescuer as we approached.

In front of us was an exit. The corridor led to the castle's courtyard. Hope filled me.

Freedom. Finally.

We were behind the castle, and far from the main gates. There were no guards in sight. Before us stood a servant carrying a basket of fresh bread. He dropped his basket when he saw us, the loaves falling into the grass, and cried out, "The prisoner!"

Quick as ever, Akael moved behind the vampire and put his hand over his mouth. The vampire struggled, but the elf kept a firm grip on the servant. I felt the air fill with mana as Akael began reciting words. At that moment, the vampire's eyes widened. He struggled even harder, desperately trying to break free. The elf's hand glowed red before flames burst forth. The vampire kicked as hard as he could, coughing and wheezing as he desperately tried to breathe. But the merciless flames continued their path, crawling up, wrapping the contours of his face, his nose. They reached his hair, which caught fire. The smell of burning flesh filled the air.

The vampire lost consciousness, forcing Akael to support the weight of his body as he continued his spell.

Keeping his hand over his mouth to continue burning him, he laid the body on the ground. Quickly, the fire spread to the servant's woolen clothes, charring and smoldering. Fortunately, the grass was damp from a light rain that had fallen earlier, so it didn't catch fire.

Akael kept his grip until the vampire's facial skin was blackened and covered in blisters. He wasn't breathing now. Only then did he remove his hand.

"I won't let anyone hurt you," he said.

I stared for a moment at this man, capable of such strength. I felt safe with him. He had protected me, and I knew he wouldn't hesitate to do so again.

"Let's hurry in case someone heard him," he urged. "I have a room at the inn. It should be safe at least for tonight. Jason swore he'd keep guards and servants away from your room the rest of the day. Anyone loyal to the queen shouldn't hear about your disappearance before tomorrow. We'll leave before dawn."

We left the courtyard without encountering anyone else. We walked through the least frequented streets, stepping over the debris, trying not to attract attention. Being two elves in a vampire city, this was not so easy. We passed a tall vampire with piercing blue eyes. His long, straight, dark hair was tied. Beside him was a short vampire with tawny skin. Her eyes were golden, and she wore a sophisticated brooch to hold her hair in place. She wore a long, refined lace dress. She was gorgeous. I noticed she was staring at us for a tad too long. It made me nervous, and I hoped she didn't intend to attack us.

Vampires were so unpredictable.

The male vampire put his arm lovingly around her waist. "Come, Esmeralda," he said as he pulled her away from us.

Her eyes fell back on him. "Yes, Aleks, my love."

I was glad to see them go further into the street. As we approached the inn, we met several vampires. However, as news of my escape had not yet spread, people gave us curious looks before continuing on their way. We finally arrived at a gray brick building. The sign read *The Last Drop* and I thought it was a perfect name for an inn. The two lanterns on either side of the door shone with a yellowish glow.

Although I would have preferred to be far away from the vampire city, it was better than the castle.

We went inside, finding the room was filled with the laughter of patrons. The smell of alcohol and blood wine filled the air, along with the smell of fresh stew, which made my stomach grumble. As if reading my mind, Akael motioned to the tavern keeper. "Bring two bowls up to my room."

The tavern keeper nodded. I followed the elf up the wooden stairs, which creaked under our weight, worn down by years of footsteps. His room was the second-to-last door on the right.

The noise from the tavern below faded as the door closed behind us. The room was modest with a single bed with freshly laid sheets, along with a small window, a wooden desk, and a round table with a chair. I breathed a sigh of relief. We were finally safe, at least for the moment.

Akael took off his coat and laid it on the bed. He was even more handsome this way. He wore a green shirt that highlighted his muscles. He stood tall, and his every movement was graceful. I mean, elves were graceful by nature, but he was even more, and I wondered who he really was. I knew nothing of him, but that didn't make it scary. I was excited and eager to discover who he was.

He had entered my life as suddenly as a flash of lightning and already had such a big impact. Now that I was alone with him in a safe place, I would finally be able to ask him all my questions.

Chapter 13 (Erendriel)

Mumbur

I left for Mumbur the same day. I had instructed Mathias to continue the experiments in my absence and to notify me in the event of an emergency. The royal peregrine falcons were at his disposal. I had brought nothing with me except my precious rune, which I kept with me at all times. It was an extension of myself. I could feel its power, its life.

It rained heavily as I walked. Each droplet struck the leaves with a sharp patter before spilling down, soaking everything beneath. My hair was plastered to my cheeks, my clothes clung to my skin, but I didn't care. The forest needed this. Leaves quivered under the weight of the water, glossy and vibrant; ferns unfurled like green tongues to drink their fill. Moss along the roots swelled, releasing the earthy scent of life renewed. Even the twisted undergrowth seemed to breathe easier, its thirsty stems bowing gratefully beneath the downpour.

Impatience tugged at me like a hand at my sleeve. I wanted—needed—to read the writings found in the ruins deep in the mines. If they truly held threads of the Oracle's prophecy, then every moment I lingered was a moment wasted.

The rain softened as I pushed deeper into the forest, the roaring storm fading to a whisper beneath the thick boughs. But little by little, the forest began to thin. The trees grew farther apart, their trunks narrower, their leaves losing their luster. Ferns surrendered to scraggly shrubs, and moss gave way to brittle patches of dry earth. The air warmed, and the wind changed. It was hotter, harsher, and carrying the faint sting of grit.

By the time I reached the last line of trees, the rain had ceased entirely. Behind me lay a world of green dripping with life, but before me stretched a cruel, unforgiving place: the desert. Lands of shifting sands, jagged stone, fractured ridges, and blistered ground where nothing soft could grow.

I pressed on. Dust clung to my soaked emerald cloak, turning its shine to mud. The sun blazed down, merciless and unfiltered, and I swore inwardly for not bringing anything to shield myself from its burning glare.

I walked, eager for the afternoon heat to lessen. The sun burned the stones until they shimmered with a haze that made my vision waver. Sweat pearled on my skin, and I regretted that the earlier storm didn't stretch over these wretched lands. The air finally cooled when the sky glowed with streaks of crimson. The plateau stretched before me like a battlefield abandoned by gods, its cracked skin littered with sharp rocks that threatened to twist an ankle with every step. Vultures wheeled overhead, and the distant cry of a hawk rang through the canyons, sharp as a blade's edge. *I preferred this to dragons. I could handle a handful of hawks and vultures*, I thought to myself.

In the haze rising from the desert heat, I spotted two figures, and for a moment I wondered if it was a hallucination. As I got closer, I remembered that I was on the only road connecting Mytvathyr to Mumbur across the desert. Marked by symbols carved into rocks, as sand and storms made it impossible to actually create a path. The few merchant caravans followed the marks on the rocks as they passed between our two cities. Very few people dared to venture there, given the harsh conditions of the desert, but elven and dwarf guards still patrolled to ensure the safe passage of merchants and travelers.

The silhouettes became clearer, and I recognized two elven guards on patrol. The two men watched me suspiciously as I approached. I smiled, satisfied with my guards' performance. It was their job to make sure there were no brigands to attack the merchants. They drew their swords as I approached. Their expressions suddenly changed when I was close enough for them to recognize me.

"Your Majesty," they exclaimed apologetically. "We didn't recognize you."

"You're doing a good job," I replied.

"Thank you," said the first guard.

"Have you intercepted a lot of thugs?" I asked.

"We defeated a group just yesterday," answered the second. "They were trying to get to Mumbur. We tied them up, then dragged them to Mumbur's dungeon. The guards at the palace will decide their fate."

I could transfer them to Mytvathyr and add them to my army of mutants. That might actually be a good use for the prisoners. Come to think of it, I was hoping that there were a lot of people in Mumbur's dungeon. That would bolster my army even more. I couldn't wait to get there.

"Are you going to the dwarven city?" asked the first guard.

"I am," I replied.

"What brings you to Mumbur?" asked the second one, curious.

The reason for my visit was none of their concern, and I was about to say so when the first guard gave the other a stern look. "You can't ask the king that, you idiot! You'll have us lose our heads."

Fear filled the other one as he mumbled, "I'm sorry, your majesty! Please don't fire us."

I was pleased with their reaction. "Don't worry about it. I still have a long way to go. I should keep going."

"Safe travels," said the second guard.

"Keep up the good job," I replied before going my way.

When the day finally gave way to night, I found shelter in the shadow of a boulder as tall as a tower. Goblins were the most common creatures in these lands, but they had been quiet for some time. The road was being patrolled day and night, making the place even safer. The desert sky opened above me, vast and indifferent, the stars like cold fire. I lay restless, listening to the scrape of unseen creatures across stone and the mournful hiss of wind in the cracks.

The morning dawn broke with no warmth. I opened my eyes to the sound of claws scraping stone, telling me that I wasn't alone. Shapes shifted at the edges of the rising sunlight—kobolds, their scaled hides mottled and cracked, their eyes glowing yellow. They hissed among themselves, barbed spears and jagged nets clutched in clawed hands. Creatures of cavern and mire, never desert. Their presence here was wrong, unnatural. Had they been drawn here by the dragons?

I rose to my feet, my cloak slipping from my shoulders. The power stirred in the hollow of my chest, and the rune pulsed in my pocket. "*Kill them,*" whispered the voice as it had done when we battled the dwarves. My senses willed at the voice, enthralled by the possibility of the creatures' blood spilling on the ground.

A kobold shrieked and lunged, its spear driving straight for my ribs. My hand shot out, fingers curling as if to grasp something unseen. Black fire erupted from my palm, a jet of darkness so cold the air cracked. The kobold froze mid-stride, its body withering to a brittle husk before crumbling into ash.

The others recoiled, chattering, but hunger and numbers overcame fear. They rushed from every side.

I turned, a sweep of my arm loosing another torrent of shadow fire that ripped through two kobolds at once. Their shrieks split the morning silence, cut short as their bodies dissolved into nothing. Another leaped onto my back, claws raking at my shoulders. I snarled and seized its skull. Power flared. The kobold convulsed, shrieking, until only dust sifted through my fingers.

"*Yes,*" the voice breathed inside me. "*Yes, more. Do not stop. Tear them apart, my king. Let their screams crown you.*"

I struck without hesitation now, my body moving with a grace not my own, every blast of black fire fueled by hunger. Kobolds scattered, their courage shattering under the weight of my fury, but I hunted them down one by one. Jets of darkness lanced across the rocks, leaving black trails of frost where they struck.

When the last body crumbled to ash, silence returned. I stood amid the desert, chest heaving, hands still trembling with the aftershock of power. The dawn had risen fully now, the sun's light stretching over the barren plateau, but I felt no warmth. I closed my eyes and took a deep breath. By the end of the day, I would be in Mumbur.

As the day went by, the air grew hotter, drier, as though the desert sought to strip the very breath from my lungs. I passed the carcass of an old caravan, with wagons overturned and bones scattered white, sticking out of the sand. I walked faster.

By afternoon, the desert struck one last blow. A hot wind screamed through the canyons, flinging sand and shards of grit into my eyes. The world turned red with dust. I pulled my cloak tighter, wrapping my face with it to shelter myself from the storm's fury. When the gale finally broke, silence fell heavy, broken only by the wheeze of my exhausted breath.

At last, I could see the city's walls and the giant carved dwarven king faces staring at me when the sun dipped low again. I approached the city, grateful to know I would be spending the night in a bed rather than in the desert. The destruction of the town became apparent as I approached the gates, reminding me of the damage we had caused during our attack. Nothing had been repaired yet.

I would have to ask my generals for a detailed report. Mytvathyr was more important than the dwarf city, but in time, I would see to its restoration. After all, in its current state, it was vulnerable to attack, and with war looming with the werewolves and humans, Mumbur would not last long without a stronger defense.

The guards at the gates bowed when they recognized me. "Your Majesty," they said with respect.

"Let me in," I ordered.

They opened the gates, allowing me to enter. The city was as gray as when I had come with my army. Made of stone and metal, with no vegetation, I remembered once again how much I loved my elven city compared to the boredom that was Mumbur. But for the people here, it was home. A few dwarves walked the streets, mostly women and children. The majority of the men had been killed during the attack on the city. They looked at me with fear when they saw me passing by, remembering the assault on the city when I conquered it. A few bowed respectfully. Good. They knew who was in charge.

The bodies had been collected, and the debris cleared from the roads, but reconstruction was slow. However, the shops were open, and people had food. That was good. The last thing I wanted on my hands was having to deal with famine or an epidemic.

I knew the entrance to the mines was on the northern side of the city, but I needed to talk to my generals before I went. It felt important to show that I was there for them and to get a detailed report of the situation. I followed the main road, overlooked by the castle.

As I climbed the hill, I could see the town from above. The last time I had been here, during the war, I hadn't taken the time to admire the landscape. I was so high up that I could see the rooftops stretching to the far end of the city, where the river met the land. The blue of the great river was still colored red and purple from the sunset, as if pots of paint had been spilled. A feeling of peace filled me at this sight. How long had it been since I had last taken the time to admire the beauty of nature? I surprised myself with how calm I felt despite the war about to break out.

My eyes turned to the city's commercial port. The grand jewel of this town, the prize I got by killing the dwarven king and queen. Even as night gently descended to embrace it, the place remained lively. I noticed a fleet of boats moored. Their red flags, with an orange flame at the center, mocked me. The ships of the Sun Kingdom.

I scowled. Hadn't Prince Vaelarion already left? He left earlier than I did from Mytvathyr. I hadn't spotted him on my way, so he must have arrived earlier today. Perhaps they needed to restock their supplies before leaving. This was good for us. More gold for the stores. They would travel for weeks at sea before reaching land, so it made sense.

And what a big fleet! Having put so much effort into avoiding talking to him, I hadn't even asked about the size of the people accompanying him. Their kingdom must have had a formidable army and an unrivaled fleet to send a prince abroad with so many boats. I hoped they would leave quickly. I would make sure to check that they had left tomorrow or the day after.

I continued, determined to reach the castle before the last rays of sunlight disappeared. I had much to discuss with my generals. Elven guards stood at the gates. joking among themselves and chatting rather than keeping a lookout for intruders. Although the city was fairly quiet, it was a shame to see them acting this way.

"Is this how you ensure the safety of the castle?" I asked firmly.

The two soldiers recognized me, and their faces froze with fear. "Yes, Your Majesty!" said the first.

"Um, no," corrected the second.

Their behavior was not worthy of royal guards. Either they were incompetent and would be dismissed immediately, or they had a good reason, and I wanted to know what it was. "Explain yourselves," I ordered.

"You see, we haven't had a break in ten days," explained the first, looking uncomfortable. "We sometimes work fourteen hours and can barely take time off to eat and sleep, so when it's quiet, it's nice to relax."

"Fourteen hours?" I asked in disbelief. They weren't given any days off either. At this rate, the soldiers would soon be burned out. What were my generals thinking? "Let me in. I'll make sure the schedules are changed," I said kindly.

The two soldiers looked relieved. They nodded and opened the door to let me through.

The interior of the castle was dark, but a few torches were lit. It looked deserted, and I wondered where everyone was. I headed straight for the throne room. Memories of my previous visit came flooding back. I remembered walking these halls to the throne room to slit the throats of the king and queen. I remembered the queen's strong-willed gaze even in her death, followed by the moment when, in a fit of rage, I had decimated her body. It was a sad moment when I lost my composure. I would make sure not to lose control of myself again.

The throne room was empty, only the two dwarf-sized thrones were there. But who would leave a palace with no one to watch over the throne room? My generals had better have a good reason, or they would hear from me.

As I left the room, I passed a dwarf servant who was walking by. He looked at me with a frightened expression before bowing slightly.

"Where are the generals?" I asked him.

"In the war strategy room," he replied in a small voice.

"Take me there," I ordered.

The dwarf motioned for me to follow him. He walked with quick, small steps down a corridor that led to the armory. We turned left, then right. Portraits of the former royal family were still displayed in the hallways. I made a mental note to ask that they be removed. A few suits of armor stood upright on stands. I almost expected them to come to life, like the ones we had fought.

The sound of voices reached our ears as we approached an open door. Clearly, the generals were in disagreement. I could hear them arguing about where to send resources and what to do first.

I pushed open the iron-banded doors, their hinges groaning. The generals stopped talking as I stepped inside. My boots echoed against the polished floor as I took in the room. The walls were masterpieces of dwarven craftsmanship—massive sculpted panels depicting the great battles of their history. Warriors locked in shield lines and kings sealing treaties by hammering them into anvils rather than parchment. The carved scenes were a reminiscence of the dwarves' past glory. They filled me with rage—the dwarves were no more. It was the elves' time to shine. I would have my workers replace those with elven panels instead.

"I leave a kingdom in your hands, and you act like children?" I asked, barely containing my fury.

"Your Majesty!" cried one of them. They snapped out of their stupor and bowed before me.

I looked sternly at my three generals: Lane, Dale, and Rahul. Their eyes were filled with nervousness. They all got back to their rightful seats as I approached the table to take the head chair. "I visit my city to find no reparations underway, my soldiers working fourteen hours a day without breaks, and my castle deserted? How do you explain this?" I asked.

"I told you we should have started the repairs," said Lane to the others, his long purple hair braided and chains decorating his ears.

"But we don't have enough resources to make the repairs!" argued Dale, taller and leaner than the others.

"We would if we'd mined more stone," countered Lane again, the wood elves' eyes glowed blue with emotion.

"And how do you suggest we mine stone when we don't have a soldier to spare?" challenged Rahul, the dark elf.

I pinched the bridge of my nose as the three started arguing more. This conversation was going nowhere. "Silence!" I shouted firmly.

They all stopped, shame plastered on their face. "Rahul, why is it you can't spare soldiers?" I asked. This was the first and biggest problem to address.

"The citizens have told us that there has been a troll attack at the northeast wall. We had to set up soldiers over there. With those at the west wall, and those patrolling, we're spread thin."

"But we haven't seen the troll or heard of any attacks since we posted men there," added Lane with his finger in the air.

"We can't take a chance," argued Rahul, tiny magical sparks flying from his fingertips. He noticed them and rubbed his fingers together to make them disappear, then pulled himself together.

"Why not?" asked Lane. "If there is indeed one, we just slice it, and we're done."

Rahul shook his head. "Were you raised in a cave? Everyone knows trolls can't be killed by conventional methods. They regenerate constantly."

Dale nodded. “That’s right. You need to set them on fire or throw acid on them when they’re almost dead, otherwise they’ll come back.”

Lane gave a stifled cough. ”I was raised cloistered.”

They were right. Trolls were formidable foes. It explained why the soldiers didn’t get rest and why they didn’t have time to repair the city, but still, I was mad. The city was in a poor state.

“Why am I only hearing about this today? You should have sent a message for reinforcements and informed me of the situation. I trusted you,” I said, my voice loud. “With how the city stands right now, you would be overrun at the slightest revolt or attack.”

“We didn’t want to bother you with this, your Majesty,” said Dale in a small voice.

“More like you didn’t want me to see how incompetent you are!” I exclaimed, standing up and slamming my hand on the table.

Silence filled the room. No one dared to answer or even look me in the eye. “What if the city had fallen? Do you think I would have been happy then?” I asked. I couldn’t believe my generals. They were experienced, or at least I had thought so. It was true that this was our first real war in centuries, and that filled me with dread. I sat down again with a sigh.

“I’m here now. I’ll go and see for myself if there’s a troll in the northeast, since we can’t afford to send troops. This can’t happen again.”

“Yes, Your Majesty,” replied the generals, looking grateful that I was not going to punish them further for their mistake.

“It’s getting late. Tomorrow, before I leave, I want a full report on the city’s state. I will tell you what needs to be done while I am away.”

I left the room, leaving the generals seated, digesting their emotions, and headed for the room I had occupied the last time I was here. This would be my room for the night.

Chapter 14 (Nathan)

Flowers of Death

I followed the tunnel as it climbed higher. A small stream of water flowed down the center, and I walked along one side where the ground was dry. Fresh air greeted me, so I knew I was approaching the surface. The bricks were newer and in better condition here. I passed a man walking with a hood over his head. He was dressed in a large overcoat made of animal skins that fell to his ankles. He barely raised his head to look at me, his brown eyes meeting mine for a fleeting second before returning to the floor, pressing himself against the wall to avoid touching me. Finally, the sewer opened onto a street. It was night, and I was grateful as there would be fewer eyes. Finding myself back in my city after fleeing made me realize how much this was my home, even though I was wanted. This was where I belonged. It was my city, my kingdom. I had grown up here, and I was the rightful king.

I took a deep breath. The air still smelled of smoke after the fires that had destroyed so many homes. My pulse sped, and I clenched my fists as I thought back on the destruction that had taken place. The people deserved better. I would rebuild this city once I had regained my throne, but my first priority was Emerald. She was far more important than my kingdom. No treasure could compare to her.

There were destroyed buildings all around me. Stones lay scattered on the ground. Despite everything, I recognized the street I was on. I was in a small residential street, about two blocks away from the destroyed mill.

I walked through the night, avoiding people. I was good at moving stealthily, but I was in a city of vampires with keen senses. People passed by without looking at me, but everywhere I went, I felt like the wind was whispering, *"It's the fallen king."*

I walked along the walls and turned onto the street where the slave shop was located. I could already see the broken arms of the windmill atop the buildings, at the end of the street. I walked as fast as I could, sticking to the shadows as much as I could. A woman came out of her house right in front of me, letting out a surprised gasp. I froze, and we stood there staring at each other for a moment. *If she intends to report me, I will have to kill her*, I thought. She whispered, "Your Majesty!"

I put my finger to my lips and gestured with my other hand downward to ask her to keep her voice down. She nodded, keeping her voice barely above a whisper, "I won't say anything. You must save the city."

The tension eased in my shoulders. "It's good to know that I still have people on my side in my kingdom."

"There are many," she said passionately. "Many of us hate the new queen. It's been so long since anyone has seen you that we thought you were dead. It's good to know you're still alive."

It was more than I had hoped for. I could use this to my advantage. "Get ready," I told her. "The day I need you is coming. Together, we will reclaim this city."

The woman smiled. "I'll spread the word. We'll be ready."

"Stay safe," I said before taking my leave.

"You too," she said, walking away in the opposite direction from the slave shop.

I continued on my way down the winding street, my heart filled with new hope. I needed allies. I could count on the werewolves, the Thieves' Guild, and the citizens who were still loyal to me. Things finally seemed to be looking up.

The destroyed mill grew more imposing as I approached it. There was only one more turn in the street. As I passed it, I finally saw the slave shop. To my dismay, there were about twenty royal guards posted there. So the queen already knew . . . How many of them were loyal to Samantha? I couldn't take any chances. I was stronger than the guards, but given their numbers, they could have captured me, and I couldn't allow that.

Just as I was about to turn back to find another way in, a familiar scent reached my nose. I knew it so well. It was my old friend, my advisor, Lysander. He was coming out of a house carrying bags across the street, his free hand leaning heavily on his cane. He had advised my father for many years and had practically raised me. His brown eyes met mine, and he froze. He was so taken aback that he just stared at me with his mouth open for a second. He looked left and right to see if anyone was there, then covered the distance between us at high speed.

His voice was hushed and filled with concern. "Your Majesty! What are you doing here? You'll be seen."

I smiled, his presence bringing a sense of comfort. "It's good to see you, my friend."

"Me too, but we can't stay here. Come on," he urged. I followed him into a narrow back alley between houses. It smelled of rotting food, but I ignored it. Once we were out of sight, he continued, "If you only knew what it's like at the castle since Samantha arrived. I have no choice but to obey, but enough about me. I thought you were dead!"

I chuckled and told my friend how I had escaped from the castle and how Emerald had been kidnapped.

"Your vassal?" he asked.

"Not just my vassal. My *mate*," I replied with emphasis on the last word as I followed him through the alleys. Rats scurried through the boxes lying on the ground.

He gasped. "Your mate!" he exclaimed as he struggled to step over a puddle.

"That's why I have to go to the slave shop. She's there," I explained.

His tone hardened. "I see."

"The queen must have known. I've never seen so many guards for a simple shop," I added, hoping he could tell me how much the queen knew about my whereabouts.

The vampire continued walking, still looking ahead. "I don't know if the queen knows. I was at the seamstress's all day trying on and picking up some new clothes. My old ones wore down. That's where you found me."

We came to a place where the alley was wider. On either side were the courtyards of better-toothed houses. Tall hedges lined the gardens, some of which had oil lamps lit, giving off a faint yellow glow in the darkness of the night. We continued, walking more easily. In my excitement at finding my old friend, I hadn't paid attention to the path we had taken.

"Where are we going?" I asked Lysander.

The old vampire smiled and opened the gate to a large garden. "This way," was all he said.

The courtyard was huge, and the garden was well-maintained. There was a fountain in the middle and several benches. The roses, closed for the night, must have been magnificent during the day. It was surely the house of a noble vampire.

"I know a way to get into the slave shop," said Lysander. He pointed to a bench. "Wait for me here."

"That's nonsense. I'll go with you," I replied, but the old vampire shook his head.

"My old friend is wary of new people—his mind is starting to go. It's better if I go myself."

I nodded and watched Lysander walk away.

I decided to stay where I was, studying a group of tuberose flowers. The delicate white petals kissed the moonlight. A few moths fluttered around them, attracted by their sweet, creamy, exotic scent. I was captivated by their narcotic scent, wanting my sweet Emerald in my arms more than ever.

A sound came from behind me, and I turned around. I saw Lysander returning with four vampires. My senses prickled. Something was wrong, and as they neared, I saw that they were dressed in leather armor. I tensed up.

Lysander stopped and let the four young vampires approach.

"What is the meaning of this?" I asked.

But the old vampire didn't answer. He just leaned on his cane and watched as the others closed in on me. The first one carried a metal hammer that he had to lift with both hands. The second and the third carried daggers, while the final, a menacing vampire with a shaved head and tattoos, possessed a sword.

The tattooed vampire lunged at me before I could think. I hissed from the burning sensation as steel sliced my forearm. I roared and backhanded the attacker, sending the vampire crashing through a stone bench in a shower of shards. Another with a dagger was already at my throat before I could react. His nails raked across my chest, hot blood spilling down my torso, but I didn't have time to think about this when the dagger from the other cut low, deep into my thigh. My body faltered, pain flaring white-hot.

The wolf surged within me. He wouldn't let himself be defeated like that without seeing our mate again. The shift came swiftly, taking the vampires by surprise. My vision sharpened, and my breath thundered. He demanded violence, and I gave in to his will.

I caught one vampire mid-air, locking my jaw around his neck. He lost balance, and I smashed him into the cobblestones. I drove him down until his skull met the ground with a loud crack, debilitating him.

The one with the hammer attacked next. I easily avoided his attacks in my wolf form as I was swift and agile. In the confusion, the tattooed vampire swung his blade forward and ended up lodging the blade in the one who held the hammer. He cursed, and I slashed at them while they were distracted. My claws sliced through the vampire's flesh with the hammer, creating rivers of red. He staggered and fell backward. Meanwhile, Lysander hadn't moved. I caught a glimpse of worry in his face, but he remained still, leaning on his cane.

The last two vampires roared and attacked together: one dug his dagger into my shoulder blade, the other into my leg. My wolf whimpered from the pain, but instinct took over. I tore through the throat of the dagger-holding vampire with my claws, blood spraying across our faces, but as that happened, the last vampire slashed my back open. A shockwave of molten pain bloomed outward and forced me to shift back into my vampire form, naked. Every breath made the pain in the wound on my back shoot through me, as if it were getting bigger with every inhalation. I lay on the ground for a moment, trying to catch my senses.

The tattooed vampire hit me in the face with his boot as I lay there. The pain was blinding. My vampiric healing powers, coupled with my werewolf's, worked in sync, and I felt the skin fusing back together. It wasn't fully healed and still stung, but I was able to stand.

The tattooed vampire backed up, stunned. I took advantage of this to grab his head firmly and twist it until the neck snapped like dry wood. The corpse fell, twitching.

Only Lysander and I remained in the courtyard. He stared at me without flinching. If he was afraid, he hid it well. I grabbed the sword and a pair of pants from one of the fallen vampires, my eyes never leaving Lysander.

"You should have never existed," he spoke, cold as ice. All those years, all just to hear those words. His betrayal hurt more than any blade. "Your father was supposed to marry my oldest daughter. But no, he had to go and fall in love with your mother. *A werewolf.* The pain was such that my daughter took her own life."

My chest clenched, and my breath caught. I wanted to answer, but no sound came.

Lysander continued, "I may not be as skilled as my assassins, but I can still hold a fight."

He pulled the end of his cane, revealing a concealed blade. He launched himself at me. I parried his blows, steel against steel. Every strike ripped flesh, every counter rattled bone. Each blow brought back a memory, paralyzing me in the pain of his betrayal. A slash across my ribs. A kick to my chest. A blade across my cheek. My blood flowed from my wounds, already weakened from the fight before. He kept slicing relentlessly, pouring his rage into me.

I wanted to scream for him to stop, but I couldn't breathe the words. It was clear he wouldn't stop until I was dead. My sword struck deep into his flesh. Lysander staggered, blood spilling, yet his eyes remained cold.

"You are a mistake of nature. An obscenity of fate," he declared.

I plunged my sword into Lysander's throat. The old vampire emitted a gurgle, and blood fell from his mouth. His breaths became ragged and whistling, then shallow. He fell to the ground, and I dropped on top of him, unfinished. I punched at the words he had spat so disdainfully. I punched to forget his treason. I punched until the betrayal stopped hurting in my soul. When I was done, the vampire was long gone, his eyes staring at oblivion.

I swayed, drenched in blood. My own, my old friend's, the assassins' blood. My lungs burned, my body shook, and it felt like fire licked every wound. I staggered through the gates, each step heavier than the last, into the alley. I had been injured more seriously than I thought. My blood was flowing freely. The wound on my back had reopened.

The cobblestones tilted under me, and my vision blurred. I fell against a fence, slid down, breath rattling. In my mind, all I could think of was Emerald.

The last thing I heard was my own blood dripping on stone.

Then the world went black.

Chapter 15 (Samantha)

Skyfall Temple

I stood before the dark water, the ruins of the Skyfall Temple rising like broken teeth from the marsh. My breath came shallow, mist curling from my lips as I whispered the words of the water-breathing spell Alastor taught me. The air trembled, and a faint shimmer rippled across my skin—a thin veil of magic sliding over my mouth and nose. The next breath came smooth and cold, the air of another world.

I stepped forward.

The water closed over me as I followed the steps down inside the temple, silencing the night. Everything slowed. My hair floated like dark silk, my armor glinting in the faint light that filtered down from above. The white stone that had once been radiant had dulled to the color of old bones. Strange shapes drifted past: fragments of old stone, collapsed columns, the bones of those who had come before and failed.

The room I ventured into had collapsed inward. Remnants of statues stood against its walls, and fragments of broken marble littered the floor. The head of a statue stared at me. Eaten away by algae and decay, its face was no longer serene. Its wings lay further away, half buried in sand and sediment. An altar stood in the center of the room, still standing despite a collapsed column that had crushed it.

The deeper I swam, the colder it grew. Pressure built around me, but my spell held. The temple looked ghostly, its once-golden spires now strangled by moss and barnacles. Statues of kings of all races lined one path, their faces eroded, hands forever reaching upward toward a light that no longer shone. I recognized deities as well, like Hecate, the vampire goddess. I frowned. Once again, Alastor was not represented. This was further evidence that my almighty god had been neglected for thousands of years. It was high time to rectify this, and it would be done when his prophecy was fulfilled.

I moved from room to room, hoping that the water-breathing spell would hold. Perhaps it would be wise to recite it again to renew it, but that was risky. I didn't know how long it would last, and it had taken up a good portion of my mana. I estimated I could recite it at most two other times before running out of mana.

I arrived at a large room that looked like a council chamber. In the center of the room was a huge stone table partially covered with sediment, rusticles, and algae. I could imagine how grand the room must have once been. I walked around, pushing myself against stones to help me move through the water, searching everywhere, hoping to find the relic here, but to no avail.

I went outside and walked down a corridor. It led me to a much smaller and more modest room. The doors were cracked open, as if forced from within during some ancient battle. I slipped through, my hands trailing along the carvings on the door, scenes of saints walking among kings, their wings stretched wide, light streaming from their hands.

In this room, I found several rusty swords, corroded and partially covered with seaweed. No light filtered in this room. I moved carefully, not needing light to see in the dark. Faded murals adorned the walls. Although they had spent years underwater, the blue was still clearly visible, along with traces of yellow, white, and green. It was still possible to make out what they depicted, as they had been carved directly into the stone walls of the temple: a kingdom kneeling before radiant beings, a winged figure brandishing a shield toward the heavens, while dragons coiled in the clouds.

The relic.

The shield of the last saint. A faint tremor stirred through the temple. I turned sharply. The silence here was too complete, too watchful. Something was awake. I was sure of it.

I pressed onward, searching for a chest, a pedestal, anything that could have held the relic. But in the distance, where the corridor opened into the temple's drowned heart, something vast moved—coiling, ancient, and not quite dead. The saints' resting place had not been left undefended.

I adjusted my grip on my blade. I didn't care what was guarding the relic. I would not leave the depths without it.

The tremors intensified, and pieces of rock fell from the ceiling, forcing me out of the room and into another with a gaping hole. The moonlight filtered through the broken waters above. The walls were carved with wings and stars, now distorted by the slow breath of the current. In the center was an altar, half buried in silt, and behind it stood a massive statue, or at least what I thought was one. Until it moved.

The motion was subtle at first, a tremor rippling through the mud. Then, from behind the altar, a shape began to rise—skeletal wings spreading wide, the remains of feathers long decayed, replaced by strands of shadow and bone. Its body was twisted, draped in remnants of armor fused with coral and stone. Its face, once human, was split by lines of blackened veins and the faint glow of magic gone wrong.

When it spoke, its voice came like water echoing through stone: hollow, ancient, and aching with pain.

"So . . . another seeker comes."

I didn't expect the creature to be able to speak underwater until I realized the room was imbued with such magic that sound traveled through it rather than air.

I raised my blade. "I come for the relic," I said, my voice steady even though my pulse thundered in my ears.

A deep, hollow laugh rippled through the water.

"You seek the shield of the winged saint, as did your kings before you. But you are too late. The temple fell by betrayal, and I—"

Its head tilted, the faint green glow of its eyes piercing me.

"—I am what remains of its guardian."

The creature drifted closer, its form both fluid and terrible.

"The traitor's curse binds me. My wings were stripped, my soul tethered to this ruin. For thousands of years, I have guarded what cannot be redeemed."

I gasped as I realized that this was Alexander, the last saint, or at least what remained of him. Transformed into this undead guard, it was bound to this place, condemned to protect it for eternity. Nothing remained of the saint it once was.

"You guard nothing but bones and rot."

The creature's claws curled, stirring the current. "I guard *his will*. And his will is to suffer until the pure reclaim the relic. But you . . ."

It leaned forward, its voice like a whisper inside my skull. "Your heart is not pure. You are a queen of darkness, tainted by evil."

I clenched my teeth, rage building inside me. "You know nothing of my heart or of my faith."

"I *know* the weight of blood on your hands. I smell it in the water."

The words struck deep because they were true. I had killed plenty: men, beasts, and even innocents, but purity meant nothing now. Survival, destiny, and fulfilling the prophecy, these were my truths.

The guardian spread its bony wings, filling the chamber with a storm of silt and shadow.

"Then prove your worth, usurper. Redeem the blood you have spilled . . . or drown beneath the curse that damned me."

The water boiled violently as it attacked, its skeletal wings cutting through the current, its claws sharp as swords. I dodged while murmuring an incantation, sending a wave of burning energy through the water. The clash was silent but devastating, light against shadow, will against curse.

The guardian struck again, its claws slicing through my armor, burrowing into my skin. I winced, my blood mixing with the water. When my gaze returned to the guardian, its wings glowed with an aura, making the white of its bones sparkle. A series of bone materialized between each of its wings, appearing out of nowhere. I didn't have time to wonder what kind of magic this was before the guardian made a gesture with its hand, simultaneously throwing the bones in my direction. One of them lodged itself in my leg, while another pierced my cloak. They were as sharp as daggers.

I grabbed the bone with both hands and pulled. It was embedded deep in the muscle, and I cried as I pulled it out. The creature laughed once more.

"Don't you see how pointless this is? You've already lost."

I cast a magic wave in its direction, but it did nothing. If my magic couldn't reach it, then my knife would have to.

I approached, but it swam much faster than I did. The creature flapped its wings intensely, and the current pinned me against a wall. The guardian approached, unafraid and toying with me, like a predator with its prey. But I wasn't going to be intimidated. I waited until it was close enough and plunged my knife into its chest. The blade sank into the armor, and I smiled, thrilled to have the upper hand. I pulled out the knife, preparing for a second assault, when I saw the wound close up.

The guardian smiled maliciously at my dismay. "You can't kill what's already dead!"

Its claw struck me, slashing my cheek and sending me flying across the room, through the ruins of rotten wooden cabinets. I lay there for a moment, contemplating the situation. My magic did not affect it, nor did my knife. How was I supposed to defeat it? My eyes fell on the ceiling, which opened onto the water of the marsh. Could I swim fast enough and escape? But what good would it do me to run away without the relic? *Alastor, I need your guidance.*

Floating above in the water, the guardian materialized another set of bones. I was dead if I stayed there. I waited until it was ready to throw them and hid behind a column at the last minute, narrowly avoiding the attack.

The guardian was trapped here by a curse. Then I remembered a spell I had learned as a young priestess. It was my last chance. I recited the words, and my blade burst into white flames. It was not a fire of destruction, but a fire of liberation.

"If I can't kill you, then I will *free* you."

I lodged the knife into the creature's chest, and the light burst outward. The guardian screamed in agony. Its wings dissolved into ash and bubbles, the bones beneath turning to dust that spiraled upward toward the faint shimmer of moonlight above as the curse was broken and the saint was put to rest.

The temple fell silent once more. Only I remained, kneeling in the still water. Before me, where the guardian had stood, the altar glowed faintly. Within it rested the relic, an orb of pale metal, etched with wings and veins of light, its surface unbroken and free from algae despite the centuries that had passed.

I reached out, my fingers trembling as they brushed against it, afraid that some magic might protect it. A comforting warmth spread through my arm, though. It was mesmerizing, the most beautiful thing I had ever seen. I could feel the power emanating from it. So strong. So pure.

I carefully placed it in my bag. I felt a tightness in my chest and realized that I was having trouble breathing. The spell was beginning to wear off. Quickly, I recited the spell's words again, but I had used mana in the fight against the guardian. As a result, I had just enough left to cast the spell a second time. Fortunately, I had what I had come for.

Reassured that I would have enough air, I decided to swim through the broken roof of the temple until I reached the surface. Above water, the night was calm.

I hoisted myself onto one of the wooden planks, happy to be back on land and to have the relic in my possession. The fatigue from everything fell on me. I was eager to return to the castle to rest. I quickened my pace.

Chapter 16 (Elaine)

Veneficus Dei

I was alone with Akael. Cool air was coming in through the open window, yet I felt as if it was too warm in the room. I had butterflies in my stomach, and I longed for his touch.

"You must have a lot of questions," he said to break the silence.

Everything that had just happened came back to me. From his arrival at the castle to rescue me to our escape. I wanted to know everything. He was just a mysterious stranger to me, yet I felt like I knew him and could trust him. And I would never dare confess to those thoughts, which had been consuming me since I first laid eyes on him.

"I don't even know where to start," I admitted.

He laughed in a smooth voice that I found seductive. "Let me start from the beginning, then. I am Akael Vaelarion, prince of the Sun Kingdom."

My eyes widened. "Prince?" I interrupted.

This explained why he moved with such grace, or why he addressed the servants we encountered with such effortless authority. He smiled even more at my question. What could a prince possibly want from me?

"Yes, I am the youngest prince of my kingdom."

"But the Sun Kingdom is far from here," I commented, recalling the city's details from scrolls I'd reviewed. As Grand Wizard, it was expected that I knew about the surrounding kingdoms to be aware of any possible conflicts. "Why come all the way here?"

"Indeed, it is far. Since my birth, the Oracle had predicted that my soul mate was not in my kingdom. I was told that she was the mage of the gods and that she lived in a distant kingdom."

My heart twitched at the words "soul mate". I had never been the kind to believe in predetermined fate, but I couldn't deny the attraction I felt for Akael. I had no choice but to admit that soul mates existed.

"Are you saying that I'm your soul mate?" I asked, even though I already knew the answer.

He nodded, giving the most beautiful smile, melting my heart. "This defies everything I thought I knew. However, my soul also longs for yours. But this is happening so fast," I admitted.

"I will gladly wait for all the time you need, My Lady. When your heart is ready, then I'll be there."

I was grateful for his answer. Love wasn't something that should be rushed, even if he was my soul mate.

"The world is vast. How did you find me?" I asked.

"I sent messengers to all the kingdoms on every continent. I knew from the Oracle that I had to find the mage of the gods, so that's what I looked for. Then finally, in Mytvathyr, I heard about the *veneficus dei*. I knew it was you."

It was true that the servants had called me like that forever, but it was a lot to accept. My hands shook, and my heart raced.

"So then, you came all the way here, travelling for weeks, only to find me?" I replied.

"That would have been a goal worth the trip. However, I have come because the Oracle has said that you and I were to wage war against the great darkness that threatened to spread to the world."

This seemed like a tall order. I was just one mage. "I . . . I'm not sure I'm strong enough to do this."

"It doesn't matter if you believe or not that you can. The gods believe in you. *I* believe in you."

It was too much for me to bear all at once. Restoring the elven magic had been a heavy burden, but it was a task that fell to a mage, and I had done it. However, I did not want the fate of the world resting on my shoulders.

"I could have died at any moment at the hands of the queen, trapped in this castle without my magical powers. I'm just an ordinary elf. I don't want to be involved with gods!"

Akael grabbed my hands. His touch was warm, comforting. I immediately calmed, but a single tear rolled down my cheek. He wiped it softly.

"Think about it, Elaine. You say you're just an ordinary elf, yet I see those two embedded magic jewels. Those are known to be powerful, and I haven't heard of anyone able to wear two and survive. How can you not see the person that you are?"

I felt like my legs would give out from under me. I guess it showed because Akael pulled me gently toward the table. I sat down on the cold wooden chair and took a deep breath.

There was a knock on the door. Akael opened it, grabbed the two bowls of stew from the tavern keeper, and closed it. He brought me mine and ate his bowl while standing, as there was only one chair.

"Eat while it's hot," he said between mouthfuls.

The shock had been enough to make me forget I was hungry, but the smell of the stew reawakened it. The stew was delicious, especially after eating only dry bread for the past few days. I ate in silence while my thoughts ran rampant in my head.

Akael put his empty bowl on the table. His deep green eyes stared at me with kindness, or maybe it was tenderness? I wondered if I was imagining things. He said he was my soul mate. I had always heard that soul mates could recognize each other. I had never believed in any of that crap, let alone gods! Though I couldn't deny how I felt about him. I felt as though all my bearings, all the certainties on which I had based my life, were suddenly false—that everything I had believed impossible was true. And now I was faced with a destiny I had not chosen, did not desire.

"When I arrived in Mytvathy," he said as I ate, "I asked for an audience with the king. I immediately knew something was suspicious about the way he answered my questions. He said you were away to the dwarves' city to do something with magic."

"What?" I asked, almost choking on my food.

"Yes, I knew it was a lie. Dwarves don't have magic. It didn't make sense, and the way he hesitated as he spoke said it all. So I said I'd wait for your return and stayed at the castle. I knew he'd have to offer hospitality. I am a prince, after all.

"But while I stayed at the castle, I asked the servants about your whereabouts. Sylvia eventually told me everything."

I smiled at the name of the old servant. I loved her like a mother.

"She told me that the king had sent you to the vampiric city as a prisoner to be delivered to the queen. That no one had seen you since then, and that she was very worried for her *veneficus dei.* That you had been gone for too long, and you were their sole hope.

"I left the castle on the same day and traveled here to find you. It wasn't easy, but I was able to make connections with a few in the palace. I waited for the queen to be out of town before rescuing you. It was safer that way."

I was speechless. The king had lied about my whereabouts. It wasn't such a big surprise, but it still hurt. After all, he had betrayed me the day he sent me to deliver the prisoner to Ichoryllia, but this was yet another example that added to the wound. I would have to thank Sylvia when I returned to the castle. If I ever returned to the castle, that is, since I could no longer trust the king.

"Thank you for rescuing me," I finally said.

Akael kneeled and grabbed my hand. He landed a soft kiss on top that brought heat to my cheeks.

"It's the least I could do for you, My Lady. You are my soul mate. I would have gone to the end of the world to find you."

His words came back to mind. "But how are we supposed to fight back darkness with only you and me? We don't even know what it is?" I asked.

"I didn't come alone. I have an army awaiting me at Mumbur's port. Another fleet has anchored south, the soldiers hidden in the forest."

I thought for a moment. I knew the king had fallen to darkness. I had felt the dark magic seep into the castle, into him. Or maybe it referred to Samantha and the Miłonblooders.

Scorchfire's words came to my mind. "*Zarvok Drel'kaan*. That's what the dragon said before he died. That, and *Ruun to ruun. Mor'thuun noth*."

"The dragon spoke to you?" asked Akael, still kneeling.

"Yes, I heard him talk to me before he died. It may be nothing but . . ."

"Dragons don't talk just to anyone," the prince cut in.

"Do you know what it means?" I asked, hoping that his kingdom's knowledge of dragons was better than mine.

He shook his head, grinning. "No, but we'll just need to find a dragon who knows."

"Are you suggesting we go see a dragon?" I asked in disbelief. I had seen what those creatures could do to a city. "What if they attack us?"

Akael stood up and shrugged. "We'll just need to find one who'll agree to talk to you."

"And where do you suggest we find a dragon?" I asked.

He pointed to the window. "There are dragons everywhere outside, my dear."

He was right. "Yes, we should do that tomorrow," I replied.

I had eaten well and felt full. The fatigue of the day overtook me.

"Do you have any more questions?" he asked me. "Because I'd like to find out everything about you!"

This made me happy and set my heart racing. "Yes, what do you want to know?" I asked.

"Tell me about yourself. What you like, who you are."

I thought for a moment before answering, trying to choose what I wanted to say. Being a grand wizard had been such an important part of my life that it felt natural to start there, "I started working for the king when I was only five years old, chosen for my magical powers."

"So young?" Akael interrupted.

I was surprised by his reaction, as anyone living in Mytvathyr would know about it, but then again, he had been raised in the Sun Kingdom, so it would make sense that he didn't know about it.

"The king selects the most magically talented elves at this age. It's the same for all the elves in the kingdom," I replied.

"Wouldn't you have preferred to stay with your family?" asked the prince.

His question took me aback. "I never even considered that as a possibility. It's tradition," I replied.

"And if you were queen, would you keep this tradition?" he asked, his eyes locked with mine.

I turned the question over in my mind. I had never questioned the way things were. I remembered the families who refused to send their children to the castle, risking their lives by hiding them. It may have been tradition, but I realized it broke many hearts. What harm would there be in keeping the children with their families?

"I'm not sure I would," I replied.

Akael smiled. "Good, we'll do as you wish when you're queen by my side."

Hearing him say it out loud seemed unthinkable. "I still find it hard to believe that I'll be queen one day."

He reached for my hand, his touch warm, and squeezed it. "You are my soul mate. Of course, I would like you to be my wife one day, but I am patient. I want us to have time to get to know each other, and I will respect your choice."

"Thank you for not putting pressure on me," I said. I was eager to discover Akael's personality. I liked what I saw so far. I felt like I could tell him anything.

I yawned despite myself, the fatigue too strong.

Akael smiled. "We've had a long day. You should get some rest," he said, pointing to the only bed in the room.

"What about you?" I asked, suddenly blushing as I realized the implications of my question.

His lips curled up in a smile. "As much as I would love to sleep close to my gorgeous soul mate, I will sleep on the floor. We'll have the rest of our lives to get to know each other. We will leave before dawn."

I nodded. I used the small shower attached to the room. There was no hot water, but I considered myself lucky to have running water. With my mana already being half-restored, I heated the water directly through the pipe. It felt amazing to finally wash away all the dirt that had accumulated during my time at the castle and on my journey. It felt like it had been forever since I could enjoy water on my skin.

Once I got out, I took the time to clean my studded leather robe. I laid the clothes out on a chair to dry and kept only my undergarments on. I ran my fingers through my curly hair to try to untangle it a little. Looking in the bathroom mirror, I thought to myself that I looked a little more presentable than earlier, maybe even pretty.

Akael's gaze was heavy with desire when he saw me come out in my undergarments. I smiled, happy with the effect I had on the prince. He made me feel like the most gorgeous elf in the kingdom. I couldn't wait to get to know him better.

"Good night, Akael," I said as I went to bed.

The elf was already preparing to sleep on the hardwood beside the bed. "Good night, My Lady."

I closed my eyes, grateful to sleep away from the castle, my head full of what was to come.

Chapter 17 (Nathan)

The Trap

The sun was warm on my skin. My muscles felt bruised even without moving, but I knew my wounds had begun to heal. All around me, footsteps echoed. Were there more assassins sent to finish me off? I opened my eyes and sat up suddenly, preparing to fight. Two children screamed and ran to take refuge behind a woman's skirt. I relaxed when I saw there were no immediate threats. My head hurt, and my body disagreed with my sudden movement. I looked around. I was in a courtyard, under the roof of an outdoor tent-like canopy. I wondered how I had gotten here. I was sure I had fallen asleep on the street.

A woman approached. She wore a large apron over her long, loose blue skirt. Her red hair was tied back, and she smiled warmly. Small hands clung to the back of her skirt, and I could see the fearful but curious looks on the faces of the two children who had screamed.

"Come on, children, I told you not to bother His Majesty," she scolded gently. Her blue eyes fell back on me. "How are you feeling?"

"Better," I said hoarsely. That wasn't entirely true, but my healing powers would soon have me completely recovered.

"Go get Maria," she told the kids. The two ran off toward the large house at the end of the courtyard. "My name is Sherry. We found you on the street a little further down at dawn. We dragged you under the outdoor shelter before the first guard patrols came by."

At the back of the courtyard, I saw the doors leading to the alley where I had collapsed after the fight.

"Thank you," I said. If guards had seen me, I would be dead or a prisoner. I wasn't sure which one was better.

The two children returned, accompanied by a vampiress. She was dressed similarly to Sherry. A dozen children, both vampires and humans, accompanied her. They ran around, curious and cautious, whispering to each other.

"Ah, you're awake," she said with a smile. "Welcome to our orphanage."

"An orphanage?" I asked. I didn't remember there being such an establishment in Ichoryllia during my reign. It must have been very recent.

As if reading my mind, she went on and explained, "It was Lord Legeais's house before he was murdered. He had no children or heir. We were overjoyed when we discovered he had left his fortune to us, his servants. We decided to turn the mansion into an orphanage."

Sherry continued, "The parents of the children you see here were either killed, sent to human breeding facilities, or sent to Krelgraz."

"To Krelgraz!" I exclaimed. "The island is overpopulated with wild, armed orcs. They will be slaughtered."

Some of the kids covered their faces as I said the words, and I regretted telling them. Sherry's disapproving look said it all.

"That's not what I meant," I began, trying to correct myself in front of the children.

Maria said, "It's fine. Though these children don't know when or if they'll see their parents again, they are safe here. They have friendship and a family."

Sherry added, her voice full of hatred, "The queen destroyed the lives of so many."

A little girl with hair as blond as wheat approached, interrupting the conversation. "Is it true you have a wolf inside you?"

A young boy, no more than six years old, joined her, his dark hair tousled. "I heard you had magic."

"Children, please!" said Sherry, but I waved her off. These kids had lost so much and witnessed too much sadness for their young age. Yet, they kept their innocence, and it was beautiful to see.

"It's fine, really," I said to the woman, who looked happy with my answer. "I do have a wolf inside me and magic. All vampires have magic."

Another boy came closer, his fangs showing slightly as he spoke. "But I've heard that yours is different."

I nodded. "That is true. My magic is different."

By this time, all the children had gathered around me to listen, the fear seemingly gone or too curious to stay away.

"Can we see your wolf?" asked the vampire boy.

"Can I pet him?" asked the little girl.

I laughed. "Let's keep the demonstration for another day, shall we?"

They were disappointed but nodded. I got up and spoke to the women. "Why did you help me? I don't have much to offer."

Maria shook her head. "On the contrary, you have everything to offer, Your Majesty. We only ask that you remove the queen from the throne."

She spoke about it as if it were just a simple task. I had the hope of so many people on my shoulders, and I wouldn't let them down. "I can see why you despise the queen. Yes, I intend to reclaim my throne," I said, the words resonating through my soul.

The children cheered in joy, and the two women smiled warmly. Maria wiped a tear from her cheek. She mouthed *thank you* without making a sound.

"There's something I need to do first, though," I added. "I'm looking for someone, and I think she's at the slave shop."

They nodded, and Sherry gestured toward the house. "You should eat before you leave. It will allow you to heal more and gather strength. It would be an honor to have you with us for breakfast."

There was a large area covered with flat beige slabs next to the house. A long, worn-out-looking table sat atop the stones, surrounded by a group of chairs of varying sizes. Two men brought plates, while a woman brought food to the table.

"We eat breakfast every morning outside when it's warm and sunny," said a little girl.

I figured I ought to keep them company for a little longer. I needed the food anyway. "Well then, let's go eat breakfast," I answered.

The children ran to the table, excited to have a guest. "It is a gift to the children to have you with us," said Sherry as we walked.

"I'm the one who should be thanking you. Not only did you save me, but you're also offering me food. When I reclaim my throne, I promise to help you."

I would have a lot of people to help when I was a king again. So much had been destroyed, and so many had been hurt in a remarkably short period. I only despised Samantha more for what she had done.

I sat in one of the regular-sized chairs. The little girl from earlier sat down next to me in a small chair that could have been made for a doll. "I'm Molly," she said casually, replacing her blond strands as she spoke. "This is my chair. The others don't fit in it, so it's reserved just for me. It makes me feel special," she concluded.

"Well, even without the chair, you are special," I answered.

Molly beamed while the other kids sat down. Some boys fought over one chair until Sherry separated them and assigned their seats. Sherry sat beside me, and Maria sat at the other end of the table so that they could keep an eye on everyone. The other servants, or should I call them masters of the mansion, sat around the table. Baskets of fresh fruit, breads and brioches, as well as poached eggs adorned the table. Joyful conversations sprang all around as everyone ate. We were hidden from the main road by the manor and set back far enough that we couldn't be seen from the alleyway. I let myself be swayed away, forgetting my worries for the time of a meal.

"What's it like to live in a castle?" asked Molly as we ate.

The first thing that came to mind was the obligations it entailed. My every move being scrutinized by everyone. Checking over my shoulder to make sure no one backstabbed me. But these were kids. They probably dreamt of dresses and balls, horses, sword fights, and shiny armor. I decided not to dampen their dreams.

"You learn to wield a sword at an early age. You read books and learn how to think like a king. Your duty is to serve your kingdom and care for the people. It's an important role." The children's eyes sparkled as I spoke.

"Do you dance with princesses?" asked Molly.

I thought back to the ball I had held to announce that I would marry Samantha. Back then, I was so happy. I had met my half-brother there, though I didn't know who he was at the time. I still remember how gorgeous Samantha looked in her dark red satin dress. How naïve I had been at the time.

"Yes, I do. We hold balls and dance with music."

The little girl smiled. "Aww, I wish I could dance at a ball!" she exclaimed.

"How about we create our own ball?" proposed Sherry.

"Really?" Molly asked, excited. The boys didn't seem very convinced that it was a good idea. I held back my laughter, thinking that in a few years, they would probably enjoy dancing more than they could imagine. The first dance with a girl as a teenager was always so nerve-racking, but it awakened the desire for first loves.

"We'll get new dresses for the girls and nice shirts for the boys. It will be fun! And we can create our own orchestra!" added Sherry.

Cheers erupted. "Will you come?" asked Molly.

I nodded. "If you invite me."

Royal trumpets resonated through the street. Everyone stopped talking. An announcement was about to be made. We didn't need to get to the street to hear it, and I felt grateful to stay here, hidden from soldiers' sight.

A voice was heard, strong: "Hear ye, hear ye, citizens! Be it known that this afternoon, a caravan carrying human slaves will be sent as a sacrifice. There will be a public execution by fire. The queen hopes that this will bring peace with the dragons. Anyone who attempts to intervene will be considered a traitor and killed on the spot."

Emerald.

My thoughts immediately turned to her. She had been stuck in that slave shop for too long.

"She's going to kill more innocent people," Sherry hissed.

"I need to save them," I said with conviction.

"It may be a trap," suggested Maria.

"It *is* a trap. But what if she's amongst them? I can't let her be killed," I retorted. I was mad at Samantha for doing this.

"You could go to the slave shop first and see if she's there?" suggested Sherry.

I shook my head. "There's not enough time. If I don't get to the caravan fast enough, it will be too late. Intercepting it is my only option, but I can't do it alone. I expect it to be heavily guarded."

"What will you do?" asked Sherry.

I didn't have to think about it. I already knew. "I can't risk my mate getting sacrificed to dragons. I need to return to the Thieves' Guild and get their help to intercept the carriage."

Everyone had a serious look on their faces.

"Do you know how to get there?" asked Maria.

I shook my head. "I'm not sure. I've been there only once. I know how to get into the sewers, but it's a maze of tunnels."

Maria replied, "Then let me show you the way. This way you won't lose hours wandering around."

I looked at her, surprised that she knew where it was. She had a knowing smile. "Don't forget we were once servants. The Thieves' Guild helps the less fortunate, and we help them in return. There's more to it than what you might have heard when you ruled. Come."

We were back at the Thieves' Guild in no time. I first headed to the room where I had left Raphael and Simeon. The werewolf was in much better shape than the last time I had seen him. He was sitting up in bed, laughing and talking with Raphael. His eyes widened when he saw me.

"Nathan," he said warmly.

“You seem to be doing much better,” I replied.

He nodded. “I got up this morning and was able to walk around the room. It’s not over yet. The silver badly wounded my wolf, but he’s well on his way to recovery.”

“That’s good to hear,” I replied. I was genuinely happy that my friend was doing better. He had been in such a sorry state the last time I saw him.

“In the meantime, we’re enjoying the guild’s hospitality,” Raphael added. “I went out for a walk around town to see what condition it’s in. The Alpha asked us to gather intel on the vampire city.”

“You what?” I asked.

“I was careful. No one saw me,” replied Raphael hastily.

“I told you to wait for me,” Simeon reminded his lover.

“It’s just until you’re better,” he insisted.

“You’re lucky to be alive,” I told him.

“You’re a human in a vampire city. They can smell your human scent,” Simeon said.

The human rolled his eyes, but I agreed with what the werewolf was saying. “Don’t forget that you’re prey, livestock, in the eyes of vampires. Simeon is right. You shouldn’t go alone.”

The werewolf smiled at my support.

“You’re on his side, too?” Raphael asked, exasperated. “I’m just trying to be helpful.”

“You’re helpful here with him,” I replied, the werewolf nodding in agreement.

Simeon looked at the human with eyes full of tenderness. Raphael opened his mouth as if to speak, then changed his mind. The human finally replied, "You're right. This is where I belong."

A moment of silence passed before Simeon said, "Surely you didn't come just to see how I was doing."

I nodded. "Although I wish that were the case, you're right. I came because it has been announced that a caravan filled with human slaves will be sent as a sacrifice to the dragons by the queen."

The two looked at me in shock. They immediately understood that Emerald could be part of that caravan.

"You're going to get yourself killed," the werewolf replied grimly. "The queen knows you'll want to get your mate back."

I balled my hands into fists. "I know. But I'd rather die trying to save her than live without her. Could you imagine if she were in the caravan and got killed, and I had done nothing to save her?" Even just saying the words hurt. I couldn't live with myself if it were to happen.

The men nodded seriously. "I wish I could help, but I'm not healed enough to fight. The best I can do is send back information to my pack through a guild's messenger to inform them of the situation here, and for them to prepare for war," said Simeon.

I smiled. "I understand. I came here to ask for the guild's help, but I wanted to see you first."

At that moment, Vince entered the room. "Ah, Maria told me you were at the guild. I figured you'd be here."

"Perfect timing," I replied.

"I imagine you're here for the sacrifice caravan?" he asked, crossing his arms. I nodded. "I thought so. I immediately thought of you when I heard the news. Follow me."

"Take care of yourself," Raphael said as I followed the guild master out of the room.

We went through a series of corridors until we arrived in a large room. Piles of riches were in one corner, stacked behind cabinets. Although nothing was guarding them, I guessed that they belonged to the guild master and that no one would ever dare touch them.

There were several desks and tables lined up against one wall, piles of documents, and a few books on shelves. In the center of the room stood a large table. A handful of men and vampires were waiting there, some sitting, others standing for lack of chairs. A map of the city was on the table.

"Nathan, these are my best fighters. Skilled assassins or former guards, they are the best we have to rescue the slaves."

I looked at the men. They were all willing to risk their lives to rescue the innocent. A strange feeling came over me. I was now allied with those I had once hunted, and I was about to fight the guards who had once been loyal to me.

Vince pointed to the map. He had traced the caravan's presumed route in ink. It would likely start at the castle, follow the merchant road, and head for the northern entrance to the city, since a dragon carcass still blocked the southern entrance. Vince pointed to a square with his index finger. "At the third turn, when the caravan reaches the large square, that's where we'll attack. We'll have plenty of room to blend into the crowd and stop the caravan. The square is large enough for us to fight, and for the crowd to disperse and prevent other innocent people from getting hurt."

It was the last turn before the city exit. It was our best chance. "It's a good plan," I agreed.

"We don't have any time to waste. It's afternoon and the caravan is probably about to leave," Vince added. "Let's move."

We split into groups of four to avoid attracting attention and made our way through the dark alleys. Some had walls so narrow that no sunlight could penetrate them, while others had makeshift walkways of planks on the roofs, plunging the ground into eternal shadow. Finally, we arrived at the square. Dozens of people had gathered to watch the caravan pass by. Despite the large crowd, the atmosphere was rather quiet. Everyone knew that the caravan was going to its death, to be burned, for dragons who didn't give a damn. It was just another cruel act by the queen.

I recognized Sherry and Maria in the crowd, accompanied by other workers from the orphanage. I was glad that the children weren't with them. A few glances met mine. They knew who I was but didn't let on. The tension rose within me. My breathing quickened. "*Mate,*" whispered my wolf in my head, as anxious as I was. The anticipation drove me crazy. Everything came down to this moment.

Vince was in the crowd on the other side of the road that the caravan would take. The other members of the guild also mingled with the gathering. Pigeons landed on the road, cooing. They pecked at grains, unaware of the events that were about to unfold.

After what seemed like an eternity, I saw the front of the caravan approaching. At the head were four guards leading the way. A series of five closed carriages followed, each pulled by two horses and driven by two guards. I knew these carriages well. They could comfortably seat four people, or six if you crammed them in. Bringing up the rear were four more guards on horseback. Clearly, the queen had anticipated that there might be some unrest, but I had expected that. I didn't care if this was a trap. I would free my beloved Emerald.

The pigeons flew away as the caravan approached. As discussed, we waited for the first carriage to pass us. Once it was, I nodded to Vince, who nodded back. He put his fingers in his mouth and whistled loudly.

That was the signal.

I jumped toward the horses pulling the first carriage. They whinnied and stopped abruptly, one of them rearing up on its hind legs. "Hey! What are you doing?" shouted one of the guards, while the other tried to stand up, holding on to the edge of the carriage to steady himself. I drew my sword and cut the reins holding the horse closest to me. It bolted through the crowd, people jumping to avoid it.

At the same time, the others had also launched their attack, bringing the caravan to a halt. The guards left their positions to fight back while the crowd scattered, shouting. I had time to glimpse the orphanage workers joining the attack, as well as other citizens who had decided they could not let the queen sacrifice innocent people.

"How can you live with the atrocity you are committing?" I shouted at the guard leading the first carriage as he jumped to the ground to confront me with his sword, but it was a lost cause. These were not the men who once served me, probably Miłonblooders who were loyal to her.

Steel clanged against steel, the sound ringing in my ears as I drove my opponent back. The guard's fangs bared in frustration, but I was faster, stronger. My blade cut low, forcing the Miłonblooder to stumble.

One down.

But before I could finish the kill, movement flickered in my peripheral vision. The four guards who were opening the caravan closed in, their eyes burning with fury. They had probably received orders to kill me above all else.

"Get him!" one hissed, rushing forward.

My wolf growled. He wasn't about to be impressed by four vampires. I met them head-on. Steel whirled around me—slashes from every side, coordinated, precise. I ducked one swing, caught another on my blade, but a third slipped past, biting into my shoulder. I hissed as pain seared through me. Enraged, I twisted, grabbed the attacker by the throat, and sank my fangs deep.

Hot blood filled my mouth, rich and flavorful, fueling the beast inside. Strength surged in my limbs as the guard thrashed, then went limp. I flung the body aside, baring my teeth at the others. I could already feel my vampiric powers strengthened by the blood, healing the sword wound.

"Who's next?" I snarled.

Two threw themselves at me. My sword struck one down with a brutal blow that split his armor and flesh. The other pressed me with his attacks, but I drove my foot into his chest, sending him rolling to the ground.

Around me, the square was chaos. My allies clashed with the remaining guards. Vince was at the top of his game, and the others were doing well, too. We had the upper hand, and the number of guards was decreasing. The air was thick with the stench of blood. Behind the line of armored bodies, the carriages stood. We could hear the slaves screaming inside and banging on the doors.

A sharp whistle pierced the air, and a shower of arrows rained down.

I barely raised my blade in time to knock one aside. Another struck my arm, cutting through flesh. I snarled in pain. All around, men and women fell, pierced mid-swing, cries echoing against the walls.

"Keep fighting!" Vince shouted, his voice ragged.

My wolf raged, and my pulse hammered. My focus narrowed, every strike fueled by fury. I tore through the last guard, ripping the blade from his hands and driving his own sword through the vampire's chest.

And then, silence.

The guards lay scattered, broken on the stones. For a heartbeat, relief flickered.

And just as quickly, chaos returned. Arrows engulfed in flames rained down onto the carriages. They would burn them here on the square.

Flames leaped instantly, smoke curling upward as screams rose within. The smell of burning wood hit me like a fist. I would be damned if I let Emerald burn.

I sprinted forward, ignoring the agony in my arm. I drove my blade into the gap between the door and the frame, infused it with my vampiric magic, and ripped out the lock of the first carriage.

The door burst wide, and six people tumbled out, coughing, their faces pale masks of panic.

"Run!" I barked, dragging a victim to his feet and shoving him clear.

Another carriage groaned under the flames. I leaped to it, ripping out the lock again in the same way I had done for the first.

More slaves spilled into the smoke-choked air, crying out as they stumbled away. Still no sign of Emerald.

One after another, I ripped them open, my arms screaming from the strain, my lungs burning, but I didn't stop. I couldn't. Not while there were lives inside. Not when she could be inside.

Behind me, arrows still hissed down, but I shut it all out. All that mattered was the next lock, the next door, the next soul dragged from the fire.

The arrows finally stopped as I reached the last carriage and freed the slaves. Some women, and even a child, came out. But not Emerald. I stood, numbed by this realization. A mix of gratefulness and defeat filled me. My hope to find her had been crushed, but this meant she was still out there. In the slave store, waiting for me to rescue her.

A hand landed on my shoulder. Vince stood beside me with a look of pride on his face. "Assassins have taken out the archers. We did it! We saved them all."

All around us, people were applauding. The guards were dead or had fled. In the middle of the crowd, a man and a woman were desperately pushing their way toward the carriages. They burst into tears and rushed to take their child in their arms. People made their way to thank us. They were shouting, "King Nathan," recognizing my true title, but I couldn't feel any of it. My heart was dull. I needed the woman I loved.

"I'm going to the slave store," I said resolutely. I had lost way too much time already. I didn't care if the guards saw me. Let them come, I'd cut them down. I was getting my mate back, and that was it. My wolf growled in agreement.

Vince nodded seriously and signaled for a group of assassins. "We're coming with you.

Chapter 18 (Caleb)

Forever Yours

I woke up in the morning feeling better than I had in days. My muscles still ached, but only as if bruised. I felt the draconic magic within me, alive and vibrant, and a sense of acceptance. This change was so sudden that I knew it wasn't solely due to the herbalist's potions. He himself had said it: the draconic magic had a will of its own. I could only assume that the dragon's blood had decided to let me live and team up with me—whatever that meant. I could feel its magic flowing through me. I would need to learn to communicate and control it.

I sat down, wanting to get up and walk. I wanted to see Summer, to hold her in my arms, and make up for the last few days. What was I saying? Make up for all the time since I met her.

She cared for me while I was sick. It was time for me to play my role as her mate. I couldn't wait to show her who I really was.

Darryl entered the tent, his long black hair loose. He smiled when he spotted me. "I can see you're doing better."

"Much better, thank you," I answered.

"Will you still hold to your promise?" he asked.

I was only half-surprised he asked. "If there's one thing about me, it's that I always stay true to my word. I said I'd help you, and I will."

The man grinned widely, his teeth showing. "Amazing. Summer will surely drop by soon. I saw her eating in the main tent this morning."

My heart leaped at the thought of seeing her. I couldn't wait to drown myself in her big chocolate eyes.

"How about you try and stand to see how well you are in the meantime?" the man asked.

The human had seen me on the brink of death just the day before. It was normal for him to think I would need more time to rest. I obliged and got out of bed. The man rushed to me when he saw me go with a decisive pace, afraid I would fall to the ground. He stared at me, amazed when he saw me standing firmly.

I winked. "Looks like I'm all better now."

Darryl was speechless, his mouth agape. "Wow," he finally breathed. "I wouldn't have imagined this, especially after seeing the state you were in yesterday. I guess the dragon blood decided you were worthy."

I chuckled. "I guess."

"Even the king didn't recover that quickly when I healed him," he said in awe.

I wondered if it meant that I was now stronger than Nathan, but it didn't matter. I had new goals now. "You look like you care a great deal about him," I commented.

Darryl nodded. "He is a kind man. He deeply cares about his people and will help anyone who's in need. We travelled together, and I saw firsthand how much of a leader he is."

I pondered on his words. This was a side of Nathan that I didn't know about. Living in the slums, I've always only cared about the jobs, my next paycheck, and a better life. I wondered what I'd do if our paths crossed again.

A gasp came from the tent's entrance. Summer stood there, her black hair braided, and her flowery scent enthralled me. I could feel her happiness through our bond. "You're better!" she exclaimed enthusiastically.

"As you can see, little wolf," I teased her. She ran across the room, Darryl stepping back to let her pass. She ran straight into my arms, forcing me to take a step back to catch her momentum. Her embrace was full of love, and I hugged her back just as tightly.

"I missed you," I whispered, not breaking the hug.

"I've been afraid of losing you," she answered.

Her voice betrayed how difficult the last few days had been, but also the sweetness of the promise that everything would be better. Of course, we still had to save Darryl's sister, then get far away from here and find a place to hide from Aeris.

"Anne is waiting to meet with you," said Darryl. I let go of Summer and turned around.

"Anne?"

He nodded. "The captain. She's the one who found you in the orc camp and brought you here."

I remembered her. She was covered in mud and the blood of her opponents. She appeared to me as a warrior. Darryl continued, "I reported to her and said that you had agreed to help us. She asked to see you as soon as you'd be better."

"Right, then let's not make her wait," I replied. I was eager to see the woman who had saved us.

I followed Darryl and Summer out of the tent. As I did so, I assessed my condition. I had no trouble keeping up with them. My senses were heightened, my vampire instincts drawing my attention to the sounds of hearts beating around me. On the other hand, I felt a wild energy slumbering within me, waiting for the right moment to act. I was eager to see the dragon within in action. It was as if I had never been sick.

I stared around at the encampment. The war camp stretched across the ravaged plain. Smoke from small fires rose into the sky. I could see dozens of soldiers: humans, elves, and vampires. They carried the scent of old battles and the weight of too many deaths. Yet beneath their exhaustion, there was unity. The tents, mismatched in make and hue, stood shoulder to shoulder. Human tents, coarse and patched, bore the marks of hasty repairs. Elven shelters glimmered faintly where runes of preservation fought to keep the weather at bay. The vampires' tents were darker, yet even these had human stitching and elven knots along the seams—a symbol of shared labor, of hands that no longer cared who they belonged to as long as they held steady.

Paths of trampled earth wound between the rows, leading to the heart of the encampment where a single banner rose above the rest. Beneath it, a long table stood under a stretched canopy, serving as the main tent for meals and important speeches. Several people were still eating as we passed.

"People help each other," explained Darryl as we walked. "Sometimes, people forget that we are humans, elves, and vampires. It's not uncommon to see a vampire passing a cup of warmed blood to a weary human, and then realizing humans don't drink blood. Sometimes elves tell stories in their ancient language and then translate them so that others can understand. Everyone helps, regardless of their rank. Tending to the fires, sharpening the weapons, or helping someone in need. That's what keeps us strong."

"I've been lucky and been shown around the encampment while you were recovering," said Summer. "A vampire warrior, Stephan, showed me where everything was and then led me to my tent. He was very kind."

I was glad Summer had been well treated by everyone while I was stuck in bed.

We arrived at another large tent—the captain's. It was slightly apart from the others; close enough to stay among the men, but far enough to command a sense of authority. Its canvas was reinforced with thicker hides to better protect from rain and ash. The fabric had faint stains of dried mud and a few repaired tears stitched with uneven thread.

At the entrance, I noticed a human and a vampire standing guard. Darryl explained, "The captain pairs them, using their differences as strengths. The elves for the sight and magic, humans for their endurance and ingenuity, and vampires for their speed and strength. Of course, everyone's skill differs, but the captain said that mixing us provided the best results. This also helps to improve acceptance of others and our differences. We are family here."

I liked that way of thinking. I had once been happy with the queen's new rules against humans, considering them prey, but having a werewolf mate had opened my eyes. I would never consider Summer as prey. She was the most precious person in my life.

I realized that people were more than the race they were born into. You could feel it in the atmosphere in this camp. People had a purpose. They were proud. I had never seen that in my years as an assassin, and I felt that Summer belonged among them. If she belonged, then so did I.

"Well said," a female called from inside the tent. A woman appeared at the entrance of the tent, her long, blond hair tied back, her brown eyes kind yet assertive. "My name is Anne."

I remembered Darryl had mentioned her earlier.

"Captain," said Darryl respectfully to the woman.

The woman looked at us kindly. "It's good to see you in better shape than yesterday."

"Thank you for your hospitality," said Summer.

I nodded in agreement. "Thank you for saving us."

"Come," said Anne.

We followed the captain inside the tent. The air smelled of oil, steel, and smoke. A small bed rested against one side of the tent, neatly made but clearly seldom used. Beside it sat a chest of personal items. Armor rested on a stand near the bed, polished and ready for use. A few weapons lay within arm's reach: a sword, a dagger, and even a crossbow.

At the center of the tent, a rough wooden table dominated the space, scattered with maps, each weighed down with daggers and stones. Ink stains and wax drips marked the long nights spent planning. We followed the captain to the table, and she pointed to one of the maps. It was a close-up view of Krelgraz with the main encampments drawn. I wasn't used to seeing it like that and almost didn't recognize it at first.

"This is the island. Here, in the center, are the remains of the ancient human city. That's where most of the orcs are. We are here, on the southeast of the island, a little further from the main orc encampments. That's how we manage to avoid being attacked on a daily basis."

I could see a cross over an orc encampment and wondered if it was the one where we were being held. Other small camps had been marked with an X in this area. All the orc camps in the section around our encampment had been destroyed, making it a safe zone.

She continued, "Here, north of our position, is where we believe they keep their prisoners."

Darryl clenched his fists at this, and I remembered that his sister was being held captive by the orcs.

"And finally, here, somewhere to the west, is where we believe the gateway to the Underworld is. It is our ultimate goal."

"Are you kidding me?" I asked. Everyone stared at me in shock. No one would dare talk to the captain that way, but I didn't care. "This is at the heart of the orc's civilization. We will get killed if we go there."

The captain had a stern look on her face, her brown eyes cold as she spoke. "This is our main target, and the reason we have been sent here."

"I thought you were here to rescue Darryl's sister," I retorted.

Sure, it would be a lot of people just to rescue one person, but this island was so full of orcs that it would take that amount of an army to do it.

Prisoners
Gate to the Underworld?

Anne shook her head. "That is only a small task that we agreed to do in addition to our main objective."

"That's *my* main objective," Darryl clarified. "Rescuing her and the other prisoners."

"We're all for rescuing people," added the captain, "but the sole reason the queen sent us here is to close the gate to the Underworld."

"You mean the sole reason she sent you here is to be butchered and to avoid the people rebelling against her," I corrected.

Anne had daggers for eyes. I didn't care about what she thought. I wasn't the kind of person to refrain from saying it out loud. "You can hate me all you want, it's still the truth, and you know it," I added. Anyone experienced would have understood.

The woman pinched her nose and sighed. "That may be true, but it doesn't mean that I won't do everything in my power to prevent people from being killed. I think I can count on you not to talk about this outside my tent. It would crush the people's morale, and anyway, you should be grateful that we saved you rather than criticizing our mission."

Summer had a look on her face that screamed for me to shut up. The last thing I wanted was for my mate to be mad at me. "I am grateful to have been saved. You are right. I will try to help and see how I can protect everyone."

The captain nodded, satisfied with my answer. I glanced at Summer, who also looked pleased. My attention returned to Anne, who explained the strategy. We were to start by rescuing the prisoners to the north. To get there, we would take a detour east along the beach to avoid a secondary orc camp on the island. This would allow us to approach the prisoners without too much unwanted attention. We would need to keep men here to defend the encampment, but it was our best chance. Anne didn't want Darry to come. As an herbalist and healer, he usually stayed out of the battle and treated the wounded when they returned to camp, but he insisted on coming with us. If his sister were there, he wanted to be among those who saved her. The captain allowed it for this once.

It was agreed that we'd leave at dusk, to take advantage of the night. We'd need to try to sleep in the meantime.

Darryl took a deep breath as we exited the captain's tent. "I can't believe I'm going to see my sister again after more than twenty years. I have so much to tell her, so many questions. I had given up hope of ever seeing her again."

A thought crossed my mind that the orcs were ruthless with their prisoners and would not hesitate to poison or torture them, as they had done to Summer and me. I didn't dare tell him she might be dead already. It was best to keep his hopes alive.

"How will you recognize her after all that time?" asked Summer.

"An elf named Caeda came to me when I was in Mytvathyr. She told me about my sister Paisley. She and Caeda were friends, so she knew about me. Paisley was ten years old when my father left with her, but she has never forgotten about me. She's been trying to be reunited with me for years. I was too young to remember it, but I've been told my sister has long black hair and icy blue eyes. I know I'll recognize her when I see her."

This man had waited so long for this. I hoped he could find his sister.

"Let's regroup at dusk," Darryl added hastily. "I have things to prepare. Do you need directions to your tent?" he asked Summer. My heart leaped. I had been waiting to be alone with her for what seemed like an eternity.

"I'm fine. I know where it is," she answered.

The man took his leave, and I followed Summer, eager for the moment we would reach her—*our*—tent.

The sun was high in the sky. We'd have a few hours of rest before we left. Vampires didn't need much rest, but I knew werewolves needed it more than us, so I'd make sure Summer got the sleep she needed. We walked silently through the camp. Even though we had only been here for a day, Summer turned left and right as if she knew the place like the back of her hand. We passed rows of tents, greeting people as we went. Each row looked the same, but Summer described them all differently to me. The row where the head cook was, the one where the armor repairer was, the one where Stephan's tent was . . .

I jumped at the vampire's name. "You know where Stephan's tent is?"

It was silly, but I couldn't help myself. Summer chuckled softly. "I haven't been *inside* his tent. He just mentioned it in case I needed anything."

"I swear, if he tries anything, I'll rip off every finger that touches you."

She rolled her eyes. "Stop worrying, okay? You're my mate. You're the onc I love."

"It's not you I don't trust. You're so beautiful, I find it hard to believe that others could resist you."

She shook her head. "I understand. My wolf is just as possessive of you, in case you've forgotten."

I laughed and shook my head. "We can thank the fated mate bond for that, can we?"

She smiled. "Anyway, no one could ever replace you, my shadow assassin."

The corners of my lips turned up. It was the first time she had called me that, and I loved it. "Wait and see what your assassin will do to you when we're alone."

Her eyes flashed a knowing look. "I can't wait to find out," she said, pointing to the tent in front of us.

I followed her inside, excited to have her all to myself. The tent was small, but we had a cot and privacy, and that's all that mattered.

"Here we are," said Summer as she turned to me.

"You don't know how long I've been waiting to be alone with you."

"Oh, believe me, I know." The way she said it told me she'd been yearning for it as much as I had. I ran my hand through her hair. She came closer and embraced me. Lost in her love, I realized how much I had missed her. This moment was our first as mates, as a couple. I was going to make it everything it should be. A growl escaped from my chest as I grabbed her hips and held her tightly. I took a deep breath, inhaling her intoxicating scent. The warmth of her body radiated into mine, contrasting with the natural coolness of my own. Unable to resist the temptation any longer, I devoured her lips. Summer moaned into our kiss, making me melt even more. She was the only goddess I would worship.

The only one I needed.

My heart pounded, and I was dying to take her, but I wanted to make up for how our relationship had started. I lay her down on the bed and whispered, "Let me show you how much I love you."

Her smile held the promise of sin, soft as silk and sharp as sorcery. She consumed me with her eyes, and her wolf purred softly. "Mmm, with pleasure, my shadow assassin."

She wrapped her legs around me, driving me crazy. I desired her as I had never desired anyone before. This was more than just lust. Tonight was the promise that I would always care for her. I softly kissed her skin, moving down to her chest, removing her clothes as I went. Her skin bore scars from the battles she fought, but she was perfect in every way. I wrapped her in a gentle wave of magical caresses and licked the thin skin of her hip bone, giving her goose bumps. Touched by both my magic and my hands, she let out a long, sensual moan, filling me even more with yearning. She rocked her hips as I made my way back up to her breasts. The way she whimpered when I licked her erect nipples was to die for.

"Let's see how many times I can make you scream my name, and then maybe you'll beg for me to take you," I whispered, my breath hot on her skin.

I positioned myself between her legs. Her scent drove me wild, and I groaned with hunger. I eagerly devoured her soft pussy. Her moans were soft and restrained, knowing we were in a tent, but I didn't care if they heard us. Let them know to whom she belonged. Let them know how much I loved her.

I kept licking, her breath quickening. Summer's hand grabbed my hair and pulled gently as she arched her hips, panting. She was perfect, and seeing her unravel under my tongue made me her slave. I wanted nothing more than to take her, but I would wait for the right moment. I grabbed her hips, holding her in place as I revelled in her core.

Her body shook, and she screamed, "God, yes!"

I stopped licking and smirked. "It's not a god who's doing this to you, little wolf. Say it, say my name."

"Caleb," she said as she rode her wave of ecstasy, her hips rocking, yearning for my touch.

"Good girl," I purred.

I needed to remove my clothes; my cock was so ready for her, but I wanted her to ask for it. I pushed into her with my finger, finding that spot that had her squirming. I switched between her clit and her moist center. Her cries enthralled me, and she came again, her body arching against me. Fuck she was perfect.

"Come on, say it. I want to hear you beg for it," I teased.

"Fine, please take me! I beg you."

A deep rumble resonated through my chest. I bit my lower lip as I removed my clothes in haste, almost tearing them off. I slid right into her, unable to hold back a gasp.

"So wet and hot for me," I hissed.

She tightened around my cock, and I had to take a moment to avoid coming as it was too much. Through our fated mates' bond, I could feel her pleasure and love. She grabbed my shoulders, bringing me closer, deeper into her.

I grunted. My instincts kicked in, and hunger gnawed at me. I wanted more.

"You have no idea how much I want your blood. Let me mark you again. How it should have been the first time."

She pushed my head toward her neck in response, too focused on the sensations to answer me. Her hands explored my buttocks, back, and chest, as if it were never enough, discovering every inch of my body. Her nails dug into my skin as I sank my fangs into her neck. She moaned once more, her body arching with pleasure.

I groaned when the first drop touched my tongue.

Her blood was even more divine than usual, delighting the monster within me. I rocked her as I drank, enjoying every thrust, every sip, in this forbidden paradise. All I wanted was her, forever, only her. She came again, trembling, and I removed my fangs from her neck. She was as drunk from pleasure as I was. A growl escaped from her chest. Her eyes flickered, and her usual brown eyes turned golden.

"Gorgeous," I breathed in awe.

"I can't hold her back," she said, panting.

"Then don't," I replied.

Summer's canines lengthened as her wolf took control. She thrust her hips faster and stronger, taking charge despite being under me. I loved the feeling of losing control, gladly letting my mate take the lead. In a fell swoop, she dug her teeth into my neck. The pain was immediately replaced by ecstasy, and I came, unable to resist anymore. Being bitten was foreign, but I loved it. Her wolf wanted to make me mine, just as I had claimed her.

A wave of love and pride washed over me that her wolf cared about me as much as I did. I stayed there, giving her the time she needed to mark me. With her wolf in control, all sensations were primal and intense. I understood everything she felt for me. I admired the beauty of her soul for a split second before Summer regained control. Her eyes returned to their normal color as she withdrew her fangs from my skin, licking the wound, which gave me chills.

"Now you're mine," she said, satisfied.

I smiled. "Yes, little wolf. I'll be forever yours."

I lay down beside her, letting myself drift off to sleep in that perfect moment.

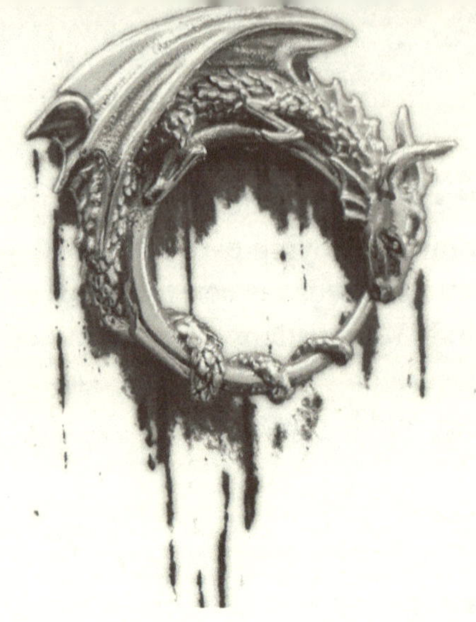

Chapter 19 (Erendriel)

The Mountain's Soul

Sleeping in the dwarves' royal bedroom was always a weird experience. The room was luxurious, but everything was too small. The bed, although made for two, was just big enough for me to lie diagonally across it. I slept well, nonetheless, as the mattress was of regal quality. Still, I was eager to return to my own castle, but I had a lot to do before I could go home. I hadn't planned on doing anything other than looking at the Oracle's writings, but the town was in such poor condition that I couldn't ignore it.

First, I had to deal with this troll business. I couldn't allow such a creature to attack Mumbur. It could cause significant damage. I slipped on some light armor taken from the stocks of my army stationed here under my robe and hood. My sword was well hidden. If there really was a troll, I had to be prepared.

Before I left to deal with the troll, I had to make sure the city was in good hands. My generals looked more confident when I reached the war strategy room. Dale's golden hair was tied back with a leather strap, his yellowish skin glowing in the morning sun. Lane still had his purple braids from the day before. As for Rahul, the dark elf had short, black hair and red eyes that shone.

"Gentlemen, have you prepared the report I asked for?"

The three nodded, and Dale got the report out and started reading. The detailed report on the city's condition was devastating. Houses had been destroyed, as had the walls and fortifications. Even the only school and the healer's home had been damaged.

"Pretty much everything that isn't commercial or for the mines has been affected," Dale added.

"I didn't realize we caused so much damage," I said pensively. It didn't make sense. Something was wrong.

Dale cleared his throat. "Me neither."

Sure, we had killed people, but we had pretty much made our way up to the castle. That's when I realized what it could be. It had to be. It was dirty, and it irritated me to no end.

"Lane. Go and investigate the town. I suspect some citizens might be sabotaging the city."

The generals looked shocked. "You think so?" they asked.

I nodded. "There's no doubt in my mind that we haven't destroyed as much of the town. Anyone found sabotaging should be killed on the spot."

"Understood," answered Lane.

"What about the reconstruction?" asked Dale.

I sighed. We lacked people. Most of the men were serving in the dwarf army, so they had been killed during the war. The remaining workers were mainly involved in shops and bakeries, providing food for the people or profits in gold. It was good to have the economy running, but we needed people to have houses to return to at the end of the day. The houses were made of rocks and metals that needed to be mined, and I had almost no miners left in the city.

"Send a letter to Mytvathyr. We need elven workers to help with the reconstruction and the mining. It will take a long time to restore Mumbur to an acceptable condition, but I have gold in my treasury that I can spare. We will start by rebuilding the healer's house and the school."

The elf nodded, taking notes as I spoke.

"As for the army," I continued, "new soldiers need to be trained. That will take years, and nothing can be done to get the soldiers ready faster. Rahul, see that all the boys over fourteen begin military training in the barracks."

The dark elf nodded. It would give them a few years of training before they were adults. It wasn't ideal. For now, I would need to keep all the elven soldiers who were here and use them sparingly. With the werewolves and humans having declared war on us, I couldn't leave the elven city defenseless.

"Anything else, your Majesty?" asked Dale.

That was already a lot. "I will take care of the troll. It will reduce the number of soldiers needed in the northeast. This way, the men will be able to rest."

"Thank you, Your Majesty," said Lane.

I motioned to leave when I remembered something else. "Another thing," I added.

The generals all waited for me to talk. "The Sun Kingdom's ships are still anchored at the port. Go ask about their business and send them off."

Dale nodded. "It will be done."

Satisfied, I turned around and left the room. I ventured into the storage room. There, I found what I was looking for: a vial of acid. As I knew I'd face a troll, I needed one of these to kill it permanently. Without it, the creature would regenerate from its wounds. At last, I had everything I needed for my journey.

The moment I stepped outside, the cool morning air greeted me. I followed the path down toward the northeastern entrance of the city, my boots crunching over broken stones. I studied the destruction. The roofs had collapsed, and the remnants of homes sagged under their own weight. I was glad I had asked for elven workers to come and help. The people deserved better than this. A few citizens picked through the ruins in silence, searching for anything salvageable. Others stood in small clusters, whispering to one another. I hoped we found who was responsible for this, as we hadn't attacked on this side of the town. I was now certain about my theory that someone was sabotaging the city and that filled me with rage.

As I continued north, the devastation gradually thinned. The rubble became scattered debris, then merely dust along the roadside. The air shifted, now less acrid, touched instead with the scent of baked bread drifting from somewhere ahead. By the time I reached the long row of shops, the transformation was striking.

This street looked as if it had been spared entirely. No shattered windows, no scorch marks, no crumbling stone. Instead, colorful awnings fluttered in the breeze, merchants swept doorsteps, and early customers exchanged coins. It was a wild contrast to the other side of the city, like stepping from night into day. The sharpness of that contrast settled heavily in my chest as I kept walking.

A dozen soldiers were posted at the northeast gate and asleep when I arrived—so much for protecting the city. I couldn't blame them, though. I knew that they were overworked. I would solve this mess, allowing the men to get proper rest and the city to be protected again. It was frightening how fragile Mumbur was at the moment. The slightest problem could cause the city to collapse and spark a revolt.

I pushed open the heavy iron doors myself, hoping to let the guards sleep, but the loud creaking of the metal woke them with a start. They scrambled to their feet, grabbing their weapon in haste.

"It's only me," I said, as if being the king were a trivial matter.

"Your Majesty!" one of them exclaimed nervously. The wood elf had baggy eyes, and her hair was a mess under her captain's hat. It was clear that the current situation was taking its toll on her.

"I'll take care of your troll. You'll be able to rest once it's done."

They paused for a moment, realizing what I had just said, lowering their bows and swords. A grateful smile spread across their faces. The captain answered, "Thank you, Your Majesty. Stay safe."

"Do you know where it is?" I asked, realizing that my generals had been stingy with details.

A second guard stepped forward. His long, dark blue hair was braided and contrasted with his light green skin. He was young, barely old enough to work as a soldier, I realized. "The citizens said it came at dusk from the tunnels to the north, in Carlpar Mountain. They said that was the creature's lair."

My eyes traced the path ahead, noting the chain of mountains to the north. I wondered if they were linked to the mines. "Thanks, I'll head there," I answered as I ventured forward.

I walked through the tall grass and bushes, making my way toward the mountain. There were a few trees. Not enough to form a dense forest, but enough to shelter animals and birds. Two squirrels ran in front of me, one chasing the other. They suddenly realized I was there and turned back, hurrying to find refuge in the trees. A few blackbirds sang in the distance. I enjoyed the fullness of nature, reminding me of the elven forest, except for the absence of the magical creatures. Everything was so quiet and normal that I began to think maybe there wasn't a troll. I had been walking for over an hour or more and hadn't seen any signs of one being nearby. Maybe the citizens had played a joke on the guards. But as I approached the mountain, I sensed that it was sick, if a mountain could be ill. I felt a humming, faint and wrong, through my boots as I got near.

The closer I got, the stronger the humming became, and the birds became silent. I finally reached the base of Carlpar Mountain. It was majestic, with its peak lost in the clouds. I would have believed there were no trolls if it weren't for the smell that came out of the tunnel. The stench was foul, and I swallowed my bile. I didn't expect the creature to let me come all the way to its lair. Trolls were known to be territorial. They usually charged travelers for passage through their lands. It was rather unusual to walk freely across their territory.

I entered the dark tunnel. I ignored the smell as best I could, my heart pounding. The humming from earlier was so strong it reverberated through my chest. I tensed, preparing for an attack from any angle. Fortunately, my night vision allowed me to see well in the dark. At least I wouldn't be ambushed.

The tunnel was tall enough for me to walk up, but it narrowed and twisted the further I went. I could feel the omnipresence of magic all around me. Stalactites hung like jagged teeth from the ceiling, forcing me to duck now and then as the path dipped and curved.

To my surprise, the further I got, the hotter it became. At first, it was only a subtle warmth, so subtle that I hadn't noticed. Caverns were supposed to be cool, even cold—the kind of places where one's breath fogged in the air and the walls wept condensation. Soon the heat grew heavy and oppressive, sliding over me like a thick, invisible cloak. Sweat beaded on my temples and trickled down my spine, and the air itself felt dense enough to drink.

A faint, rhythmic tremor pulsed through the floor every few moments, like the mountain's heartbeat.

I noticed that as it got hotter, the stones became strange. They were melted smooth in places like wax. I didn't know of any fire that could do that to stones. The only thing I could think of was the dragons. Would their return have an impact here, deep underground? I was almost certain that the humming I felt was an old magic rising from the deep. An old magic or sentient being awakened from its long sleep by the return of the dragons.

I started to fear not encountering the troll, but something else, something more dangerous. A tremor rolled beneath my feet. Dust fell like snow. Then came the sound—deep and ragged, a slow exhale through a throat of gravel. I froze, holding my breath. The troll stepped into the pathway.

It was enormous, at least three times my height. Its back was hunched, its skin fissured like blackened stone. Through the cracks ran veins of molten red, pulsing faintly with each breath. Its eyes were dull and clouded, as if filmed with ash. I regretted coming alone, but I tried to gather my courage. I was a king, and I had powerful magic at my disposal. I could do this.

I drew my sword but remained where I was, my knuckles turning white as I gripped the hilt tightly. I tried to speak to it first. "Why are you attacking the city?"

The creature didn't charge, studying me closely. It tried to answer, but only a loud grunt came out. I was stunned, as trolls were usually intelligent enough to talk. Maybe not in full structured sentences, but a few words. That's usually how they got people to pay to get permission to walk on their territory.

The troll stumbled forward, dragging its knuckles through the dust, the sound a slow scrape of rock on rock. It reached out a massive, trembling hand toward the molten channel that ran beside the tunnel. When its claws brushed the edge, a sigh escaped its chest, low and almost mournful. The humming intensified, and I felt it. A flicker of something beneath the cracked skin and terrifying look. Longing.

Then the heat surged. The molten stream brightened, and the troll's body spasmed. It roared, staggering back, its chest splitting open in a burst of steam and light. The troll collapsed to its knees, clawing at the rock, as if trying to bury itself in the mountain.

I understood then.

Whatever magic had awakened had taken hold of the troll's lair. It had fled to the city, but the guards attacked it and drove it back. The troll returned to its lair, but the magic that lingered in the mountains was seeping into its flesh, burning it from within.

The troll's head grazed the ceiling as it charged at me, screaming. The ceiling split open, and rocks rained down from the cracks. I met the creature's charge, my blade meeting his fist. His hand was so big that it could have crushed my skull with one hit. I pushed with all my strength, groaning under the effort. We were evenly matched, or at least, neither of us could gain the upper hand. He withdrew his hand, and I almost fell forward. The troll was strong, but it was slow. I took the opportunity to strike him on the arm, infusing my sword with the black fire magic I possessed. The blade split open its arm, and the creature shrieked, making the walls shake. I didn't wait and thrust my sword into its chest. Fiery blood spurted from the wounds. At that moment, he was writhing in agony. I didn't wait and kept hitting, knowing that I couldn't let it recover.

When the troll collapsed, the mountain shook with him. I knew it wasn't totally over. Trolls regenerated over time. I took a vial of acid I had brought with me. I poured it over the creature, smelling the acrid scent of its skin liquefying and disintegrating, preventing it from regenerating and finishing it off for good. The fire flowing through its veins flickered once, then went out.

I stood above it, breathless, the heat around me reduced somewhat, making everything a little more bearable. For a long time, I couldn't move. The humming was still there, and I wondered if I should go after its source. The troll had been slain, and that was what mattered for the city, but I couldn't get myself to return just yet. I wanted to know what was generating that humming. I *needed* to know. I could feel a vein pulsing beneath the skin in my neck, and my heart raced at the thought of finding the source of it. Something that could make a whole mountain hum was probably way too strong for me to kill. However, I felt that, as king, I should assess whether it posed a threat to the city.

I continued deeper into the tunnel. I felt the mountain reverberate into my whole body.

Then came the whisper.

Soft. Wordless. But alive.

It brushed through my mind like the breath of something vast and sleeping just beyond the veil of thought.

I moved deeper until I came upon a great chamber, the hollow heart of the mountain. At its center was a bright light of pure energy spiraling upward into the mountain's darkness. Around it floated shards of stone, suspended as though caught in invisible currents. I narrowed my eyes as the light was too bright, but I could discern the shape of something at the center of it all. Half-formed, half-shadow. It was a shape, but I wasn't sure what it was. The body looked like it had been carved from crystal, and its veins glowed faintly gold. Its face, if it had one, was smooth and featureless, yet somehow it *looked at me*.

The hum grew stronger, words forming at the edge of understanding.

"The fire above rekindles the fire below. The dragons breathe, and so do I."

I jerked back as it spoke. It knew I was there. The being tilted its head. I felt its thoughts invade my mind, forcing their way in, violating my most closely guarded secrets. I knelt despite myself, overwhelmed by the sheer magnitude of this being's presence. This was no creature, no elemental beast. This was the mountain's soul, awakened and bound to the same magic that had revived the dragons.

I thought of the troll for one instant, of how the magic had seeped into it. How distraught it had been. I understood then that I was next.

"All who dwell in my bones will obey," the being murmured. "Stone, flesh, and flame alike. They are mine."

My mind reeled. Dwarves. Miners. Any creature living within the mountain would be enslaved to it. I had to see if the mountain connected to the mines of Mumbur.

"You will spread," I rasped. "You will consume them all."

"Not if they serve," came the reply. "Not if *you* do."

That voice pressed against my will, vast and patient. I felt its heartbeat falter, the air shivering with heat.

Instinct, not courage, saved me. I sent a jet of black flames at the being. It was pointless—too weak to hurt it—but it broke the mind control. That was all the opening I needed.

I fled.

I didn't remember the climb back, only the trembling in my limbs, the sense of something ancient watching me retreat. I pushed as fast as I could, afraid it would catch up to me. I tried to convince myself that it couldn't reach me if I were far enough, even though the whole mountain was alive with its force. I ran with all I had until I reached the outside.

There, I finally let myself fall into the grass, catching my breath. I still heard the humming from where I was, but I felt that it couldn't reach me. Or at least I let myself believe that it couldn't. It had said, after all, that everything living within the mountain was its. Maybe its magic didn't reach outside. One thing dawned on me then: I had to hurry and check that the mines didn't connect with the mountain. I knew that the mines were in a chain of mountains, but I didn't know the region enough to be sure it didn't connect all the way to here. The city would be at risk if that were the case. That, and the writings of the Oracle in the ruins.

A second wave of energy washed over me as I realized this. I ran toward the city, my legs carrying me as if I were flying. I was lucky that the road sloped down toward the town, making the journey even easier. The sun was high in the sky but beginning to descend.

It was still afternoon when I reached the city walls. The same guards who had been there in the morning were there. One was carving a piece of wood, while others talked together. I slowed down to catch my breath, trying to look somewhat regal. A big smile appeared on the guards' faces when I arrived. The captain asked, "Did you find it?"

I put on a solemn expression, trying to hide the fear of what I had discovered. "The troll has been killed."

Another guard replied, "With all that blood on him, if the troll hadn't been dead, I don't think the king would have been able to return."

The captain looked embarrassed. I laughed at the comment. "It's nothing. It could have been the blood of another creature," I suggested.

The first guard smiled. "Is everything back to normal?" asked another.

He was clearly interested in whether they would be able to rest. I thought for a moment about the mountain's soul. First and foremost, I had to check if the mines were connected to it, but regardless of whether they were, the security at the wall here could be lessened. The guards would get some rest. I preferred not to alert them about a sentient being quite yet—I need more answers first.

"Yes, I'll talk to the generals."

The men and women looked at each other, a feeling of joy silently shared between them. "We owe you a huge debt of gratitude, Your Majesty," concluded the captain.

I nodded and continued on my way into the city. People stared at me as I passed by. I must have been a sight to behold. Still, I held my head high and made my way to the castle. There, Dale was waiting just beyond the front gates.

"Your Majesty," he said.

"I have slain the troll. Lessen the security at the wall and let the men rest, but before you do that, send a group to seal the tunnel in the mountain. No one must descend into it."

His green eyes stared at me.

"There are still mages in Mumbur, aren't there?" I asked. I had left Ambrel and Ritori here in the city. Mages were valuable resources and could turn the tide of war. Their magic could prove very useful.

"Yes," answered my general.

"Ask him to seal the tunnel from a safe distance. I am certain he has a spell that will do the trick."

"It will be done," said Dale before bowing his head.

Chapter 20 (Nathan)

The Slave Store

I walked toward the merchant street, carried by adrenaline. It was bathed in the red of the sinking sun, amplifying the color of the blood that stained my face. I wanted to see my mate. I *needed* to see her. I had wasted too much time.

Wanted posters still plastered the town, but they were useless. With the recent events of the dragons' attack on the city, more and more people wanted the queen gone. Vince and the assassins followed me, and people moved out of our way. We must have been an impressive sight. Some even bowed in respect.

"For Alastor!" shouted some Miłonblooders before throwing themselves at us, but we easily slit their throats. They were just fervent followers of the queen, caught up in their madness.

With the caravan causing a distraction, there were no guards on the streets.

We quickly arrived in front of the slave shop, its red door mocking me. The establishment was not luxurious and had no sign. It was just a dirty gray building whose bricks had been eroded by time. A little further away stood the destroyed windmill, its broken blades still hanging.

I turned the handle and found the door locked. My wolf growled. I didn't hesitate for a second to ram my shoulder into the door. Two blows were enough to break it down and give us access.

Inside stood two vampires. One was older, and the other a young adult. The older one wore a cheap jacket, probably to make himself look more important. He was surely the owner of the establishment. The younger one was probably an apprentice. I was disgusted! Who in their right mind would want to learn the trade of selling slaves?

They shouted at us for trespassing. "My store! How dare you?" yelled the older vampire.

Four armed vampires came out from the shadows, holding swords. Their shoulders were broad, and they had the look of vampires who had killed before. Whether mercenaries or guards, I didn't care. I'd kill anyone standing between Emerald and me. Vince and the assassins took three, while I took the fourth one.

The vampire was strong, lunging his sword at me, but I was faster and stronger. I deflected every blow and buried my sword in his chest several times. I was so close to finding the woman I loved. This was only delaying me further. I attacked the vampire relentlessly, even as he was too weak to strike back. I only stopped when his body fell lifeless on the floor. Vince and the others had already slain the other armed vampires and stood there, watching me, keeping an eye on the store owner and his apprentice to prevent them from fleeing.

I turned my attention to the store owner. My fangs were out, pressing against my lips as I barked, "The slaves! Take us to them."

I was two inches from the vampire's face, my sword against his throat. He backed up until he touched the wall behind him. I was so close to him that the smell of old cigars on his breath made me choke. But nothing would distract me from my goal, and the growl that escaped from my chest left no room for negotiation. I could hear the old vampire's heart beating faster and smell his sweat. Fear. Good. He was right to be afraid, because I could barely contain myself from tearing him to pieces.

"Stuart, lead the way," he said to the young one.

"Yes, Malicio," the apprentice replied, his eyes wide and his lip trembling. The young one fumbled to find the right key to open the door to the back of the shop.

The place smelled of mold and dirt. The walls were yellowed, and the floors were covered with dust.

"How can you live with yourself?" I asked as I pushed them forward, forcing them to move on and hurry up.

"I, um . . . It's a good business," stammered Malicio.

I refrained from telling him what I thought, more interested in finding Emerald than anything else.

We went down a winding staircase that barely hung to the walls and finally arrived at the first cells. They were so small that humans couldn't lie down completely. They slept on the floor without blankets, wearing only rags. With the smell of urine wafting through the floor, it was clear that they didn't have access to toilets either. Prisoners were treated better in the castle dungeon. I was outraged. No one deserved to live in these conditions. I couldn't leave them like this.

"Open the cell!" I ordered.

Stuart looked to his master for confirmation. "Do as he says," replied the old vampire, frightened.

The heavy metal door creaked as the young vampire opened it. The man in the cell took a step back, frightened at the sight of me. I tried to soften my tone despite the rage coursing through me. "You have nothing to fear. You are free. Run for your life."

The man blinked, surprised. Then he whispered before running away, "Thank you."

The other slaves had turned to us, watching what was happening. They stared gawking.

I ordered, "Open all the cells. You are all free!"

"But my trade . . ." Malicio protested.

"Is a dirty and disgusting business," I finished his sentence, gritting my teeth.

Malicio suddenly lunged, his sharp nails scratching me. His fangs were out, and he jumped on me, trying to drink my blood.

The fool.

"You think you can take on the king?" I sneered.

The old vampire was no challenge. I slashed his arm, blood gushing out. He was no more of a threat than a pestering fly. I could have broken him like a dry twig, but figured it was more fun to keep him alive. I sent a wave of energy so powerful that it threw him into the cell the man had been occupying just moments before. He was stunned by the impact, plaster falling from the old, decaying wall.

"Close the door," I ordered Stuart.

He nodded immediately, his hand trembling. "I'll open it for you later," he stammered to his master.

"Now open all the cells," I continued firmly over the cheers of the victims. I rejoiced at the thought that the old vampire would have to watch all his *business* regain their freedom without being able to do anything about it.

The young vampire did as I asked and opened the cells one by one. I followed him down the corridor, watching each woman and man walk away. They nodded as they passed me, grateful smiles on their faces. Some hurled obscenities at Malicio, a small reward for the humans who had been locked up here for weeks, before fleeing.

But none of them were Emerald.

"Where are the other cells?" I asked angrily when we reached the end, and Emerald was still nowhere to be found.

"This is the last one," answered the terrified young vampire.

"A young woman. Brown hair. Green eyes. My vassal," the word rolled off my tongue now that I knew she was my mate, but the young vampire could only know her by that title. "Where is she?"

I felt his pulse quickening. He knew who she was. "Not here," he replied.

"Where?" I asked again, moving even closer to him. "I won't hesitate to tear you to pieces if you don't have the answer."

I had already experienced hunger, that irrepressible urge to drink someone's blood that could drive us mad, but never anything as strong as my desire to destroy this vampire here and now.

He swallowed, his Adam's apple rolling in his throat. "Sold," he replied.

I punched the wall right next to his head, making the young vampire close his eyes and cry out. It took all my energy to keep my wolf from taking control in that moment. I needed more information.

"Who bought her?" I demanded.

"I can't . . ." His eyes met mine, and he changed his mind. "The king. The elven king sent his emissaries to buy her. He paid three times the price. He took her a few nights ago," he whispered. "Please spare me." Ugly tears streamed down his face, repulsive.

I owed him no mercy. He had chosen to work here, to turn a blind eye to what was happening. I sank my fangs into his neck, holding him in place with my hands, my sharp nails digging into his flesh. I tore off a chunk of muscle, Stuart letting out a shrill scream. Blood flowed greedily, but my intention was not to drink, but rather to kill. I tore flesh from his arms with my fangs, and anywhere else I could. I could have finished him off quickly with magic, but I wanted to see him suffer as he had made defenseless humans suffer. Eventually, he could no longer support his weight and collapsed to the ground. Using my magical powers, I plunged my hand into his chest, groping for his heart. When I found it, I closed my fingers around it, crushing it. It was dense and firm, warm, and liquid flowed between my fingers as I squeezed. I withdrew my hand when I felt it stop moving, satisfied. I wiped my hand on the vampire's clothes.

"What do we do now?" Vince asked.

"We're going to visit Mytvathyr. But first," I replied, glancing around us, "let's burn this place to the ground so it can never be used again."

Vince and the assassins smiled knowingly at these words. Malicio, who was still locked in the first cell, shouted, "No! You can't do that!"

"What do we do with him?" one of the assassins asked me.

I chuckled. "Let him burn with his business."

Malicio screamed. "No, no. I don't want to die."

I ignored him as I walked past his cell. He wasn't worth an answer. The assassins and Vince grabbed torches and set fire to the back of the store. The place, being old and poorly maintained, quickly caught fire, and smoke blossomed around us.

Back at the front of the store, I screamed as loudly as I could. I pushed with all my might, tears of rage streaming down my cheeks, and knocked over the wooden counter, which tore itself from the floor. I destroyed the shelves and threw all the furniture against the walls in a fit of despair. I knew it wouldn't bring Emerald back, but I needed to do it.

When I was done, I stood in the store, panting. Erendriel. That bastard. He'd better not have hurt her, or I would destroy him.

A scent caught my nose. Faint, almost nonexistent. The smell of peaches. I followed the scent and found a lock of hair lost in dust behind one of the counters I had knocked over. Emerald. She must have fought with her captors and lost it at that moment. A tear rolled down my cheek.

"Wait for me, I'm coming," I whispered.

This lock of hair, as insignificant as it seems, gave me enough strength not to lose myself. I tucked it in my pocket.

I exited the store, followed by Vince and the assassins. The store burned intensely, a testament to the rage that burned within me. Vince put his hand on my shoulder. "I'm sorry, friend. I can't follow you to the elven lands. I have tasks with the guild here."

"I understand," I answered. "Take care of my friends. I will go alone."

"We'll be here when this is done, and you're ready to reclaim your throne," added Vince as a reminder of his loyalty.

I parted with them as they made their way to the Thieves' Guild. I walked with conviction toward the northern entrance of the city. Memories of when I had fled the town with Emerald and Xavier came to mind. If only I had known then what disaster my life would become—would I have changed the decisions I made?

Nothing would stop me.

Not even the gods.

Chapter 21 (Elaine)

Dragon Queen

The soft voice of Akael awakened me. "Elaine, wake up."

A soft hand brushed my cheek, and I smiled, opening my eyes. His red curls framed his face like fire, his eyes filled with forbidden promises.

"Is it time already?" I asked.

The blinds were open. Outside, it was raining, but I could see the clouds fading on the horizon and the faint glow of the rising sun. My heart raced when I realized we'd soon be far from the vampiric city. I couldn't wait to leave.

Too much had happened in this town. Too much grief and evil. I wasn't sure where home was anymore, or where I'd go after all this, but something deep inside told me I'd be home as long as I was with Akael.

"It is. Are you ready to face your destiny?" he teased.

"When you say it like that, it makes me want to run away," I confessed.

"As long as you let me run with you," he answered.

"I don't believe in faith or in the gods, but I want to understand what Scorchfire told me, and be away from this damned town."

"That's the spirit," he said with a laugh.

I picked up my bag of belongings. Downstairs, the innkeeper was asleep in a chair, his head resting on the counter, so we slipped out quietly. The streets were deserted as most people were still asleep. The rain was light and cold, making my hair damp.

We walked through the empty streets, heading north of the city. There hadn't been any bells announcing my disappearance from the castle yet. It seemed that Jason had kept his word, but it was only a matter of hours before that changed. We needed to be out before that.

We passed an old church. The stones were blackened by time, and moss grew between them. The white doors, once magnificent, were worn and beige, yet the building retained a majestic appearance. We crossed a vast lawn with empty benches. It looked as if they were waiting for people to wake up and come visit them. It seemed that this area had been spared from the dragon attacks. Without their constant presence in the sky, one could have forgotten about them. As we approached the northern gates of the city, there was no more damage.

My breath caught in my throat as I saw the vampire guards standing at the entrance. One was tall with bronze skin, his arms and face covered in tattoos. The second was slightly shorter, with long hair and multiple rings in his ears. Akael squeezed my hand reassuringly.

He whispered, “Remember, they’re not looking for you. You have nothing to worry about.”

“Right, I had almost forgotten,” I answered, thankful for the reminder.

The guards watched us as we approached. My heart pounded in my chest, and I kept telling myself to calm down. Vampires could feel it, and I didn’t want to raise suspicion or hunger. We were two elves leaving the city of vampires. Nothing more.

“Have a good day, gentlemen,” Akael said kindly as we passed through the gate.

“Have a good day, travelers,” the guards replied simply.

I didn’t answer, too busy keeping a straight face and holding my breath. I expected them to call us back and start chasing us at any moment, but we kept walking. Nothing. When we were far enough away from the city that the gates looked small, and we finally entered the edge of the forest, I relaxed. I let out a big sigh, and the elf beside me smiled, squeezing my hand affectionately in his.

“I told you so,” he said teasingly.

I blushed slightly. “I know, but I couldn’t help worrying.”

“You worry too much,” he said, his beautiful green eyes captivating me.

“And you don’t worry enough,” I replied.

"I have faith in the Oracle. No matter what would have happened, we would have come out unscathed. You are the *veneficus dei*. There is nothing you cannot accomplish."

"That term again. You say it as if I were a goddess."

He gave me a sexy smile. "You are my goddess as much as you want to be, My Lady. I am dying to worship you."

His words took my breath away, and heat rose within me. I couldn't deny the effect the prince had on me. I stepped over a fallen tree trunk in the path, then brought my thoughts back to the discussion. "But I almost died in the vampire castle. I'm not immortal."

He nodded. "Yes, and so the prophecy brought me to you. I will protect you and make sure we fulfill our destiny."

He spoke with such conviction, but I doubted myself. All I wanted was to return to find normalcy, to be happy, but everything clung to me like vines that tightened their grip the harder I tried to break free. My life had been one disaster after another since I became Grand Wizard, and I was tired, but the prince's words resonated with me, and I understood their gravity. "Akael, I . . ." I couldn't find the words to continue my sentence. I knew he was right, whether I wanted to believe it or not.

He was so sure of himself that I decided to let myself be carried away by his madness. Maybe the gods *did* exist, and we were going to succeed. After everything that had happened to me, maybe this was finally the moment when things would work out.

"You're right," I whispered.

He smiled and brought his face closer. The next moment, his lips were on mine, like a gentle breeze that carried my heart away. He wrapped his arms around me, holding me close, and I couldn't help but melt into his embrace. All my worries vanished.

I rested my forehead against his when we broke the kiss, breathless. We stayed like that, looking at each other, words unnecessary to express what we both knew.

"Come, My Lady. Let's keep going," he finally said, pulling away.

I regretted that the moment had passed and promised myself that next time, I would tell him how I felt.

"Where?" I asked.

"To find a dragon who'll talk to you," he replied.

"Right, dragons," I repeated. It wasn't that I had forgotten, but it seemed unreal.

We had been walking for hours. The sun was high in the sky and dragons flew above us. It almost seemed as if they were following us, but that was probably just my imagination.

I was so concentrated on the dragons, looking at the sky while I walked, that I didn't notice that we weren't alone anymore.

"Your money or your life." The voice was hoarse and threatening. Before us stood a group of five men armed with knives and clad in leather armor. They thought they had the advantage, but they were only humans. Nothing we couldn't handle.

I no longer had my sword, as the vampires had taken it, but I still had the artifact. I took the knife in my hand, the handle fitting perfectly. Akael stood defensively in front of me, drawing his sword. "I won't let you touch her," he said.

The man lunged at Akael, attacking him, but Akael parried the blow. The others threw themselves at us in turn. The sound of steel against steel resonated from Akael's fight. I recited the words, happy to be able to rely on my spells again. The magic came easily, and I threw ice daggers at my attacker. The ice pierced his armor, striking vital organs. He fell dead on the floor before he could even reach me. I turned and sank my knife's blade into the flesh of another. The man collapsed immediately. I didn't understand how he fell so fast, as it was only one stab. I expected him to give more resistance. That's when I realized that the artifact contained unknown magic. I turned to find my next attacker, but realized that they were all on the ground.

I wasn't sure you could even call it a fight, as it had been so easy. The men had underestimated their enemies. Akael was barely out of breath when he turned to me.

"Are you okay?" he asked.

I grinned. "I've survived worse than this."

He pointed to the knife in my hand. "Not bad. I've never seen one like it."

"I found it in the crystal mines when I looked for something else. I'm not sure what it does, but it clearly has magical powers."

The elf nodded. "Nothing happens by chance. The artifact found you."

I chuckled and put the knife away. The forest was full of life as we walked. It wasn't as beautiful as the forest close to home, but it still filled me with joy. We came to a large clearing where white flowers grew between blades of grass.

The earth groaned. A shadow fell over me, and the forest fell silent. I held my breath in awe as a large dragon descended from the sky, its wings—*her* wings, I realized without knowing how I knew—beating with thunderous force. Akael shielded me with his body, drawing his sword. "Stay back," he said as we watched the magnificent beast.

The dragon landed in the clearing with a rush of wind that whipped my hair back, her talons carving deep furrows into the soil. The ground trembled beneath her weight as the creature folded her wings with a slow, regal sweep. Her wings were completely white, but they became purple from the middle to the tips. I realized I had seen her when I was trapped in the castle. Or maybe she had been the one watching me. I wasn't really sure which way it went anymore.

The dragon's large green eyes studied me, full of intelligence. Akael relaxed his stance when he saw that she wasn't attacking.

She was massive, ancient, and majestic.

I froze under her stare, feeling a force as old as the elven race itself. For a moment, I remembered when Scorchfire had spoken to me. *Zarvok Drel'kaan*, he had said. Just as I thought about that, I felt it again—the splitting headache and the foreign presence inside me, a mental link.

"You are right," the dragon said in my mind. *"Zarvok Drel'kaan. You are god's mage."*

I stood there, shocked. First, the servants, then Akael, the Oracle, and now the dragons were saying it. It was useless to fight it. I might as well accept my fate. I decided to try to talk to her.

"Scorchfire had said: Ruun to ruun. Mor'thuun noth. What does it mean?"

I swore I could discern a smile on the dragon's face.

"Vok'rath vekhul, zar'kaan vekul. Ruun to ruun. Mor'thuun noth," she replied. *"One flame awakens, all flame returns. Blood to blood. Death is not the end."*

I pondered on her words. One flame awakens, all flame returns. The dragon continued, curiosity and amusement filling her tone, *"It's the first time you speak to a dragon, and that's the first thing you ask?"*

"With everything happening, I figured it was kind of important," I retorted.

Smoke seeped out of her nostrils as she made a sound that resembled a laugh, or at least that's the feeling I got from her. Akael raised his hand and took a step forward.

"Can you talk to it?" he murmured.

I nodded. He gawked before smiling. "I knew it! I knew we'd find a dragon who'd talk to you."

He took another step forward. The dragon moved her tail, causing the elf to hesitate.

I motioned to Akael. "Maybe it would be better to get to know her before getting closer."

"It's a *her*?" the elf asked.

I realized that I hadn't asked the dragon before saying it, but I had felt it so strongly that I had no doubt. I looked at her for confirmation, and she nodded. *"You can call me Safira."*

"Her name is Safira," I said to Akael, who couldn't hear her.

"I have so much to tell you. Climb on my back. The skies await their queen," she told me.

I stared at the dragon, unsure, then at Akael. "She wants me to mount her."

He answered, "Then go. It is your destiny, My Lady."

"But how will I hold onto her? I have nothing. It's not like a horse with a saddle. At least if I had a rope or something to tie me to her so that I don't fall."

The elf was pensive for a moment. "How about we make a leather rope?"

"Out of what? Do you know a spell that can make it happen?"

He smirked. "I know just where to get leather. Wait for me."

I looked at Safira with an apologetic stare.

"Sorry for the delay, I just need something to hold on to you," I explained.

She blinked. *"You don't need to explain yourself. I understand. I wouldn't want you to fall from the sky. Let's see what he comes up with."*

It was only a few minutes before Akael came back running, carrying five leather armors.

"Where did you . . ." I was about to ask when I realized those were the armor of the thugs we had slain.

He smiled at my astonishment. "If we cut it like this," he said as he slashed the armor carefully with his sword, "we can create leather strips."

I realized what he meant, took out my dagger, and helped. Soon, we had a bunch of leather strips of different sizes. "Let's weave them together. It will be stronger," I suggested.

Akael nodded, and we did. When we were done, I had a long leather rope. Safira looked like she approved. I swallowed, realizing that the time had come to climb onto her back. I was so nervous, not only because of her size, but also because of the idea of flying. I had never flown before. The idea had always seemed appealing, but now that I had the opportunity to do it, my stomach knotted at the thought. I approached Safira slowly. She seemed even more imposing, yet her gaze was peaceful and reassuring.

I wasn't quite sure how to climb onto her. Seeing this, she moved her tail and leg to form an improvised staircase to help me reach her back. Her scales were cold and hard to the touch. It was formidable armor. I hauled myself over her back, and she gave me a push with her snout to help me reach the top

"Hold on to your end of the rope," said Akael from the ground. He carefully walked to the other side of Safira, then threw me the rope. I almost fell off her back trying to reach for it. "Careful!" said my prince, but I caught myself.

I was glad that the leather rope was long enough to make it all the way around Safira's neck. She had several horns sticking out at the base of her shoulders. I positioned myself between two large ones, almost like an improvised seat.

"I wanted it long enough to be around your body," I told her, afraid that the rope would hurt her, but she dismissed the idea.

"It won't bother me. We'll find something better next time."

I understood from her words that she was implying that we would fly together more than once. I wrapped the rope around my waist, securing myself to her, then tied a tight knot. I kept my hands around it and the rope that was on Safira. It was the best I could do. I hoped it would do the trick.

"You and I are bound together," she said as she prepared to fly.

My gaze fell on Akael, my heart pounding. He had taken several steps back to give us space. Probably sensing my nervousness, Safira said to me, *"Don't worry, I'll bring you back safely to him."*

I grabbed the rope and a horn with both hands, my knuckles whitening from the force I applied, surprised by Safira's movement as she spread her wings. Her movements were calculated, deliberate. Sitting on her, I could feel her incredible strength. Akael smiled, looking at us.

"Hold on tight," was the only warning I got before Safira leaped forward, her wings stretching wide. The force was so great that I felt myself crushed against her back. Each flap pushed me backward and downward. I held my legs as tightly as possible around her, and stayed close to her neck to avoid the gusts of wind. If it weren't for the rope, I'd probably fall, and I was so, so grateful for it! The sky and clouds quickly replaced the forest.

Safira climbed rapidly, passing through layers of clouds that looked like thick fog as we flew through them. Once above the clouds, the gusts calmed down. The view was magnificent, and for a moment, my fear disappeared. They covered the sky like a flock of white sheep in a meadow. I had never seen anything like it, and I was amazed.

"The one you call Scorchfire. He was one of the First, linked to the original bloodline of dragons. When he died, he gave his blood to bring us all back."

Her words brought me back to reality. I held on to her as we conversed. *"You mean one of the sacred dragon Aurelion's first descendants? The one that created the elven race with the demigoddess?"*

She followed a flow of air that descended beneath the clouds, then rose again. My stomach churned. I tried to get used to the sensation, taking deep breaths.

"If you mean our father who led to the creation of your race, then yes. Scorchfire was one of the first descendants, just like me. He let himself get killed so we could live again."

Just like that, she had explained the dragons' rebirth. I was blown away, and I had so many questions.

"Wait, you're also a descendant of the holy dragon?" I asked, suddenly realizing what she had just said.

While we flew, other dragons joined. They flew close overhead, then somersaulted around. I felt watched, but safe.

"Just like you are a direct descendant of the demigoddess Celestia. You are the last direct bloodline of the first generation of elves that the demigoddess and holy dragon have created."

Nausea rose at her words. I was so shocked that I didn't even react when she rounded the peak of a mountain that stood before us. The other dragons danced with us in the air. It was a beautiful waltz, but I couldn't accept that I was the descendant of a demigoddess. This couldn't be.

She continued, *"We're running out of time. The time for your destiny is coming, and you're going to have to live up to the gods' expectations. Otherwise . . ."*

I was overwhelmed and fought back the tears that were welling up. *"Otherwise what?"* I asked with a lump in my throat.

"Otherwise, the world will fall into darkness."

I remained silent for a moment, reflecting on everything she had just said, blinking back the tears. It seemed that Akael was right. I had already figured I might as well accept it, but this was much more. The weight of responsibility fell heavily on my shoulders. I thought back to Sylvia, whom I loved like a mother. She had always told me I was *veneficus dei*. If I were a descendant of the Celstia, then it was my duty to protect the world.

"I still don't understand how I could have been unaware of the origins of my bloodline," I said more to myself than for Safira.

She answered anyway. *"Gods never approved of Celestia's and Aurelion's love. They tried to get rid of your line for centuries. Knowing this, your parents sealed your real identity. The truth is, no other mage but you could have resurrected Scorchfire. You carry a fragment of the soul from Aurelion and Celestia inside you. You were born to lead the dragons and elves."*

I was shocked. "*Aren't gods supposed to be good? I am god's mage, ain't I?"*

The dragon spoke with the knowledge of one who had lived for several centuries. *"Gods aren't perfect. They are jealous and strive for power. Although some offer protection to mortals, not all of them are good. One in particular is scheming to bring destruction to the world. The one responsible for the darkness in the elven king."*

A sudden burst of wind almost threw me off of Safira's back, and I held her horn tighter. *"I had sensed his darkness. He is no longer the king I grew up with. He is cold and hostile."*

The dragon snorted. *"The tainted king must fall. You are the rightful ruler. Zar'kaan shal vektharn drel. From the broken line, whole flame returns. The daughter of the oath-born soul shall call the flame, and gods shall burn."*

Safira sent me images that were foreign to me. Images of bygone eras and wars. I saw ancestors I had never known fighting to protect our lineage from enemies. I saw dragons being decimated. And finally, I saw my mother reciting a spell. I heard my father whisper to her that he hoped it would be enough to let me survive. I hadn't seen them since I was enlisted as a mage in the king's service. I barely remembered what they looked like. I understood how much they loved me.

"How do you know so much?" I asked.

A dragon roared beside us, and others followed his call. I wondered what it meant.

"I have lived for thousands of years, surrounded by my kin who passed on their knowledge to me," she answered.

"Am I to fight a god?" I asked. This sounded like a daunting task.

"Don't forget that you now control dragons. You also have the Shard of Blood Right."

"The Shard of Blood Right?" I asked.

"I sensed it in your belongings. A dagger imbued with the force from your ancestors, passed down from generation to generation. It had been lost generations ago, but it found its way back to you."

I immediately thought back of the dagger artifact I had found in the crystal fields. I thought of how it looked like it was made of hardened dragon hide. I had suspected it might have been linked to the dragons.

Around me, the dragons roared and danced in the air, as if trying to get my attention. *"What are they doing?"* I asked.

Safira answered, *"They're pledging themselves to their queen."*

I stared in awe. Proudness and peace filled me. A great task lay ahead, but I wasn't alone. I had an army of dragons. I thought of Akael, waiting for me in the clearing. He also had his army with him. With my soul mate by my side, and dragons and my bloodline powers, I knew that I could do it.

I would rule over dragons and elves, and bring down the corrupted king.

"Come, let us return to your beloved," said Safira.

We returned to the clearing. My heart beat faster when I saw Akael's smile, waiting for us. The ground shook when we landed, sending leaves and dust flying.

I went straight into the embrace my prince had for me. It was warm and comforting, and I found myself yearning to be closer to him. I kissed his lips.

"How was it?" he asked.

"The kiss or the flight?" I teased.

He smiled at my question. "Both."

I told him everything Safira had said to me. He listened with great interest. When I had finally finished, he paused for a moment. He breathed one word, "Impressive!"

I giggled. "I was overwhelmed at first, but now it sounds as if it could be possible."

He nodded. "We must go and join my troops. They are waiting for us further into the forest, south of the elven city. They are at the spot where two fallen trees form a cross, but it's very far from here. I fear we won't make it before nightfall."

"Do you know where that is?" I asked the dragon.

She lowered her wing, motioning for me to climb on. *"Come, I'll take you there. It'll be quicker."*

"Can I come too?" asked Akael. I looked at her and felt her affirmation.

"Yes, she agrees," I replied.

We took to the sky, covering the distance quickly. As we did, I could feel that Safira was communicating with other dragons. She was rallying them to our cause, telling them to follow. As they drew near, I could hear them speaking to me. It was weaker than my link with Safira, but I could understand them. All said the same thing, *"It is an honor, my queen."*

"As you are destined to rule over us and you possess a fragment of Aurelion's soul, you can communicate with all dragons," explained Safira, knowing I would ask the question.

There were so many that when we got to the spot where Akael's troops were camping, we now had over fifty dragons with us.

"More will join," added Safira. *"We will await your signal."*

"Thank you," I answered as we got down from her back. The dragons landed in the clearing beside Safira. My muscles ached, and I realized it would take some time to get used to riding a dragon.

We walked the short distance between the clearing and the forest where the elven soldiers were camped. They were panicking when we arrived. One of them advanced toward us. His armor had a badge on it, and I guessed he was the captain. He had long white hair, and his eyes glowed orange, and his skin was slightly yellow. He was surely a high elf, or at least one of his parents was. The captain recognized the prince and bowed before running toward us.

"Your Majesty! You are safe and sound. Prepare yourselves, there are dragons. We must protect ourselves," he said in fear.

Akael stopped them with a wave of his hand. "You have nothing to be afraid of. The dragons are with us."

The soldiers' eyes widened. "They are?" he asked.

The prince nodded. "Now bow before your queen."

They all looked at me for a moment, then bowed low. I blushed. I wasn't used to this.

"Please rise," I said.

They obeyed. The captain put his hand on his heart. "It is an honor to serve you, my queen," he said.

Akael put his hand on the captain's shoulder. "She is my soul mate. You will do well to protect her, Sephirot."

The light was already lowering, and the birds sang in the trees, preparing for the night. "Let us eat. I'm starving," said Akael.

It had been a long day, and I couldn't agree more. Sephirot led us to the camp. The aroma of wild boar roasting in a large pot of broth with vegetables filled the air as we approached the tent where meals were served. *"Will you be okay?"* I asked Safira through our link as we walked away.

"Don't worry about me," she answered. *"We will hunt and spend the night here."*

I sat down next to Akael by the fire, a bowl of stew in hand. This morning's breakfast seemed so long ago, and the meal was delicious.

"We camped just far enough away to avoid being detected by Erendriel," Akael explained as we ate. "At least, that was the goal," he added, looking at his captain.

"I confirm that, Your Majesty. Our scouts have seen patrols passing by, but none have ventured this far. The king has no idea we are here," confirmed Sephirot.

"Excellent," replied the prince.

"Shall we attack tomorrow?" the captain asked.

"What do you think, My Lady?" asked Akael.

I was proud he'd ask for my advice. It warmed my heart that he trusted my opinion.

I thought back to how easily the king had conquered the dwarves a few weeks ago. I knew we had to confront Erendriel, but I was afraid that with all the mages and the army, we could lose a lot of souls. Attacking from multiple sources could help spread their soldiers thin and give us an advantage.

"You have troops in Mumbur too?" I asked for confirmation, remembering what Akael had said before.

The prince nodded.

"We could cause a diversion there first," I suggested.

"What do you suggest?" he asked.

"We attack Mumbur first. That will force Erendriel to send troops to defend the city. We wait for that to happen, then we strike Mytvathyr. Attacked on both sides, his forces will be scattered."

"That's a good plan," said Akael.

We sat down by the fire. I watched my prince talk with his troops. I could see the friendship between them; despite his title, years of working together had brought them close. This was a stark contrast to how Erendriel worked with his troops.

I couldn't wait to find out more about Akael. He was my soul mate, but I didn't know much about him yet. This was the first time we could relax and enjoy time together since we fled the vampire castle. Akael put his arm around me, pulling me closer as he spoke cheerfully. The elves introduced themselves and their hobbies to me; one loved to make bracelets, another played the guitar, they all wanted to pay their respect to their new queen. I wasn't used to so much attention.

The evening eventually turned festive. Some sang around the fire, while a few even danced. For a while, I forgot the task that weighed on my shoulders.

But as the night wore on, fatigue overtook me. "Let us retire," I said to Akael, wanting to be alone with him.

The most beautiful smile appeared on his face. He told the soldiers we were retiring for the night, leaving them to celebrate together.

"My tent is this way. My troops had prepared it, knowing I was to return with you," he said as we left the others.

The prince's tent stood near the center of the military camp. Its silk canvas was a deep charcoal black, edged with gold thread. In the light of the nearby torches, the fabric shimmered faintly, like embers beneath the ashes. At its peak flew his banner: an orange flame on a black background, flickering in the night wind as if it were alive. I found that the symbol of his kingdom reflected my prince's personality: full of passion and power.

Guards flanked the entrance, but even they kept a respectful distance. They nodded at us when we passed. Inside, the world softened. The ground was covered in thick furs and woven carpets. It was warm and inviting. A low table held a few rolled maps, a silver goblet, and a half-melted candle. Akael took off his boots as he entered, letting out a sigh of relief. I did the same, feeling the soft fur beneath my feet and releasing the pressure that had built up during the day's journey.

"How are you feeling?" he asked.

I took a deep breath. So much had happened today, but I felt better than I thought I would.

"That's a lot of revelations in one day, but I'm fine. My thighs and shoulders hurt from riding," I replied.

"Let me help you," he offered.

He walked around me and stood behind. His chest pressed against me as he leaned forward to undo the top of my studded leather dress. I let him do it. His fingers, rough from battle, gently removed the fabric and pushed my hair aside, revealing the bare skin of my shoulders. He traced my skin gently with his index finger, sending shivers down my spine. His lips left warm kisses on my shoulders, and I closed my eyes, losing myself in the sensation that overwhelmed me. His large hands rested on my shoulders and massaged them. My tense muscles relaxed as the knots unraveled. It was gentle and strong, just where I needed it.

Akael's voice was warm against my skin. "Be careful, My Lady. If you sigh like that, I might not be able to resist you."

Desire rose within me from those words. I glanced at the cot. It was larger and finer than any soldier's bed, draped in heavy linens and trimmed with fur, wide enough for two.

"Maybe I don't want you to resist me," I whispered boldly.

The prince let out a deep groan. "Oh, you won't have to tell me twice."

He stopped massaging and turned me around in his arms so that I faced him. His green eyes burned with yearning. I realized how much I wanted him too, my heart pounding.

He grabbed my face and pressed his lips against mine. Our clothes were quickly on the floor. My hands slid down his muscles, discovering his body for the first time as he claimed mine. I admired the beauty of his body, sculpted by combat. Each scar told a story, and I couldn't wait to hear them all, but not tonight. Tonight, I wanted him.

He covered me with kisses. "You're so perfect," he whispered, and in that moment, I believed him. Surrounded by his caresses, drowning in his scent, I felt like the most beautiful elf in the world.

Akael lay me down on the cot, his erection pressed against me. He was so close. I just wanted him. Now.

"Akael, take me."

"Not yet, My Lady. You deserve to be worshipped like the queen you are."

With those words, his mouth traveled down my body, leaving kisses and licks in its wake. He teased my hard nipples, heat rising within me as he made his way to my hot center. I gasped when his tongue found my clit, circling it one way, then changing direction. I moaned, caught in a storm of pleasure. My pulse quickened as he continued, my hips thrusting.

"More," I moaned.

"Oh yes," replied the prince between licks. "Gladly."

He was devouring me now. I grabbed the sheets with my hands, my legs trembling. It felt so good.

He added, "Go on, My Lady. Let me hear your seductive song."

He inserted a finger inside me, redoubling his efforts with his tongue, triggering a wave that was impossible to hold back. I cried out his name in ecstasy, "Akael!"

"So seductive," he whispered.

He continued to lick, pushing his finger into me, my walls pulsing against him. I thrust my hips, unable to hold back.

"Take me," I gasped. I wanted to feel him inside me. I wanted to hear him moan in turn.

That was all the motivation he needed. He withdrew his finger and licked it. His lips immediately found mine, the taste of my wetness lingering in his mouth. He penetrated me in one stroke, his cock sliding easily inside me. He was hard and the perfect size, hitting me just the right way. I had another orgasm almost instantly as he thrust into me. His body and mine fit together as if we were made for each other. He groaned, pushing harder and harder. I felt the pressure build again, my erect nipples rubbing against his chest, my walls tightening around him. He pushed again, his hot breath rolling against me.

I pulsed as ecstasy washed over me one more time, Akael finding his release simultaneously. His thrusts slowed until he gently on top of me, careful not to put all his weight on me.

He took a moment to catch his breath. His smile was utterly charming, and I knew then that I could never live without him.

"I love you," I whispered.

"Oh, My Lady. I love you more than I have ever loved," he confessed.

He kissed me again. We slipped under the covers, and I gazed at the elf beside me. He was my soul mate, my everything, my prince. With him, I felt safe, beautiful, and loved. Akael embraced me, and I lost myself in his affection.

Chapter 22 (Caleb)

Paisley

We got up just as the sun was setting. I was still energized from my moment with Summer, still remembering her wolf and her wild and delicious instinct. A purr came from her chest, soft and comforting. "I enjoyed it, too," she said, a smile on her face.

"Too bad we can't do it again right now," I answered.

She laughed. "Let's go take care of the orcs. We'll have plenty of opportunities to do it again. I'll bite you as much as you want."

She winked at the last words. The thought of her biting me excited me more than I wanted to admit. "With pleasure, little wolf."

We rejoined the others.

The air felt heavy, thick with tension, as we prepared to move. The fires were doused one by one, their embers crushed beneath boots, until only one remained. A couple of people would stay at the camp, the chef and a handful of fighters to protect it. They would keep a low profile and hope not to attract the orcs' attention while the rest of us were gone. Orders were given in hushed tones.

Darryl looked at me with a serious expression. "I've been waiting for this moment for so long," he said, more to himself than to me.

I nodded, understanding how much he wanted to save his sister. I hoped she was still alive.

The sky above still held the faint blush of sunset, fading into indigo. Soon it would be dark enough to hide us—dark enough to pass unseen through the lands no sane army dared cross. The orc territory was filled with ambushes and watchfires. To skirt around it, around the biggest encampments, was our only chance.

At the front, the elven scouts led the way, their eyes already glowing faintly in the dim light. They moved silently, their cloaks blending into the twilight. Behind them came the humans, steady and solid, the sound of their armor muffled beneath fabrics. The vampires brought up the rear. We were perfectly suited to nighttime travel, our pale faces little more than glimmers in the darkness. Summer stayed by my side, and I realized that she was the only other werewolf in the group.

No one spoke. The only sound was the soft rhythm of boots, the creak of leather, and the faint rustle of branches as we slipped into the eastern wilds. After some discussion, it had been decided to avoid walking directly on the beach. It would have been too easy to spot us. Staying in the forest was slower due to roots and obstacles, but safer. The air grew colder, damp with mist rising from the floor and the nearby river. Somewhere far to the west, a low drumbeat rolled across the hills—the orcs' war signals, distant yet close enough to chill the blood. I held my breath, thinking the same thing as everyone else: I hoped our camp was safe. It was too late to turn back. There was nothing else to do but move forward, so we did.

We passed the ancient ruins of the human city that had once stood on these lands. I stared at the remnants of this forgotten civilization: rubble, standing walls, and half-collapsed houses. I didn't like this. Any building still standing could serve as a hiding place for enemies. I used my sharp vampire senses, trying to detect the slightest sound, my nerves on edge. Fortunately, I detected nothing. The place seemed deserted.

"I don't smell anything either. That's a good thing," Summer sent through our bond. Her wolf was also worried, on edge, ready to pounce on anything that moved.

"Don't worry, I'll protect you," I whispered to her, even though I knew she was capable ofdefending herself.

Her wolf calmed down, her heart rate slowed. Summer replied, *"We'll protect each other."*

I sent a wave of affection her way. *"I wouldn't have it any other way, my little wolf."*

The elves abruptly stopped walking. At the same time, I heard hearts beating not far from us, just to our left. There was an orc encampment. They were just on the other side of some bushes and rundown walls. I suddenly found myself grateful for the ruins.

That encampment wasn't supposed to be there, it wasn't on the map, and if an encampment was near, so were the traps.

We adjusted our course immediately, angling further east, deeper into the uneven terrain where jagged stones and twisted roots slowed our steps. It was safer this way, hidden beneath the heavy branches where moonlight barely reached. The elves, masters of the woods, marked the safest paths for us to follow.

By the time the moon crested the horizon, our camp was long gone from sight. Through the darkness of the night, the woods felt haunted. We spotted the occasional flicker of an orc campfire in the distance. A few orc patrols walked near us—too near for comfort. Each time we spotted one, we froze, hearts pounding, until the patrols moved on. Luckily for us, these creatures didn't possess magic powers. We could take down an orc patrol, but that would alert their encampment when the patrol didn't return. We needed to stay low until we found the prisoners.

We walked farther, even though some of us started to show signs of fatigue. I put my arm around Summer, supporting her, and she leaned her head against me. I spotted vampires supporting tired humans or elves helping others who had fallen. Those small gestures sometimes went unnoticed, but kept everyone going. Under the veil of night, our mismatched army became something rare and unspoken: a single entity.

We slipped into a ditch and stopped just before the last row of trees. The orc camp stretched out before us like a dark wound across the plain: halos of smoke around the guard fires, squat tents surrounded by sharp stakes, and the dull reflection of armor where the torches struck the metal. No cages were visible from here, only a maze of shapes and the slow, gruff movements of the patrols. Everyone held their breath, as if the night itself might swallow us.

"Where are the prisoners?" whispered Darryl to me, as if I had the answer.

“They’re probably further,” suggested Summer.

“We need to know where they are,” replied Darryl.

I agreed with him. Just as I thought about going to talk to her, Anne walked near us. “Stay put,” she instructed Darryl. “I know you’re thinking of rushing there to save your sister, but you’ll get killed if you do. We’ll scout the area first.”

The man had a guilty look on his face. Desperation could cause men to do stupid things. “I’ll make sure he stays with us,” I said.

The captain nodded, satisfied. She motioned for an elven mage to come by. He was thin as a reed, his face hooded, but his eyes glowed purple. “You know what to do, Thalion,” the captain told him.

Thalion didn’t answer anything. With a small, practiced motion, he drew a sigil in the air and whispered old words. The air around him shivered, and a pale translucence crawled over his skin. The invisibility took him like mist, and he melted into the dark. I was amazed. I had never seen anyone use an invisibility spell.

“That’s impressive,” I said.

Anne nodded. “Very useful,” she commented.

“Isn’t there a way to cast it on everyone?” I asked. This could be much more beneficial this way.

The captain shook her head. “No, and before you ask, the spell wears off if you try to interact with anything. Like opening a door, stealing an object, or killing something. Using it for scouting ahead is the most effective use of it.”

As a skilled assassin, I was a master of the shadows, but even *I* didn't have the ability to become invisible. I wondered if there was a way for me to learn it.

The minutes ticked by. We waited, each man and woman allowing themselves to sit down for a moment. Yet despite the relaxed exterior, I could see human fingers clenched around the hilts of their swords, elves with narrowed eyes, and vampires, teeth elongated, waiting, ready to drink the blood of their enemies.

A distant orc laugh echoed across the field, but no sound of battle. Darryl was becoming uneasy. Summer spoke with him about pleasantries, trying to keep his mind busy.

I wasn't sure exactly when the mage returned, only that he was still unseen. Thalion flicked back into sight with the last syllable of the spell, just beside us. Everyone gathered close, especially Darryl, who was dying to hear about his sister.

"The camp is larger than the map showed," he said. He drew with his fingers in the dirt. "Two outer rings of tents, thirty to forty warriors on watch in those rings. Outer sentries post pairs. Inside those rings are supply pits—barrels, hides—and three heavy fires that mark the inner hold. At the center stands a platform of crude timber with a circle of iron cages around it. I could see the prisoners huddled in two rows of cages. There were more, but I couldn't get closer."

"Did you see a woman with long black hair and blue eyes?" interrupted Darryl.

The elf shook his head. "I'm sorry, I couldn't discern faces," he answered before continuing his description, "The inner ring is guarded by the largest orcs, thicker-armed, many with throwing hooks and lit shields. An orc with a horn patrols the camp. There are rudimentary alarm bells, designed to warn the orcs in the camp, but they are not loud enough to alert everyone in the surrounding area. Our concern is that orc with the horn."

Silence fell after the report, the gravity of it pressing like cold iron.

"No way to sneak them out," the captain said quietly, fingers tightening. "Not without tearing through that center. If we try to take one cage at a time, the alarm will bring the rest down on us. We can't risk the prisoners' lives."

A vampire on the flank bared a smile that was not amused. "There's no honor in letting innocents die because we were timid."

I laid a hand on the Thalion's shoulder, saying out loud what everyone was thinking. "Then we do what must be done. We hit the heart and end this tonight—silent, sharp, and quick. We spare no mercy for those who guard the cages."

All the eyes fell on the captain. She looked at me and nodded.

She prepared an attack plan. "We need to take the orc with the horn first. You will cast the invisible spell again and sneak behind him."

"I don't have enough mana to cast it again," Thalion answered.

Another elf raised his hand. "Then I'll do it."

Anne nodded. "Thank you, Eldrin. We will split up and prepare. We'll wait for two hourglasses before attacking. That should give enough time to kill him and not leave you exposed once the invisibility spell wears off."

She motioned to us. "We will split into three groups. I want one group of archers and warriors for the first outer ring, one for the second, and I need warriors for the inner circle and the prisoners. Each group will be responsible for deactivating the alarms and bells right away to avoid reinforcements from coming."

The people split into three groups. I joined the one heading toward the inner circle, accompanied by Summer and Darryl. There were about twenty of us. Our group was mainly composed of vampires, as we were stronger than humans and elves. Anne was also with us.

Before we left, she gave us one last instruction. "Once you have accomplished your objective and eliminated the enemies, go and help the next group. If the attack turns into a disaster, retreat to our camp, but make sure no orc follows."

Everyone understood what she meant. We were all ready to give our lives, but hoped it didn't come to that.

We waited while Eldrin cast the invisibility spell on himself. Anne flipped the hourglass. Archers prepared their arrows, and the others got their weapons ready. We all watched the sands of grains fall steadily.

Some mouthed framed prayers, others cursed softly, the gravity of the situation showing on their faces. They knew what the end would be—steel for steel, blood for blood. But they also knew that returning empty-handed and with dead hopes would be worse.

The moon slid across a fraction of the sky and threw a sliver of silver down on the path. The last grain of sand fell for the second time.

We hadn't heard a horn, which was a good thing. It also meant we needed to hurry. Orcs would quickly overrun a single mage, and his invisibility spell would have worn off the moment he killed the patrol.

We moved like shadows, driven by the desperate goal of reducing the camp to ashes and saving the survivors. Night swallowed us, but not for long. The outer sentries were quickly dispatched. I watched as the first group entered the outer ring. I continued past them, with Summer by my side. Darryl followed a little further behind.

I slit the throat of another sentry with ease. There was some commotion coming from the second outer ring. I turned to see Eldrin fighting with orc warriors. The corpse of the orc with the horn lay on the ground further in the second outer ring. The mage tried to prevent the other orcs from getting to the horn, but he was overwhelmed. He wouldn't last long.

"Hurry," I urged the second group, pointing to the fight.

The group sprinted there, and some elves were already aiming their arrows at the orcs, helping from afar. I wanted to stay, but I couldn't divert from the plan. It looked like the fight was already turning to our advantage. I made my way to the inner ring with the others.

Fires were lit inside the inner ring, and the orcs standing guard were heavily armored. I could read Summer's intention through our bond. We jumped on the first one, attacking together without exchanging a word. We were fast, silent, brutal. The first orc fell quickly to the ground.

I turned my focus on the next orc. We killed every orc crossing our path. My strength was unlike anything I had felt before, and I was amazed. This was surely a gift from the dragon blood I had consumed.

Sparks flew as my blade met crude iron. One by one, the orcs fell. Behind me, I could hear the sound of the others slaying orcs. For a split second, I watched Summer fight as if she were the very heart of the battle. Her movements were raw and instinctive.

I smiled, impressed by her, remembering how lucky I was to have her as my mate.

I narrowly parried a blow as an orc attacked me with his flail. I was stronger than him and pushed his blow away. I sank my teeth into the orc's throat and drank a large gulp of his blood. It was sour and bitter. Disgusting. Still, I drank his life until he collapsed.

There were fewer orcs now, and I shouted, "Get the cages open!"

Darryl was already there, on his knees beside the first lock, his pack of vials and tools spilling out over the dirt. The smell of smoke and alchemical acid mixed in the air. His fingers worked with feverish precision, uncorking a small vial that hissed when it touched metal. The lock melted into a stream of blackened liquid.

The first prisoners stumbled free, their eyes wide and empty with shock. I caught a man before he could fall, steadying him with a hand that was still slick with blood. "Get to the camp entrance," I ordered.

We moved from cage to cage, Darryl's potions cutting through locks like a blade through ice, Summer holding the line, and I shielding them from every charge. The night echoed with grunts, steel, and the dull thud of collapsing bodies.

"Paisley," shouted Darryl as he opened one of the cages. A woman stood in the cage with long black hair. Her bright blue eyes contrasted with the night's darkness. She looked fragile, tired, yet alive, and bore a striking resemblance to her brother.

"Darryl, is that you?" she asked with hesitation. The man nodded, and the woman ran into his arms. Tears streamed down their cheeks. It was a sweet reunion, twenty-seven years later, and though I was happy for them, I reminded them, "There's no time. We need to get everyone out."

They nodded. Paisley stayed close to Darryl as he opened the remaining cages. Just as he opened the last one, a feeling of victory came over me. We had succeeded, we had rescued the prisoners and found Darryl's sister. All that remained was to return to camp.

Then the sound came.

Not the deep, rolling horn that would summon every orc in the valley—but the sharp, metallic clang of a bell. Small, frantic, close.

My head snapped toward the noise, eyes narrowing. Across the camp, a dying orc hung from a rope that led to a crude warning bell. Even bleeding, the creature had pulled it. The clang still rang in the cold air, carried by the wind.

"Damn it," I hissed. "They'll be on us in minutes."

I could already hear the distant roar of orc voices and the thunder of boots from the outer camps.

"Hurry!" said Summer to the last prisoners. They ran with all their strength to the entrance.

"Fall back," ordered Anne.

Everyone ran toward the entrance. Just as I was about to follow, I noticed that Darryl and Paisley weren't coming.

"What's wrong?" I asked urgently.

"She can't run, she's too weak," Darryl explained.

I swore at our situation. I knew that man wouldn't leave her behind, and there was no time to waste. We had to retreat immediately, or we wouldn't make it. I didn't want to lose either of them.

"I'll carry her," I said.

Summer came back to us, who had gone ahead and noticed that we were lagging. "They're already here. Anne and the others killed enough orcs to allow the prisoners to escape, but there are too many of them and they fled. The four of us need to find another way out."

I frantically searched for an idea. The situation had quickly gone from excellent to dire. Given Paisley's condition, we wouldn't stand a chance against the orcs. "Then we'll go the other way," I said.

"But that's in the opposite direction from our camp," said Darryl.

"We have no choice," I barked.

The man realized the obvious. We ran away as fast as we could. The path to the other side of the camp was very lightly guarded. Most of the orcs had been drawn to the fighting earlier and were already lying on the ground. Summer killed a stray sentry while I carried Paisley in my arms, who weighed almost nothing. Darryl kept saying he had potions to heal his sister, but there was no time for that. It would have to wait.

We finally left the camp on the opposite side from where we had entered. If we were lucky, we could bypass it through the forest and reach our camp quickly. The sun was rising on the horizon. Soon, we would no longer be able to take advantage of the cover of night and would be even more exposed.

We began our journey through the forest. Paisley insisted she could walk, so I let her. This freed my arms in case we were attacked, but it also slowed our pace, as she walked with difficulty. When we were under the cover of the trees and far enough away from the orcs, I allowed Darryl to search through his potions for one that would help his sister.

"How did you find me?" she asked as he rummaged through his satchel.

"It's thanks to Caeda," he replied, handing her a potion with green liquid. The woman's eyes widened as she recognized the name of her friend. She pinched her nose before drinking it all.

"Oh, I have so many questions and so much to tell you," she said, handing the empty bottle back.

"Me too," added Darryl.

Their conversation could have easily lasted hours. The potion had been drunk, and we had to get back on the road. I interrupted them. "This was just a short break; we can't afford to stay too long. It's already morning. We have to get back to camp. You can talk when we're in a safe place."

They both nodded. Summer took my hand and squeezed it as we walked. Her skin was warm, and all I wanted was to be back in her arms alone. Darryl followed behind us with his sister.

The morning was warm, and I estimated we would be back at the encampment by noon if we were lucky. A cold shiver suddenly ran through my veins.

Then I felt her.

My body trembled, and I swallowed. I knew this magic. My pulse raced, and I fought the urge to run. It would be useless.

"Why are we stopping?" asked Darryl.

"What's going on?" asked Summer. She could feel my terror.

"She found us," I said.

I breathed memories of the goddess into her mind, and she froze in fear. "Oh no," were the only words that came out of her mouth.

"Would someone explain what's going on?" asked Darryl and Paisley, who had no idea of what was happening.

I didn't have to explain. A voice rang loud and cold. "So, you thought you could hide from me."

Chapter 23 (Samantha)

Reunion

The castle gates opened as dusk fell. I crossed the courtyard, covered in mud, with hollow eyes, and my cloak torn. I was beyond exhaustion. The guards blocked my way.

"Halt!" they said.

I gave them a stern look. "Can't you recognize your queen?" I asked. They were only doing their job, and I should have been grateful, but at that moment, all I wanted was to get back into my castle.

They studied me and their mouths opened in astonishment. They looked at each other and whispered. I had been gone for nearly two full days. I must have looked terrible, unworthy of a queen, but I was too tired to care.

"We did not recognize you, Your Majesty," one of them said apologetically. They stepped aside and let me in. I said nothing. I just waved as I passed.

Viktor met me halfway across the courtyard, running toward me. For a heartbeat, his composure cracked. Relief and disbelief warred on his face before he reached for my hands, his voice low and trembling.

"You're alive."

A few words that clearly revealed his true feelings. I was grateful to see him. My lips curved faintly, weary but proud. "Barely."

He drew me in, armor and all, his embrace firm and warm against my cold skin. I let myself breathe. The smell of the marsh still clung to me, earth and decay and smoke.

When I stepped back, I unfastened the strap across my chest and drew from beneath my cloak the relic. The light reflected off its pale metallic surface, highlighting the luminous veins and engraved wings.

Viktor stared, awed. "You found it . . ."

"I did." My voice was quiet, reverent. "The temple is real. The legends are true."

He reached out as if to touch it, then hesitated. "It feels alive."

I nodded, exhaustion softening my expression. "It is. And it knows me now."

For a moment, silence settled between us—heavy with all that had been risked and all that might come. Then Viktor smiled, gently brushing a lock of wet hair from my cheek.

"Come. You're shaking. Let me take care of you."

I nodded, happy to let him take the lead. He led me through the corridors, past startled attendants and hushed courtiers, until we reached the royal baths. Steam curled above the water, perfumed with herbs and oils. I hesitated only a moment before allowing him to unbuckle the ruined armor, piece by piece, each clasp falling away with a dull clink that echoed in the still air.

Viktor's hands were tender. I was no longer a queen. I was just a vampire in the arms of her lover, and nothing else mattered. The bruises along my ribs, the dried blood on my arms—all the marks of battle faded beneath the warm water. He said little, but his gaze told me everything—the fear he'd carried since I'd left, the awe at my return, and the relief that I still stood before him.

When he finally joined me in the water, he pulled me close. The tension that had bound us both slowly melted, leaving only the quiet rhythm of our breathing and the soft ripple of water between us.

For a while, the world outside the steam and warmth ceased to exist. No relics, no thrones, no looming war—only two souls reunited.

Later, when I was too weary to stand, he carried me to our chamber. I tried to speak—to tell him what I had seen, the guardian, the curse—but the words dissolved on my tongue.

"Tomorrow," he whispered. "You can tell me everything tomorrow."

I nodded, surrendering to the exhaustion that had stalked me since the marshes. As my eyes drifted shut, Viktor brushed a kiss against my forehead, the faint glow of the relic still pulsing on the table beside us—silent, watchful, and waiting.

Sunlight streamed through the high windows, pale and cold. The scent of rain lingered in the air—it had fallen during the night, washing the courtyard clean but leaving the sky heavy with clouds. I smiled, happy to be in my chamber.

My muscles ached when I got up, but my vampire regeneration powers had already healed the most serious injuries. I sat by the fireplace, wrapped in a robe of dark silk, my hair loose around my shoulders. The relic rested on the table beside me, wrapped in white linen that could not hide the faint glow pulsing beneath. When Viktor entered, I did not look up immediately.

The smell of eggs and ham filled the room, reminding me it had been a long time since my last meal. I was grateful that he brought me breakfast.

"Thank you," I said as he handed me a serving tray. Fresh fruits and bread accompanied the meal.

Viktor poured two cups of coffee before sitting across from me, smiling. "You looked like you needed the extra sleep," he said softly.

I looked at him. "You should hear what I saw."

And I told him between mouthfuls. Everything—the descent through the dark waters, the battle with the marrowyrn, the guardian's voice echoing through the temple, and the battle that had nearly taken my life. Viktor listened without interruption, his eyes fixed on me, his hand occasionally tightening around his cup. When I finished, silence fell.

Finally, he exhaled. "I should have come with you. I could have protected you. I don't know what I would have done if you had died." His voice was full of sorrow and tenderness.

For a while, neither of us spoke. Then I straightened slightly, my tone sharpening, my meal finished. "Now tell me. What happened here while I was gone?"

Viktor hesitated only a heartbeat, but I caught it.

"A great deal," he said. "The elven king has sent envoys. He calls upon our alliance in the war."

I gave a short, mirthless laugh. "Let him call. I owe him nothing."

Viktor's brow furrowed. "Ignoring him will not go unnoticed."

"I don't care to be noticed anymore," I replied, my tone like steel. "Let the elves fight their own war. I'm so close to fulfilling Alastor's prophecy."

He looked into his cup. "As you wish."

My next words were quieter, but laced with intent. "And Nathan?"

The question seemed to hang in the air. Viktor's jaw tightened. "He escaped."

My head snapped toward him. "Escaped?"

"He slaughtered the guards. Every one of them. Freed the slaves from the caravan, burned the slave store to ash, and vanished before reinforcements arrived."

I cursed. My hand flexed on the arm of my chair, the faint hum of restrained magic flickering beneath my skin. "That annoying fool." I hissed. "He keeps slipping through my fingers. The next time, I'll deal with him myself."

"The reports say he fought like nothing before," Viktor added, watching me carefully. "Stronger and faster."

The elven king's words came back to mind. He had spoken of the Oracle and a prophecy when I had first met him. I hadn't put much thought into it when we made the deal on that faithful night before the wedding. If the Oracle's words were true, Nathan could become more than just a nuisance.

My anger burned quiet and cold—not the fury of a ruler slighted, but the fury of a woman who'd lost a piece of her plan.

I needed that man dead.

After a long silence, I asked, hoping for better news, "And Elaine, has she found anything?"

Viktor shook his head. "Not yet. With everything that's happened, I haven't had the time to visit her myself. The servants say she's being well tended to."

"She should not be tended to," I snapped. "She should be working. Every hour, every breath, until she has an answer."

My voice softened a moment later, but the edge remained. "I will visit her. I want to hear what she's discovered, or what she's hiding."

Viktor nodded. "As you wish."

I rose, determined to get dressed and check on the progress of the elf. "You did a good job while I was away. Have the guards summon everyone. They need to know I have the relic. Hopefully, that will calm them."

Viktor smiled seductively. "Do you need help getting dressed?" he asked, raising an eyebrow.

"If you can keep your playful fingers under control, maybe," I replied in the same tone.

The vampire laughed, approaching me and kissing me on the lips. "I can't promise anything."

I grabbed his hand and led him to the wardrobe. Between kisses and caresses, I was finally dressed in a long black royal gown trimmed with gold.

I walked through the familiar corridors, people bowing respectfully as I passed. It was good to be back in my castle. I made my way to the corridor where Elaine's room was located. My blood ran cold when I saw that there were no guards outside her door.

I unlocked the door and threw it open. My eyes scanned the room, confirming my suspicion.

Elaine was gone.

"Lysander!" I shouted.

My pet was walking down a corridor further away. "Jason," I called out.

The human jumped nervously. "Your Majesty," he said eagerly, coming over. "You're back!"

I dismissed his comment. "Bring Lysander here immediately!"

"He hasn't returned, Your Majesty," he stammered.

I recalled the events that had transpired before I departed from the castle. Lysander was in town, and Jason had been helping out at the castle.

"What do you mean he hasn't returned? For several days?"

"Yes, Your Majesty," the man said nervously.

This day was spiraling out of control. I'd send guards to search for him. In the meantime, with Lysander gone, I had to appoint someone else to lead the servants.

"What happened to the prisoner?" I asked, hoping the human would know.

"I have no idea," he said. "How is she?"

"Gone. That's how she is," I spat back too harshly. My pet recoiled, frightened. I took a breath. This wasn't his fault, and I didn't want him to be afraid of me—it would spoil his blood. It had taken me long enough to tame him.

I softened my tone. "Do you know why there were no guards, Jason?"

The man fidgeted with his fingers, avoiding my eyes. "No, Your Majesty."

"Did you know she was gone? Who brought her meals?" I asked. The servants had been instructed to bring her meals every day. One of them must have noticed her disappearance. Unless she had killed the servant today. Or . . . I had a traitor in the castle.

"I don't know, Your Majesty," answered Jason nervously. The man clearly hadn't seen anything, and I didn't want to lash my anger on him. I smiled at him as best as I could due to the circumstances.

"It's fine," I said gently to ease the human. I heard his heart slow down at these words. Two guards passed by in the hallway at that moment. "Guards!"

They turned to me. "Yes, Your Majesty."

"Ring the bell, the prisoner has escaped. Send regiments to search for her. I want her back in her room—and find me the servants who were in charge of her food, and the guards who were supposed to be in front of her door. I want to see them in the throne room this afternoon."

They nodded fearfully. "At your command."

"Send men to find Lysander. He's been gone for too long."

They nodded again and waited. "There's nothing else. Go," I spat angrily.

I sighed as I watched them leave. This was definitely not my morning. Without the mage, I had no clue as to why the dragons had returned. I approached the bedroom window and noticed that there wasn't a single one left in the sky above the city. I had been so exhausted when I returned the night before that I didn't notice.

I turned to Jason, who had followed me to the window.

"When did the dragons leave?" I asked pensively.

The man stared curiously. "I haven't noticed. My bedroom doesn't have a window."

"And what were you doing in the hallway?" I asked. Not that he wasn't allowed to move around the castle. My pet could move around as he pleased, as he had proven his loyalty. I was just hoping to change the subject so my day wasn't completely ruined.

"I was going to help in the laundry room," he said.

I shook my head, disapproving. "You're still helping."

"Yes, because Lysander is away," he explained.

That wasn't the role of a pet. I looked at the man, taking in his scent, staring at his skin, sensing the heat emanating from him. Thirst overwhelmed me. I knew how to make sure this day wasn't ruined.

"Jason," I said, moving closer to him. My fangs were already lengthening. "I don't mind you helping out once in a while, but you're not a servant at the castle. Let them do the chores."

The man backed away quietly, following my movement as I urged him toward the bed Elaine had occupied the previous nights. The human swallowed, and his heartbeat quickened. It was fast, loud, mesmerizing. I licked my lips. It had been several days since I had indulged, and suddenly, nothing else mattered.

"It's time I reminded you of your place in the castle," I said, pushing the human gently onto the bed.

He sighed with anticipation. I climbed on top of him and smiled when I felt the bulge in his pants. He had clearly missed me. "Good boy," I said, licking the skin on his neck. He grabbed my waist, holding me tightly against him.

"Do you want it, Jason?" I asked, my lips caressing his skin as they moved.

"Yes, mistress," he begged, pushing his hips against me.

I sank my fangs into his neck. The man cried out in euphoria. I moaned with pleasure as the first drops hit my tongue, connected to him, feeling his ecstasy.

Nothing compared to fresh blood. Jason was still asleep in the bed, exhausted from the blood loss and from having a vampire ride him to ecstasy so many times. I smirked. Humans had such low stamina compared to us.

I left and headed for the throne room. I ran into Viktor as I passed the castle entrance. "There you are!" he said. "So, did she find anything about the dragons?"

Reminding me of this stirred up my anger. "She escaped," I replied gruffly.

"How?" he asked.

"I don't know, but I intend to find out," I replied.

"Well, I wanted to let you know that the message has been delivered to the citizens by the guards. They will be in the castle courtyard this afternoon to hear your announcement."

"Perfect," I replied. *At least one thing was going well*, I thought to myself.

"I had your meal brought up to the music room," Viktor added.

His thoughtfulness made me happy. I suddenly realized how long it had been since I had taken the time to go there. I would have plenty of time to relax once Alastor's prophecy was fulfilled, I reminded myself.

"Thank you, you know me so well," I replied.

He offered me his arm, and I gladly took it. I enjoyed his company as we made our way to the room. I smiled at the sight of the piano—the only thing that could make me forget the stress of ruling. Sitting on the bench was one of the castle's maids, who looked at Viktor intently. He nodded, and she began to play a soft melody.

In the corner of the room was a small table with two plates with a single rose in a small vase.

Viktor led me to the table. "I thought this might make you happy. You're always so busy."

I was moved by how much time the vampire had taken to consider everything I loved. "It's my favorite piece of music, my favorite meal, and my favorite flower. Viktor, this is so touching." A tear rolled down my cheek as I put my hand to my heart.

The king smiled broadly. "That's an even better reaction than I hoped." He took my hand and kissed it before pulling out my chair.

I sat down and waited a moment for Viktor to join me. He may have been young, but he had transformed entirely since becoming king. I had to admit that I couldn't live without him anymore. I would enjoy continuing my life by his side when all this was over. A simpler life. Maybe even having children, as he so desired.

The meal was delicious, and the blood wine was of high quality. It was rich and flavorful. We ate while listening to the sweet symphony played on the piano. For a moment, I forgot my problems.

"Thank you for all this," I whispered to Viktor.

"It's only natural for the vampiress I love," he replied.

A blueberry pie was served for dessert while a waltz was now being played on the piano. When we had finished, I noticed voices coming from outside, from the balcony entrance.

"They're waiting for you," Viktor said.

He held out his hand to me, and I took it. We walked to the balcony, and I saw hundreds of people gathered there waiting for me. I recognized Lord Dumoulin, my piano repairer, in the crowd with his mate. She stood out with her long dress of silk and lace. She almost looked like a princess. The lord clearly spoiled her, but I smiled, happy for their love and that he had changed her into a vampire without problems.

The scent of werewolf struck me, and I searched the crowd, looking for the source of it. My eyes fell on a tall, bald man, accompanied by a round, short human, and an ebony-skinned man.

Viktor motioned to go back inside to leave me all the space as usual, but I held him back. "Stay with me. It's only natural for the king to accompany his queen."

The vampire smiled proudly. "With pleasure."

My heart suddenly began to race when I realized that the relic had been left in my bedroom. "I forgot the relic," I whispered to Viktor.

He smiled. "I thought of it."

Behind him, a servant emerged carrying a large white silk cushion. In the center, under a cloth, I could make out the relic, its magic pulsing discreetly.

"Thank you," I replied. I was definitely grateful that Viktor was by my side today.

Some people had stopped talking, pointing to us on the balcony, waiting for us to speak, while others hadn't noticed.

"People of Ichoryllia," I said, my voice strong. I waited as the others hushed. When the crowd was silent, I continued, weighing each word carefully, adding silence between my sentences.

"What we have experienced is a tragedy. You have lost children, wives, families, and friends to the dragons' attack. You are afraid and angry, and you have the right to be, but I have listened to you. I have traveled, fought creatures, and risked my life."

I waited to see if anyone would react or say anything, but they remained silent. I motioned to Viktor. He took the silk cushion from the servant and came to my side.

"Behold," I said with a strong voice and lifted the cloth. "The relic imbued with the bones and will of the last winged saint. A shield against dragons."

The orb glimmered under the sunlight. The people observed in utter silence. I waited. I had expected a reaction, a clap maybe, or an acclamation. Nothing. I had risked my life for them, to show them I cared. To prove that I wasn't the cause of their suffering. And what did they do? They didn't even show appreciation.

"Maybe you should activate it," whispered Viktor in my ear.

What a splendid idea, but I realized that I didn't know how to do so.

Alastor, give me the strength.

Words resonated through my mind. *"Reliquiae praeteritorum, activa. Protege nos ab igne qui de caelo pluit."*

I recited them. The orb sparkled, rising from the cushion, levitating into the sky above the courtyard. Some people cried out in admiration, others hid, afraid. A group of children concealed themselves behind the skirt of the woman accompanying them. The orb emitted a whoosh, and a light stretched across the sky above the city. It was thin and transparent, yet it shimmered; a protective cover placed above us.

"Behold, the magic that now protects us from the dragons," I said in a solemn voice.

Some people started a slow clap, and then everyone followed. Soon, the crowd erupted in cheers. I watched, satisfied.

But the cheers were short-lived.

A dozen orcs burst into the courtyard. Screams rang out from all around. Parents protected their children. The strongest fought the creatures while others fled. Some flew into the sky because too many people blocked the exits on the ground. However, the young, the sick, and the humans could not fly. So they tried to make their way through the fray. Several bodies already lay on the ground.

"Send reinforcements to the guards outside!" I shouted to the servants.

They hurried to do so. The guards who were already outside were fighting the creatures. Soon, there would be reinforcements. Viktor grabbed me in his arms and led me inside. "We mustn't stay here."

I took one last look at the people being slaughtered. The guards were arriving. They would soon deal with the orcs.

"You're right. I already risked my life to get the relic. That's enough," I said, following him inside.

Chapter 24 (Erendriel)

The Prophecy

I entered Mumbur's castle and saw a dwarf servant passing by. I stopped him. "Prepare a plate for me and bring it to my study."

The servant bowed low and obeyed. I made my way directly to the royal chamber I was occupying.

The shower was refreshing, and it felt good to wash all that dirt off me. However, I didn't linger, knowing full well that a meal was waiting for me. I put on my royal silk clothes, which I had asked to be cleaned. With my long white hair neatly pinned back with a brooch and my crown, I finally looked like a king. My gray-blue eyes reflected confidence and authority as I stared into the mirror.

The delicious smell of quail and spices wafted up to my nose as I entered my study. As requested, the servant brought a plate, a glass of wine, and a decanter of water. It was only when I took the first bite that I realized how hungry I had been. I quickly devoured everything, washing it down with a generous sip of wine.

It was late afternoon, but I was eager to visit the mines and see the Oracle's message. However, it was imperative to check whether the mines were connected to the mountain.

I left the study and headed for the strategy room. As I expected, I found Rahul, Dale, and Lane there. The three elves turned toward me when I entered.

"Do we have a map of the area?" I asked, not wasting time. We had some at Mytvathyr's Castle, but they only had rough details of the dwarf kingdom.

"Yes, Your Majesty," Dale replied. He walked over to a desk against the back wall. He pulled out a large drawer and took out a map, which he unrolled on the table in the center of the room.

It took me a moment to get my bearings, as the dwarven map was not labeled the same way as ours. I finally found Carlpar Mountain, whose letters were slightly faded. Fortunately, it wasn't connected to the mines. The mines were located within the Vuradun mountain range, which stretched across the northern part of Mumbur. Fortunately, the mountains stopped just before Carlpar, and a valley separated them. With any luck, that would be enough to prevent the creature from taking control of the kingdom and the miners.

"Did you want to check something, Your Majesty?" Lane asked hesitantly.

I decided to tell my generals everything. They should be aware in case something happened to the city while I was away.

“That’s terrible,” Rahul said with a concerned voice.

“As I told you, I don’t believe the being can leave the mountain. That’s why we’re going to block the tunnel, to prevent anyone from entering. The city should be safe.” I wasn’t sure if I was trying to convince them or myself. Burying a problem didn’t solve it, and I was sure it would come back eventually, but we couldn’t deal with it now.

Dale nodded, understanding.

“Also, don’t tell anyone about this. We don’t need the citizens panicking, and the guards need to rest. Let’s train an army and rebuild the city, so we’re ready in case of attack.”

“Yes, Your Majesty,” Rahul replied.

“Now. Let’s move on to the real reason I came here,” I added, thinking that in light of everything that had happened, it was a very good thing that I was here. “You sent a message about ancient writings that were discovered.”

“Yes, that was me, Your Majesty,” Lane replied.

“Good, show me the way.”

I followed Lane through the city as we headed northwest, where the mines of Vuradun were half-buried beneath the cliffs. Although the dwarves maintained them, the wind blew constantly in this region, carrying dust, sand, and debris that accumulated at the mine entrance, which had to be cleared every week to prevent it from becoming blocked.

Remembering what the letter had said, I was very excited. “You’re certain of what you found?” I asked.

“Certain enough to bring you here,” Lane replied. His torchlight flickered against the walls, revealing faint carvings—lines and sigils unlike anything dwarven. “They dug too deep in these tunnels and broke through into something far older. An entire ruin buried under the mountain."

I frowned. "How old?"

Lane's lips pressed together. "Older than the kingdoms of men. Older than the first songs of the elves."

We descended for hours, the air growing colder, heavier. The narrow passage widened suddenly into a vast hollow, and our voices came back to us warped by echo. I stopped short, my breath catching.

Before us lay a sunken city—or what remained of one. Pillars lay toppled in the dark, half-swallowed by stone, bridges of carved basalt stretched over deep chasms, and faint blue light shimmered beneath, reflected from veins of crystal threading the rock.

"This is not the work of dwarves," I said softly, noticing that the rock had been carved in places in a way that couldn't have been done with a pickaxe or hammer.

Lane nodded. "The miners said the same. The walls are fused at the seams, as if shaped by magic. There are glyphs everywhere."

His torchlight passed over one such inscription—curling, fluid symbols that seemed to move when we weren't looking.

"It feels . . . alive," Lane whispered.

"Everything ancient does," I murmured, studying the glyphs. These weren't elven either. "But you said our mages were able to decipher them?" I asked eagerly, thinking back to the letter.

Lane nodded as we pressed onward, crossing a narrow bridge where water dripped from the ceiling into a silent pool far below. "Yes, they said this was likely the home of the El'thors."

I was amazed. I had only heard about the El'thors as a child through history books. They were an ancient civilization that lived thousands of years ago. The few scrolls that mention them say that they had very powerful magical abilities, that it was potentially the most advanced ever to exist. Several of its members had divination powers. It was believed that all the Oracles over the centuries were descendants of these people.

"How did they come to this conclusion?" I asked.

Lane answered, "Ambrel has read all the texts in the mage library in Mytvathyr about them. He recognized some of the glyphs and transcribed them into his personal spellbook."

"That's rather useful," I commented.

Lane chuckled. "That's what I thought, too. It seems that ancient glyphs are his passion. He does this with all the writings he finds about ancient civilizations."

Lane led the way, consulting a leather-bound journal filled with sketches. "We followed the markings east," he explained as we walked. "They form a path. Every doorway, every column leading toward a central point. We think it's a temple."

I glanced at him. "You think?"

His mouth curved faintly. "It certainly looks like it."

I smirked. "Well, let's go see it, then."

The temple stood at the heart of the ruins, carved from a single slab of obsidian-veined stone. Its gates were massive, half-collapsed, the carvings upon them worn smooth by time, but still visible was a figure cloaked in stars, arms raised toward a sun that burned from within.

Lane traced a hand over the door. "They called this place *Eshal-Varan*, the Voice of Eternity, according to the fragments we could read."

"And inside?"

"The Oracle's texts, or so the mages claim. They say the walls whisper when you stand too close."

I said nothing and pushed against the gate. The stone groaned but yielded, a whisper of stale air spilling forth—dry, ancient, laced with the scent of dust and incense that hadn't burned in a thousand years.

The hall beyond was vast. Torches sputtered against black marble that caught the light like water. At its far end stood a dais, surrounded by murals of fire and winged beasts—dragons.

My breath caught. The resemblance was unmistakable. "They knew," I murmured. "Whoever built this place, they knew the dragons would return."

Lane stepped closer to the dais, his torchlight grazing faint inscriptions carved into the floor. "These are the Oracle's words," he whispered. "The ones we found broken on the tablets above. This is the complete text."

I knelt beside him, brushing away the dust. The glyphs were unreadable to me. "Do you have the translation?" I asked.

Lane nodded and opened his leather-bound journal and read aloud, his voice trembling:

"When the fire breathes again, the world shall wake.

The earth will tremble with the memory of its birth.

From beneath the stone, the sleepers shall rise—

and from their ashes, the age of dragons will begin anew."

The torches hissed. The faint hum of the crystals under the ruins pulsed once.

Lane looked up at me, eyes wide. "They prophesied the return of dragons."

I stood slowly, my gaze fixed on the mural—dragons soaring above cities now turned to dust. "No," I said softly. "They warned us."

The words hung in the air long after my voice faded. Dust motes swirled in the dim light, shimmering like fragments of broken stars.

I stepped toward the dais. "There's more," I said. "Look at the base. The runes don't end here."

Lane knelt beside me, brushing his fingers along the stone. The lines of script spiraled downward, vanishing beneath a layer of collapsed debris. Together, we carefully cleared it until another slab revealed itself. The symbols carved into it pulsed faintly, as if stirred by our touch.

"This isn't the same language," Lane whispered. "It's elven."

I frowned. "Maybe from another Oracle? There have been records of many elven Oracles."

Lane nodded. "Perhaps. It's the ancient elven language. I can make most of it. These markings speak of the return of a ruler bound by both the moon and shadow."

The torches flickered, dimmed. Somewhere deep in the ruins, a low tremor rolled through the earth. The air grew warmer, vibrating with an unseen rhythm.

Lane's voice faltered as he translated the new glyphs as he went along, using the leather-bound journal to decipher them:

"When fire and blood entwine,

the heir of ruin shall rise.

Neither beast nor man,

but both, and neither again.

When fire rains from the sky,

and the sun kisses the purest,

his crown shall bleed the heavens,

his reign shall shatter thrones.

From his shadow, kingdoms fall,

and the world ends not in flame —

but in silence.

All under the One rightful ruler."

A chill crawled up my spine. I stared at the words, their faint light dancing over my armor.

I pondered on their meaning. "Neither beast nor man, but both, and neither again . . . The hybrid king. I knew he would end the world. There it is again."

Lane nodded slowly, pale beneath the torchlight. "If the first verse foretold the dragons' return, then this one speaks of what follows. Their ruler." He hesitated. "And if the dragons have already risen—"

"Then the rest is coming," I finished grimly.

The humming grew louder, reverberating through the floor. The murals along the walls, once still, seemed to shimmer. The painted dragons twisted, turning their heads toward the dais as if awakening.

Lane stumbled back, clutching his torch. "Have you seen this? The painting! It's reacting to the prophecy."

"No," I said softly. "It's recognizing it."

For a heartbeat, I thought I saw something move beyond the edge of the chamber, a flicker of gold scales vanishing into shadow. The air throbbed with power, ancient and furious.

I turned to Lane. "Take what you can. Copy the glyphs, the text, everything. We can't leave it buried again."

He hesitated. "Your Majesty . . . if this is true, if the hybrid king rises, what happens to us?"

I looked once more at the prophecy, its last lines burning faintly like embers ready to consume the world.

"Then our kingdom will burn," I said, "and the rest will follow."

Chapter 25 (Nathan)

The Battle Against Dragons

The vampire city faded behind me like a fever dream—cold stone, darker memories, and the echo of blood. I didn't look back. My body had healed, flesh and bones mended, but the scars inside had not. I had one purpose left—to reach the elven city and find her. I wouldn't come back until the elven king was dead and she was with me.

It would be faster if I flew, but with the recent reappearance of dragons, it was safer to walk than to fight those beasts. The forest swallowed me whole as birds sang in the trees, but I didn't pay them attention. The early morning sun felt cold on my skin. Being apart from my mate had numbed me.

I stayed clear of the forsaken river. Memories of Emerald came back to me. She had saved me from the dreaded siren. Even with all my powers, I didn't stand a chance against them, so I took the long path through the trees, silent and alone.

It was then that I noticed the change.

At first, it was only the air—thicker, charged with something ancient. Then came the shadows moving high above, wings beating against the clouds. I looked up, and my heart tightened.

Dragons. A lot of them.

I slowed, watching one swoop low between the treetops. Its scales glimmered like molten bronze, its eyes burning. I didn't understand why there were so many. The sky was almost blackened by the number of them. The hairs on the back of my neck stood on end.

As I walked, the forest grew thinner until it gave way to a vast plain that stretched to the mountains separating the Valley of Nysa from the forest.

Before I could take ten steps into the open, a low growl rolled across the land. I turned to find three dragons descending from the clouds. One red as blood, another dark as obsidian, the third pale as bone. They landed in a storm of dust and wind, folding their wings.

I clenched my teeth, my claws lengthening, dropping into a low stance. It was naïve to think I even had a chance against three dragons, but I was surrounded. I would be damned if I died before I found Emerald.

The wolf growled within me. *Fight*, he said.

The first dragon lunged. I darted aside, claws slashing across its foreleg. Scales split, blood flowed, but the wound was shallow. The creature roared in frustration.

The second came from above, its tail sweeping. I jumped, barely clearing the blow, but the wind from it sent me tumbling through the grass. The third exhaled, not fire but raw heat, searing the air. The ground smoked where it touched.

I sprang at the dark one, claws digging between scales, climbing up its chest. The dragon thrashed, throwing me skyward. I hit the ground hard, breath driven from my lungs. Pain flashed through my ribs.

Still, I rose, driven by the urge to survive.

I sank my fangs into a wing, not to drink, but to tear it apart. The dragon screamed, staggering back, but the others closed in. A tail slammed into me, too fast for me to use magic to protect myself. I was sent skidding across the plain. Blood filled my mouth.

I tried to get up, but my body reacted slowly, too slowly. The dragons circled me, vast shadows hiding the sun.

One roared, the sound splitting the air, and I braced myself. It was over, and I was overcome with sadness at the thought that I would never be able to hold Emerald in my arms again. My wolf snarled in defiance, but even his strength was fading.

The pale dragon rushed forward, talons closing around me. My claws scraped helplessly against the scaled grip as the ground fell away. The plain dwindled beneath me, the forest swelling into a sea of green.

I lost track of time as we flew, too hurt to keep track. Maybe I had blacked out, I wasn't sure. Finally, the dragon descended into a strange grove.

The trees were tightly packed, too close to pass through, forming a kind of barrier that prevented escape. It was like a living cage. Every space between the trees was occupied by another dragon.

Trees shifted to create an opening. The pale dragon dropped me roughly onto the ground. Dirt and roots came flying toward me, and I let out a cry of pain upon impact. My body hurt, but I knew I had to try to get away. Before I could rise, the trees shifted again and closed tighter, sealing me in.

No chains. Just the forest itself, alive and intent on keeping me.

I looked up. Dragons circled the clearing, silent and observing. I had escaped vampires, kings, and gods. But here, surrounded by dragons, I felt something colder than fear—insignificance.

I drew one ragged breath, glaring at the pale dragon that had taken me.

"You mean to kill me?" I rasped.

The dragon stared. It didn't respond, didn't even make an effort to roar.

I was still breathing hard, crouched low in the dirt, when the dragons stirred. Their great heads lifted as one, turning toward the edge of the living cage.

Light rippled through the forest. It flowed like water through the branches, bending the shadows away. Magical light.

Then she stepped into the clearing. An elf.

She moved with that impossible grace they all had—not human, not divine, but something caught between. Her cloak brushed against the roots, her hair a mix of white and purple, and she had magical jewels embedded into her skin. The dragons bowed their heads as she passed, the light following her. I once enjoyed the presence of elves, but my recent whereabouts with Erendriel had changed my view of them.

I rose slowly, dried blood on my jaw, eyes narrowing.

So that was it. The dragons had brought me here for her.

"Another elf," I rasped, voice rough as gravel. "Is that how it is? You caught me to deliver me to your king?"

Her eyes studied me in silence. She ignored my question. "So, you're the one they found."

I barked a mirthless laugh. "You say it like it's a disease."

"I had my share of troubles with vampires. You're vampire and wolf—born of darkness both. Nothing good can come out of your presence."

I took a step forward, rage tightening inside me. I wanted to lunge at her and free myself, but the dragons would kill me in no time.

"Spare me your sanctimonious tone. Your kind calls themselves pure, but I've seen your king's purity." I spat at the ground. "He bought her. Like cattle. A woman who deserved more than all your gilded palaces."

Her expression flickered—a small, almost imperceptible reaction. "Who?"

"The woman I love," I growled. "Taken by your king. Imprisoned like a trophy." My eyes burned crimson. "And if you think I'm going to stop because dragons are growling or elves are shooting arrows at me, you're wrong. I'll rip your cities apart stone by stone. I'll fight a thousand dragons if I must. I'll kill your king and take her back."

My words echoed through the grove, and the dragons shifted, their scales scraping like thunder.

But the elf didn't flinch. She only regarded me with quiet intensity—as if weighing something unseen.

Finally, she said, "The Oracle spoke of you. You are dangerous."

I froze. I knew where this was going. It was never a good thing when people spoke of the Oracle.

"She spoke of the one who carries both curse and crown. The one who would bring the end of the world."

Her tone wasn't mocking. It was careful—controlled.

I bared my teeth in a humorless smile. "I ruled to keep the peace for centuries before being usurped by a traitor. All I want is to get the woman I love back. Let me out!"

She studied me a moment longer—something conflicted flashing in her gaze. Then she turned to the dragons, her voice cutting through the air.

"Keep him here," she ordered. "Do not harm him. Do not let him leave. I will decide his fate."

The dragons bowed low, their eyes glinting gold.

I took a step forward, fists clenching. "You think you can decide my fate?"

But she was already walking away, light spilling in her wake, her voice fading like mist.

"No," she said quietly. "Your fate has already been decided for you even before you were born."

And then she was gone, leaving me surrounded by dragons and trees that breathed like sentinels, and a silence heavy enough to crush the heart. I cursed and hit the ground with my fist. I couldn't escape the cage. I couldn't fly away. I was powerless. I screamed in rage, screamed with all my might. I pounded until my knuckles bled and the ground was carved with the shape of my fist. Finally, I resigned myself to waiting, to see what *Fate* had decided for me, as she said, as there was nothing more for me to do.

Chapter 26 (Caleb)

Aeris

Aeris stood there, angrier than I had ever seen her. A murderous aura emanated from her, her eyes black, her wings spread wide. At her side stood a group of harpies and orcs. She must have alerted the surrounding camp. Her wings fluttered as she paced back and forth.

"I don't know how you managed to break our bond, but I will not forgive you for this."

I wasn't sure either. My best guess was that it was the fated mate bond with Summer, but I wasn't about to tell her that the bond given by the Moon Goddess, her sister, whom she hated, was the cause of this. I remained silent and waited for her to continue speaking.

"I admit I never imagined you would come here, of all places. Well done. You escaped death for a few days, but now you will pay the price for your betrayal."

Her last words were so full of resentment that I could feel it hanging in the air.

"Kill them, but leave Caleb to me," she said angrily.

The harpies and orcs threw themselves at us. We were vastly outnumbered, but I managed to kill the first orcs that attacked us. Darryl hastily applied an acid potion to his weapon before slicing through the enemies. Paisley was defenseless, hiding behind us, too weak to fight. Summer transformed into her wolf and tore the attackers' skin with her sharp teeth and claws. We held strong against the first few waves.

I didn't even have time to react before I found myself on the ground, Aeris on top of me, pinning me.

"You think you're so strong, do you?" she asked with a snicker. "But you're not strong enough," she spat.

She hit with the force of a storm. I gritted my teeth, refraining from screaming as it would give her satisfaction. The familiar taste of blood filled my mouth. This wasn't good. At this rate, I might get killed. For the first time in centuries, I felt small.

"Hang on, I'm coming," I heard Summer say through our bond, and I could sense how much she struggled against the other attackers. She'd get killed if she interfered between the goddess and me.

"Don't," I pushed back.

Aeris smiled wickedly when she spotted her. "So, the werewolf is alive. I should kill her."

My blood boiled at those words. It felt as if I had molten lava flowing through my veins.

I roared, "You will not touch her."

A force pushed out of me, shoving the goddess off me, taken by surprise. I forced myself up, trembling. My head was filled with thoughts of fire and raw destruction. A sound like distant wings filled the morning. Scales of light flickered over my skin before fading. When I looked at my shadow, I could see smoke wings, though there was nothing if I looked at my back.

The ground rippled beneath my feet. Aeris looked at me in shock.

When she struck again, I met her with a growl. The impact sent waves of energy outward, gouging a furrow in the earth and snapping trees like twigs. She stumbled, her divine grace faltering under the sudden assault. I advanced, faster, harder, relentless.

"You annoying worm," she spat. "I will not rest until I get rid of you and that bitch."

That's when I realized I had to kill the goddess, if it was even possible. I would never be able to live peacefully with Summer if the goddess were alive.

I doubled my attacks, and she did the same. Each blow I struck burned brighter than the last, the dragon's fire setting the air ablaze. The goddess let out a shrill cry, her arm splitting open where my blade had pierced her flesh, a wound that smoked and bled light. She staggered backward in disbelief, and even I was wondering what was happening to me.

"How are you so strong?"

I was sure it was related to the dragon blood. I stepped forward, my fangs bared, my sword dripping with divine blood. I said resolutely. "Your death is overdue."

She faltered, retreating before my power. "This isn't over," she spat before running away.

I turned my attention to Summer, Darryl, and Paisley. The orcs continued to attack, and they were barely holding on. I lunged at them and decimated the enemies.

"There are too many of them, come on!" I shouted.

I covered their backs as we fled. I was glad to see that the potion Darryl had given his sister allowed her to run. At least we had a chance to escape the orcs, but they were everywhere. No matter how many I killed, more came. It bought us a little time at best. We fled without looking where we were going. I no longer knew which direction our camp was in. I could have flown away with Summer, but that would have meant abandoning Darryl and Paisley to their deaths. I would never have done that.

We finally arrived at the entrance to an underground passage. It had once been a human structure, but now it was nothing more than a ruin leading underground.

"Inside," I ordered.

Summer signaled to Darryl and Paisley to ensure they had heard.

"But we'll be trapped," Darryl pleaded through the orcs' cries.

"It's the only way," I replied.

We ventured into the ruins. Outside light came from old, half-broken windows embedded in the ceiling, which was several dozen feet high. We descended several steps into a wide tunnel with concrete walls, on which remnants of colorful ceramic mosaic murals remained. This deep, we only had faint light coming from above, but it was enough even for Darryl and his sister to see where we were going. We eventually came to an intersection after descending very deep underground, finding dozens of collapsed tunnels. Only one was intact. I wondered for a moment what this place had once been used for, but didn't have time to think about it. There was only one path to follow.

The tunnel was smaller, made of brick, and full of cobwebs. The outside light didn't reach us here. Darryl rummaged around in his bag and got two vials out. He mixed them together in the larger one. The liquid immediately began to glow with a greenish light.

"That should provide light for several hours," he said with a smile.

A strong smell of mold filled my nose. Clearly, no one had been here recently, except for the rats, who scattered as we passed. The tunnel's height allowed us to keep running, but as we went on, it narrowed further. We soon had to walk, and even crawl.

I brought up the rear, making sure the orcs didn't catch up with us. I could still hear them chasing us. The only thing that reassured me was that they were bigger and heavier than we were, so they would have more trouble navigating these tunnels than we did. That should give us an advantage.

Suddenly, the ground shook, forcing us to stop. Dirt and rocks fell on our heads. I rushed to protect Summer, covering her with my body, fearing that the ceiling would collapse on us. Paisley took refuge in her brother's arms.

The seconds felt like eternity as larger rocks fell, the ground shaking harder with a deafening rumble. I hoped this old tunnel wouldn't become our grave. I held Summer tightly in my arms, her heart pounding into mine. I saw a rock the size of a cannonball tumble toward Darryl. Quickly, I used my vampire powers to deflect the rock. When the ground finally stopped shaking, the silence was deafening.

"We have to get out of here," Summer said.

I nodded. I could no longer hear the orcs. I took a few steps back to see if they were still following us. I noticed that the tunnel behind us had collapsed entirely. At least we were no longer in danger of being attacked. I just hoped we would find a way out further on.

"Well, looks like there's only one way to go," Paisley murmured in a grim tone.

"Let's hurry," I pressed.

The further we went, the less structured the tunnel became. The carefully stacked bricks gave way to piles of rocks and earth. The smell of sulfur gradually replaced that of mold.

We walked in silence, no one daring to speak, for fear of saying aloud what we were all thinking: that there would be no way out. We eventually came to a strange structure that marked the entrance to . . . something. The top looked like the head of a giant rock creature. Its eyes were round, and it looked frightened. Its mouth was wide open, revealing only two sharp fangs at the top. A foul odor emanated from its mouth. There was no other path than the one leading into its mouth, where stairs disappeared into darkness. In any case, turning back was out of the question.

"There's only one way," I said.

Darryl's hand landed on my arm, stopping me from venturing in. "Stop. It's the entrance to the gate to the Underworld."

I stared at the entrance. "I would have expected something grander than this."

The man was outraged. "Are you kidding me? This is the entrance mentioned in the old books. It's too dangerous to go there."

"Well, didn't you say you were tasked with closing it?" I asked.

The man nodded nervously. "In reality, I only joined the battalion to save my sister. I was planning to leave before it got to closing the gate."

"You did?" Paisley asked.

The man nodded. "Ever since I learned that you were still alive, I have been wanting to find you. Maybe even meet with our father, even if I hate him for running away with you."

She stared at the ground. "Our father was sacrificed by the high priestess Samantha years ago. A gift to appease the gods."

Darryl clenched his fists in anger.

I sighed at the mention of Samantha. It seemed that every time her name was mentioned, it was because she had caused trouble. The two of them chatted away. The urgency to find a way out pulled at me, but I knew it was important for everyone to get some rest.

Eventually, when they were done talking, I asked, "Does anyone have food?"

"I have some rations," said Darryl.

I was relieved by the man's answer. We would have been in trouble otherwise.

He opened his bag and got some dried meat and fruit. He handed me a portion, but I refused. "I'll be fine," I said, wanting to keep the food for my mate and the humans. They needed it more than I did. In any case, I could drink blood if I were too starved.

I sat, wrapping my arms around Summer while she ate with the others. I felt as safe as one could be near the entrance to the Underworld.

Darryl had much to tell his sister. We listened to the man's tale. Nathan was mentioned several times, and I realized how much the ex-king meant to him. Then we listened to Paisley's tale of everything she'd seen and endured with the Miłonblooders. I had never been a follower of the religion, but now that I had heard everything she had to say, I despised them. When everyone was done talking, I offered to take the first watch so they could rest. And so I listened to their steady breathing as I kept an eye on the gaping entrance, expecting to see orcs or demons come out at any moment.

Chapter 27 (Elaine)

Facing Destiny

I returned to our tent, trembling. The dragons had captured someone near our camp. At first, I thought it was one of the queen's vampires searching for me. She must have known by now that I was gone. I was shocked when I saw it was Nathan. I never expected to find him here. I assumed he had the worst intentions, because of the Oracle. But when I heard his reasons for being here . . . that he was going to Mytvathyr, and that Erendriel had bought the woman he loved. *Bought* her. Like she was an object, and now he *owned* her.

The thought disgusted me.

What was the king thinking? This confirmed the prophecy. At first, I had thought I had to fight the Miłonblooders. But now that I saw how far he had strayed from the just and pure king I had once known, I realized that it was Erendriel I had to fight, and it broke my heart. He had raised me almost like a father.

"Well?" asked Akael when I arrived. He had gone to discuss with his generals, so he hadn't accompanied me. His smile faded when he saw the state I was in. He rushed toward me and wrapped his arms around me. I relaxed in his comforting embrace, laying my head on his shoulder.

"Are you alright?" he whispered in my ear.

"The prisoner. It's the Cursed King," I answered.

I didn't need to add any details. The title alone was enough. My nerves shot back up, and I paced as I recounted everything. "The prophecy said he would bring the world's end. I thought he was an enemy. That he was a mindless killer, a *monster*. But that's not the man I saw."

"Really, then what is it that you saw?" Akael asked.

I took a deep breath. "He's broken, fueled by the hope of claiming back the woman he loves from the clutches of Erendriel. I'm so confused."

Akael scratched his chin as he thought. "The prophecy did say that he would bring about the end of the world, but the prophecy did not specify what or how."

I frowned, hands on my hips. "What do you mean by that?"

Akael's lips curled into a smile.

"Well, Erendriel conquered the dwarves, didn't he? In a sense, you could say that it's the end of the world compared to what it was before. And if we overthrow the elven king, that would be another radical change that could be described as such. When you think about it, are all ends of the world bad? Or can they be positive?"

I paused, thinking about what he had just said. "That actually makes a lot of sense. So what you're saying is that Nathan could bring something to the world that's not necessarily bad."

He nodded. "Having a vampire-werewolf hybrid on our side might be useful. If the prophecy tells the truth, then he is probably very powerful."

I took a deep breath, weighing our options and the prophecy. The choice was obvious, and we faced a common enemy. "We should offer him an alliance."

The elf beside me smiled. "I agree. In what condition is he?" he asked.

"Wounded and dirty," I replied, thinking back to how the hybrid had looked in his prison. "And not in a very good mood, rather aggressive."

Akael tilted his head to one side, his long hair falling, his eyes playful. "Quite understandable, given how the dragons apprehended him."

I nodded, a slight smile playing on my face. "We should bring him something to eat and to clean himself up with," I suggested.

"A healing spell?" added Akael.

I shook my head. "He's a vampire and a werewolf. It's common knowledge that both races have healing powers. He should be fine."

The elf nodded, and we left together. I was in a better mood, though apprehensive. Our previous encounter hadn't gone well. We stopped at the tent where meals were being prepared and took a portion for our prisoner. Akael took a damp cloth and brought it with him.

When we returned to the cell, the dragons and branches parted to let us in. Nathan was kneeling on the ground. I could see marks dug into the dirt, shaped like his knuckles. He was in a terrible mood, his eyes still filled with rage. I didn't know exactly what I had expected, but he was even more irritated than I had imagined.

"We've come to bring you some food," I said, not quite sure how to start this awkward conversation.

"And a cloth to wash away the dust and dirt," added Akael kindly.

Nathan stared, a growl escaping from his chest. I wondered if he was going to lunge at us. As a vampire, I was sure he could pick up on my nerves, but I tried to hide it anyway.

"I'm Elaine, and this is Prince Akael," I continued, trying to think of something to say.

"Are you expecting a bow, *Your Majesty*?" he asked mockingly, almost spitting the last words.

I sighed. This wasn't the reaction I had hoped for. I hadn't intended for it to sound that way. "No," replied Akael. "We're here to talk."

"Talk about what? What fate has decided for me?" he retorted.

I took a breath. This was all my fault, and it was my duty to get us out of this mess. "The Oracle did speak of you, it's true. She predicted you would end the world. But here's the thing: if it means the end of Erendriel's reign, then it's an end of the world that I also long for."

Nathan's eyes widened in surprise, and his tone softened slightly. Akael stepped forward and offered him the damp cloth. He looked at it for a moment, then reached for it. He began to clean his face, which was stained with blood and dirt.

I continued, "The king has been tainted with darkness. You're right, elves are no better than vampires, and I've been unfair. My experience with the vampire queen hasn't been good. Show me that not all vampires are bad. My goal is to put an end to Erendriel's reign."

Nathan's hazel eyes were now staring intently at me. His gaze was animated by a deep fire, filled with determination. Without the blood and dirt, I found myself thinking that he was handsome.

He handed the cloth to Akael, who took it.

Nathan gestured toward me, and I had to restrain myself from backing away. I was still nervous, but his aggressiveness was gone. He took the plate I had brought, which I had almost forgotten I was holding in my hands.

"We want to offer you an alliance," said Akael as Nathan ate a grapefruit.

"All the alliances I've recently had ended in attempts on my life," he replied bitterly.

"Understandable," Akael said. "Being royalty tends to lower your life expectancy." He sounded like he spoke from experience, and I felt bad for him. I made a mental note to ask about it when we'd be alone.

Nathan continued between bites. "You imprison me, then expect me to trust you based on your word that you want to get rid of Erendriel?"

"How do you plan to defeat an army alone?" challenged Akael.

"Do you have an army at your disposal?" retorted Nathan, looking around himself.

The prince nodded with a smile. "We have an encampment nearby. An army of elves and dragons."

I added, "Our sentries report that Erendriel now has an army of mutants at his disposal. A few have been spotted."

"Mutants?" Nathan asked, frowning.

"We're not entirely sure how he came into possession of them, but we're no longer dealing with just elves," I replied.

We told Nathan about the prophecy and how Akael had found me imprisoned in the vampire castle, and how I was the queen of dragons, destined to rule over the elves. Nathan listened to every detail. He told us how Samantha had usurped his throne, how Emerald had disappeared, and how Erendriel had bought her from a slave trader. We spoke for quite some time. When everything was said, we remained silent for a moment. A dragon flew low over the forest, completely blocking the sunlight filtering through the trees, its shadow momentarily covering us.

A faint smile finally appeared on Nathan's face. "Alright, I'm willing to try to trust you. The dragons will be valuable allies against an army of mutants, which I have very little chance of defeating on my own anyway."

He held his hand out to me. "For Erendriel's death."

I smiled and grabbed his hand. "For the king's death."

"Come on, let's get out of here," said Akael. We showed Nathan around the camp, then headed to our tent. There, we prepared our strategy. One of Akael's generals was already waiting for us. He gave us all the necessary details.

"Our attack will be in two stages. We already have troops in Mumbur. We will launch the assault there to draw the troops to that location. Once the attack is underway, we will advance toward Mytvathyr, charging from the south. That way, our two armies can advance to meet somewhere and take both kingdoms from the elven king."

"And then what?" asked Nathan. "Rule over both kingdoms?"

I shook my head. "I want to restore the dwarven kingdom to its people. The royal family has been decimated, but there must be someone worthy left who wants to rebuild their country."

Nathan smiled at my answer. "As a king, this is exactly what I would have done."

A question popped into my mind. "You were king before. What will you do once you've found the woman you love?"

His stare darkened, and he clenched his fists. "I will take back my throne, and I will restore the laws as they should be. Respect for humans among vampires, peace with other races."

"That is a noble cause with good intentions," said Akael.

Nathan added, "The werewolves and humans have already given me their support."

I didn't need to ask Akael for his opinion. I knew that he would agree with me. The vampires had allied with Erendriel in the war after all. The vampire queen, the Miłonblooders, and the war were an integral part of the darkness that I needed to fight. "Then you will also have our support."

Nathan's smile was sincere and pure. "I am grateful to you."

A soldier came running up. "My prince, we are ready to send the message to Mumbur."

Akael nodded, satisfied. "Ah, just in time. Let's go."

I followed him, with the general and Nathan behind us. On the way, I spotted a juvenile dragon with blue scales, the size of a carriage, lounging next to a supply tent. His eyes were half-closed in bliss, while a young elf soldier brushed his jaws with a comb carved from bone. Every few strokes, the dragon's enormous tail would strike the ground in pleasure, nearly knocking over a passing scribe who darted aside with a curse. I held back my laughter, finding the scene amusing. It was a welcome respite from the severity of the moment. The juvenile dragon sensed my presence and opened his eyes as I passed by.

We arrived in front of a tent. Inside, the air was thick with mana, and in the center stood a mage with a grimoire in front of him. I could have sent the message myself, and I had even offered to do so to Akael, but he had insisted. As the future queen, he wanted to save my mana for things more important than sending a message. I didn't argue with him, gradually adjusting to my higher rank.

At Akael's signal, the mage recited the words. It was a simple spell that I knew by heart. Moments later, a glass-like portal opened in the air. On the other side, we could see a room that was probably a ship. The wood was polished, and the small windows were trimmed with brass. There was a large table with a map, a compass, and scrolls, all held in place by stones. An unlit lantern hung from the ceiling. Seated at the table was an elf. Her long blond hair was tied back under a red scarf adorned with an orange flame.

"It's good to see you, Your Majesty," she said when she saw us, her red eyes shining.

"Captain Highdrich. As you can see, I am well, and I have found the one I was looking for," he said, motioning to me.

The elf smiled and replied, "It is an honor to meet my queen."

I realized she was addressing me. "And the pleasure is mine," I replied.

"Are the troops ready?" asked Akael.

"Yes, Your Majesty. The elven king sent a note yesterday asking us to weigh anchor and depart, but we pretended we needed to fill the ships with provisions. It's still early morning, but we anticipate that they'll ask again."

Akael answered, "Let's not delay then. Prepare the troops and begin the attack. We are in position and will advance on the city. We will be there by tomorrow morning. This will give the king's troops time to leave Mytvathyr and then fall back when we arrive. With good timing, this will basically leave both cities defenseless."

"Understood," replied the elf before bowing and leaving.

The mage in the tent stopped casting his spell. I took a deep breath, nervous. So much had happened so quickly. I was still learning how to work as a team with Safira, and all this didn't leave me much time. Tomorrow, we would attack my home, my city. I would face my destiny, and we would see whether the prophecy was right that I was *veneficus dei*.

Chapter 28 (Erendriel)

Storm of Ash and Treason

Morning light spilled across the stone courtyard as I stepped outside, the cool breeze brushing against my face. Sleep had dulled the edge of exhaustion but sharpened the memories instead. The troll's death, the humming beneath the earth, the Oracle's prophecy carved in ancient stone—all of it weighed on me like a second cloak. My only chance in avoiding the prophecy was to kill Nathan, and fast. Luckily, I had the perfect bait to get him to come and see me. Emerald had probably arrived in Mytvathyr by now. It was only a matter of time before he went to the castle. I needed to be ready for when he came.

The town was still quiet. The mountain air carried scents of damp stone, metal, and the distant water. When I reached the outer ramparts, I paused. Below, the dwarven port shimmered in the gold-blue haze of dawn.

And there, undeniably, the prince's ships were still anchored, their sails decorated with their iconic orange flame, ruining the view.

I frowned.

I told the generals to send them off yesterday.

I descended toward the port.

Merchants prepared their stalls for the fast-approaching morning, moving crates, filling their stalls, while dwarf children ran and played among the goods, threatening to knock over stacks of crates. Destruction hadn't hit here. For the first time in days, I felt a flicker of warmth at the simple bustle of life.

Crewmen of the prince's fleet moved with disciplined speed. A sailor noticed me approaching and bowed sharply. "Your Majesty."

"I would like to speak to the prince," I announced, prepared to board the biggest boat, the one that would hold Akael.

The sailor had an apologetic look on his face. "I'm afraid His Majesty is busy with final preparations. We're almost loaded. Departure is imminent."

This was irritating, but it was good that they would leave soon. It made sense that the prince was probably busy checking the supplies before leaving. I studied the sailor. A polite façade, but tension simmered beneath. I nodded and let it go. He was probably not accustomed to speaking with foreign royalty.

"See that you depart before noon," I said sternly.

"Yes, Your Majesty. It will be done," the sailor answered politely.

I turned back toward the castle. I had much to discuss with my generals.

The meeting with my generals dragged into its third hour. Maps littered the table, marked with lines of destruction, and parchments of costs and required help. Dwarven engineers argued about collapsed tunnels, captains reported shortages, stone masons pleaded for more men.

I listened, responded, and planned. The message had been sent to Mytvathyr. We would get some help, but it would take days.

A pounding of boots shattered the discussion. A guard burst through the doors, breathless, helmet askew.

"Your Majesty," he gasped, "we're under attack!"

The room froze.

"From where?" I demanded, already rising from my seat. Were the werewolves and humans attacking from the desert, as I had suspected? They were acting sooner than I had anticipated. We'd need our mages to cast fire on the desert to block them.

"From the prince's fleet, sire. His soldiers have disembarked from the ships. They're storming the port district."

Silence fell, sharp as a blade.

Fury surged through my veins. The memory of his sailor this morning came back to me. I would crush his head if I saw him again.

"So this was his intention all along," I muttered.

I wasted no time. I gathered Ritori, one of our mages, a slender woman dressed in a dark blue robe.

"Send a message to Mytvathyr *now*. Inform them that the Sun Kingdom has betrayed our hospitality and launched an assault."

The mage raised her hands and began the incantation.

I strode to the balcony that overlooked the courtyard. "And fetch me a peregrine flacon," I ordered a passing guard.

Within minutes, a large blue-gray falcon landed on the leather armguard protecting my arm, its eyes shining like polished obsidian. I tied a sealed letter to its leg—a letter laced with iron-edged words.

"To the vampire queen," I said aloud, ensuring every general in the room heard. "Inform her that our alliance is being tested. She will send assistance *immediately*. If she refuses . . ."

I tightened the knot around the parchment.

"I will expose her attempt on Nathan's life, and the false attack she staged to hide it."

The bird of prey blinked once.

"Go," I murmured.

It launched into the air, its wings cutting across the sky.

Below, the distant sound of battle reached us—screams, metal clashing, smoke rising. After the initial attack we had perpetrated on the city to conquer it, this was the last thing we needed.

My jaw hardened.

Now, the sea brought war. If only I had my army of mutants here, but I needed them in Mytvathyr. They had to be ready. The war against the humans and werewolves in Mytvathyr would be much greater than a clash against the forces of the Sun Kingdom. I couldn't afford to move my troops.

There was no time to lose. I drew my sword and plunged into the streets, the echoes of combat pulling me toward the port like a tide. Smoke rolled between the stone houses, thick with the scent of burning tar and blood. Dwarven militia, or what was left of it, and elven soldiers clashed with the prince's soldiers beneath banners that had still flown in peace that morning. Now they burned.

My heart hammered as I sprinted down the sloping avenue. A group of guards stumbled past, dragging a bleeding comrade. One looked up and gasped.

"Your Majesty, they broke through the lower gates—"

"I will hold them," I growled. "Fall back to the upper line!"

They obeyed instantly.

I emerged onto the vast stone expanse overlooking the port and froze. The prince had not only come here with many ships, but he had also brought an army.

Sleek ships lined the piers, unloading wave after wave of armored soldiers, shields gleaming like polished obsidian. War mages stood on the decks, hurling arcs of lightning into the defenses. The port's outer walls were cracked, sagging under the force of repeated blasts. We were vastly outnumbered.

I raised my hand. Black fire coiled around my fingers, swirling like smoke and night. The flame roared from my palm, erupting into a sweeping discharge that consumed a line of enemy soldiers. Some screamed, while others vanished in a burst of ash.

But more surged forward.

I charged into the melee.

Steel clashed with steel. My sword carved through armor, and when blades pressed too close, I unleashed bursts of black fire that sent men flying backward. I had to find the prince. I was going to wipe that smug smile off his face forever.

A massive dwarf, covered in blood and wielding a double-axe, appeared at my side—one of the survivors from the dwarven army.

"Your Majesty! We stand with you!"

We fought back-to-back. We held our ground against fifty men, bodies piling beneath us. My black flames rained destruction. My arms trembled, and my throat burned from shouting commands.

For a moment—a heartbeat—hope flickered.

Then a horn blasted from the sea.

I turned.

Cannons shot fire. Hundreds more soldiers crowded the decks. My heart sank. There was no winning this.

Not here. Not today.

A crack of lightning struck the parapet beside me, sending dwarves tumbling. A second blast scorched the stone at my feet, throwing me to one knee. The rock was blackened by magic, and a smell like gunpowder hung in the air. The dwarf captain grabbed my arm.

"Your Majesty, fall back! They'll cut us off!"

I hesitated, then forced myself to look around. Bodies, smoke, fire—my people dying in the streets I'd sworn to protect.

I clenched my jaw until it hurt, a mix of shame and failure raging inside me. "Retreat," I whispered.

The dwarf stared at me, unsure of what I had said. "Sire?"

I rose, my sword dripping blackened embers. "*RETREAT!*" I roared.

The order rippled outward, and horns sounded. Dwarven and elven warriors disengaged, dragging the wounded behind them. I unleashed a final torrent of dark flames to buy us seconds, then sprinted up the avenue as more enemy troops poured into the lower city.

Stones cracked under my boots, and arrows hissed past my face. I reached the upper gate and slammed it shut with the help of dozens of soldiers, sealing off the burning port.

The enemy hammered at the lower walls, their war cry rising like a tidal wave. I looked back toward the castle looming above.

A siege was beginning.

I wiped blood—someone else's—off my cheek and ordered the elven captain beside me, "Prepare the inner defenses. Barricade every entrance. Hide what provisions we have left, and ready the mountain tunnels. If we fall here, the city must not."

The elven bowed grimly. "Aye, Your Majesty."

I took a long breath, tasting ash and the faint metallic tang of my own dark magic. I whispered to myself, "We will hold, Mumbur. I swear it, even if the mountain devours me next."

Behind me, the drums of the prince's army began to pound.

Chapter 29 (Samantha)

Threats, War, Death

I was still in my room, lying in bed with Viktor. His masculine scent intoxicated me. He was busy perfecting my pleasure with his fingers and tongue, caught up in a languid dance that I didn't want to break away from.

A knock came at the door.

I disregarded it, too lost in the moment to care about it.

But it came again. Persistent. Again and again, to a point where I couldn't ignore it anymore.

"Who is it?" I asked from the bed, trying to control my voice.

"A messenger, Your Majesty. It's urgent," the voice answered, sounding panicked.

I sighed. My moment with Viktor would have to wait. He had a sorry but understanding look on his face.

"Duty calls," he joked.

I half-smiled as I rose from the bed, dressing myself up. I waited for Viktor to put on his pants before answering. The messenger stood behind the door, pale, shaking, boots covered in mud. He bowed and offered me a sealed letter bearing the sigil of the elven king.

I huffed and broke the wax with a flick of my thumb. My jaw clenched, my fingers whitening around the parchment as I read.

The message was short—a demand and threat, but more importantly, a reminder.

Assist us in this war, as your oath binds you, or I will reveal the truth of Nathan's attempted execution—and the cover you crafted in blood.

My breath left me in a slow, controlled hiss. Magic sparks escaped my fingers.

"He dares," I whispered. "He *dares* think he can hold my own secrets over me?"

Viktor stepped closer, uneasy. "What will you do?"

I stared into the light filtering through the tall windows. "What I must. At least for now."

I would not kneel, but I would pretend.

"I must fulfill Alastor's prophecy, then I will make that bastard pay for the insult. Send our banners to the elven fronts," I instructed. "Enough soldiers to look cooperative. No more. Let him think I bend."

"Even though you swore we would not?" Viktor asked cautiously.

My smile was thin and venomous. "I swore an alliance. I will honor it for now. And then I will break him."

My mood soured, and I left the room, issuing orders to the guards. Word of the troops leaving spread through the town like wildfire. And with that came *murmurs*.

People questioned my judgment during the time of the dragons' attack. They questioned why a queen who claimed to protect them with a saint's relic would send their sons and daughters to die in an elven war.

Doubt festered. Anger simmered.

By dusk, protestors had gathered in the square with torches and crude banners. I watched them from the balcony, my eyes cold and unreadable as I heard their chants.

"These people forget who keeps them safe," I grumbled.

Viktor, beside me, shifted uncomfortably. "Perhaps they only need reassurance—"

"They need *order*," I said sharply. It was time to remind them of the cost of questioning me.

"Guards, with me," I said. I flew directly from the balcony toward the protesters, the guards following me. The protesters were too filled with rage to be afraid, as they should have been.

A haughty-looking vampire pointed at me and shouted, "Enough of the bloody queen!"

I dove straight at him. The crowd parted out of my way, but he stood his ground, thinking he could intimidate me with his polearm. The guards formed a security circle around me. My hand closed around the vampire's throat, taking him by surprise with my royal speed.

"With all the obscenities coming out of your mouth, I think it's high time you learned what it costs," I hissed.

The man tried to break free, but to no avail. I tried to force his mouth open, but the vampire struggled too much. I signaled to the guards to come and help me. They held the vampire in place, preventing him from moving. With both hands, I managed to open his mouth. I took out my knife and pulled the vampire's tongue out with my other hand. He desperately tried to close his mouth.

I whispered to him, "If you move too much, my knife will gouge your eyes out."

He froze at these words, cries of fear escaping his mouth. "When you dare talk against your queen, at least face the consequences with dignity," I huffed in annoyance.

I sliced his tongue with the blade of my knife as if it were butter. Blood filled his mouth, flowing greedily down his chin to his clothes while he coughed.

I said in a loud voice for everyone to hear, “This is what I do to dirty mouths who speak against me.”

People were indignant and screaming, but nothing could drown out the cries of agony coming from the vampire struggling in the guard’s grip. The tongue suddenly detached itself from the vampire, caught between my fingers like a piece of still-warm meat. I walked away from him, satisfied. “You can let him go,” I said to the guard.

The vampire fell to his knees, blood spurting from his mouth all over the floor. I held up the lifeless tongue in my hand to the protesters, who were shocked with horror. “Let this be a lesson to you.”

They were paralyzed, too stunned to move. I said to the guards, “Catch a few of them to set an example.”

At these words, the people ran. I flew to my balcony, satisfied, throwing the tongue away like trash. Viktor stood speechless when I returned.

“That’ll teach them,” I simply said.

He swallowed and nodded slowly. Viktor usually supported me. I’d have to explain to him the sacrifices required to rule so he would understand.

The next morning, the square held a different crowd—quieter, cowed, and pressed close together as royal guards lined the edges with drawn spears.

Five prisoners knelt on the stone platform. Some were agitators. While others were accused of spreading rumors. One of them, a baker, had refused to pay his taxes, demanding that I explain where the soldiers were going and why.

No one dared protest now.

I stepped onto the platform, dressed in my dark armor for the occasion. I had tried to be kind to them. I even risked my life to get a relic, but there was just no pleasing them. I was done being nice. It was time to remind them that their queen was also a fighter, someone not to be trifled with.

"For those who challenge stability," I announced, my voice carrying like a blade through the square, "there will be no mercy."

Fear was where true power lay, the only way to really maintain control. The executions were swift, brutal, and very, very public. By noon, the whispers had died. By nightfall, fear had a grip on the city like a closed fist.

Chapter 30 (Caleb)

The gate to the Underworld

The night had not been restful. I had heard noises coming from the gate to the Underworld several times. Each time, I had prepared myself to see a creature emerge, but there was nothing. However, it was becoming clear that we were not alone. There was something in there—something we would encounter when we ventured inside. For everyone's sake, I just hoped we would find an easy way out and avoid a fight. Paisley was in no shape to fight, and I didn't know how much Darryl could take. That left only Summer and me, and we couldn't take a whole army with just the two of us.

I remembered Anne's words. They had been tasked to close the gate to stop the flood of orcs from entering the land of the living. Ridiculous—they had no chance of doing it. I hated the queen for sending them here, and I regretted ever allying myself with her. I wondered how the old me had accepted doing her bidding. But who was I kidding? The old me would have agreed to anything as long as there was money.

Summer woke up slowly. “You should cuddle instead of overthinking,” she said.

I smiled. “You’re right,” I replied, joining her on the cold floor. Not the most comfortable bed, but beside her, it didn’t matter. The warmth of her body snuggled against mine eased my worries.

I had dozed off a little when Darryl and Paisley began to stir. Despite the darkness of the tunnel, I imagined it was morning.

“Do you have more glowing light?” asked Paisley to her brother.

Summer and I could see well in the dark since we were vampires and werewolves, but the two humans must have seen nothing but darkness.

“No,” the man replied sadly. “Are you feeling better?” he asked his sister.

Summer and I sat up, realizing there was no way we could sleep any longer, resigned to getting up.

Paisley nodded. “I think so.” She took a few seconds to assess her body. “Better than I have in weeks.”

“That’s good to hear,” replied the man.

Summer tore out some of the roots that were hanging down. “Do we have something to light this up?” she asked.

Darryl handed her a sharp stone and a piece of steel. Summer took them and rubbed them together with expert hands, quickly creating sparks, and set the roots alight. Darryl took some herbs from his bag and added them, creating a small fire that helped him and his sister see better.

"What's the plan for today?" asked Paisley.

"First, you need to eat. Do you still have rations?" I asked Darryl.

He opened his bag and searched around. "Yes, but I don't have much left."

"Okay. You eat, I'll wait," I replied.

"No way," Summer objected. "You didn't eat last night either."

I shook my head. "It's more important that you eat. I'm a vampire, I need less food than you do." It was only half true, but I would gladly let myself starve if it meant she was fine, but Summer's stare said it all. She had no intention of letting me do this.

"I'm fine," I lied.

She rolled her eyes. "Bullshit."

I shrugged my shoulders, trying to appear casual. "I'm not hungry, really. Just eat already."

Summer moved closer until her face was just inches from mine, her gaze hard. She was headstrong, and I loved that trait in her.

"If you don't eat, then you'll drink my blood before we leave. I won't have it any other way."

My mouth watered at the thought. She knew how to get to me. "I can't say no to that," I replied.

She smiled, satisfied. I stayed with them as they ate breakfast. My stomach disagreed with me not eating, but I didn't want to admit it. I waited patiently for them to be done.

As I got up to leave, Summer motioned to me. We walked a few steps back for more privacy.

"I won't take too much," I whispered.

Summer put her hand on my shoulder, pulling me closer. "Take as much as you need. I wouldn't want anything to happen to you. I love you."

Her words delighted me. I kissed her greedily, losing myself in the moment. "I love you too," I replied.

She hugged me. As she did so, she tilted her head to one side and pushed her beautiful black hair away from her neck, revealing her tempting skin. So irresistible. My teeth were already elongated, yearning for her.

She moaned when I bit her, her nails digging into the skin of my arm. My senses sharpened, and a primal need overcame me. I devoured her greedily, gulp after gulp. She was *mine*. I would not let anything come between us. She filled me in ways I couldn't describe, sating my thirst and hunger, amplifying my strength and powers, and making me fall under her spell and in love even more. My bloodlust calmed down as the hunger subsided. I suddenly realized that I had not paid attention to how much I had drunk. I hurried to remove my fangs from Summer's neck, letting my tongue linger to heal the spot. She was still holding on to me tightly, panting.

"Are you okay?" I asked, concerned that I might have drunk too much.

Her eyes rested on me, heavy with desire. Her breath was hot on my skin as she purred, "Yes."

How I wished I could take her right then and there.

"Did I take too much?" I felt the need to ask, even though I could sense her wolf was fine. She moved closer and kissed my neck, sending shivers down my spine.

"No, but I wished we were alone right now so I could do all the things I'd like to do to you."

Her heart beat fast. She teased my skin, running her fingers over it, and I sucked in a breath. I just wanted to be her slave, but we were trapped in that damn tunnel, so I held her tight. "I promise when this is all over, I'll be yours as many times as you want."

She nodded, biting her lower lip. "I know. It's too bad that we can't right now."

We joined Darryl and his sister, aware that we had only one way out of here and that we couldn't waste any more time. We had to be out of here by tomorrow; otherwise, we would run out of rations.

We cautiously entered the strange opening. I went first, and the others followed, joining hands so they knew where to go as it was pitch dark. If something were to attack, I would be the strongest to throw it off. The tunnel stretched endlessly, damp, dark, and echoing. As we moved forward, the walls were carved from a dull red ore, and light illuminated the space, coming from further away. At least Darryl and Paisley could see. Beads of dark water gathered on the ceiling and dripped in slow rhythms; the beginning of stalagmites. A small lizard ran by and hid in a crevice. The smell was a thick mixture of sulfur, metal, and decay, like flowers left too long in a closed room. It got hotter with every step I took.

We arrived at a crossroads where two paths diverged. Hope filled me when I caught the faint scent of fresh air coming from the tunnel to the right. Too faint for humans to get it, but I had no trouble picking it up. An escape waiting just beyond reach. To the left, a low rumble shook the earth, followed by a distant, inhuman scream. The light came from the tunnel to the left.

"The way out is just there," I told them, pointing to the right.

"I know, my wolf smelled it, too," answered Summer, a wide smile plastering her face.

The others nodded. "That's great, we can get out of here!" rejoiced Paisley.

Darryl hesitated, conflicted. He sighed. "I don't really want to do it, but we should check the other tunnel."

The others had a stunned look on their faces, but I nodded. "Agreed. We have come this far, and I doubt Anne and the soldiers could get all this way here without being butchered. We should check if we can close the gate to the Underworld."

They hesitated, but finally, Paisley nodded. She would follow her brother anywhere, even if she appeared frightened.

"We can always turn back and escape through the other tunnel if it's too dangerous," I added to reassure her. This was for the best.

We jumped as another loud growl came from further down. I clenched my fists and took the lead, and the others followed. We crept close enough to see a vast chamber. My breath caught.

A colossal arch of black magic glistened, its contours outlined by a line of white magic that shone in the darkness. Its surface swirled with shadow and fire. Through it, I could see the waters of the Styx, desolate and fiery landscapes, and an army of demons. All around the portal, on this side, the enemy gathered--hundreds of orcs armed for war, lower demons hunched on clawed limbs, and harpies clinging to the ceiling like grotesque birds.

At this rate, it was a miracle that only orcs rampaged on Krelgraz. It looked like they were getting ready to take on the world.

Summer whispered, “There are too many. We’ll never make it through.”

Darryl’s face had gone pale. “It’s even worse than I feared. If we leave it open, they’ll pour through.”

“What if they come in through another way?” asked Paisley.

Darryl shook his head. “The map said there was only one gate left open.”

My jaw tensed. He was right. It was only a matter of time before the army attacked. Judging by their numbers, they wouldn’t be satisfied with taking just one city. We were on the brink of a world war.

I turned to Darryl. “You were part of all the discussions with the battalion. Do you know how to close it?”

“There’s an incantation—a sealing rite. We were all taught it so that whoever reached the gate could close it. It’ll take several minutes.” Darryl’s voice wavered as he looked at his trembling hands. “It doesn’t require mana as it calls upon the gods to close the gate. I can do it, but I’ll need protection.”

I turned my gaze back to the horde, the swirling gate, and the tide of shadows gathering, then I looked at Summer. She was my future, my everything. Her chocolate eyes met mine, and in that instant, everything was said without words.

I had to protect her, no matter what.

“I’ll hold them off,” I said.

"Caleb, no—" she started. I felt her worry through our bond.

"Someone has to." My voice softened, my hand brushed her cheek. "You make sure he finishes that spell. Don't stop. No matter what happens."

Summer's eyes shone wet. "Please . . ."

I smiled faintly. "I'm harder to kill than I look."

Darryl knelt by the edge of the abyss and began to chant. I walked down the slope toward the gate, gathering my strength and magic—everything I had. I cleared my head of doubts, leaving only rage and conviction. It came down to this moment. For the world, for my mate, our future. I couldn't afford to lose. The air rippled around my body. They didn't even notice me when I reached them. I struck first, my sword cutting through the front ranks of orcs in an explosion of power.

The cavern erupted into chaos.

Demons shrieked, and harpies dove from above, claws outstretched. I was everywhere, my blade flashing, power blazing. The chamber became an inferno of magic fueled by the enemies and the blood of the dead. They were endless. For every one I killed, two more took their place.

From her cover, I felt Summers's eyes on me. From our bond, I felt her nerves screaming. She wanted to run to me, to tear through them, but she had to protect Darryl. I couldn't hear his voice from where I was, but I could see the effects of his incantation. The gate howled, light and shadow twisting violently as he spoke. Some creatures were searching for the source of the threat to their precious gate. I killed them immediately, trying to hide Darryl and the others for as long as possible.

Then, suddenly, the tide shifted.

A dozen demons chanted in unison, their eyes burning violet. The ground beneath me cracked, and chains of black fire burst upward, wrapping around my arms and legs too quickly for me to react. I was pinned to my knees, my arms raised toward the ceiling. I roared, pulling, but the magic held tight.

"No!" Summer shrieked, her voice weak amid the madness.

A handful of orcs heard her cry and headed toward her. I cursed. I couldn't kill them. I was trapped, powerless, but I had faith in my mate. She could hold them off as long as they were few in number.

I pulled on the chains as much as I could, but couldn't get myself free. I channeled the magic in me, but it was of no use. I was a prisoner of the demons and surrounded by orc blades, demon claws, and harpy talons. They lashed at me, stabbing, slashing, rejoicing at the sight of my blood flowing. I gritted my teeth, enduring the pain as they struck and stabbed, again and again. How many stabs had I endured? I had lost count. A hundred, maybe more . . . My ears were filled with the sound of steel digging into my own flesh, echoing through the tunnel, mingled with the creatures' cries of joy. My body convulsed with each blow, and blood flowed across the floor in dark rivers. The pain was so intense that I lost feeling, wavering between consciousness and death. How sweet a reward it seemed to die at that moment.

"Caleb!" Summer's voice broke in my head. I saw her in the distance, barely able to lift my head, through the bodies of the creatures swirling around me. The bodies of the orcs lay at her feet. *She had slain them. Good,* I thought. I saw her sprint toward me, but the ground shook. The gate drew in wind and dust. Though I couldn't hear it, I knew through our bond that Darryl's chant grew louder, faster, desperate.

My vision blurred. Pain became fire, fire became nothing. My strength was failing. The dragon's magic inside me faltered, then flared. A sound tore from my throat—not vampire, but something older, something that had slept beneath mountains and storms. My chains shattered as the sight of shadow wings came to be. My wounds still bled, but the fire inside me refused to die. The dragon blood wouldn't let me die.

The gate began to collapse.

A pull like a hurricane tore through the chamber. Orcs screamed as they were dragged backward into the vortex, their bodies twisting into shadow. Harpies clawed at the air before being ripped apart. Even the demons howled as their forms unraveled into smoke and ash.

And then it was over.

Silence fell—broken only by the soft crackle of dying fire. The gate was gone, sealed by Darryl's final word.

The chains disappeared. I collapsed to the ground and closed my eyes. Our duty was done. For once in my life, I had done something for the greater good rather than for myself. It was weird to feel this way. I felt . . . proud.

I heard footsteps running toward me. I knew without looking that it was her. I wanted to rise, to stare at her, to tell her I was fine, but I couldn't. Behind her came the sound of other footsteps.

It smelled of jasmine when she knelt beside me.

"The blood. There's so much—Caleb . . ." Her voice wavered as she spoke urgently. She turned me over, her hands shaking. My eyes fluttered open. I was glad to see her. She was so beautiful, so wonderful, and safe. My mate. My love.

"You're so pale," she commented.

I smiled weakly. "Told you . . . I'm hard to kill."

Tears streamed down her face as she pressed her forehead to mine. "Don't you dare die on me."

I lifted a trembling hand to her cheek, my touch barely there. "Not while you still need me."

"You need blood," she said instantly.

I shook my head. "No, I already drank from you today."

"There's no way I'm letting you die!" she raged, her last words ending in a roar from her wolf.

But I wouldn't drink from her, and she knew it. To do so would put her life at risk. Blood loss was dangerous. She turned around, looking distressed.

"Drink mine," said Darryl, who had joined us. "It's the least I can do for what you did."

Before I could say anything, Summer grabbed Darryl's forearm and brought it to my mouth. I couldn't object or say anything. My teeth lengthened as my survival instinct took over. It was like they were spoonfeeding me blood. I sank my teeth into the man's arm, and he let out a muffled cry.

His blood tasted like echinacea laced with mint. His thoughts connected with mine, and I understood the fire that burned within him. His deepest secrets were revealed to me. His father's abandonment, the life of misery he had lived, his hatred for Samantha, his faith in Nathan to restore order, and his relief at finding his sister. As I drank his blood, I was startled by a strange feeling that I hadn't expected to find: friendship. The fact that I was a vampire, that my past was dark, didn't matter to him. He accepted me as I was. I wasn't used to this. I was an assassin, had been for as long as I remembered. Assassins didn't have friends.

I withdrew my fangs from the man's arm, not wanting to take more. I could already feel the effects of the blood on me; my regenerative powers were amplified, and my wounds were already starting to heal.

Lost in my thoughts and Darryl's, which still lingered, I made a decision: to do everything in my power to help him restore Nathan to the throne and oppose the queen. The man had so much faith in him.

"Thank you," I said simply.

I lay there for a moment, regaining my strength, but I knew we couldn't stay there too long. We had almost no food rations left. We had to get out. Summer slowly helped me up, tears streaming down her cheeks, a broad smile on her face. It hurt, but I pushed through the pain.

"I will never abandon you," I told her as I kissed her, happy to be alive by her side. I was the luckiest vampire in the world. It was, in a way, a rebirth for me. The beginning of a second life, burying away my past as an assassin.

We looked up at the tunnel above us, knowing that the exit awaited us. I put my arm around Summer's waist.

"Come on, let's get out of here," I said. We started walking toward our freedom.

Chapter 31 (Erendriel)

We Will Not Fall

We had resisted the prince's siege for a day, but it was becoming increasingly clear that we would not win. The city was still wounded from my conquest, the soldiers were exhausted, and we had few supplies. I blamed myself for not being more wary of the Sun Kingdom. Sleep eluded me. I spent the night wondering if there had been signs I had missed, if I could have done things differently. As a result, my eyes were dry, and I struggled to read the map in front of me. The only thing keeping me awake was adrenaline and stress.

My hand trembled as I brought the cup of tea to my mouth. My generals listed the supplies we had. We could hold out for at most a week—so much for resisting the invader. It was a lost cause. Yet I stubbornly searched for a way out. There had to be one.

A mage burst into the council chamber, the door slamming shut with a crash, making me jump. I cursed as I spilled hot tea on myself, burning through the fabric of my pants. I put down my cup, my gaze turning to the mage before me, who seemed to understand what had just happened.

Her face was pale, and she held a scroll in her hand. It must have been urgent for her to burst into the room like that. I just hoped it was good news, even though I knew deep down that good news didn't arrive on a scroll in the hands of a panicked mage.

"A message from Mytvathyr, Your Majesty. It arrived by falcon."

My stomach tightened. I broke the seal. The words inside were sharp as blades:

"Humans and werewolves have been sighted south of the city. And dragons. They advance in great numbers. The war is starting. We can't send help to Mumbur."

I closed my eyes. A single breath escaped me—half grief, half fury. I had known this war was coming, but this was the worst possible timing ever. Was this the prophecy's doing?

I remembered the words: *"When fire rains from the sky, and the sun kisses the purest."*

If the sun represented the Sun Kingdom, then who was the purest? I shook my head. It didn't matter now.

Even if I wanted to fight on both fronts, I had to face the fact that Mumbur had already fallen. Given the state the city was in, there was no point in persevering. Mytvathyr was much more important and in better condition. It was my home, my kingdom.

I would die defending it if I had to. I lifted my gaze to the generals gathered around me. "We leave," I said. "Now. Mumbur is lost."

Gasps. A few curses. One elf slammed his fist on the table, beard trembling with rage. "But—"

"We cannot die here," I cut in, voice iron. "Not when the world is changing beneath our feet. We regroup at Mytvathyr and prepare for war."

No one argued again.

Orders flew and horns sounded. What was left of the Mumbur defenders gathered what they could: weapons, children, and injured comrades carried on makeshift litters. Some of the dwarves followed us, while others stayed here. It was their home, after all. I didn't care if they died defending it or surrendered to the enemy at this point. Smoke still rose from the lower city as we evacuated through the mountain gate.

I paused only once—turning back to look at the ancient dwarven stronghold. The port where I had fought, the walls I had bled for, were now swallowed by the invader. The orange flame on their armor and banners mocked me, ruining the sight.

"I will return," I whispered.

The escape route was safe, safer than trying to cross the desert. It was impossible to know if enemies waited for us in the sandy dunes. The mountain gate would allow us to avoid enemy troops since it was a path known only to dwarves, dug in ancient times.

"How many days before we reach Mytvathyr?" I asked.

One of the dwarf soldiers counted. "Three or four days, Your Majesty."

When war was at our doorstep, this wasn't good. "I need to get there faster," I barked.

Ritori approached, her hands trembling around a crystal shard pulsing faintly with light.

"This is the last teleportation spell I possess, Your Majesty. It will take only you."

I nodded once. It was necessary. "Do it."

The mage traced a rune with the crystal shard around me. The rune circle flared beneath my feet—white, then blue, then violet. A high-pitched whistling sound, like wind blowing through broken glass, filled the air. Then the world shattered and reformed.

I staggered as my boots struck carved marble. The familiar smell of Mytvathyr's forests drifted through the open archways—pine, earth, a faint sweetness from blooming moonvine.

I was home, in the palace.

A roar echoed from the training grounds. Not elven a not wholly beasts, either. I strode out onto the balcony overlooking the valley below the elven city.

My army of mutants waited there—twisted, powerful, loyal. Born from the runes' magic, shaped for war. Some bore scales like stone, while others wielded unnatural strength, wings folded, claws gleaming. A massive hybrid knelt when I appeared, bowing its horned head.

"My king," it rumbled.

My chest tightened with pride.

We were stronger than ever—stronger than when I left. And every one of them was waiting for my orders.

Jules stood apart, contemplating the army, a scroll in hand to take notes. He ran toward me when he saw me.

"You're back," he said breathlessly.

My lips curled into a smile. "You did well," I praised.

From the southern ridge, smoke rose, forming thin dark trails like fingers clawing at the sky. The enemy was already approaching. Humans and werewolves, while dragons blackened the sky like a threatening storm. Whatever alliance had been forged in the south, it was marching toward Mytvathyr with greed.

But this time, we wouldn't be caught unprepared. They weren't the only ones with winged creatures. With my mutants, we would prevail. Even dragons didn't scare me.

I stood tall, black fire curling around my fingers like eager serpents.

"Let them come," I said to Jules.

My mutants roared back—so loud the very trees trembled. A smile curled my lips upward, sharp and confident. "It is here," I whispered to the wind, "that we will stand. And this time, we will *not* fall."

Chapter 32 (Samantha)

Unexpected Ally

Even after the executions, the city refused to be quiet. Whispers slithered through taverns and around market stalls. Lanterns lit the night streets, not in celebration, but in vigilance.

The relic's faint glow didn't reassure anyone—they spoke of it with suspicion, fear, even resentment. I even overheard two of my servants say, *"Dragons may have vanished again, but the queen's tyranny is a danger of its own."* I killed the one who had spoken with my own hands in front of the other. The second woman didn't dare say anything after that.

More than once, guards dragged agitators from the crowds. Some openly accused me of selling the kingdom's future to elven wars, and others claimed the relic was cursed. Some even dared to whisper I was no longer the woman I once was.

I felt the tension like a tightening coil.

I still lacked the two essences needed to fulfill Alastor's prophecy: that of the human and that of the werewolf. Without them, the prophecy remained incomplete, and my grasp over the kingdom remained fragile. The orcs still launched attack after attack on the outskirts of the city. I was pissed at them, and at the battalion I had sent. They should have taken care of this already. Entire villages fled toward the capital gates; refugees crammed the streets, frightened, furious, desperate.

My soldiers struggled to keep the peace. My rule trembled beneath the weight of too many crises.

And all the while, I could feel Alastor stirring inside me—pushing me toward urgency, demanding I finish what I began.

If I failed . . . Alastor's rise would crumble. And I with it.

The night was moonless, the stars swallowed by a heavy, unnatural darkness. The palace torches flickered as though suffocating. I sat alone in my war chamber, staring at maps scattered across the table. Orc raids were marked in red, and rebellions in black.

The candle beside me went out, and a cold wind brushed my neck. A knock echoed.

"Come in," I said.

My pet entered, his human scent arousing no desire in me, so preoccupied was I. We still hadn't found Lysander, but given the current state of the city, I wouldn't trust anyone to take his place. There were enough people who wanted me dead; there was no way I was going to let one of them into my inner circle.

"A visitor wishes to see you, Your Majesty," he said.

At this hour? This was rather unusual. I frowned. "Who?"

He hesitated. "She asked to speak to you directly without revealing her name. She's unlike anything I've ever seen before, like she's made of . . ." He thought for a moment before finishing his sentence. "Made of clay. She has wings, too."

I was shocked by the description he gave of my visitor. "Wings, you say? That certainly sounds like someone I'd want to meet. You did well, Jason."

The man grinned at my praise.

"Bring her to the throne room. I will meet her there," I said. Viktor was out in town, trying to pick up on the new rumors so we could counter them.

Jason bowed and went away as I walked to the throne room. She was already waiting for me when I arrived, standing in a shadowy corner of the room. She looked just as Jason had described her. Her presence made me uneasy for reasons I didn't understand. She didn't kneel or move when I sat, but I felt her slow heartbeat through my vampire senses. It was slower than any living being I knew of. She was incredibly beautiful, but she was cold, both figuratively and literally. I considered asking her to bow and respect my title, but decided against it. I was more interested in knowing what she was.

"You look tired, my queen," she whispered—smooth, velvety, and chilling.

Her words felt like a warning, and I rose abruptly, hand on my dagger. “Step in the light.”

The woman stepped forward. She was battered and bruised, but still, she held herself high. Her wings quivered in the light, her eyes animated with incredible strength.

A small smile curved her lips. “I have waited a long time to meet you,” she said.

I stiffened, unsure of who she was or what she might want from me. “Why?”

The woman dipped her head, dragging something behind her. I realized it was an unconscious human being tied up with ropes. I had been so focused on her that I hadn't even noticed or heard the man's heartbeat. “We share a common goal, Your Majesty. I simply wish to help you.”

Her smile was wicked, and I didn't like it. “Which goal?”

Her smile widened even more, to a point where I wondered how it was physically possible. It gave her a crazy, diabolical look, and it made the hairs on the back of my neck stand. I gripped the handle of my dagger even tighter.

“Orc raids. Rebellion. A kingdom slipping beyond your grasp, and yet you lack what you need most—the human essence for Alastor's prophecy.”

My heartbeat quickened, suspicion and hunger tangling together. This was too good, too sudden. It didn't make sense. Surely this had to be a trap. Still, I couldn't pass up the chance that it might be true. “Are you a Miłonblooder?” I asked.

"Oh, child," the woman purred. "I knew Alastor long before you learned to walk. His visions still whisper through the void. And I have come to help you finish his work."

I stared, breath caught. She knew Alastor. What did that make her? She pulled the human forward.

"Who or what are you?" I asked, frowning.

The woman bowed slightly. "I am the goddess Aeris. This is my gift to you," she answered.

I couldn't hold back the gasp that escaped me at these words. I was talking to a goddess. This was beyond anything I had ever experienced before. Of course, Alastor had spoken to me when I prayed, but I had never seen a deity in the flesh. I reached out to the human, hesitant but hungry. I wanted him, *needed* him. I needed to fulfill Alastor's prophecy.

"Why?" I asked. "What do you want in return?"

Aeris's expression softened into something almost affectionate and infinitely dangerous. "To stand beside the queen who will reshape the world," she whispered. "To guide you. To watch you ascend."

"And the cost?" I pressed. Nothing was free in this world.

Aeris leaned in close, her breath cool as frost. "When Caleb comes, crush him like the bug he is."

The incompetent vampire I had hired to kill Nathan, who had failed. I would take pleasure in ending his life. He would be no problem.

I swallowed hard—fear, excitement, and the prophecy roaring in my blood. With the human essence, all I'd need to fulfill

Alastor's prophecy would be the werewolf essence. He would be happy with me. I would finally be able to resurrect him and be the vessel I was meant to be.

Chapter 33 (Nathan)

The Assault on Mytvathyr

Adrenaline rushed through me as we walked through the forest in silence. The dragons flew above us, following their queen. I still found it hard to fully realize that these majestic beasts were in our army. It seemed unreal, like I was in a dream. I pushed aside a fir branch and stepped over a fallen log. The night was quiet, and the insects sang, unaware of the gravity of our goal. I took a deep breath, enjoying the silvery light of the moon on my skin. I knew the sun would soon rise, and with it would come the chaos.

Akael's generals reported that the attack on Mumbur had begun in the afternoon and had been a huge success. It seemed that the city was almost defenseless, offering little to no resistance.

With the resources stored in the ships, they could hold out for weeks. With this distraction, Erendriel should be disorganized. That should give us the advantage during the assault on Mytvathyr.

Our forces were impressive. We had encountered the humans and werewolves along the way. I was glad to see that Brooke, from the Luscious Woods pack, had recovered and was standing proudly beside her Alpha. They had joined Etienne and his pack, along with dozens of other packs from all around. St. Selena's human army was also with them. Their armor had been reinforced to counter spells, glowing with a faint blue light that was easily recognizable.

In total, our three armies had several thousand soldiers. I could never have hoped to have so many at our disposal.

My wolf grew restless as we drew nearer. At last, we were heading for the elven city. At last, I would recover the woman of my life.

Hang in there, I thought, hoping she could hear me. I put my hand in my pocket, found the strand of hair, and touched it without realizing it. Not being able to talk to her and know how she was doing was driving me crazy. If our bond had been sealed, it would have made this much easier. I would have her in my arms already. When I found her again, I would mark her and make her mine, so that this would never happen again.

The events of the previous day came back to me. Elaine had seemed so cold when we first met. I was bruised and battered, helpless, and subjugated by the dragons. I had expected her to announce my death when she returned. I was ready to jump on her even though I knew the dragons would tear me apart with their talons.

I was thankful to find an ally in her, though. As master of the dragons, alongside the prince, she would be a powerful ally. Her cause was noble, and I could sense the purity in her. As for Akael, he was fire, that much was obvious. Together, they would rule over the dragons and the elves, liberate the dwarves. It was the right thing to do.

"How do you communicate with them?" I asked as we walked.

"I'm not sure how to explain it. It just happens naturally."

I nodded. "Then it's exactly how I communicate with my wolf," I replied.

Her eyes widened. "Oh, really? It's obvious now that you mention it, but I never thought about it."

"Can you feel their emotions, too?" I asked.

"Only Safira's."

My eyes turned to the sky, to the white dragon that was following us closest. She had told me how they were connected. "It makes sense. You're so close to her."

"We're approaching the city," Akael shouted.

Normally, we would be silent before an attack, but with an army of dragons following us from the sky, it was pointless. I could already see people panicking on the city's defensive walls. They shot arrows and cast spells at the beasts. Ballistae fired, and the dragons dove to avoid the shots.

The city was as elegant as ever, bathed in beauty, but the soldiers standing on its ramparts were another matter. Some were elf-like in form, though a malevolent energy emanated from them, palpable even from a distance. They had become something sinister and deadly. Their eyes glowed with the king's colorless magic.

As for the others . . . Elaine's sources had told the truth. Transformed, with extra limbs, they were nothing more than bloodthirsty creatures, mutants. It was horrific. The city was well protected despite the diversion at Mumbur. It was going to be a difficult fight, but I was confident in our forces.

The ground shook when Safira landed. Elaine immediately climbed onto her back, and a private conversation ensued between them. They took off, while the prince remained on the ground to lead the attack. I watched them rise to the sky. A pale golden light crept over the horizon, reflecting off armor and scales, glinting off drawn blades. The air was cold, crisp, almost painfully clear. I tightened my grip on my sword, my breath steady, waiting for the signal.

On the brink of chaos, we all felt the weight on our shoulders.

"Attack!" shouted Akael, raising his sword to the sky.

We let out a battle cry that echoed throughout the valley. We ran toward the city. The dragons were already attacking from the air, keeping the enemy soldiers busy. It was only when we approached like a tsunami wave that they noticed us.

To my left, the wolves ran on all fours, their teeth bared, ready to bite. I was tempted to transform and join them, but I told myself I would be stronger in my vampire form. My wolf agreed, lending me his strength and letting me know he would be there if I found myself in danger. To my right, Akael's archers shot arrows at the city while soldiers, humans, and elves ran with their shields raised to protect themselves from the city's projectiles. Above us, dragons grabbed rocks and threw them at the town in a counterattack, while others spat magic.

The gates did not open.

But we did not let ourselves be crushed by arrows and magic. Safira dove from the sky, claws first. She crashed through the gates, spitting fire and clawing furiously. The wood caught fire and shattered. The metal reinforcements bent under the dragon's weight, allowing us to swarm the city.

I charged forward with the army, ravaging everything in our path. A mutant with three arms lunged at me. I could still recognize that it had once been an elf, even though its mouth was now just two rows of razor-sharp teeth. My sword pierced its throat, but the creature continued to advance, unperturbed. Its blood was black and thick, warm on my wrist. The mutant's skin was hard, and I wondered how best to kill it. I stabbed it with my sword, but that didn't seem to have any effect either. The creature struck me, knocking the wind out of me. It tried to grab me with two of its arms, attacking with the other. If my sword didn't bother it, I would use my magic.

I got as close as I could, my palm almost touching its chest, and used my royal vampire magic. The blow was so powerful that the mutant was sent flying, the sound of cracking bones echoing through the air as it fell to the ground at an unnatural angle. The screech that came out of its mouth was distressing, and I almost felt pity for it. I watched as it tried to get up but was unable. It wasn't dead, but that would do.

Another mutant jumped on me from above, and I fell under his weight. His foul smell of sweat and sulfur caught in my throat. I pushed with all my strength and managed to get out from under him. This one was less massive than the first but faster. He lunged at me immediately. I spun around, claws shooting out from my fingertips, slicing clean through his outstretched arm. His skin was also easier to cut, I noticed.

The battle swallowed everything. Each mutant was different from the others, and I had to adapt my fighting style to their weakness. The sound of screams and steel filled the air, accompanied by spells that flashed like lightning, as dragons crashed into buildings, reducing them to clouds of stone and dust. The mutants were numerous and offered great resistance, but we still advanced through the city.

A dragon fell from the sky, crashing on the town below.

We arrived in the center of the city. It was a large square with a fountain, and a great number of enemies awaited us there. Safira approached, breathing fire on them, but it wasn't just fire—it was a breath filled with draconic magic. The enemies caught fire, the draconic magic sticking to their armor, unforgiving. The mutants fought Safira even as they burned alive. We rushed at them, decimating them and putting an end to their suffering. Soon, the square was filled with charred bodies. Safira landed, and Elaine climbed down. The dragon took flight again, continuing her attack from the air.

"We have a problem. The magic guild is over there," she said, pointing to a street. "They are putting up formidable resistance. The best mages in the city have banded together. They killed a dragon and are blocking our way. We need to talk to them. The king probably lied to them. It would be advantageous for us to have them on our side."

We followed the path and quickly saw the magic guild. The building was taller than most of the shops around. On each side of the big double-sided wooden door stood two tall statues of mages, each holding a staff. Dozens of mages stood on the roof and balconies of the building, and some were outside in front of the door. A blue protective bubble surrounded the guild and its occupants from magical attacks. It was remarkable. Given its size, it probably took many powerful mages to cast this spell. The dragon's body lay on the ground, amid the rubble of destroyed houses and debris.

"For Mytvathyr!" they shouted when they saw us.

Magic spells began to fly from all directions. The dragons dodged the shots and retaliated, but their attack was countered by the shield. Any attempt to fly over the building was also futile, as the mages hurried to cast lightning bolts and freezing spells at anyone who tried. Even my magic was powerless against the shield they had put up. On the ground, the soldiers couldn't get close with their swords, as enchanted arrows were fired by mages. Fortunately, we had elves who enchanted the shields, allowing us to at least repel the enhanced attacks.

They were stronger and more skilled in magic than we were. They didn't have unlimited mana, but it could be a long time before they tired, especially if they had restoration potions inside the guild. Waiting for them to exhaust their magic was out of the question, but our shields wouldn't hold up forever either. If we didn't find a solution quickly, we would be forced to turn back.

"I need to get to them," Elaine shouted to Akael and me through the noise.

"They'll kill you," I retorted.

Akael shook his head. "I have faith in Elaine. Her strength was not forged in fire, but in endurance. I have seen it. If anyone can convince the mages to stop, it will be her."

I nodded confidently. Elaine wrapped herself in a shield and marched in front of the army, standing alone in front of the magic guild.

The mages pointed at her and stopped attacking as she approached. I realized they recognized her. They passed the word around until they were all frozen, their eyes fixed on her. One of them stepped forward. He was tall, had short gray hair, and a long green cloak.

"Elaine?" he said incredulously. "That's impossible. The king said you were dead."

"Do I look dead?" she asked defiantly.

"He said . . . He said that you had been taken to the shadow valleys of the Underworld."

She spoke with force, "Look around you. The mutants reek of darkness. The king lied to you. He's the one who's corrupt."

They looked at each other in silence. "Is it true?" asked another mage. "Why would the king lie?"

"I have been the great wizard for years. I have worked with many of you over the last century. You have always trusted me. Can't you see the truth?"

Murmurs rose from them as their faith in their king was shaken. Evidence of the king's lies was all around them.

"Join us. Together against the king," Elaine shouted.

The mages withdrew their shields. They knew Elaine was one of them and that she was being honest. They joined us, and the balance of victory shifted in our favor. We pushed through market streets now turned battlegrounds, stepping over broken carts and shattered crystal lanterns. Dragons tore through rooftops, wolves leaped across balconies, and arrows fell like winter rain.

We fought block by block, pushing deeper, forcing the king's creations back into the shadows.

The deeper we went, the more the city changed, and the more my wolf grew restless. He could feel her. She was there, and we were getting closer. *Mate*, he begged.

For a split second, I heard her in my mind. *Nathan*.

My heart raced. Finally, I was in the right place, close enough that our bond, though unsealed, allowed us to talk. We had spent enough years together for our hearts to recognize each other. I could sense how much she had lost hope, how much she had cried, and how incredulous she was to feel me there. *I'm coming*, I pushed to her, knowing she would hear it.

The streets grew cleaner, and the stone glowed faintly with enchantments. The air warmed, as if protected by layers of magic. And at last, rising above all, stood the castle.

I remembered the first time I came here—how beautiful it had all been. How foolish I was at that time, thinking Erendriel would be my ally.

The castle was no longer the serene place it had once been. Lines of grotesque mutants stood in formation before the gates, dozens upon dozens. Above them, elven soldiers loyal to the king lined the balconies, bows drawn. The massive mage tower pulsed with dark light—a spell in progress, or perhaps the king himself gathering power.

I felt it in my bones—this was where it had all started. I stepped forward, my gaze fixed on the castle doors where she was imprisoned.

I searched the courtyard, looking for Erendriel, but he was nowhere to be found. The coward.

The bows were drawn, ready to shoot their arrows. The dragons above prepared to fold their wings and dive. Wolves growled, claws digging into stone. Humans steadied shields. Elves readied their spells.

The courtyard was charged like clouds before a thunderstorm. I bared my fangs.

"For the king's downfall," I growled.

Our army roared as one.

The last time I had seen Emerald was in this damned city, betrayed by my own blood. Now, I would get her back.

A word from the author

I hope you enjoyed Dragons' Rebirth. Please take the time to leave a review and talk about it with your bookish friends. This is the best way to help authors and show your appreciation.

The story will continue and end in the final book of the series: *The King at World's End.*

What an adventure writing this book has been! Thank you for your patience. Life means that I don't always have as much time as I would like to write.

Thank you for your support! It's thanks to you that I continue to write. A book without readers has no purpose.

While waiting for the next book, have a look at my short stories or other series you haven't read. *The Vampire's Pet* is already available. *The Goddess's Wards* tells of the origins of witched. *Age-Old Enemies* is considered for a movie adaptation.

Thank you!

Danielle

Characters

Nathan

Age: 334 years old

Race: Half-Vampire, Half-Werewolf

Hair: Brown

Eyes: Hazel

Facial hair: Goatee

Size: About six feet

Biography:

The former king of the vampire city Ichoryllia. He is also called the Cursed King. He was overthrown but is determined to regain his rightful place as ruler of Ichoryllia. His fated mate has disappeared, and he will tear anyone to find her back.

Son of Damien, previous vampire ruler of Ichoryllia, and Kate, werewolf, daughter of the Alpha. Kate and Damien fought during the Great War against Eurynomos to unite vampires and werewolves and defeat the demon. Although werewolves live less longer than vampires, Kate had been granted a prolonged lifespan by the Moon Goddess. *(See Longing Mates series)*

Samantha Delacour

Age: 282 years old

Race: Vampire

Hair: Black

Eyes: Black

Size: About five feet eight

Biography:

Queen of Ichoryllia, daughter of an Earl, well respected among the nobility. She is the Miłonblooders' high priestess. She believes her god, Alastor, has asked her to fulfill the Great Prophecy. She is to assemble Alastor's essence, which has been split into six beings, and become the vessel of his reincarnation.

Fun facts:

She hates having her hair wet from the rain. It gets frizzy.

Elaine

Age: 200 years old

Race: Elf

Hair: Curly white hair, purple at the bottom

Eyes: Green

Size: About five feet six

Biography:

Has been chosen at the age of five years old by the king to join the castle's mage tower. She is now the grand wizard for the elven king Erendriel. Magic jewels are embedded in her forehead and neck, allowing her to harness vast amounts of mana.

Although she doesn't believe in gods, the castle's servants call her "veneficus dei", believing she is god's mage, sent to protect and save them.

She is tasked with saving elven magic and keeping the magical order of things.

Fun facts:

She doesn't like vampires.

Caleb

Age: Unknown

Race: Vampire

Hair: Blond

Eyes: Blue – Silver since he bonded with the goddess Aeris

Size: About six feet tall

Biography:

Loves to dress stylishly. He's a for-hire vampire assassin who likes to fuck women before killing them. He has mastered the art of controlling his bloodlust monster, allowing him to harness its strength, but he needs to kill regularly to keep it under control. He likes whiskey and human taverns. The Thieves' Guild of Ichoryllia is the only family he really ever had.

He was reborn as the son of the Goddess Aeris after bonding with her, granting him more strength and power. His goal is to find Nathan and kill him, as he is his target, but he has slipped away.

Fun facts:

Caleb will never kill a child, even if the contract pays well.

Erendriel

Age: Unknown

Race: Elf

Hair: Unknown

Eyes: Unknown

Size: About five feet ten

Biography:

King of the elven city Mytvathyr. He believes in what the Oracle has foretold about the end of the world: that Nathan will bring about the world's destruction if he awakens his powers. Therefore, his primary goal is to stop Nathan at all costs.

He gained powers through the goddess Aeris, which gave him the power to conquer the dwarf town of Mumbur. Now ruling over both the elven and the dwarf towns, he is preparing for war. He is building an army of mutants thanks to magical runes he found.

Secondary-Characters

Xavier

Nathan's half-brother (half-human, half-vampire). Was killed by Nathan after betraying him and admitting to being the reason for Emerald's disappearance.

Emerald

Green eyes. Brown hair. 30 years old human. Vassal of Nathan and his fated mate. Has disappeared.

Summer

Werewolf. She has chocolate eyes, long black hair, and a scent of jasmine. She is in her early twenties, and she is Caleb's fated mate. Caleb betrayed a goddess to save her. Now they're fleeing together.

Lysander

Brown eyes. Black long hair. Walks with a cane because of an old battle injury. He was the closest advisor of Nathan when he was king. He is now working for the Queen. Also, he is Viktor's father.

Darryl Everett

27-year-old human. Owner of the herbalist shop in Ichoryllia. Slender man. Black hair tied in a bun—a childhood human friend of Emerald.

His father left to join the Miłonblooders with his big sister when he was but a baby. He recently discovered that his sister is being held hostage by the orcs and has volunteered to go to Krelgraz to rescue her.

Paisley Everett

Darryl's sister. She has long black hair and blue eyes. She was 10 years old when her father left with her to join the Miłonblooders.

Jason

Human. Vassal of Samantha. Has short black hair, dark brown eyes, and white skin. Is not very muscular. Plays the guitar and the lute.

Prince Akael Vaelarion

Elven Prince Vaelarion of the Sun Kingdom. They resided very far to the east, on another continent. He has curly red hair and deep green eyes. Freckles dot his face.

Races

There are six main races: humans, werewolves, elves, vampires, nymphs, and dwarves.

There are six evil races: orcs, goblins, succubi, centaurs, harpies, and lesser demons.

There are three holy races: gods, demigods, angels

Vampires

Millennia ago, vampires hid among humans, mostly in hiding, trying to conceal their nature. Humans didn't want to be used as food, and although vampires were more powerful than humans, they far outnumbered us. For years, humans would drive a stake through a vampire's heart before beheading them. A shiver ran down my spine at the thought.

It took centuries for vampires to create a great revolution, uniting together and bringing humans to their knees. Today, a balance had been found, with vampires evolving into a respectable society.

Fairies

Fairies watched over the natural balance of things. Some were in charge of flowers, others of animals and insects. A fragile balance that was necessary to our world, and fairies governed all nature

Elves

They are a graceful race, renowned for their magic. They live in harmony with nature and protect it. They are usually agile and love to hunt with bows. If they take a sword, it is usually a dagger or short sword. They can live over seven hundred years old, some of them even reaching over a thousand years old.

Magical Level

All the elves are born with some level of magic.

M-1 is the lowest level of magic. The elves at this level can usually use only one element to a very low level of strength. For example, they can calm animals, or call the rain on their fields. They can't wield multiple spells.

To be a mage working at the tower, you need to be at least level M-8, the highest level being M-10.

There are seven sub-races of elves.

Dark Elves

Black ebony skin. Glowing eyes, ranging from ice blue to dark red.

Gray Elves

Gray skin. White hair.

High Elves

Yellowish skin. Renowned to be the best at magic but liked to stay amongst themselves.

Moon Elves

White skin with a slightly blue hue to it. Their eyes range from blue to brown and they have all colors of hair.

Snow Elves

Very little is known about snow elves. They live in snowy mountains rather than with the other elves.

Wood Elves

The most common type of elves.

Winged Elves

Very rare subclass of elf. No one knows where they come from or why they have wings.

Dwarves

Dwarves are smaller and bulkier than humans. They usually prefer to fight with an axe. They don't have magical powers but are great merchants. They are ingenious and construct machines to help with tasks. They value gold greatly and exploit the riches of their lands. Their mines are amongst the best, and they have a commercial port in their city. Most of them are shorter than four feet tall. The men generally have beards. Dwarves live for about 150 to 250 years.

El'thors

An ancient civilization that existed thousands of years ago. The few scrolls that mention them say that they had very powerful magical abilities. The civilization was potentially the most advanced ever to exist. Several of its members had Oracle powers. No one knows how they disappeared, but the few Oracles who appeared hundreds of years later and who still appear occasionally are said to be descendants of these people.

Gods and Demigods

Aerdrie

Queen of the Avariel, was an elven goddess of the Seldarine.

Hecate

Goddess of vampires. She is the goddess of magic, witchcraft, ghosts, and many more.

Aeris

Goddess of deception and betrayal. She is Selena's half-sister. She wants to bond with Alastor, the spirit of vengeance, to assert her vengeance over her family and the world.

Selena

Moon Goddess, worshipped by werewolves.

Deep Sashelas

Elven god of the sea.

Creatures

Dragons

Legendary winged beasts breathing magic, whether fire, electricity, ice, holy, or anything really, as we hadn't discovered all of them. Mature dragons can weigh up to 40k to 50k pounds. There used to be many of them, although they preferred to live secluded from people. Their numbers unexpectedly decreased a few years ago, without anyone really knowing why. Today, they are considered extinct; however, Elaine and Samantha have resurrected one.

Scorchfire

Scorchfire was the last known dragon. He was a fire-breathing dragon, living peacefully on the top of a precarious mountain until one day, he decided to attack the human part of Ichoryllia and burn down many houses. Vampire and humans had teamed up and killed the beast. That day, people cheered their victory but mourned the death of the last dragon. A big ceremony had been held to honor the lost lives and the lost dragon. To this day, no one understands what had driven the dragon to attack the city.

Marrowyrn

A serpent-like creature. Their eyes glow. They usually live in marshes. Can reach 10-15 feet long, with bodies as thick as trees. They have a powerful roar. They are very fast swimmers and masters of the water.

Trolls

Trolls are tall creatures, nine to twelve feet tall. They regenerate constantly, so they can't be killed through conventional methods. They need to be set on fire or have acid thrown on them when they're almost dead so that they remain dead. They have a low level of intelligence and can't cast spells, but have formidable strength.

Factions, groups, and religion

United Races Committee

Delegation of people from all races, humans, werewolves, elves, dwarves, and vampires, committed to keeping the peace.

Miłonblood

The Miłonblooders as followers of the Miłonblood religion. They worship the demon Alastor. They are preaching a strict and uncompromising interpretation of their faith. These individuals believed that their deity had chosen them as instruments of divine wrath, entrusted with the task of purging the world of perceived sinners and heretics.

Alastor

Demon – Spirit of vengeance. Avenger of evil deeds, specifically familial bloodshed – the inflicting of vengeance upon younger generations for the crimes of their forefathers. He is especially cruel. He is related to the Erinyes, the avengers of murder, but the retaliation which Alastor presided over is directed against the murderer's family rather than the murderer himself.

Alastor, a prince of Pylos. Son of King Neleus and Chloris, daughter of Amphion. Chloris and Neleus had several children together, Alastor being one of those children. After Neleus refused to clear a blood debt, Heracles killed him and all his sons except for Nestor.

In death, Alastor became the spirit of vengeance, enticing and spurring blood feuds between families. He also ensured that the stakes were so high that the spirit of vengeance passed down from generation to generation. In this way, he ensured that the cruelty of his death would not go unnoticed and that his story would survive several lineages.

The Shadow weavers

A dark elvish magic cult that believes that true power lies within the shadows and darkness. They see it as a wellspring of untapped magical energy that can be harnessed and channeled for their purposes. The cult members delve deep into forbidden and ancient elven rituals, seeking to unlock the secrets of shadow magic.

The Shadow weavers yearn for immortality and eternal darkness. They believe that by delving deeper into the secrets of shadow magic and dark rituals, they can unlock the path to eternal life. They seek forbidden artifacts, ancient texts, and dark artifacts that hold the key to transcending the boundaries of mortal existence.

Terms/Slang

Exsanguination

To die of blood loss. Ex: when a vampire drinks all the blood from a human, he dies of exsanguination.

Sucked dry

To suck someone dry

Slang used by the vampires for exsanguination. Sucking all the blood from a person.

Artifacts and Objects

Rod of Origins

A long, straight rod with crystals. Created by an ancient civilization that was highly advanced in magic, it allows one to control time itself.

Shard of Blood Right

A dagger imbued with the force from dragon riders, passed down from generation to generation. The tip is sharp and slightly hooked, made for ritual as much as for war, made from high-quality steel. Wrapped in interlaced strips of hardened dragonhide, blackened and scaled, warm to the touch.

Events

Great War against Eurynomos

This refers to the war that happened in the Longing Mates series, when the demon Eurynomos tried to take over the world of the living about three centuries earlier. Many people were killed during this war, but all races joined forces to drive back the demon and his army.

Read the Longing Mates series for all the details.

Places

Krelgraz

City of the orcs, on an island. Some name it: Underworld's Attic.

Ichoryllia

In ancient Greece, ichor was believed to be the God's blood, which was believed to be different than human blood, hence the name of the city. Name of the vampire kingdom, and of the main city, ruled by Nathan.

Dark forest pack

One of the most ancient packs of werewolves. They are said to be the original werewolf pack gifted fated mates by the Moon Goddess and bestowed the task of being the goddess's wards.

St.-Selena

Human town, named in honor of the Moon Goddess. Holds a big basilica in her honor.

Mytvathyr

Elven city, ruled by Erendriel. Home to the oldest magic guilds. A refuge for all races of elves, and a few outsiders.

Mumbur

Dwarven city. Great trade center and commercial port.

Skyfall Temple

The Skyfall Temple was once said to be where the saints lived. It was said that its summit formed a bridge between the Elysian Plains and the world of the living. Kings would consult the saints about the problems of the living. Only the most powerful people were allowed to enter, and even then, their hearts had to be pure. But the temple collapsed thousands of years ago during an attack by a traitor. History forgot his identity. It's now drowned in the marshes.

Magic

Gifts or talents

True vision

Strong magical beings, such as mages and magical creatures, have a natural talent called true vision. This talent allows them to see past illusion spells and the true nature of things. Its force varies depending on each person's magical strength.

Evocation

The evocation school of magic included spells that manipulated energy or tapped an unseen power source to produce a desired end. In effect, they created something out of nothing.

Sending

You send a short message to a person/creature with which you are familiar. The person/creature hears the message in its mind and recognizes you as the sender if it knows you. You can send the message across any distance.

Transmutation

Transmutation is manipulating and changing the physical world. It is usually used for defense and utility in combat. For example, you can change your skin into rock.

Magical portals

Transmutation magic includes the ability to bend space-time and allow the user to open a magical portal, allowing the mage to move to a specific place or plane, such as the ethereal plane.

Levitation

One creature or object you can see within range rises vertically, up to 20 feet, and remains suspended for up to 10 minutes. The spell can levitate a target that weighs up to 500 pounds.

Water breathing

This spell grants up to ten willing creatures you can see within range the ability to breathe underwater until the spell ends. Affected creatures also retain their normal mode of respiration. Only advanced mages or beings with high magical force can cast this spell, as it requires a lot of mana. The duration of its effect varies depending on the power of the person casting the spell.

Alteration

Alteration is an upgrade of Transmutation. With it, you can warp reality on a massive scale and even bend the laws of physics.

Telekinesis

A Telekinesis spell, part of the Alteration magic family, can weigh up to a thousand lbs. The spell works for a maximum of 10 minutes and requires a lot of mana as it is an advanced spell. The mage can lift and move an object for up to 60 feet.

Permutation

Permutation magic allows the size of objects or creatures to be changed, making them smaller or bigger.

Divination

The divination school of magic contains spells that enable the caster to learn long-forgotten secrets, interpret dreams, predict the future, find hidden things, or foil deceptive spells.

Speed

In speed and skill, there is power. You grant yourself or another creature greater speed. The effect varies depending on the creature's natural dexterity, and the duration depends on the mage's magical strength in casting the spell. The higher the mage, the longer the duration.

Restoration

The restoration school of magic contains spells that remove sicknesses and negative effects (like poison) and spells that heal wounds and ailments.

Slow Ailment

A spell that slows the spread of an ailment for up to one hour. If the affliction is in the blood, such as poison or venom, then it will slow the blood flow.

Illusion

The illusion school of magic contains spells that make objects invisible or change how others see something, like making a woman appear as a dangerous creature.

Invisibility

A creature you touch becomes invisible until the spell ends. Anything the target is wearing or carrying is invisible as long as it is on the target's person. The spell ends for a target that attacks or casts a spell. If the person doesn't attack or cast a spell, then the spell lasts up to four hours.

Imaginary Wall

You summon an imaginary wall, making it look that behind the wall was any natural terrain, up to the winds and light. Thus, open fields or a road can resemble a swamp, hill, crevasse, or difficult or impassable terrain. Magical beings sometimes can see the wall depending on their power. They will see it as a picture or a curtain over the area. Creatures can enter the area; when they do, they will see what's there. This spell lasts up to 24 hours and has a range of about 300 feet.

Camouflage

A spell that grants a single person or creature the ability to alter its coloration to match its background, including changing and shifting to match that background. Certain creatures with true vision or a high enough dexterity can see through the camouflage. The spell lasts for an hour.

Necromancy

Gentle Respose

For the duration of the spell, about two weeks, any corpse is protected from decay. It also can't become undead or being revived.

Check out the rest of my work.

All my books are available on Amazon. They are also available in Barn & Noble's stores and other libraries across the world.

$0.99 Short stories collection

- The Vampire's Pet
- The Vampire's Pet Part Two
- The Werewolf's Revenge

Longing mates Series

Considered for a movie adaptation!

A powerful, alluring vampire prince. The strong daughter of the Alpha. Born enemies, tied by an unbreakable bond.

Worldwide Best Sellers. Read the series that started it all.

1. Age-Old Enemies - ISBN 978–1777572136
2. A Beloved Sin - ISBN 978–1777572150
3. The Fallen - ISBN 978-1-7782178-5-2

Related to the Longing Mates series

Read the **Award-Winning** dark fantasy romance today!

The Goddess's Wards: Origins of the werewolf-witches rogue pack - ISBN 978-1-7782178-8-3

Blood and Kisses Series

1. Cursed King - ISBN 978-1-7388313-2-6
2. The Awakening – ISBN 978-1-998458-00-4
3. Dragons' Rebirth – ISBN 978-1-998458-11-0
4. The King at World's End – Coming soon

Half-angel's Daughter Series

1. Devoured by Darkness – coming soon

www.ingramcontent.com/pod-product-compliance
Lightning Source LLC
LaVergne TN
LVHW050920080826
845145LV00001B/144

* 9 7 8 1 9 9 8 4 5 8 1 1 0 *